IN

Seek thrills. Solve crimes. Justice served.

Texas Bodyguard: Chance
Janie Crouch

High Mountain Terror
Janice Kay Johnson

MILLS & BOON

DID YOU PURCHASE THIS BOOK WITHOUT A COVER?
If you did, you should be aware it is **stolen property** as it was reported 'unsold and destroyed' by a retailer.
Neither the author nor the publisher has received any payment for this book.

TEXAS BODYGUARD: CHANCE
© 2023 by Janie Crouch
Philippine Copyright 2023
Australian Copyright 2023
New Zealand Copyright 2023

First Published 2023
First Australian Paperback Edition 2023
ISBN 978 1 867 28910 4

HIGH MOUNTAIN TERROR
© 2023 by Janice Kay Johnson
Philippine Copyright 2023
Australian Copyright 2023
New Zealand Copyright 2023

First Published 2023
First Australian Paperback Edition 2023
ISBN 978 1 867 28910 4

® and ™ (apart from those relating to FSC®) are trademarks of Harlequin Enterprises (Australia) Pty Limited or its corporate affiliates. Trademarks indicated with ® are registered in Australia, New Zealand and in other countries.
Contact admin_legal@Harlequin.ca for details.

Except for use in any review, the reproduction or utilisation of this work in whole or in part in any form by any electronic, mechanical or other means, now known or hereafter invented, including xerography, photocopying and recording, or in any information storage or retrieval system, is forbidden without the permission of the publisher, Harlequin Mills & Boon.

This book is sold subject to the condition that it shall not, by way of trade or otherwise, be lent, resold, hired out or otherwise circulated without the prior consent of the publisher in any form or binding or cover other than that in which it is published and without a similar condition including this condition being imposed on the subsequent purchaser.

All rights reserved including the right of reproduction in whole or in part in any form. This edition is published in arrangement with Harlequin Books S.A..

This is a work of fiction. Names, characters, places, and incidents are either the product of the author's imagination or are used fictitiously, and any resemblance to actual persons, living or dead, business establishments, events, or locales is entirely coincidental.

MIX
Paper | Supporting responsible forestry
FSC® C001695

Published by
Harlequin Mills & Boon
An imprint of Harlequin Enterprises (Australia) Pty Limited
(ABN 47 001 180 918), a subsidiary of HarperCollins
Publishers Australia Pty Limited
(ABN 36 009 913 517)
Level 19, 201 Elizabeth Street
SYDNEY NSW 2000 AUSTRALIA

Cover art used by arrangement with Harlequin Books S.A.. All rights reserved.

Printed and bound in Australia by McPherson's Printing Group

Texas Bodyguard: Chance
Janie Crouch

MILLS & BOON

Janie Crouch writes passionate romantic suspense for readers who still believe in heroes. After a lifetime on the East Coast—and a six-year stint in Germany—this *USA TODAY* bestselling author has settled into her dream home in Front Range of the Colorado Rockies. She loves engaging in all sorts of adventures (triathlons! two-hundred-mile relay races! mountain treks!), travelling and surviving life with four kids. You can find out more about her at janiecrouch.com.

Visit the Author Profile page
at millsandboon.com.au.

DEDICATION

Since this book is about family, it's dedicated to my Kiddo #4. I am delighted to see the woman you're becoming, but you are, and always will be, my baby. Your artistic talent and bullheaded stubbornness amaze me on a constant basis. Go out and do great things in the world!

CAST OF CHARACTERS

Chance Patterson—One of the four boys adopted as a teenager by Clinton and Sheila Patterson. The most strategic. The caretaker. Owns San Antonio Security with his brothers.

Maci Ford—San Antonio Security office manager.

Weston Patterson—The most quiet and serious of the Patterson brothers. Engaged to Kayleigh.

Brax Patterson—The most charming and outgoing of the Patterson brothers. Married to Tessa, father to Walker.

Luke Patterson—Gruffest of the Patterson brothers. Willing to do whatever needs to be done to protect his family. Married to Claire.

Stella LeBlanc—Spoiled social media influencer who has attracted a stalker.

Nicholas LeBlanc—Stella's father and real estate tycoon billionaire.

Dorian Cane—Head of security for Nicholas LeBlanc.

Rich Carlisle—Stella's companion and part-time bodyguard.

Evelyn Ford—Maci's mother, an addict.

Sheila and Clinton Patterson—Adoptive parents of the four Patterson brothers.

Prologue

The moment his alarm rang, despite the fact that the sun wasn't quite cresting the horizon, Chance was up. He didn't have time to waste on snoozing.

He needed to help everyone with breakfast, washing and hair and teeth brushing. Everyone had to be outside for the bus by eight. While the others were eating, he'd check homework and make sure their backpacks were ready to go. Snacks for the younger kids. Change of clothes for the preschool—

"Chance, breakfast is ready!"

Chance froze midway through pulling on his pants and blinked at the darkened room around him.

His room. His alone.

He wasn't in the group home anymore like he'd been for the past four years. There was no small army of other kids around him. No one he needed to help get out the door every morning.

He was at the Pattersons' house. He'd been here for five months now.

He finished getting dressed and walked down the stairs. He didn't need to make breakfast for a bunch of hungry little kids. Sheila had made breakfast for *him*.

She smiled at him as he walked in the kitchen. "Pancakes. Strawberries on the side for you. The other boys should be up in a minute. Sit and eat."

"Um, thanks." He sat down, still trying to adjust to someone feeding him rather than him being responsible for feeding others. "Do you need help packing lunches or anything?"

Sheila smiled. "Already taken care of. Thank you for asking though."

Right. Already taken care of.

When Sheila shooed him onward, Chance nodded and sat at the six-seater table in the breakfast nook. The room was silent for less than a minute before the others started trickling in.

"Morning, Mom." Brax, Sheila and Clinton's biracial adopted son, kissed Sheila's cheek as he grabbed his plate and sat down next to Chance. "Thanks for breakfast. I'm starving."

"Yes, pancakes!" Luke, their adopted White son came in next, taking his plate and shoving a whole pancake in his mouth before he sat down. Chance winced at the painfully large gulp he took to swallow it, but the others just laughed.

"And that's why I always make yours smaller." Sheila grinned.

The last ones down were Clinton and Weston, who talked quietly on their way into the kitchen. Weston had arrived a few weeks ago, after Chance. The Black boy hardly ever said anything, and worked out in the garden all the time, but Chance liked him.

He liked Clinton too. Sheila's husband was big and Black and funny. He was always respectful to Sheila and didn't yell. He worked as an accountant for some business here in San Antonio.

Sheila joined the rest of the family at the table once they'd all sat down. "Anyone have after-school plans?"

She took a bite of her own pancakes and looked pointedly at Chance's untouched plate. He'd waited for the rest of them too. She didn't say anything, but she didn't have to. With a small grin, he took a bite, knowing it was what she wanted.

What would it be like to have Sheila Patterson as a mom? She was Hispanic like him, so they already looked similar.

Sheila and Clinton had started some of the preliminary paperwork for adopting Chance, but he wasn't holding his breath.

Minds changed. Circumstances changed. Systems changed.

It was why Chance liked to take care of others rather than someone take care of him. That way, if *things changed*, he'd still be okay.

He could take care of himself. He could take care of everyone.

Silence crossed over the table and he looked up, startling when he caught everyone's eyes on him. He'd missed something.

What were they talking about? *Plans*.

"I don't have any plans," he said when the others kept looking at him. He hadn't realized they'd been asking him.

"Do you want to come hang out with us? We're going to a movie," Luke said, stuffing another pancake in his mouth, only to swallow quickly and painfully again.

Clinton chuckled into his coffee while Sheila pointed at Luke with her fork. "I appreciate that you enjoy my cooking, but you'll eat with some manners at my table."

"Yes, ma'am," Luke said, throwing Chance a wink when she wasn't looking. He laughed under his breath.

"So, movie?" Brax asked.

Chance thought about the cash he'd squirreled away doing odd jobs over the summer. Mowing lawns and whatever side jobs he could get here. He liked having money saved in case he needed it for something.

He did the math in his head. The movie would

take a bit of it, but he'd still have plenty left over if he needed to buy new clothes or school supplies once he went back to the group home.

"We're paying for everything, and you could use an afternoon out," Clinton said. "You should go, Chance."

Sheila smiled kindly. "Go be a kid for a change."

Chance wasn't sure he'd ever felt like a kid. There was always too much that needed to be done. Too many people who needed taking care of. Too many bad things to plan for in case they happened.

And in Chance's experience, the bad things always happened.

But he was smart. He knew saying no now would be upsetting to everyone. So he nodded at his foster family. "Okay. A movie sounds good."

The other boys high-fived and started talking about what they would see. Sheila and Clinton smiled at each other.

Chance took another bite of his pancake.

He'd have a good time and enjoy the movie. But despite the happy faces around him, he still knew the truth.

The only one he could rely on was himself.

Chapter One

Abrupt knocking startled Chance Patterson into spilling hot coffee across the back of his hand as he poured it into his mug. He muttered a curse. This wasn't how he'd wanted to start his Monday morning.

The San Antonio Security office—the company Chance had started with his brothers five years ago—didn't open for another hour. He'd come in early in hopes of getting some time to work without interruptions. Obviously, that wasn't going to happen.

Throwing a towel over the puddle on the counter, he pulled out his phone, swiping to look at the doorbell camera.

On the office's stoop stood a man dressed in a suit, carrying a briefcase. Thanks to the HD camera, Chance could see him clearly enough despite the early morning's naturally low light. He had a medium build and was middle-aged and somewhat pale—not unusual for someone who worked in an office full-time.

"May I help you?" Instead of going to greet the man, Chance used the microphone feature on the doorbell. Security Business 101 was not to open the door to just anyone, regardless of how official they looked.

"Is this one of the Patterson brothers?" The man's voice was clipped and his words concise. Like he was used to only saying what he needed to and not a single word more.

"It is, but we don't open for another hour. If you want to come back then—"

"I can't," he said stiffly, not at all bothered by cutting Chance off or speaking through the microphone. "I'm here as a proxy for someone who wants to hire your services. To whom am I speaking?"

"Chance Patterson. Look, have your employer call us, and we can schedule a time to talk."

"I can't do that either. My employer is busy, and the issue is incredibly time sensitive."

Chance barely refrained from pointing out that he was busy too. He ran his burned hand under some cool water at the sink next to him, while pouring a new mug of coffee with the other. "Who is your employer?"

"I can't provide that information until you've signed a nondisclosure agreement." He waved a manila folder in front of the camera. "His need for privacy is very real, which you will understand if you sign. For now, I can tell you that my name is Benjamin Torres and that your business came highly recommended to my employer by

Leo Delacruz. Once you sign the NDA, I can provide further info."

Chance turned the water off and dried his hand. Leo Delacruz was basically extended family at this point. The man had hired San Antonio Security—specifically Chance's brother Weston—to guard his daughter, Kayleigh, to protect her when a merger got dangerous a few months ago.

Leo was a well-known Texas businessman and associated with a lot of people, so knowing he'd recommended their company didn't narrow down who Benjamin worked for.

The man didn't shuffle or fidget in the silence while Chance thought this through. He came across as not impatient, but efficient. He had things to do and needed his answer.

Chance couldn't give him one under these circumstances. "I'm not comfortable signing something that would require me to keep secrets from my brothers."

The Patterson brothers didn't keep secrets from one another.

Chance grit his teeth. Actually, he'd been keeping a pretty damned big one from them for the past few months.

Benjamin shook his head. "The NDA will permit you to tell your brothers anything you deem necessary, but requires you to keep the identity of my employer and anything he discusses with you confidential, even if you choose not to take the assignment."

"Put the NDA through the mail slot. I'll look it over."

A quick read proved it to be a standard document, with the only changes being what he'd outlined. He could share information with his brothers and their employees as necessary, but no one outside the company. There were no penalties or clauses that would make things difficult if they didn't take the assignment either, so he signed it and unlocked the door, handing the stack of papers back to Benjamin.

"Thank you, Mr. Patterson." The older man tucked the contract into his briefcase and stepped back. "Mr. LeBlanc will be pleased. He's anxious to meet with you all to discuss the situation."

"Nicholas LeBlanc?" The Texas real estate tycoon? He was *big* money. "What exactly does he want to hire San Antonio Security for?"

Someone of LeBlanc's stature would have his own full-time security team.

"Mr. LeBlanc would prefer to give you the details himself. If this afternoon works, he has an availability at 3:00 p.m. Top floor of the Van-Point Tower."

"We'll be there."

With an efficient nod, Benjamin left, getting into the back seat of a town car at the edge of the sidewalk. Chance watched him go, then turned back into the office. He needed to find out as much as he could about Nicholas LeBlanc and get everyone into the office stat.

Looked like a quiet morning working on his own was not in the cards.

"WHY ARE WE all here again?" Luke asked as they stepped into the glass elevator in the Van-Point Tower's lobby later that afternoon.

Chance looked out at the pristine building. "Because Nicholas LeBlanc is the type of client whose recommendation could set us up for years."

Chance and his brothers had started San Antonio Security five years ago. They'd wanted to work together and, between the four of them, had years of prior military and law enforcement experience. At the beginning of their business journey, they'd had to take whatever assignments they could get, which included a lot of following cheating spouses and hunting bail jumpers.

But in the last couple of years, San Antonio Security had grown to become one of the most respected firms in their hometown. Now they did a lot of personal and corporate security—not only the bodyguarding, but situational awareness and tactical defense.

They were brought in by companies and individuals to find and fix the holes in their security, to stop the bad things before they happened.

But sometimes the bad things were already in motion when San Antonio Security was brought in. Chance was afraid that was the case now with Nicholas LeBlanc.

The elevator gave Chance and his brothers a view of the indoor complex that housed a virtual warren of businesses. LeBlanc Holdings held the top two floors—announcing its prestige and prosperity without ever saying a word.

The elevator doors opened, releasing them into a large lobby. People were everywhere, talking, walking, typing. Phones were ringing all over the place, but there was order even in the chaos.

"Mr. Patterson?"

Chance turned and found the man who had showed up at the office this morning. "Yes."

"I was under the impression that you were bringing your brothers with you, not employees. Security downstairs listed you all as Pattersons."

"That's because we are. These are my brothers—Brax, Luke and Weston Patterson."

It was a common misconception, since none of them looked alike.

"I see. My apologies for the error." Once again, Benjamin was all efficiency. "Mr. LeBlanc is waiting for you. Follow me."

Chance followed behind everyone else, taking in the office and the atmosphere. Though the office was guarded downstairs, he saw a man stationed near the elevator and another near the stairs. Both security guards had a line of sight to the door Benjamin was knocking on.

Was it LeBlanc who was in danger then, or was that standard practice?

"Come in." Benjamin pushed the door open, and Chance found himself in a corner office with more windows than walls. The city was sprawled out, with buildings dotting the horizon and tiny people and cars jostling about like ants.

It was the view of someone who had money and power and liked both.

Beyond that, the rest of the room was taken over by a massive desk covered in neat stacks of paper. Everything else in the office, from the carpet to the chairs to the paintings, was done in warm, masculine neutrals. Deep navy and warm gray mixed with the dark mahogany of the bookcases to create a type of space that fit the CEO and founder of a multimillion dollar company.

"Mr. LeBlanc, these are the Patterson brothers, owners of San Antonio Security."

Nicholas LeBlanc stood from behind his desk. "Thank you for coming, gentlemen. Leo Delacruz speaks highly of you. Please sit. Benjamin will get you whatever drinks you want."

Chance took note of the expensive watch and tailored suit jacket. Everything on LeBlanc's body—and in his office—was both extravagant and orderly.

Chance had no problem with either. But once again he was trying to figure out why someone like LeBlanc was interested in a security firm like theirs, even with Leo's recommendation.

Nicholas motioned everyone to a sitting area off to the side of his behemoth desk. They all declined the offer of drinks.

"What can San Antonio Security do for you, Mr. LeBlanc?" Brax asked. As the most charming of the Patterson brothers, he tended to do the initial talking. He had a way of making people feel at ease.

Chance preferred to let Brax talk so he could observe.

"Leo told me that you four were the best at what you do."

"Thank you. We work very hard and pride ourselves on our solid reputation." Brax tipped his head in acknowledgment. "Are you needing more personal security? It seems like you've got plenty."

"Not exactly." Nicholas sighed. "My daughter, Stella, is having an issue. She's a social media influencer, and recently she's become the target of a stalker."

Chance leaned forward, leaning his elbows on his knees. "What kind of stalker?"

"At first it was messages on her social media, comments and DMs from dummy accounts. Then it turned into actual letters being sent to the house with no clue how the individual got the address. Recently it has been bizarre gifts and more. She wants to use what she receives to further build her social media following. Obviously, she doesn't understand the severity of the issue."

"Tell us what you perceive that severity to be," Brax said gently, nodding at Nicholas.

If it was just letters, there wasn't much anyone could do to stop them. Even the police rarely prosecuted stalking cases. There was too much ambiguity to make them stick in court.

Gifts were the same, as long as they didn't cause harm. Icky wasn't illegal.

Nicholas rubbed the back of his neck. "The problem is, no matter what our security measures are, her stalker keeps getting through. We've had Stella on lockdown and they've still gotten letters inside the compound to her. We've gone through three security teams and none of them have been able to stop her from receiving the notes. I'm worried that things are going to get worse, and I don't want my daughter caught in the crosshairs."

Brax sat back, resting an ankle on his knee. "So, you want us to bodyguard Stella?"

Nicholas shrugged. "Yes and no. She has guards on her at all times, though she's not often aware of it. Her constant companion, Rich Carlisle, is someone I hired a few years ago as a social secretary/babysitter. He's also trained in defense, although that's not his primary purpose."

It sounded like Stella had a full team. "Where would we come in?"

"While you might do some guarding and security setup, I'd really like you to focus on finding the stalker. Since we don't have proof of anyone physically harming or threatening Stella, the police can't do anything but write reports. I need someone out there looking for whoever is behind this."

Chance caught his brothers' eyes. They all knew how beneficial this assignment could be for their business overall, but for something like this, everyone needed to be in agreement before they took it on.

Things had changed for his brothers over the past few months. Luke and Brax both had wives now. Brax even had a kid. Weston was engaged to Leo Delacruz's daughter, Kayleigh.

Chance was the only one still alone.

An assignment of this magnitude would take a lot of man hours for everyone, even if Chance took the lead.

It would also mean Chance would be spending a lot more time in the office. A lot more time around Maci Ford, the San Antonio Security office manager.

Who he saw every day, while both of them pretended she hadn't snuck out of his bed in the middle of the night a couple months ago.

All his brothers gave him subtle nods, so he knew they were okay with taking the LeBlanc assignment. Chance gave his full attention back to Nicholas.

"If we do this, we'll have to split our time between bodyguarding and investigating. It's going to take a lot of planning and strategy."

"I'm willing to pay whatever it takes. You kept Leo's situation quiet, and that's what I need—someone with both discretion and skill."

"This isn't necessarily about the money. What about your own security team?" Brax asked. "Will they feel threatened by us coming in here on top of them? That sort of divided energy makes a difficult situation even harder."

They'd dealt with that exact situation with

Leo Delacruz, and it had ended in bloodshed. None of them wanted to take that on again.

Nicholas shook his head. "No, it won't be like that at all. I would not even be here talking to you if my team hadn't vetted you. As a matter of fact..."

Nicholas walked over to his desk and typed something. A few seconds later a man walked through the office door.

He was maybe in his late forties, with salt-and-pepper hair styled neatly to match his black suit. It was tailored, but not designer, and the slightly worn quality of his shoes told Chance he didn't sit behind a desk all day like LeBlanc. He was on his feet a lot.

"This is Dorian Cane, my head of security. Dorian's been with me since I started the company, and he's known Stella her whole life. Dorian, these are the Patterson brothers."

Dorian stepped forward and shook everyone's hand as they introduced themselves. When it was Chance's turn, he watched Dorian's calculating eyes run over him, stopping briefly at the places where Chance had a weapon of some sort stashed. He only missed one, which said Dorian Cane was good at his job.

Chance sat and cleared his throat. "In your opinion, how dangerous is the stalking situation, Dorian? Based on your experience, are these pranks, someone seeking attention or something worse?"

To his credit, the other man thought before he spoke. "It definitely felt like a game at first, but the messages have been getting stranger as time wears on. I'm worried about escalation becoming a very real possibility in the future."

It was one thing for a concerned father to say he thought a stalker was dangerous. It was completely different for someone of Dorian Cane's experience to say the same.

And Nicholas was right. There was nothing about the other man's actions or mannerisms that suggested he felt threatened or angered by their presence.

But Chance asked him anyway. "You're alright with Nicholas bringing us in?"

"My top priority is figuring out who this stalker is. Something about him—although it could be a her—has got all my internal alarms going off. You guys are good. I checked you out myself."

Chance had no doubt that was true.

"I can't let Nicholas's other security concerns fall to the side while concentrating on the stalker. Bringing in people we can trust, who can keep it quiet, is the best solution."

"If we take this job, we'll need to know that Stella will actually listen to us," Weston said. He was the quietest of all the brothers, but he knew from personal experience that trying to guard someone who didn't want to be guarded could be dangerous for everyone. "From what you've said, she may not be interested in that."

Dorian looked over at Nicholas, who gestured for him to go ahead and answer. "Stella is spoiled. She's used to getting what she wants, and she doesn't understand that this stalker isn't something to joke about. It's unsafe and getting more dangerous by the day."

Nicholas adjusted his tie. "Dorian's not wrong. I've definitely spoiled and sheltered her more than I should have, but she's my whole world."

Nicholas reached for one of two framed photos on his desk and held it out to Chance. He took it, nearly doing a double take.

Ah, hell.

"We'll accept the job," Chance said. The picture solidified any doubt he had in his mind.

All three of his brothers looked at him with raised brows until he turned the picture around. Chance wasn't the type to blindly accept any deal without analyzing the details of the contract, but this time was different.

Stella LeBlanc looked exactly like Maci Ford.

And there was no way anyone who had Maci's face was getting stalked on Chance's watch.

Chapter Two

"I've been waiting for this all day."

The soft-spoken words tickled the skin of Maci's rib cage as the feel of warm, calloused hands on her waist made her shiver. She writhed as those hands slid down to her hips, pulling her closer, and those lips climbed to brush her neck and shoulders. She couldn't stop her groan at a soft swipe of a tongue along the hollow of her throat.

"Maci, you taste so good."

Chance's voice was so low it was barely a sound, and the heat of his breath on her skin gave her goose bumps. Threading her fingers through his hair, all Maci wanted to do was feel.

Here in her room there was no work, no clients, no danger. There was only the two of them surrounded by darkness. The pressing weight of him on top of her, the slow glide of their bodies coming together, the touches that anchored them together as they climbed.

Everywhere he touched, her skin burned. It had never been like this with anyone else. She shouldn't have been surprised. There was no one else in the world like Chance Patterson.

Even when he drove her mad, he made her feel more than she ever had before.

It always made her wonder how hard it would be to survive when he eventually got tired of her, when he realized how bad she was for him.

He nipped his teeth against her collarbone, his palm warm against the side of her throat. "Stay with me, Maci."

He knew her. He may not have known the details of her past, but he knew her need to overthink things that could get the best of her during inopportune moments.

She pressed her lips to his temple. "I'm here. I'm here."

He pressed a kiss over her throat, then continued along the side of her neck, driving her higher until she was gasping for breath. Her nails dug into Chance's back as she found herself falling over the edge. He whispered praises with every sweep of his hips until they were calling each other's names.

As always, there was a moment afterward where they clung to one another. Their breaths mingling, their bodies soft and warm and pliant.

Their hearts unguarded.

It was both too much and never enough for Maci when Chance looked at her then. She had too many secrets to guard, and he was too close to discovering them. Too close to walking away once he did.

Sated and relaxed, Chance pressed a kiss to her head, rolled to the side and tugged her into his arms. Maci tried to pull away, to give them some sort of space so the lines wouldn't blur come morning.

She needed a minute. Just one to rebuild the walls he so easily broke through every time they were together like this. Usually, he let her have some space, but this time he was having none of it.

"Stay with me," he whispered into her hair.

She wanted to. How she wanted to. No matter how short this passion with him lasted, she wanted him with a fierceness that made her feel weak.

Maci Ford was weak for almost nothing, but Chance Patterson was the exception to that hard-won rule. It was as surprising as it was oddly delightful.

When he squeezed her tighter, she smiled and let him drag her close enough that there was no space between them. "I'm not going anywhere."

She didn't want to go anywhere.

She wanted to stay with him.

She rested in his arms and let contentedness wash over her.

But as he fell asleep and the darkness around

them became heavier, she knew she couldn't stay. Knew she should've never let this happen again, no matter how much she wanted it. Knew she had to walk away from him—from this.

It was the only way.

Wakefulness came in fits as Maci reached her arm across the bed, expecting Chance's warm skin. At the feel of cold cotton sheets, she frowned and pried her eyes open.

She was alone. Of course she was. She hadn't been with Chance in that way since she'd snuck out of his bed two months ago. She'd made sure he'd known the physical aspect of their relationship couldn't happen again. Even though that had been damn near the hardest thing she'd ever done.

Second only to seeing him every day at the office and trying to pretend like she wasn't interested in him. That they were nothing more than professional colleagues.

She peeked at the alarm clock on the bedside table and groaned. 5:45 a.m. Not enough time to go back to sleep if she wanted to get to the office on time. She spent five minutes glaring at the ceiling—frustrated and wishing that dream had been real—before she tossed the covers off her body. She made her way out of bed and to the kitchen and started the coffee with half-opened eyes.

At least the coffee would give her enough energy to get through the day. Another day with Chance.

Maybe she should get a new job.

She shut down the thought almost immediately. She couldn't do that. Wouldn't. She owed the Patterson brothers for being so good to her. Who else would have hired a twenty-five-year-old with a shiny new GED and no experience?

No one. The Patterson brothers were all upstanding, honorable men. Even before she'd slept with Chance and they were bickering all the time she'd still respected him. She respected all of them. She didn't want to give up her job.

She would have to find a way to continue working for San Antonio Security despite her very nonprofessional feelings for Chance. Which she thought was becoming easier until whatever had happened yesterday when the guys went to meet with Nicholas LeBlanc.

Chance had come back staring at her, even more grumpy with her than usual. No explanation, just a demand that she pull everything she could on the real estate tycoon and his company.

It had been all Maci could do not to tap her heels and salute. She was trying her best not to pick fights with Chance. Jabbing at each other at the office had been fun at first but now had taken a turn for a little more bitter since she'd snuck out of his bed.

She took her shower and got ready for the day, washing the memories of Chance down her drain like she tried to do every morning. Some day she hoped it wouldn't be necessary. But she wasn't holding her breath.

By the time she was ready to go, she was already half a coffee pot into her day and desperately in need of some food before the shakes took over. Still, it was nice pulling into the lot of San Antonio Security as an employee. She loved her job. Loved sorting the guys' paperwork chaos into systems that were tidy and manageable. Loved taking things off their hands and greeting and helping customers.

It was nice to be needed and feel like she was *capable*. That was definitely a first.

She turned off her car and glanced at her cell phone. Swiping away the notifications from her calendar and news apps, she froze. Two missed calls and a text, all from her mother. She stared at the phone, wishing she could toss it out the window.

Delete. She didn't listen to the voice mails. Nothing good came from her mother's mouth before eight in the morning.

Nothing good came from her mother's mouth any time of day.

She glanced at the text from her before deleting it also.

Need to talk to you.

"Of course you do." Maci tossed her phone back into her bag, yanked her keys out of the ignition and opened up her car door.

She fought not to let the text ruin a day that hadn't even started yet. Her relationship with Evelyn had been *strained* for years. Suffering from addiction her whole life, Evelyn treated Maci like a glorified ATM, showing up just long enough to get cash for her next fix before leaving again.

Taking a fortifying breath, Maci got out of her car, holding the handle up—the only way to get the door to stay closed on this vehicle that had seen better years. Evelyn wasn't her problem today.

"Hi, baby girl."

Or…maybe Evelyn *was* her problem today. The sound of her mother's voice was enough to snap Maci's spine straight. Turning quickly, she put her back to the car and stared at the slightly older reflection in front of her.

Evelyn Ford had once been the type of beautiful that people gawked after. Long blond hair that hung in silky waves, icy blue eyes rimmed with thick lashes and an hourglass figure that didn't care what she ate.

Back then, she'd been movie star beautiful. Now, she just looked tired. Almost thirty years of addiction did that to a person. Her hair was still long, but fried and stringy, her eyelashes sparse around dulled eyes. Now her body was thin with scabs from itching. It was like the disease had eaten away at her.

It was everything Maci was terrified of becoming. Everything she'd come way too close to becoming.

It was Evelyn who had sent Maci into such a horrific tailspin that she'd ended things with Chance. A single text threatening to show up had been enough to send Maci packing.

Chance didn't need someone like Maci dragging him down. He had a good family, a job he loved and a great life. There was no room for a high school dropout who'd spent her formative years following in her mother's footsteps. The drugs, the men, the mistakes. Not exactly the type of daughter-in-law Clinton and Sheila Patterson were used to.

No, Chance was better without her and her messy history. No matter how painful it was for Maci.

"You can't be here." Maci leaned against the car door, blocking her mother from view of anyone coming into San Antonio Security. The office wasn't open yet, but the urge to keep this part of her life hidden was stronger than ever. The Pattersons—Chance especially—didn't need to know what Maci came from and who she had to fight not to become.

"You didn't answer my calls." As if it was normal for Maci to be on the phone at 3:00 a.m.

"I was sleeping."

Her mother huffed. "Well, I need your help."

Maci stared at her. If Evelyn wanted help in the form of rehab or counseling, Maci would do whatever was in her power to assist. But that was never the case.

When Evelyn said *help*, she wanted funds to feed her habit, to drown herself in her current drug obsession. "You need money."

Evelyn nodded. She didn't even seem ashamed. Why would she when Maci had been cleaning up her messes since she could hold a broom?

"How much?" It wasn't how Maci would normally handle this but she needed to get Evelyn out of here now before someone saw her and started asking questions. That was the problem with working for a bunch of highly-trained security guys.

Her mother shifted on her feet, now looking sheepish. It was an act, one Maci was all too familiar with. Gritting her teeth, Maci wished she could just walk away from Evelyn. But she would follow. Telling her she shouldn't be here would just ensure she showed up again.

"Three hundred."

Maci sighed but was once again grateful she'd gotten her life together. Three hundred dollars was a lot, but Maci had made sure she had money in savings and enough in her checking to cover three months of bills if she needed.

There had been way too long when she had absolutely nothing.

"How's Pop?"

Evelyn waved one bony hand. "Same old, same old."

Hugo Ford's drug of choice was alcohol. The last time Maci had seen him had been the week after she turned eighteen. He'd thrown her out of the house in a booze-filled rage, and she'd never returned. Still, she'd never been able to put him out of her mind. It was exhausting constantly worrying about people who didn't care about themselves or her.

The rumbling sound of a familiar engine pushed Maci into action. She thrust her hand into her purse and pulled out her wallet, quickly counting out as much cash as she had. Maci held out the stack of bills, but didn't let go when Evelyn grabbed it. "This is all I have, Mom. You're wiping me out."

"Yeah, yeah. I know. This is the last time."

Maci didn't believe that even for a second. She let go of the money as Evelyn nodded then tucked the bills in her pocket and her hair behind her ear. Then without a word she was gone.

No hug, no thanks. It should hurt, but all Maci felt was relief that she was gone.

"Who was that?"

Everything in her body responded to the deep timbre of Chance Patterson's voice. She'd been helpless against it from the very first day.

She spun, just as affected by his appearance. All long legs and broad shoulders, as if he could easily carry the weight of the world—and Maci knew for a fact he tried regularly to do. His face was too rough to be traditionally handsome—jaw and cheekbones hard and unforgiving.

The only thing soft about him were his eyes. Brown, but not a traditional brown—a lighter color, more of a molten honey.

She knew full well how those eyes could pin someone. Make them feel like they were the only person in the world when Chance's attention was on them.

"Who was that?" he asked again.

"Good morning to you too," she said, straightening her purse strap on her shoulder. There was no way she was going to explain the situation with her mother to him.

Those honey eyes narrowed. "Was that lady bothering you?"

She shook her head and started walking toward the office door. "No. Just wanted to know where she could buy tampons."

Chance had three brothers and no sisters. Maci was betting on the fact that the word *tampon* would shut him up.

It worked. He let it go, walking with her toward the office.

"The Nicholas LeBlanc case might get messy," Chance said. "Let one of us know if anything is happening out of the norm."

She had no idea why he would think the LeBlanc case would affect her, but she nodded. She didn't want to start the morning with a fight.

Chance unlocked the door and held it open for her. She walked through, heading toward her desk in the lobby.

"Maci," he said and she stopped, turning to him.

Those eyes pinned her for a long moment. She wanted to be unaffected but knew that was the opposite from the truth.

"Yes?" she finally asked when he didn't say anything else.

He still kept looking at her.

I've been waiting for this all day.

This morning's dream came crashing back into her mind, as well as the heat that went along with it.

They were alone here in the office. Chance was always early. Nobody else would be here for at least another forty-five minutes.

She took a step toward him as if she was being pulled by a string.

"Chance?" she whispered.

He took a step toward her also.

She shouldn't do this—shouldn't let the moment build between them. But she was powerless to stop it. Powerless to resist those eyes. That jaw. Those cheekbones.

The man.

They both took another step, but then Chance blinked and stopped. He stiffened, backing away from her.

The moment was lost.

"Good morning," he said. Then without another word, he turned and walked to his office, closing the door behind him.

Chapter Three

In all her time of working for them, Maci had never seen the Patterson brothers as flustered as they were working the LeBlanc case.

After their meeting with Nicholas LeBlanc, they'd camped out at the conference room table with the case notes from the tycoon's head of security. Dorian Cane and his team had collected all the stalker's letters and gifts as evidence, storing them carefully since LeBlanc hadn't wanted to bring in law enforcement. That meant one wall of the San Antonio Security conference room was now piled high with boxes of letters, notes and printed photographs, plus the reports to go along with everything.

Three days and too many pots of coffee later, they were all frustrated, exhausted and no closer to having any leads on the stalker or any clue how to keep Stella LeBlanc safe. Every day that they didn't have a plan, Chance became more stressed, the furrow between his brows more pronounced.

It'd only gotten worse when another of the stalker's letters found its way into Stella's mail. Whatever the letter contained was bad enough that Maci thought Chance might put his fist through the wall.

She had no idea why he was taking this so personally—he hadn't seemed to do that for most of their other cases since she'd worked here. Maybe stalking was a sore subject for him.

And whether Chance was taking this personally or not didn't matter. All of them needed help, so she'd done what she could. She'd secretly ferried sustenance of all kinds to the brothers in between her own phone calls and office work. Nutritional snacks and meals, since none of them were eating well.

Despite her best efforts to keep them functioning, they all had bags under their eyes the size of Volvos, with attitudes to match. It would have been almost funny if she hadn't been so exhausted herself.

She'd somehow gotten some sort of stomach bug that wouldn't quit right when the guys needed her most. She couldn't take a sick day right now, so she hid it as best she could. She sprayed down everything with disinfectant and powered through.

"He could've killed her," Luke said, rubbing his eyes as he tossed down a stack of photos from the most recent stalker incident. Maci tidied them, then walked around the table, replacing the tray of sandwiches and bringing a fresh pot of coffee.

Chance hit play on the video images. "I don't think that was the intent. Stella and her driver were followed home from a local boutique she was doing a spotlight on for her YouTube channel." He paused the video as all the guys studied it. "See how the other car nicked the trunk? He could've done a lot more damage."

"See how the driver keeps his face averted?" Chance pointed to the image. "He knew we'd pull all photo and video footage we could get. It was a carefully constructed hit."

Chance resumed the footage, and Maci winced as the vehicle containing Stella and her driver went into a tailspin. Thankfully, the guardrail stopped it before there was any major damage.

"This is a break in the pattern," Chance said. "The first incident of actual violence."

They all watched the footage again. Then again, sandwiches and coffee ignored.

It was Weston who finally stopped it. "We need a break. Watching this on repeat isn't changing anything. Dorian has Stella on lockdown. Nothing is going to change tonight."

Luke stood up. "I concur. I'm heading home to see my wife and get some sleep. Let's meet back early and tackle this with fresh eyes."

Maci could tell Chance wanted to argue but knew they were probably right.

"I need to see my tiny terror." Brax stacked up some files in front of him. "He's running Tessa ragged."

It wasn't long before they were heading out of the conference room.

"You coming, Chance?" Weston asked.

"I'm just going to look this over one more time and then I'll leave." The brothers didn't respond to him with anything but eye rolls. If he had it his way, Chance would stay at the table until his body gave out or he found a solution. They knew better than to argue with him.

"You head out too, Maci. We'll help clean up this mess in the morning," Brax said with a mock glare and a wave.

Despite Brax's words, as soon as the door locked behind them, she started gathering up the cups from the conference room. If she cleaned it up, they'd be able to think clearer. Starting again fresh tomorrow was a good idea.

"You're exhausted. You should go home too," she said when Chance threw down the pictures Luke had been looking through.

It was the first time she caught a good glimpse of Stella LeBlanc, and she stopped in shock.

Holy hell, the woman could have been Maci's twin.

Stella had slightly longer hair in a more elaborate style, and her fashion and makeup were much more complex than what Maci wore, but they could easily have been sisters.

It was almost creepy how similar they looked.

"Yeah, I know I need to go home." Chance scrubbed a hand down his face. "But this car accident doesn't make sense. For so long, the stalker didn't change his tactics. When they stopped working, he just found new ways to get his messages to Stella. He could've gotten dangerous much sooner...so why now? What caused him to attack her like that? And in a way that's not terribly personal or inventive."

Maci forced herself to look away from the photos of Stella. "Could the stalker have been upset about something? Maybe it was a warning."

She stacked the cups and took them to the office's small kitchen sink. She was rinsing them out, startled when she found Chance just behind her. She hadn't heard him follow her—the man could be so damned silent when he wanted to be.

But he'd followed her into the kitchen to continue talking to her. That was something.

He sat down at the small table in the middle of the room. Her entire body was aware of how close he was.

"What the stalker did doesn't feel like an emotional response. It feels like something else."

She shut off the water and dried her hands. "Like what?" She gave in to her urges and stepped closer.

As if her hand was being powered by someone else's brain, she ran her fingers through his soft hair. Chance tensed, and for a moment she thought he'd pull away. Then he relaxed into her touch, letting his head fall back to rest against her stomach. She nearly groaned, having forgotten how good it felt to touch Chance casually. The soft sigh as she scratched his scalp was enough for her to keep going.

"I don't know. If the motive was profit, the stalker would've taken her and tried for a ransom. He—and I use that pronoun because statistically that's the case, not because we know for sure—seems to want to get close to Stella, but not too close."

"Could revenge on Nicholas LeBlanc be a motive?"

"Possibly, but if so, he's moved very slowly over the past few weeks. Maybe the stalker is just toying with her."

"That's not generally the case, right?" Maci didn't know much about stalking, but she did know that stalkers who did it just to toy with their victims were the minority.

He let out a sigh and leaned more fully against her. "Yeah. Generally, stalkers crave the emotional response the invasions of privacy forces on their victims. Someone doing it just to mess with Stella or Nicholas would be much more unpredictable."

"Maybe it's jealousy. She's successful in her own right as an influencer, so maybe someone's coming after her for that. Or they could feel slighted that she doesn't see their support for her or something. A fan who has gone a little over the edge."

Chance didn't answer, but Maci could tell he was thinking, so she didn't push. She just let him think.

"Maybe." He pulled away, then turned to look at her. "How are you doing?"

She looked down at him, brows furrowed. "Me? You're the one who hasn't slept in days."

Chance stood and cupped her cheek, running a thumb under her eye. "That may be true, but you haven't been feeling well lately either. Are you okay?"

She knew she'd pay for it later but she let herself lean into Chance's touch. Even in the middle of the week's chaos, and with things so strained between them, he'd been watching.

Checking on her. "Maybe we're both working too hard."

His eyes tracked over her, cataloging everything from her limp hair to her baggy clothes. She really hadn't been feeling great, and her look was definitely more casual than usual. She almost apologized, but he shook his head. "You should go home, Maci. Get some rest."

"I will if you will," she joked, poking him in the stomach. When he pulled her into his arms unexpectedly, she knew she should pull away, but couldn't force herself to do so. She couldn't remember the last time he'd held her, and even though her brain was screaming at her to take a step back, to walk away, she couldn't deny how well they fit together.

Of course, fitting together physically had never been their problem.

He trailed his nose across her cheek and down until it rested in the crook of her neck.

"Come home with me," he whispered. His lips were so close to her skin, but he didn't kiss her, and Maci wasn't sure if she wanted him to or not. "We can just sleep if you want, but I want you in my bed again, Maci. I never wanted you to leave."

There was no hiding the shiver that coursed through her body at his words, just like there was no hiding the gasp that came when he finally brushed his lips so softly against her skin.

Don't let your libido cloud your judgment. Think before you act, Maci Ford.

Especially since her impulsiveness was what had gotten them into their awkward situation in the first place.

But his proposal was so tempting. She wanted to go home with Chance. She really did. She wanted to crawl into his cool sheets and fall asleep wrapped in his arms. She wanted to wake up in the morning to find him staring at her again. She wanted his hands on her after the two-month hiatus she'd forced on them.

But nothing had changed. Her mother showing up here in the parking lot a couple days ago was a reminder of that. Giving in, going home with him after so long, would make things even more muddied.

And honestly, she wasn't sure how many more times she had the strength to walk away from him. She wanted him so much.

He wanted her too. He wanted her to say yes.

She was so tempted.

But when he found out about her past—who she'd come from, the things she'd done—it would be *him* walking away.

Not just him.

Maci's breath froze in her lungs. Losing

Chance would be terrible, but losing her job and the family she'd built here at San Antonio Security? That would be devastating.

She not only cared about Chance's brothers but all their significant others... Tessa, Claire, Kayleigh. Maci loved baby Walker and Sheila and Clinton Patterson too.

It was already difficult to have a working relationship when no one knew what had actually happened between her and Chance. If she wanted to keep her life and job intact, Maci had to do her best to stay away from him. Even when every part of her body was begging her to stay.

"It's better if I don't," Maci said, stepping out of his embrace even though it was agony.

He stiffened and let her go. "Okay. I'll walk you to your car."

He sounded so defeated that Maci almost took it back. She bit her tongue, holding back the words she wanted to say.

When he didn't speak either, the two silently grabbed their things, locked the door and headed into the night together. Chance stuck close as they walked across the parking lot and checked the backseat after she unlocked the doors. Once he was sure the car was safe, he opened the door for her.

"Get home safe," he said before closing her into

the car. He didn't move or look away until she was pulling out of the lot. Maci slowed, watching as he climbed into his truck and drove off.

Even after she'd rejected him, he'd still made sure she was safe. He was a protector in his very DNA. A good man.

And she was definitely the wrong woman for him.

Chapter Four

Maci stepped into the office the next morning with a cup of tea wrapped firmly in her shaking hand. She'd thrown up twice before she left the house thanks to her stomach bug, but there was no way she was going to take the day off.

Not when she had a plan that could work to help with the Stella LeBlanc situation.

Chance and his brothers were already in the office, huddled around the conference room table once again. "Good morning. Is everyone feeling better?"

The guys all grunted unintelligibly and threw up random waves in her direction. To her surprise, everyone looked like they'd actually gotten some sleep—even Chance.

Someone had already started a pot of coffee in the conference room, but it was nearly empty, so she dropped her purse at her desk and started a new pot. When she looked up, she found Chance studying her.

"Our coffee not good enough for you now?"

Maci grimaced at the cup she'd set down. "Tea, actually."

Tea was nowhere near as good as coffee, but

she knew there was no way her stomach could tolerate her normal brew.

Chance stood and walked over to her. "Still not feeling well?" he asked, low enough that his brothers wouldn't hear.

She shrugged. "It's a bug. It'll go away soon enough."

"If you need to take the day off—"

"I'm good," she interrupted, smiling to soften the blow. When he just stared at her, she sighed. "If I need to go home and rest, I will. I promise."

"Okay. We're meeting in ten to discuss new options on the case." Maci nodded and looked away, trying to settle the nerves in her stomach. She didn't normally offer many tactical suggestions. Between the four Patterson brothers, they pretty much had that market cornered.

She had no idea how they'd take her suggestion. But ten minutes gave her just enough time to do what she needed to build her case.

She stepped into the bathroom and pulled out her special occasion makeup. She'd watched a few online tutorials last night, one from Stella LeBlanc herself.

When she left the bathroom ten minutes later, she looked less like Maci and more like Stella.

Chance and Brax were in the same seats as yesterday, sleeves rolled up and eyes focused. Luke and Weston were poring over a tablet, pointing out things to each other. She walked to one of the conference room chairs and sat, firing up her laptop so she could take notes like she usually did. She wasn't sure when she should bring up her idea.

"Is everybody ready to officially start?" Chance asked. "We're not leaving here today until we have a plan for catching Stella's stalker. Nicholas is demanding action."

"Can't blame him for that," Weston muttered. The rest of the brothers agreed.

Brax used a remote to turn on the large-screen television near the head of the table. "Should we start by looking at the wreck again with fresh eyes?"

Once they got into that it might be difficult to drag them back out. Now was the time to tell them her plan. "Actually, before you do, I have something to run by you."

All the eyes in the room zeroed in on her.

Luke shook his head in what looked like genuine fear. "Please don't tell us you're quitting. We'll never get unburied from the paperwork."

"No, not that." Maci laughed. "I have an idea for the Stella LeBlanc case."

Luke's relief was palpable as he slumped back into his chair and heaved a breath. His aversion to paperwork was near legendary.

"What kind of idea?" Brax crossed his arms and sat back in his chair.

"Why do you look like that?" Chance asked gruffly before she could answer Brax's question. "Your makeup. It's…"

She ignored him, knowing she had to get to her point before things derailed. "I think you should employ a decoy. Someone to take Stella's place publicly to draw out the danger and eliminate it."

"You want to be the decoy," Weston guessed. Maci nodded.

A heavy silence followed, but it only lasted for three seconds before Chance exploded. "That's what the makeup is about, isn't it? Showing how much you look like Stella. There is absolutely no way we're using you."

Brax leaned forward, eyeing Maci critically. "It's not a bad plan, actually. And the makeup does make them look remarkably similar. Since Stella doesn't have a sister, that would make it even more likely to work."

"Did you hear me?" Chance glared at Brax. "I said no."

Maci took a breath to answer, but Luke shook his head across the table. She didn't argue because she could see the beginnings of a sibling "chat" brewing, and she was better off staying out of it.

"Last I looked, San Antonio Security was an equal partnership, Chance." Brax's nonchalant brush-off caused a vein in Chance's forehead to pulse. "Not a dictatorship."

Luke nodded. "We're in the business of protection. We would make sure Maci is safe. If we use her as a decoy, we'd plan it right so that no one gets hurt."

Chance scrubbed his hand down his face. "You're all out of your mind. We're not sending Maci out untrained so we can catch a stalker."

Maci had had enough. "You aren't sending me anywhere. I'm volunteering," she snapped.

Chance glared at her from his chair. "You don't know the first thing about being in the field."

"So, train her, Chance." Luke leaned forward across the table so that Chance's attention was forced onto him. "She's already more tactically aware than most civilians. She's smart and self-reliant. Give her some physical defense lessons—quick and dirty basics—and let's do this."

Chance turned to Weston, who, in normal form, hadn't yet said anything. "Will you please help me get them to see reason?"

Weston studied Maci for a long moment, then looked back at Chance. The two of them were super close. "I get why you're worried. Maci is part of the family, and we don't like the thought of any family member in potential harm's way."

Hearing Weston say she was part of the family warmed something inside Maci. Chance turned to her, and for a moment she was afraid he was going to blow the whistle on her. To explain that, since she'd snuck out of his bed in the middle of the night two months ago, maybe *family* didn't apply to her.

But if anything, Chance's gaze was more protective. More possessive. More...*everything*.

The warmth she'd felt ratcheted up to a full heat.

"It's the best plan we've come up with yet," Brax said. "Let's at least keep it on the table while we continue looking at other options."

Chance finally looked away from her and nodded. "Okay. But if we send her out, we're going to damn well make sure she's safe."

All three brothers offered their agreement.

"Stella always has some sort of bodyguards around, right?" Luke asked.

Chance let out a small sigh, as if he knew he'd already lost this battle. "Yes. She has at least three nearby at all times."

"Great," Luke said. "So, we ship the original Stella off on an international vacation, so she's out of any danger."

Weston nodded. "And also so we can control

the situation more. We can send our new Stella only to events that we can have a greater measure of control over."

Brax grinned. "Plus, Maci isn't spoiled like Stella. She's an asset, not a liability. Especially will be after some defense training and running potential scenarios so she knows what to look out for."

"Fine," Chance said finally. That one word was low and gritty, like it was painful for him to speak at all. Maci's stomach swooped deliciously at the sound, and she inwardly cursed her body for responding to it. "I'll agree to this plan if you take at least three days of self-defense training with me. I'll also be with you every step of the way when you're undercover."

Maci's eyes widened. Staying in close confines with Chance day after day? That wasn't going to be easy. "I'm sure I could learn the basics from anyone. You don't have to do it all yourself."

"They've all got people waiting for them at home. You and I are the single ones of the bunch. That makes us the best people for an undercover job like this. It's me, or we scrap the plan altogether."

Chance's smile was tight. He knew she was stuck. She would always agree to anything that let the others go home to their families, but she was also desperate for a reason for her and Chance not to be alone. She had to preserve the distance between them.

She knew how easily that distance could disappear.

"What do you say, Maci?" Chance finally said. "Are you ready to work together?"

Anyone could see that he was waiting for her to say no, but she wasn't going to do it. "I'm sure it'll be a blast."

"Oh, there will be a blast somewhere," Luke muttered. Brax and Weston laughed under their breaths while Chance watched and waited. He wanted a real answer, and she could tell he wasn't going to leave without it.

Maci was simultaneously ecstatic and panicked, but she shoved it all down. Nothing else mattered but finishing the job. She had to help Stella get her life back before something—or someone—wrecked it forever.

She stared into Chance's brown eyes. "I'm in."

Maci felt like she'd just signed her soul to the devil but had no idea why.

As MACI CLOSED up the office later that afternoon, she still couldn't believe the guys had agreed to her plan. She hadn't seen any of them for most of the day. They'd been too busy going over the plan with LeBlanc's security team, working on the details of getting Stella out of the country and narrowing down the social events where Maci would take Stella's place.

Maci was really going to do it. She was going to take an active part in capturing a stalker and making a young woman safe again. Maybe it could even count as penance for some of her own past sins.

If only that was the way it worked.

Pushing those thoughts aside, she locked the door to the office and drove to the popular Thai restaurant down the street from her place to grab the order she'd put in. A big bowl of noodle soup and too many appetizers sounded like the perfect dinner to celebrate becoming an undercover super-agent.

At least her stomach could handle it. Thankfully it had settled since this morning. Hopefully the bug was gone for good.

The last thing she needed was the flu plus three days of one-on-one with Chance. It was going to be hard enough to keep her wits about her at full strength.

Thai food would help.

She'd just put the bags on the floor of the passenger seat when her phone rang. It was Claire, Luke's fiancée.

"What's going on, woman?" Maci and Claire

had become good friends when Claire had needed Luke's help a couple years ago. He and the other Patterson brothers had helped clear her name of murder.

"You have no idea how much money I would give to have seen you talk Chance Patterson into using you as bait for this stalker."

Maci winced as she put the phone on speaker so she could drive. "I'm not using myself as bait. Chance would've freaked out. I'm a decoy."

Claire chuckled. "You and Stella do look a lot alike. I still would've liked to have seen you talk him into it."

"Actually, I just suggested it and played up my makeup to look a little more similar to her. The other brothers were the ones being reasonable and listening."

"Chance is not known for his reasonableness when it comes to you."

Maci knew Claire suspected the truth. Her friend had never asked Maci outright if she and Chance had slept together, but she'd been closer than anyone else to putting the pieces together.

"Probably the most dangerous part of this entire operation will be the next few days with Chance attempting to train me. After that, a swarm of ninjas would probably be a breeze."

More laughter from Claire. "You be careful. And if it all starts to feel like too much, let someone know. Heck, you can let me know and I'll make sure Luke understands. You don't have to do anything you're uncomfortable with."

"I know. None of them would want that, even if using me is the best option. But I'm actually excited about it." She pulled up to her apartment and grabbed the bags from the passenger side.

"Good."

Maci heard some purring over the phone. "Is that my buddy Khan I hear?"

Claire's giant Maine coon acted more like a dog than a cat, and Claire loved him to pieces.

"Yeah, he's hanging here on the couch with me. I've got awful cramps and he's my emotional support animal for the day."

"He's a good one to have. Okay, I'm home. I'll talk to you later." She disconnected the call and headed inside, hoping her own period wasn't going to make the next few days even more difficult.

She froze in the process of setting her food on the counter.

Maci couldn't remember the last time she'd had cramps.

Dread bubbled up in her stomach. Her period had been regular since she was thirteen, and for the first time ever, it was off.

"No, no, no," she whispered, swiping to her period tracking app only to groan again. She'd missed not one but *two* periods. One month she could chalk up to the stress of everything that had been going on, but two?

Two was unprecedented, and something in her gut said she was out of her depth.

Don't freak out when you aren't sure what's happening. The first step is to pee on a stick.

The next thing Maci knew, she was standing in the drugstore with no idea how she'd gotten there. She threw test after test into her basket. One test wasn't enough. It could be a false positive. That happened sometimes.

Checking out and the drive home were also blurs in her timeline. She shoved the Thai into the fridge—there was no way she was going to eat now—and dumped every test she'd bought onto the bathroom counter. She picked up a random one and opened it, shoving the rest into a very un-Maci-like pile to the side.

A quick pee and two minutes later, she was curled up with her back against the tub and the test clenched between her shaking hands.

Two lines.

"No. This cannot be happening," she told herself. "Take another one. You have to be..." Positive. The mental pun was just terrible enough to send Maci into near-crying laughter.

The next test was one of the smart tests, so

when the timer went off, there were no lines, just a single word...

Pregnant.

Pregnancy had never been in her plans. She wasn't fit to be anyone's mother.

And Chance... Just the thought of him had her stomach lurching. She barely made it to her knees in time to throw up in the toilet.

He was going to think she'd trapped him. How could he not?

Now he was stuck in her life forever. After all the effort to keep him away from her, their lives were intertwined all because she was keeping this baby.

Amazing how no other option even boded consideration. Even if he didn't want anything to do with her and the baby, she still wasn't making any other choice.

You're going to be a terrible mother. You'll ruin your kid like you ruined your life.

She tried to fight back against the malicious thoughts, but she couldn't. She didn't know anything about motherhood. Her own mother used her as an ATM.

Maybe Chance might fight her for custody. Maci thought about what had happened to Brax's wife, Tessa, and how she'd briefly lost custody of her own child.

No, Chance wouldn't do what Tessa's ex had done. That had been lies and manipulation.

But maybe he would decide she wasn't worthy of his child.

There's nothing to do about it yet. Focus on the pregnancy and work—

Work. Of course, what should have been a great day had ended in such chaos. The plan for Stella's protection hinged on her and now she was pregnant. She didn't know whether to quit the plan already or...

"No. I'm doing this," she told herself, hunching over the sink to wash her face. "I'm going to decoy for Stella because she needs it, and I'm not going to worry about it. Chance will keep me safe just like he always has, and when everything's over, I'll tell him about the baby. It's going to be fine."

Maci stared at herself in the mirror and wished for the first time in ages that she had someone she could call. A real mother who could give her advice.

But she didn't have that.

She straightened, taking a deep breath. She may not have any parental figures in her life, but she didn't drink or do drugs. She was organized and clean and would do her damnedest to take care of this baby.

Feeling marginally better, she pulled out her

phone and made an emergency appointment through her doctor's scheduling app for in the morning. She needed to get an official test done and check how far along she was. Then she needed to see if self-defense training was going to be a problem.

She walked into the kitchen and pulled out her food. She wasn't hungry, but not eating now wasn't an option. Then she grabbed a notebook from the junk drawer. Between bites she listed everything she needed to ask the doctor before she went to work in the morning.

She'd just follow the list, stick to her plan, and everything would be okay.

She hoped.

Chapter Five

The next morning, Chance was getting the plan ready for Maci's training when she texted about a last-minute doctor's appointment. Good. He hoped she could get some meds for that bug she had.

Or, even better, that bug would mean she couldn't take part in this plan at all.

Chance had always been logical and strategic in his thinking. That, combined with his protective instincts, had meant he'd spent a lot of time taking care of the younger kids at the group homes he'd lived in before being adopted by Sheila and Clinton.

He'd been the one to plan things out and make sure everyone had what they needed. He'd been the one able to anticipate unexpected events and pivot to plan B, C or Z.

Those logical and strategic parts of his brain knew that Maci's decoy plan was the most likely to be successful. Wasn't the fact that she and Stella looked so much alike the reason he'd been compelled to take the case in the first place? And despite the fact they fought all the time, he knew Maci was intelligent, competent and situationally aware, like his brothers had argued.

But the logical and strategic parts of his brain weren't what he wanted to listen to. He wanted Maci as far away from potential danger as possible.

And if the safest place was in his bed—*him with her*—was that really a bad thing?

But he'd agreed. He'd stand by his word and make sure she was as prepared as she could be.

Unused to the extra time, he picked up a cup of coffee for himself, adding a tea for Maci at the last minute. She could heat it up later if she wanted.

He'd rented a private room from his favorite local boxing gym. It was quiet and familiar, which was what he needed when it came to being around Maci. Being in the office with her was tough enough, but here there would be no brothers holding him back from saying things he should leave in the past.

There would be no offices to shut himself in to stop himself from demanding once again why she'd called their relationship off with no explanation.

It would just be the two of them and a few layers of cotton and Lycra separating skin from skin.

It was going to be torture.

When Maci walked through the doors, Chance could already tell she was distracted.

Bloodshot eyes and bite-chapped lips were framed by messy hair, like she'd shoved her hands through it endlessly.

He caught her at the door and led her toward their training room. "How'd your appointment go? Find out anything interesting?"

Her blue eyes grew wide. "Wh-what?"

"Your doctor's appointment. Your sickness? Are you okay to move forward with this plan?"

"Oh." She forced a laugh. "I'm fine. Just a little…upset stomach. Doctor gave me a little nausea medicine, which should help."

She was lying or at least wasn't telling the full truth. He'd been studying that beautiful face and those cobalt eyes for way too long not to recognize it.

Maci was stubborn as hell and didn't like to talk about her feelings. She was blowing him off; nothing he said was going to get her to share what was really going on.

He should be used to her shutting him out by now, but he wasn't. The best he could do was ignore the burn of the slice. "Good. Then let's get you warmed up and ready to go. I got you some tea if you need it."

He led her through his favorite stretches, letting her modify them when they agitated her sensitive stomach and making a note to avoid touching that part of her body if at all possible. He wanted to train her, not make things worse.

The stretching should've helped her relax, but by the time he got her on the floor stretching her hips, she was nearly vibrating with stress.

"Maci, have you changed your mind? There's no problem if you have." There was nothing he'd like more.

"No, I haven't changed my mind." She shook her head, leaning forward to stretch her hamstrings, keeping her face averted.

He didn't like that she felt like she had to hide herself from him. A thought struck him and he had to swallow down the lump in his throat before he could verbalize it.

Finally, he pushed the words out. "Would you like someone else to train you? If you're uncomfortable with me being here, we can swap Luke or Weston out."

It would gut him to do it, but her safety was the most important thing. If she would be more comfortable with someone else, Chance needed to step aside.

"No. It's fine. I just… I've got a lot on my mind."

"If you're sure—"

"I am. I want you to train me, Chance. I trust you." Her blue eyes pinned him.

Something eased inside him. She trusted him.

She had no idea how much that meant. Hell, he'd hardly understood how much that meant until the words had come out of her mouth.

He walked her through the final stretches and warm-ups before she stood there catching her breath and waiting for instructions.

"Before we get started, let's level your expectations. I'm not going to teach you to fight."

Her face screwed up in an adorable frown. "Why not?"

"We don't have the time to get you to a comfortable proficiency with fighting. That means your goal is always going to be getting to safety. Survival is always the most important thing. Say it."

"Survival is always the most important thing."

"So, to that end, we're going to utilize your size and stature to get out of some common scenarios."

Maci stared at him with a quirked eyebrow and her usual sassy grin. He was surprised at how much he liked seeing it. The last few days—hell, *weeks*—she always seemed to be stressed. He'd missed the sass.

"You realize I'm not exactly tall, right?"

Oh, he realized it. He gave her a grin of his own as he dragged his gaze down the length of her body, grinning wider when a hint of pink colored her cheeks.

Maci wasn't terribly short, but the fact that she fit under his chin was something he'd always enjoyed. "Exactly. Your height means that any attackers who are taller than you will have to contort their body to grab you. That gives us a small window of time to get you out and away."

She considered that and nodded. "Okay."

"We'll go through a few holds and how to break them today. Tomorrow, we'll work on escaping a few common restraints and reiterating what we learned today. The last day is basic self-defense moves that any person should know."

"It doesn't seem like a lot," she said doubtfully.

Chance agreed. "Like I said, the goal isn't for you to win a close-quarter fight. It's for you to get enough room between you and the danger to escape."

"Alright, Sensei. Teach me."

"The most important thing you have to do in any attack is keep your head. That sounds easier than it really is." And was a situation nearly impossible to replicate in training, but he wanted to mention it.

"Okay."

"You're smart and a quick thinker. Use that to your advantage."

She blushed. "Thanks."

He wasn't saying it to flatter her. "In a battle against someone stronger than you or with more fighting experience, you have to use your strengths. For you, that's going to have nothing to do with your physical muscles and everything to do with your brain."

She was listening and taking this seriously. That was good.

"Okay, let's start with a hold from behind. An attacker is likely going to wrap around you in an effort to either pick you up or hold your arms still. They won't want you to be able to fight back since this position is mostly about the element of surprise."

She nodded, taking it all in. "Okay."

He spun a finger to signal for her to turn. He then stepped behind her, forcing himself to keep focus on the task at hand and not the closeness of her body.

"If the bad guy's arms are around you, that leaves you with your legs. Go for the soft spots and try to unbalance him. Groin attacks, knee shots, anything. If you can twist your body around, you have the ability to claw at their eyes or headbutt them. Whatever you do, it's not going to look pretty, so don't worry about form. Just make sure it's effective."

He showed her the best places to kick the kneecap, and how high up on the inner thigh to aim for maximum pain if she couldn't hit the groin.

She seemed riveted as he taught her the weakest parts of the ankle and how to rotate herself so that she could slither out of his grasp. None of it was perfect, but she managed the basics well enough, and every time she succeeded, she got happier.

Making Maci Ford happy was a heady feeling. One he wished she'd let him try to do full-time.

"Alright," he finally said after they'd been at it for a couple hours. "Break free one more time and we'll move on to other things."

Chance wrapped his arms around her, hands on either bicep, but for a moment Maci didn't move and he didn't want her to. He had his arms wrapped around her for the first time in months and he was in no hurry for her to escape them again.

He tried to commit the moment to memory. The softness of her shirt sleeves under his fingers, the sound of her breathing as he kept her close to his body. He even pressed his nose to the crown of her head and took in the smell of the shampoo she loved so much. When he was sure he'd remember it for good, he squeezed her arms lightly, a reminder to focus and escape.

Maci took a deep breath and dropped her bodyweight. It was unexpected enough that he nearly released her, and she used it to her advantage. She twisted, grabbed the back of his knee and shoved her shoulder into his stomach like a football star. As soon as he was on his way down, she let go of him and scuttled to the back wall of the room.

"Perfect. That's exactly what I wanted to see. Use whatever means necessary to surprise your attacker and put yourself in a position to escape. Let's take a break for a bit then get back at it."

Chance grabbed his water bottle and did everything in his power to focus on rehydrating rather than on Maci eating some granola bar and drinking her cooled tea on the other side of the room.

Even with dried sweat plastering her hair to her head and in shorts and a T-shirt she was damned beautiful.

How had things gone so wrong between them?

How could he make them right again?

How was he going to survive two and a half more days of being this close to her?

After the break she walked back over. She

was looking a little tired, not that he could blame her. Maybe they'd take it easier this afternoon. They ran quickly through what they'd already worked on. The more it could become muscle memory for her, the better it would be.

Then it was time to move on to frontal attacks. "Alright, next up we'll go over what to do for a choke hold. In this case, you'll have eyes on your assailant and—"

He reached for her throat, but before he could connect, Maci flinched. Her whole body shifted away from him and her eyes closed. The furrow of her brow and the tight set of her mouth told him that it wasn't a voluntary response—it was some sort of unexpected reaction.

And he had no idea why she'd had it.

Instantly, he dropped his hands and stepped back. Maci had never flinched from him before. Not in the time when they'd been lovers and not when they sniped and snarled at one another.

He couldn't recall a single moment where she'd looked scared or fearful of her physical safety with him. Seeing this flinch, even though it wasn't an extreme reaction, shattered something inside him.

"Maci? Are you okay?"

Those blue eyes popped open, and she seemed to realize what had happened. "I—I'm sorry."

"Are you scared of me?"

He hated that he had to ask, but he needed to know.

"No."

"Are you sure?" Had he been misreading her all morning long, thinking she was doing okay when really she'd been hiding fear? "I don't want you trying to push through some mental block. If this training is triggering for you then—"

"It's not. I'm not scared of you."

Her voice was firm and it sent a wave of relief rushing through him, one that was almost immediately taken over by confusion. If she wasn't afraid of him, then why did she flinch? Had someone hurt her in the past?

And why the hell didn't he know the answer to that question? He barely knew anything about her past at all.

He wanted to ask. Wanted to demand to know what that flinch had been about, but knew it would lead to a fight. The real kind with them yelling at each other, not the self-defense training kind.

"I think we've done enough for today," he finally said. "Let's call it quits."

"No."

"Can you tell me what caused you to flinch like that?"

He expected her to shut him down or joke

around the question. When she remained silent, he thought maybe she wouldn't answer at all.

"My parents would sometimes get violent with each other. Both ways. I guess choking was part of it, although I didn't actively remember that until you came at me."

Chance was stunned. He'd never heard her talk about her parents. Had no idea she'd had a less than ideal home life.

He didn't talk much about his parents either. Maci had met Clinton and Sheila and knew what great people they were. But Chance had never really known his biological parents at all, so there wasn't much to say about them.

"Mace, I—"

She held out a hand to stop him. He wasn't sure what he was going to say anyway. "We're on the clock. A woman's life is at stake. I flinched but I'm fine now. Let's keep working."

"Are you sure?"

"There's a lot of things I'm not sure about, but this isn't one of them."

Chapter Six

Chance stared down at Maci in the sparring ring. Both of them were near snarling.

It was the end of the final day of training. Tomorrow she'd be heading undercover as Stella at some bigwig art gala. Whether she was ready or not.

Chance knew she was ready, or as ready as someone could get in just three days. There was so much they'd been trying to cram into the limited time. The hours of defense training may have been the most physically demanding, but all the other elements took their toll also.

Maci had spent hours studying footage of Stella's mannerisms and nonverbal communication in order to effectively impersonate her. Weston's fiancée, Kayleigh Delacruz, had come by the office to help Maci style her hair and makeup as close as possible to Stella's.

Maci, Chance and his brothers had spent an ungodly amount of time studying the people who would be at the gala, as well as friends and acquaintances of Stella's. There were a few friends—surprisingly few—who would recognize Maci wasn't Stella. Nicholas had helped make sure those friends wouldn't be in attendance—mostly by offering them a weekend trip to the French Alps.

Must be nice to have those sorts of resources.

Rich Carlisle, Stella's companion, had come in to coach Maci on how she would act with different groups of people. That entire process was distasteful. Not only was Stella basically a self-centered snob to most people, Rich was slick and handsy with Maci.

Chance had to stop himself from breaking the man's fingers every time he tucked a strand of Maci's hair behind her ear or touched her shoulder. Every time he gave her one of his charming smiles, Chance wanted to punch him in his perfect teeth.

Logically, he knew Rich was behaving the same way he did with Stella. He was trying to help the best he could. He would actually be the biggest part of selling this whole ruse—Stella rarely went anywhere without Rich.

But Chance still found his hands balling into fists way too often around the other man. Especially when Maci laughed at something charming he said.

To avoid bloodshed, his brothers had put him on layout duty—which honestly played to Chance's strengths anyway. He'd studied the layout of the gala building, determining potential places the stalker might make some sort of attempt to get near Maci. Dorian Cane had offered backup guards to place at any locations they were needed.

Chance had studied the exits and made sure Maci knew about them. And backup exits. Ignoring everyone's rolling eyes, he'd even pointed out a couple of large air shafts she could use to hide in if needed.

Long after everyone had gone home each night, he'd run possible scenarios in his head. How he would react to different threat types. How he would get Maci to safety.

Over and over. As many situations as his mind could come up with. He wanted to be as prepared as possible. It was how his mind worked. Always had been.

But now, looking down into Maci's blue eyes, he was afraid they might kill each other before the stalker had the opportunity to do any damage.

It was a stressful situation and they both were exhausted, but that wasn't really the issue here.

She was hiding something from him.

Hell, not *something*…everything. The more he thought about that flinch on the first day and what it had revealed, the more he realized how little he actually knew about this woman.

He knew they were combustible in bed. Knew

that everything about her stimulated him mentally and physically.

But she had very carefully kept the details of her past from him. And the more he thought about it, the more he was convinced that it had something to do with why she'd run from his bed two months ago.

She still wanted him. And he damned well wanted her. Training so closely together over the past few days had proven that on both sides. There'd been way too many times when they'd had to take a step back from each other—both of them breathing hard and not just from exertion—to settle down.

Multiple times he'd tried to get her to talk about anything—them, her past, why she was keeping so much from him. But she'd avoided his attempts every time.

"That's it," he said, dropping his hands from her and stepping back. He'd been teaching her how to break a wrist lock, and he'd spent the entire time feeling the racing of her heartbeat under his fingers.

"What's it?" Maci asked, stepping back herself. He hated the distance. "Did I mess up?"

"No, you're doing great, but I want to talk."

Immediately, the open expression she'd been wearing morphed and he felt her shutting him out. Again.

"Let's just get this lesson done with, okay?"

"We're going to finish it, but we're going to talk too. I can protect you more effectively if you stop trying to keep silent about every personal thing about yourself."

Her shoulders tightened, creeping up toward her ears. "Chance, we've been doing so well. Just don't."

"Think about that flinch when I came at you the first time in a choke hold. It totally caught me off guard."

She shrugged. "It caught me off guard too. But we worked through it and I don't flinch anymore."

"But what if something happens while you're undercover? Something else triggers you."

"We can't possibly work through every possible scenario that might trigger me. It's impossible for anyone."

She was right. There were always internal factors at play in undercover work that could momentarily cripple even the most seasoned agent. There was no way to prepare for them all.

But this was different. His very gut told him so. "I want you to answer me one question."

Her eyes narrowed as she planted her hands on her hips. "What?"

"You're deliberately hiding something from me, aren't you. Something important."

The blood drained from her face, and he knew he'd hit his mark. Maci Ford was hiding something.

"Let's just finish the lesson, Patterson. I'm tired and tomorrow is a big day."

She was exhausted—he could see it in the bags under her eyes and the tight set of her mouth. He knew she'd been sick at least once a day despite her medication.

He should let this go, but couldn't. He had to know.

"I'll make you a deal. You break out of my hold in under two minutes and I'll leave it all alone."

"And if I don't?"

"Then you tell me why you keep saying you don't want to be with me when we both know we can hardly stay away from each other."

He saw her throat working as she gulped. "I don't think—"

Chance stepped into her space and ran a fingertip down her cheek. "I should've pushed way before now. But I didn't want you to feel like you were pressured into being with me," he whispered. "That you had to sleep with me for job security."

She blinked in shock. "I never felt that way."

"Good." They were so close, it wouldn't take much to bend down and kiss her. He was so tempted. "I thought maybe you'd just lost interest in me, which was a blow to the ego, but acceptable. You've done a good job of hiding that you're still attracted to me, but the last couple days I could fairly taste it in the air between us. You still want me, Maci Ford."

She swallowed, drawing his eyes to her throat where he desperately wanted to press his lips, but didn't answer.

"So, if you can't break my hold in under two minutes, then you tell me why you're so damned determined to keep away from me."

"And if I don't take the bet?"

"Then I'll be knocking on your door every day until I find out the truth. Your call."

Either way he was going to get the truth.

"Fine." She took a step back, stretching her neck from side to side. "Let's do this."

Chance set a timer on his phone and gave her a three-second warning before he lunged. He kept them both on their feet, coming at her from the side to trap her arms with his own. It made it harder for her to reach him with a kick. As she struggled, Chance kept an eye on the timer.

One minute left. Maci was breathing hard and grunting with her every move. He could see the panic setting in, and he wasn't sure if it was his arms restraining her or that she knew she was going to lose. Either way, it pushed her to fight harder. Her nails dug into his stomach where they could reach and her teeth gnashed at his arms.

Good for her. It hurt, but she was using the tools they'd worked on.

Thirty seconds left. Her energy flagged, which he'd been counting on. In a real fight against someone bigger, she'd have to use bursts of speed and power.

They were down to the last twenty seconds when the gym door opened and Brax walked in with his phone in his hand.

"Hey, Maci. There's an issue at the office. We need to get you back."

They both looked over at him, and Chance's arms loosened just enough that she collapsed hard to the ground then wrenched herself away.

The alarm went off, but she'd already won.

They stared at each other for a long moment before she turned and rushed toward the locker room.

"Everything okay?" Brax asked, glancing between Chance and the door she'd disappeared behind. "You look like you need to actually spar rather than work on training basics."

There was no doubt about that. Chance's arms were nearly quivering with the need to hit something. "Let's go."

Within a few minutes they were geared up and circling each other in the sparring ring.

"What was the emergency at the office?" Chance asked, keeping a close eye on his brother. Bastard was fast.

"There wasn't one. You two were so involved in your conversation, you didn't hear me come in the first time."

Chance stopped. "How much did you hear?"

"Just the end. The bet if she couldn't break out in two minutes or less, she would tell you why she's been keeping away from you."

That wasn't as bad as it could've been, but it was bad enough. "Brax..."

"What's going on with Maci?" Brax jumped forward and threw out a cross and jab with his gloved fists.

Chance dodged the first, but took the second on his geared chin. "Nothing's going on."

Brax snorted. "Never pegged you for a liar. Are you sleeping with her?"

Chance's glove sailed toward Brax's nose, only to miss when his brother skipped out of the way. "Things between Maci and I are complicated, but no, we are not currently involved with each other."

"Currently." Brax threw another swing. "That implies that you were involved. Is that why you threw such a fit about her going undercover?"

"She doesn't know what she's doing." It wasn't a lie, but it wasn't a real answer either.

"Her risk is minimal, given the circumstances and us being glued to her every second."

"Still a risk. How would you feel if it was Tessa?"

At hearing his wife's name, Brax stopped messing around. His blows became quicker. So did Chance's. They both dodged what punches they could and took the ones they couldn't.

Eventually Chance began to withdraw. This could go on for a long time. He and Brax were too evenly matched and knew each other too well. Brax slowed down too.

"This isn't a good use of our time," Chance said. He dropped his hands. He knew his brother could get a dirty swing in if he wanted, but also knew Brax wouldn't do that.

"Agreed. We need to be firing on all cylinders tomorrow. I'm glad Maci went home. She looks like she needs some rest."

Chance just grunted as he used his teeth to loosen his sparring gloves. He was well aware at how pale and tired she'd looked.

"You going to tell me what's going on between you two?"

"There's nothing—"

"Don't lie. We've all seen the way you look at her. I just wasn't aware that it had progressed."

Chance ripped off his sparring helmet and ran a hand through his hair. "Progressed then completely stalled."

Brax shot him a boyish grin. "Maybe you should look for a girl somewhere else, man. Maci doesn't seem interested."

"I can't," he eventually answered. It was the best he could do for his brother. There were too many things unsaid for him to walk away from Maci, even if she'd already done it to him. There was too much potential between them, and Chance had never been one to squander a good thing. "I'll try not to let it mess with work though."

Brax threw him a bottle of water and they both took a sip. "I think you and Maci would be good together."

Chance sputtered his water, coughing when it went down the wrong pipe. "But you just said to look for someone else."

"That was just a test to see if you were truly interested in her. Seems like you are."

"Are you telling me you wanted to check my intentions with her? I thought I was *your* brother."

Brax grinned. "You are, but Maci's family too, and she doesn't have anyone else to step in for her."

How the hell did Brax know more about Maci than Chance did?

Because Chance had been so caught up in the physical aspect of their relationship that he hadn't started talking to her about important stuff. He'd thought he'd have more time. That they would take it slow and get to know everything about each other.

It definitely hadn't been because he didn't want to know.

They both grabbed their gym bags and headed toward the door. Brax slapped him on the back. "I had to make sure you were ready for the long haul, because a woman like Maci Ford is a lifelong commitment."

"Don't I know it," Chance muttered. Brax laughed and changed the subject to details about tomorrow's operation. Chance barely heard him, consumed in his thoughts.

What was he going to do about Maci Ford and the secrets she clutched so tightly?

Chapter Seven

"Maci, breathe. You can do this."

She was glad for Chance's voice in her ear through the comm unit. It was the only thing keeping her even remotely grounded.

She didn't look like herself, didn't sound like herself. Didn't feel like herself.

And despite the fact that she should be focusing on this mission, her thoughts kept coming back to her pregnancy and her near-showdown with Chance yesterday.

The urge to cover her stomach made her fingers twitch, and it was all she could do to stop herself. Though she couldn't see them, all four of the Pattersons were close by. She couldn't give her secret away yet. It wasn't time.

But she knew she couldn't keep it from Chance forever. He was a pit bull when it came to solving mysteries, and she'd somehow made herself a mystery he was determined to solve.

She would tell him about the pregnancy after they caught this stalker. Right now, despite not looking or feeling like herself, she had to focus on what she was doing.

"I'm okay," she murmured into the hidden

comm unit. "These are just not my normal type of people."

Chance chuckled. "I hear that."

He was in full support mode for this mission—leaving behind their personal conflicts—and she appreciated it. He'd been the one to show her how the comm unit worked and had been the voice in her ear all evening.

"Most of these people seem so fake," she murmured.

She'd known an art gallery was way out of her norm and had expected to feel out of place and generally clueless about the art. But it wasn't the art that made her uncomfortable, it was how the people were acting.

The gala was for a new contemporary artist, an in-your-face, Banksy-type multimedia creator. Maci would be the first to admit that she didn't understand any of it.

But it didn't seem to matter. The people here were less about the art and more about making sure they were seen and photographed from all different angles. Social media was the true artist here.

Rich was by Maci's side, constantly touching her—like he would Stella—but it grated on Maci's nerves. She ignored it, focusing on her smile and posing for pictures herself. They already had some pictures of the real Stella that would be superimposed over shots of the gala. Those were what would be posted online.

But right now, Maci had to be Stella enough to fool the stalker.

An hour later, despite her best attempts and Rich all but fawning over her, Maci was convinced she was failing. Hardly anyone was talking to her.

She gripped the glass of champagne she wasn't drinking tighter. This was a mistake. She'd never considered herself a good actress even when she wasn't distracted, so why had she thought she could do this? Mingling with the elite, with their designer clothing and bejeweled shoes. Even dressed to the nines in Stella's clothes, she felt separate from everyone else. It wasn't her world and it never would be.

The urge to run, to admit her mistake and leave the room—and the case—to the professionals had her looking for the nearest exit.

"Relax, Mace," Chance told her, his voice tinny through the comm in her ear. "You look like you're going to bolt."

"I almost think it would be preferable to all of this," she mumbled into her glass.

The huff of Chance's laughter was a balm to her nerves, as was the reminder that he and the others were close by. They wouldn't let her fail, and despite the potential danger being Stella attracted, Maci couldn't help but feel safe with Chance nearby.

"Who pays this much to get in then basically ignores the art?" she murmured as Rich turned to talk to someone a few feet away.

The price tag to get in the door had been over a thousand dollars per person. San Antonio Security hadn't had to pay that, of course, but still, the thought that everyone else here had done so and then were hardly paying attention to the art...

"People who are willing to spend thousands of dollars for a single social media post," Chance answered. "Or the opportunity to network. To be seen somewhere important."

She barely refrained from rolling her eyes. The money people paid to get in here tonight could've been used for much better causes.

An arm wrapped around her waist, and lips pressed against her hair. "There you are, Stella darling."

Even knowing it was Rich and that he was supposed to do this, she had to force herself not to stiffen.

She heard Chance growl and struggled not to smile. They may have all been on the same team in trying to catch the stalker, but Chance didn't like Rich at all.

Rich was on LeBlanc's payroll even though

he didn't need the money, and even Chance had admitted the man made a great secret weapon. He'd grown up in the same elite society as Stella, so it wasn't an issue for him to show up to the same events as her best friend, making him the perfect incognito bodyguard.

Or at least Maci assumed he was. She'd never actually seen him in bodyguard action, only in flirt mode. He flirted with anything that moved, including Maci. With golden hair and a tall, lean-muscled body to match, it was no surprise that his charming behavior caused people to write him off as nothing more than a playboy.

Still, Maci wished he wouldn't touch her quite so much.

Rich dipped his head, letting his breath warm Maci's hair. "You look uncomfortable. Is everything okay?"

"Fine, just needed a second. It's all an adjustment," Maci said honestly, taking a half step back to give herself some breathing room.

"You're doing great." He stopped, his arm slipping around her waist as he plastered her body to his side. "Incoming. Amy and Angelina Kendrick. Twin influencers on YouTube. They're a couple of Stella's biggest competitors. Definite frenemies."

Maci nodded, giving him a flash of Stella's signature smile, one that had taken her hours of practice in the mirror. It felt wrong on her face, but she knew she'd gotten it right when Rich winked. "You're sure they won't recognize me as not being Stella?"

"Nah. They'll want to move on quickly, get ahead of Stella in terms of photo ops and talking to important names. I can sell this."

Maci nodded.

"Ladies, so lovely to see you again," Rich said, kissing the sisters' hands and leading the conversation like he was born for it. He kept their focus on him and away from the Stella imposter at his side.

She kept her shoulders back, chin up and bored smile on her face. "Maybe you two would like to have lunch with us sometime," Angelina said. "We could talk shop."

"I'll have to check my schedule." Maci kept everything about herself loose, adopting the pretentious, distant air Stella perpetually seemed to have in public in all the footage Maci had studied.

The twins' eyes narrowed for a moment and nerves made Maci's stomach pitch and roil. Had she messed up? Said something wrong? She wanted to look to Rich, but knew it would be a giveaway. Stella didn't look to others when making decisions, she simply made them and left everyone else to deal with the consequences.

"I'm going to get a drink. I need something much stronger than this champagne." She turned without looking at the two women and left, praying it was the right thing to do.

Rich caught up with her at the bar. "That was great! I would've sworn you were Stella if I didn't know better."

"I agree, Maci," Chance said in her ear. "You handled that like a champ."

Too bad her stomach didn't think so. It twisted and ached as Rich turned to get her a drink.

"Whoa, you okay?" He slid a drink toward her. "You really did do great. That will help sell you as Stella."

Maci couldn't pay attention to his words or the drink. All she could focus on was the nausea clawing at her insides.

Oh, no. She hadn't taken any morning sickness medicine today, since she'd felt fine this morning for the first time in a couple weeks. Evidently morning sickness wasn't limited to just the early hours of the day.

"Excuse me." She walked away from Rich, her mind whirling as she desperately tried to remember where the bathrooms were. Chance had made sure she knew where seven different exits were out of this building, but nothing about bathrooms.

Her stomach gave another lurch, and she cursed under her breath.

"Maci, you okay?" Chance asked. "Why did you leave Rich? Did he do something?"

Maci didn't want to say anything, afraid that just opening her mouth would be enough to trigger her stomach, but she knew Chance would assume the worst if she didn't. "I'm going to be sick. I need a bathroom."

She could hear Chance and his brothers talking, trying to figure out where she was going, but she didn't pay attention once she saw a sign for the bathroom. All her focus was on getting to it before she made a scene.

The relief she felt when she found the door was almost enough to send her stumbling. She shoved through, thankful there was no one else inside, although not caring if there had been, and fell to her knees inside a stall just as her dinner came up.

They really shouldn't call it morning sickness when it could happen anytime.

Maci didn't know how long she knelt there before she felt cool hands brushing her temples as they gathered up her hair, helping to soothe her overheated skin. She couldn't even be startled, could only try to remain upright as her stomach tried to empty more, even though there was nothing left.

"You're going to be okay."

Chance.

He crouched behind her, whispering soft words as his big hand rubbed soothing circles across her back.

She had no idea how she was going to explain this.

Eventually, the urge to puke disappeared and all that was left was the weariness that came from it. With one hand on the wall, Maci got to her feet, grateful when Chance's hand on her elbow stabilized her.

The first thing she did when she got out of the stall was rinse her mouth out with water and wish she had a toothbrush. Or at least some mints in her purse.

"Thanks," she muttered. She felt much better—as she always did—just weak.

"Are you alright?" Chance hadn't moved far from the stall, his arms crossed over his chest as he studied her.

She didn't have it in her to turn around and face him head-on, so she lifted her exhausted eyes to his in the mirror. "I'm fine."

"You aren't. We need to call this off."

"No."

"There will be other events, Maci."

Her eyes flashed to his in warning as she looked under the stalls. No shoes, so they were most likely alone, but still, he shouldn't be mentioning the mission.

"I locked the door behind me when I came in. We're alone."

Of course he had. The grand strategist always had a plan.

"I'm fine to keep going. It was just nerves." There was truth to that, although she knew that wasn't truly what had just happened.

She turned back to her reflection and opened her clutch, grateful for the touch-up makeup kit she'd thrown in last minute. With her makeup fixed and all signs of her bathroom interlude wiped away, she looked and felt a million times better. "How do I look?"

He took a step closer. "Are you sure you still want to do this? We can try again another night."

"I'm fine," she said. "I feel much better now."

She moved for the door, but he stepped in front of her. She could feel his gaze on her face like it was a touch, and she had to fight the urge to flinch away. Or move closer.

Those brown eyes of his were trying to dig her secrets out of their hiding spots. It was unnerving, especially when her biggest one involved him.

"The sooner we go out there, the sooner we

can be done," she whispered. "The sooner Stella is safe."

He held her gaze for a moment, then another. Finally, he walked out the door, holding it open for her. "If this happens again, we're calling it."

She nodded and slipped back into the crowd.

For the rest of the night, Maci played it safe. She talked with all kinds of people, sticking close to Rich. It was Brax in her ear now rather than Chance. She thought he might be mad at her until she caught him moving around the gala with the other patrons—blending in perfectly in his black pants and shirt.

He was staying near her in case she needed him. The thought both warmed and terrified her.

By the time the gala was winding up—no sign of anything suspicious from anyone—Maci was exhausted.

"We're done for the night, Maci," Brax said through the comm. "If the stalker was going to try something he would've already done so. You and Rich head to the car, then we'll make the switch."

She was staying at Stella's penthouse apartment to further the ruse. The place was much fancier than her own, but right now that didn't matter. She just wanted a bed and to sleep for a hundred hours.

"Who has babysitting duty tonight?"

"You get me, the best Patterson brother," Brax said. "That okay?"

She forced a smile. "You know it."

Not Chance. Probably for the best. Being alone in an apartment with him would just make everything more complicated and sleep probably impossible.

But still, she couldn't stop the disappointment pooling in her gut. She liked all the Patterson brothers, but Chance was always the one she would choose to have nearby.

Even when she knew that would spell disaster.

Chapter Eight

Nothing.

Three public events over the next four nights and they were no closer to catching the stalker than they had been when Maci first went undercover. It certainly wasn't Maci's fault. She was playing the role of Stella damn near perfectly.

And Chance hated it.

He disliked seeing her face made up to look like someone else—someone not nearly as spunky and *real* as Maci. He even disliked the clothing she wore. The outfits may have been much more expensive than her normal wear, but he preferred her in her jeans and blouses over these gowns and heels.

And Rich... If Chance had to watch that man touch the small of Maci's back—the very place Chance's fingers itched to be—much longer, he wasn't sure he could be responsible for his actions.

"Any sign?" Chance asked his brothers.

"None." Brax's frustrated voice matched his own. "Is this guy playing with us?"

"I don't know." Chance rubbed the back of his neck.

Tonight he was in the control room and Brax

was out on the floor as immediate backup for Maci should she need it. He and his brothers had taken turns, so no one would remember seeing them at other events.

The pattern had been the same. They showed up, Maci played her role remarkably well, and they studied everyone around her. Anybody who talked to Maci got checked. Hell, anybody who'd looked in her general direction got checked.

Dorian Cane and his team had provided assistance—checking identities and running unknown people through facial recognition software. Dorian himself had sat in the control room with Weston yesterday in case he might recognize anything they were missing. As an experienced security professional who kept his ego out of the situation, his presence had been appreciated by all of the Pattersons.

But still nothing.

"I think maybe the stalker is on to us and knows Maci isn't really Stella. To continue to parade her around isn't going to change anything," Chance said.

They'd already had this talk with Dorian. He had upped the security on Stella in Europe, although there hadn't been any suspicious events there either.

"I agree," Weston said into the comm unit.

He was positioned at the staff entrance near the back of the building. "There's something we're missing. Guy is ahead of us."

There'd been nothing at each event, nothing as they followed Rich each night as he drove Maci back to Stella's apartment, and nothing as she stayed there for a couple hours before sneaking out a private basement entrance to go home.

Even worse than the nothing was the strain the situation was putting on Maci. Each time, as the hours wound down, she was slower to move, her smile a little less bright. By the end, she was exhausted and nearly weaving on her feet despite being completely sober.

Chance had had enough. "Maci's done," he said into the private channel only his brothers could hear. "Let's call it."

"Roger that," Weston responded. "I'll go make sure the apartment is clear."

Chance could hear the exhaustion plain in his brother's voice too, so he made a decision for them all.

"No, you all head home and get some rest once we get Maci to the car. I'm going to let her go home rather than go to Stella's apartment. Luring him out isn't working, so tomorrow we need to figure out a new plan."

None of his brothers argued. They all knew this wasn't working the way they'd hoped.

"Call if you need anything," Luke said. "We won't be far."

Chance switched over to the channel Maci could hear. "Maci, we're calling it quits for tonight."

On the screen, he watched her turn discreetly so she could talk to him without anyone noticing. "We're heading back to the apartment?"

"No. For whatever reason, this method isn't working. I'm going to take you home. Everyone needs a good night's sleep."

He watched her rub her eyes. "I feel like I let you down."

"No, don't say that. You've been a stellar Stella."

He watched the corners of her mouth turn up at his horrible joke. "I wish it would've worked."

"Don't worry. We're going to get him. You and Rich start to move toward the car."

Brax agreed to stay and watch until the end of the event and oversee packing up all equipment. Chance met Rich and Maci in the parking garage. Maci was already inside the car.

"Giving up?" Rich asked.

Chance narrowed his eyes. "Maybe for tonight. No use beating a dead horse."

Rich's smile was full of charm. "I try not to get beat ever. Let me know what the next step in the plan is."

Chance watched Rich saunter away before getting in the driver's seat of the car. He looked over to ask Maci how she was doing.

She was fast asleep, cheek leaning heavily against the door. He stared at her for a long moment. They'd definitely made the right choice by ending early tonight. Enough was enough.

Chance didn't drive fast. Maci needed the sleep and at least here he got to be close to her. She was still keeping secrets he wanted to get to the root of. Maybe if she wasn't actively part of the investigation he could focus on that—something he'd been thinking about since that last day of training.

But maybe instead of trying to crash through her walls, he needed to try to *gentle* his way through them. Not his strong suit, but he would try. She was worth trying that for.

They were only a few minutes from the party when Chance noticed a car that seemed to be following them. Not wanting to wake Maci without reason, he took a roundabout way that led them back toward Stella's apartment. If someone was following them, that's where they'd expect the car to be going.

At a red light, Chance made a last-minute turn, hoping the car would simply drive on.

It followed.

Nerves prickling at the back of his neck, he

continued to drive around in a circle. Each turn he made, the car did too.

Definitely following.

"Maci. Maci, wake up."

"Are we there yet?" her sweet, sleepy voice asked.

As much as he hated to do it, she needed the truth. "We're being followed."

Her head jerked up. "What do we do?"

He dialed Weston on the car's speakerphone. "We're okay. Just stay low."

"What's wrong?" Weston answered his phone with the question.

Chance rattled off their location. "Black sedan is following us. As soon as I spotted them I headed toward Stella's place to keep them on us."

"On our way." Chance could hear the squeal of tires as Weston spun his car around. "Luke is with me."

"I need to get Maci into the apartment. I want to take this on the offensive."

Maybe it could all end tonight. There was nothing Chance wanted more.

"I'll just stay in the car with you," she said. "You don't have to drop me off."

"No." There was absolutely no damned way. If this turned into something ugly, he didn't want her anywhere around it.

He slowed down just slightly to buy them more time. A few lights later he turned again and the car followed.

"We're blocks behind you," Weston said. "Luke sees the sedan. They're definitely following you. We'll block them while you drop her off."

A few moments later, Weston smoothly cut around and in front of the sedan, blocking its view just as Stella's building came up on the right.

He looked over at Maci as he stopped the car. "Run inside. Don't stop for anyone. Get into the apartment and lock the door. We'll be back as soon as we can."

Thankfully, she didn't argue. "Be careful."

Chance watched until the doorman let her in the building, then pulled away fast. He got a glimpse of the black sedan as it sped past his brothers' car, and watched them lurch after it.

"I think they're on to us. They're speeding up." Weston told him. "We're heading south on Market."

"Stay with them. I'll be caught up to you in less than a minute."

"Damn it," Luke said. "They just turned south on Fourth, heading toward the interstate. They're trying to lose us."

Chance was less than three blocks away. He

jerked the wheel in a sharp right into an alley, hoping it would allow him to gain speed and cut off the sedan. "I'm coming in hot from the east in a parallel alley."

"What's your plan?" Weston asked.

"Get in front of them and make them stop."

"That's a terrible plan," Luke and Weston said at the same time.

It was the only one he had.

He gunned the engine and pulled out of the alley. He'd done it—the sedan was speeding toward him.

"We see you!" Luke yelled.

They were now in the more industrial section of town, which worked to Chance's advantage—there was little other traffic at this time of night. He positioned his car in the middle of the street so there was no way to go around it, then got out.

He spared a moment to wonder if they'd try to ram his car, but the car slammed to a halt instead. Chance's brief flare of relief died when not one but two doors opened, the people inside the car bailing and running in opposite directions.

Luke and Weston squealed up behind them.

"I'll get the driver," Chance shouted, taking off in a sprint. "You get the other one."

The driver ran back through the alley Chance

had just driven through, trying to get back to the main street. Chance had to stop him before he did that. He forced speed from his legs, gaining on the smaller man. Finally he leaped, hitting the man in a flying tackle, taking them both down.

They both hit the ground hard, but for the first time since he noticed the sedan, Chance felt like he could breathe.

Finally.

He dragged the man back through the dark alley to the cars, glad when he didn't put up much of a fight. Luke and Weston had gotten their perp too. From the light of the streetlamp Chance finally got a look at the pair.

Holy hell. They were *teenagers*.

He looked over at Weston and Luke and realized they were thinking the same thing.

It had been damned *teenagers* stalking Stella LeBlanc?

"How old are you?" Chance demanded.

"Seventeen." The driver tipped his chin up defiantly, and Chance could see the rosy edges of his eyes.

"What's your name?"

The kid rolled his eyes. "I'm Bert." He hooked his thumb toward his friend. "This is Ernie."

Chance's jaw tightened, but he let it go. They

would get IDs later. He looked closer at the boys' red-rimmed eyes.

"Are you high?"

That didn't make sense. How had a stoned kid managed to slip past so many layers of security over the past few weeks?

"Who wants to know?" Ernie asked with a smirk.

Chance crouched down beside them, ignoring the question. "Why were you following us?"

Bert scoffed. "We're not telling you anything."

"Fine." Luke took a step closer. "We'll call some friends of ours with the San Antonio PD and get you transferred to lockup. Harassment, speeding, DWI. You broke enough laws that they could take your license permanently. And seventeen is old enough to go to real jail for a couple of nights. Maybe you can make a few friends. I hear they like fresh meat."

Both boys paled. "Look, we didn't want to hurt anyone."

"So why were you following Stella LeBlanc?" Weston asked.

"Who?" Bert asked. "We don't know who we were following."

Ernie shook his head, looking like he was about to pee his pants. "Yeah, someone paid us to follow your car and make sure you knew we were doing it. We didn't think you'd get all psycho!"

Chance met eyes with Weston. This didn't make sense. "Start over. What exactly did they pay you for?"

"Just to follow the car. They said you'd probably find us, so we should keep the chase going as long as we could."

"Who?" Luke took a step forward, scaring the kids even more.

"I don't know!" they both shouted.

Chance grabbed Bert by the collar. "Who hired you? A man? Woman? What did they look like?"

Bert started shaking. "A man. We were hanging out outside the convenience store, and he offered us five hundred dollars to mess with you guys when your car pulled out of the garage. He stayed in the dark. I didn't see him."

"Why would someone do that?" Weston asked. "He didn't pay you to hurt or chase a woman who would be in the car?"

The boys shook their heads. "No, not hurt anyone. Just follow and be sneaky."

Chance looked over at Weston, his stomach sinking. "They were a distraction. I sent Maci inside alone."

Alone in an apartment that the stalker had already proven he could get into.

Chance was moving before he'd even finished his sentence, sprinting to his car. He could hear his brothers talking to each other about who would stay with the kids, but didn't care.

He drove as fast as he could back toward Stella's apartment building, dialing Maci's number as he went.

No answer.

Not the first time he called. Not the second. Not the third.

A couple of miles had never seemed longer as he drove at reckless speeds. Finally, he pulled up to the building and left the car illegally parked at the front.

The doorman stared at him as he sprinted to the elevator and pressed the button for the penthouse. Anxious energy prickled across his body, his fingers twitching as the floors passed in no time.

Maci was okay. She had to be okay. She'd been so tired. She'd probably fallen back to sleep.

Why didn't he believe that?

The second the elevator doors opened, he knew he was too late. The door to Stella's apartment was cracked open. Lock the door, he'd said. He didn't know if Maci had even had a chance to try.

Please let her be alive. He pulled his gun from under his jacket and pushed through the door.

Please let her be alive.

The stillness of the apartment made the hair on Chance's neck stand up. He wanted to call out for Maci, but he didn't want to risk alerting anyone that he'd arrived before he was in place to take them out. He quickly and silently glanced around the living room, then headed down the hallway toward the bedrooms.

He heard a slight noise behind him and spun back with his weapon raised. He lowered it when he saw it was Weston.

Weston gave him a brief nod, his own gun in hand. Without a word they both moved silently down the hall. Chance cleared the guest bedroom; Weston cleared the office.

Where was Maci?

She wasn't in the master bedroom or any of the bathrooms. Had she been taken?

They made their way back out to the living area. When he caught sight of her foot lying limply on the floor of the kitchen in the doorway, he dropped all pretense of silence and ran to her.

If it wasn't for the cut on her forehead, he could've believed she was just sleeping right there in front of the dishwasher. Ignoring the blood, since head wounds always bled a lot,

Chance dropped to his knees beside her. His fingers shook as he searched for a pulse.

Please. Please. Please.

"Is she—" Weston didn't finish.

A pulse. Thank God. "She's alive."

Chance pulled out his phone, and his voice cracked when the operator asked about his emergency. "We need an ambulance."

Chapter Nine

Maci woke slowly to the sound of steady beeping and the realization that she wasn't where she was supposed to be. Before she could figure out why, the incessant tone stole her attention again.

Had she left on an alarm?

"Make it stop," she croaked. Her mouth was dry and her voice sounded weird. She heard rustling nearby and forced her eyelids open, wincing at the bright light. Lights too bright for her apartment or Stella's. "Where am I?"

"You're in the hospital." Chance. Just the sound of his voice was enough to help calm her.

At least until she looked at him. Stubble lined his cheeks, and his eyes were bright red with exhaustion. His dark hair stood up on end as if he had been running his fingers through it for hours.

Then his words hit her. *Hospital*. Instinct had her hands flying to her stomach to protect the baby. Was something wrong? Had she lost it?

Did he know?

"Are you going to be sick?" He stepped closer, then paused at her side.

"No. How long have I been here? Am... I okay?"

"Two hours. You've been in and out the whole time." Nervous energy crackled around him, and Maci wasn't surprised when he started to pace. "You got hit on the head in Stella's apartment. Do you remember that?"

The apartment. Getting inside and deciding to make some tea.

The man.

"There was a man inside Stella's apartment," she whispered. "I didn't see him."

Her breath hitched. All that self-defense stuff she'd done with Chance and she'd never even had an opportunity to use it.

Chance reached for her hand, squeezing it. "It's okay. You're safe now."

A nurse walked in. "Awake for good this time, it looks like. How are you feeling?" She shined a small light in Maci's eyes and had Maci follow her fingers with her eyes.

"My head hurts, but otherwise I think I'm okay. Is everything okay?"

Maci had no idea how to ask about the baby with Chance in the room. She looked nervously over at him.

The nurse caught her look. "Do you want to be alone? We let Mr. Patterson in because he was listed as your emergency contact, but some people feel like they recover better on their own."

Maci shook her head, then stopped at the ache. "No, it's okay. I'd like Chance to stay." She didn't want to be alone right now.

The nurse smiled. "Your pupils are responding well and you're quite coherent—both good signs. Dr. Ashburn will be in soon and will probably want a CT scan to see if we're dealing with a concussion."

"Have I had any bleeding or anything, um, not on my head?" Maci wasn't sure how to ask about her pregnancy outside of stating it outright. "Any other problems anywhere else in my body?"

The nurse smiled. "Everything else looks fine. You're young and healthy."

That didn't answer the question exactly but reassured her a little.

The nurse left and Chance sat down next to her.

"I'm so glad to see you fully awake and talking. When Weston and I found you in that kitchen…" He scrubbed his hand down his face.

"The guy was already there when I came in. He had to have been waiting for me."

"Are you okay to talk about it or do you want to just rest?"

She let out a sigh. "I'm okay to talk. I know that will help with the case."

His eyes met hers. "The case isn't as important as you and how you're feeling."

She couldn't look away from him if she tried. "I'm okay to talk about it. I promise."

"The guys are out in the waiting room. Do you mind if I bring them in or is that too much?"

"It's okay."

He stepped out and a few moments later came back with Brax, Weston and Luke. All four brothers looked pretty haggard.

"There she is." Brax rushed over and kissed her on the cheek. "Thank goodness. Luke was out sobbing over having to file paperwork himself."

Luke grunted with a smile. "That's not completely untrue. We're glad you're okay, Maci."

Weston, solemn as always, nodded. "You gave us quite a scare."

"She's feeling up to talking about what she remembers, before the doctor comes back in," Chance said.

He sat back down next to her and grabbed her hand. It gave her the strength she needed to tell what had happened.

"You dropped me off and I rushed upstairs. I was so nervous the whole way up, but I knew once I saw the door, I was okay. I got inside Stella's apartment and locked it, but he must've already been inside."

Chance squeezed her hand and she concentrated on that.

"I went into the kitchen to grab some tea and he came up behind me. Pushed me against the wall and told me he knew I wasn't Stella."

"Did he say anything else to you?" Chance asked.

"Yeah. But his voice was weird. A low whisper." She grit her teeth. She was never going to forget how his voice sounded, how terrified she was, the words he said. She dropped her voice in an imitation of his. "How stupid do you think I am? I know you aren't her. A pale imitation of the real thing. Then again, there's strength in you. You stayed to battle while she ran. There's honor in that."

She looked at each of the Pattersons. "Those maybe weren't the exact words, but it's pretty close."

"How did you get hurt?" Weston asked quietly.

"He shoved me into the cabinet and I hit the knob." Maci remembered the pain of hitting the sharp metal, the warmth of blood dripping down her face. The man had scoffed at it, and when she lost her balance, he let her fall. "When he saw me bleeding, he let me go. I don't even remember seeing him leave. I passed out. I don't know if he meant to take me or not."

"He might have but then once you were hurt it changed his plans. Harder to hide in plain sight with a bleeding woman." Brax's frown said he didn't like the idea.

"Maybe worried about a blood trail leading us to him?" Luke guessed.

"He may have gotten word from the driver that we'd caught up to them." Weston and Chance looked at each other, but neither looked convinced. "We'll take a look at surveillance around the apartment and see what we can find."

A knock interrupted and an older woman in a white coat stepped in. "Hello, Maci. I'm Dr. Ashburn. It's good to see you awake and alert."

She did the same routine as the nurse, shining a small light in Maci's eyes and having her follow the finger.

"We did an initial CT scan when you first came in and that showed very minor swelling—good news. Your tox screen and blood work came back normal."

"CT scan?" Maci could feel herself tensing. "Could that be…bad for me?"

The doctor seemed to understand what Maci was truly asking about and shook her head kindly. "CT scans pose very minimal risks."

"I had CT scans all the time when I played sports in high school." Brax knocked on his head. "I wasn't great about avoiding concussions, but a CT scan was never any issue."

"Everything about you is just as healthy as it was yesterday," Dr. Ashburn said. "Except for the bump on your head."

"Is there anything we need to look out for?" Chance's fingers tightened on Maci's briefly, but he kept his focus on the doctor.

"Other than signs of a worsening concussion, no. The cut is superficial. It won't even need stitches. The butterfly bandage will keep it closed so it heals on its own."

"Should we watch her overnight or something?"

As much as she liked how protective he was, Maci didn't need Chance focused on her. It would be so much harder to hide the baby. "Chance, I'm fine."

"But what happens if—"

"Chance." He looked at her, and Maci saw the fear that drove him to nearly smother her. She'd been hurt on his watch and he was suffering for it. She squeezed his hand softly. "I'm fine. Tell him, Doc."

"We'll send you home with instructions for the next few days, but all in all, Ms. Ford is fine. She's in great health." She turned to Maci. "You don't need to be concerned about anything but your head. Okay? Everything else is fine."

But Chance wasn't letting it go. "What about the fact that she's been throwing up multiple times over the past few weeks? She's exhausted all the time and is crazy sensitive to certain smells. Even the flu shouldn't last this long. Plus, sometimes she seems fine and then it just comes on her without warning."

She squeezed his hand. She'd had no idea he'd been paying such close attention. "Chance, it's okay. I'm okay. Let's just worry about the concussion and getting this case solved."

He brushed a strand of hair back from her forehead. "You're here at the hospital. You might as well let them run some tests or whatever. If something is wrong with you, let's find out now. Find out early. Whatever it is, I'm here."

"Dr. Ashburn said my bloodwork came back normal. I'm okay."

He leaned closer, his brown eyes pleading. "Mace, you and I both know something is wrong. Let them check you over while you're here. What if it's cancer or something like that?"

"I don't have cancer."

"How do you know?" he whispered. "I've been watching you suffer and I can't stand it anymore."

She had to tell him. It wasn't ever going to get easier. "I'm not sick, Chance. I'm pregnant. About ten weeks along."

Chance's eyes got big, but thankfully he didn't let go of her hand.

"And I can attest that the fetus is fine, even despite the bump to the head," Dr. Ashburn said. "Maci, let me know if you have further questions. We'll do one more CT scan, then release you if everything looks good."

The doctor said goodbye to everyone and headed out the door, but Maci couldn't focus on that. All she could focus on was the raw shock on Chance and his brothers' faces.

Her secret was out.

Pregnant.

The word kicked around in Chance's brain. *Maci is pregnant.*

Had she known when she made the suggestion that she go undercover?

Was it his?

That question stuck around the longest. Was the baby she carried one they'd made together? They'd used protection, but it wasn't always perfect. Birth control failed and condoms broke. The how wasn't the issue, the *who* was.

Who was the baby's father and what would Chance do if it wasn't him? He and Maci had no commitments to each other—although that hadn't been by his choice.

"Give us the room, guys."

His brothers knew him well enough not to argue in any way.

"You owe me ten dollars," Luke muttered to Brax as they left. "I told you there was no way there wasn't something between them."

Weston was the last one out, laying a grounding hand on Chance's shoulder. "Be gentle, brother. She's been through a lot tonight."

He didn't say anything as Weston left and shut the door behind him. If there was any word that didn't fit the way Chance currently felt, it was *gentle*.

Off balance, amazed, fearful, angry... But not gentle.

Although he would find it. He knew right now that was what Maci needed, so he would find it.

Maci adjusted herself in the hospital bed, and it brought Chance's focus back.

"Is it mine?" For some reason, he couldn't look her in the face when he asked, so he stared at his lap instead. "You and I never had any commitments, so I don't want to assume..."

"Yes, it's yours. I haven't been sleeping around with a bunch of people."

Now his eyes flew to hers. "I didn't mean it that way at all. Truly. I didn't think you were involved with anyone else, but I thought it would be more rude just to assume the baby was mine."

She nodded, but he felt like an ass when a tear leaked out of her eye and she wiped it away quickly.

"I'm sorry," he whispered.

"It's okay."

Holy hell. Maci Ford was pregnant with his baby.

"Are you keeping it?" He tried to keep this as neutral as possible too. He refused to influence her decision, but he was flooded with relief when she nodded.

He was going to be a dad.

For minutes, neither of them said anything, Chance just trying to take it all in. Then his brain restarted and suddenly he had dozens of questions.

"How long have you known?"

Maci looked away, and his blunt fingernails dug into his palm. He wasn't going to like this answer. "A few days."

"A few?"

She turned back to him then, the fire that was normally so bright in her eyes nothing but embers. She looked tired, and Chance had the urge to wrap her in his arms while she slept, but he had to get some info first.

"I found out for sure the day before we started training."

The last-minute doctor's appointment. Fear

and anger tightened Chance's throat, and he had to take a deep breath just to curb them. His voice was rougher than gravel when he spoke. "You did all that training and went undercover knowing you were pregnant."

He thought back to the moves he'd taught her. None of them should've affected her belly area at all, but he hadn't been taking extra care like he would've if he'd known.

And then the attack tonight...

There was guilt all over her expression and in the way her shoulders slumped. "The doctor said it was fine. I specifically asked about the self-defense training, and he said at this stage I was fine as long as I wasn't taking direct hits to the stomach. He said even then my body would work to protect the baby even at risk to myself."

That barely made him feel better. "You went undercover on a case where your doppelgänger was getting stalked by a newly-violent offender while you were pregnant with my child. Tell me you understand why I'm having an issue with this, Mace."

"I promise you, I was being careful. You guys were there to—"

"You were attacked!" The need to move pushed Chance out of his chair. "You're sitting in a hospital bed, hurt."

"That isn't fair. We both know this isn't my fault." Chance's heart dropped to his stomach. She was right. It wasn't her fault, it was *his*. He'd left her to go upstairs alone, certain he was needed somewhere else.

He'd left her defenseless.

His whole life had been spent taking care of others, and then one mistake had nearly cost him Maci and their child. What would've happened if he hadn't gotten back in time, or if the stalker had decided to take Maci with him?

What if he'd decided to kill her right there in that kitchen when he found out she wasn't Stella?

For a moment there wasn't enough oxygen in the world.

"Chance, stop it," she snapped. She snatched his wrist, yanking him back into his chair. "This is not your fault. You didn't know that the stalker was waiting for me, and who knows if you being there would have actually helped. He might have killed you."

"You can't know that." He sat back, a bone-deep exhaustion pulling at him. So much more than from just a sleepless night.

"I'm okay. The baby is okay. That's all that matters."

That was true, but he still couldn't shake the

terror wrapped around him. "No more undercover. You're done."

Maci's eyes widened at his tone, only to narrow into slits. "You don't get to command me, Chance Patterson. I'm not yours to control."

"Like hell am I allowing the mother of my child to work in a situation that's already proven to be out of control. It's not happening." Maci opened her mouth to respond, but he continued. "Besides, your cover is blown. You said it yourself…the guy knew you weren't Stella."

"Then you ask me. You don't demand."

Chance's jaw was tight. He drew on every bit of love and respect he'd ever seen between his mom and dad. Clinton and Sheila had some fights, but in the end, their respect and admiration for each other won out over any arguments.

He grabbed Maci's hand gently, grateful when she didn't snatch it away. "Maci, your cover is blown. If it was any of my brothers I would say the same thing. We need to regroup and come at this a different way. Please help us do that."

"What about Stella?"

"She's still out of the country. Between us and her other security team, we'll keep an eye on the situation and find the stalker before she comes back in the country. She's safe, we've got time, but you going undercover is no longer viable. Agreed?"

Maci sighed. "Agreed."

That took one problem off Chance's list. Now only a thousand more to go.

Chapter Ten

After another round of vital checks and a clear CT, Dr. Ashburn agreed to release Maci. While the rest of his family went home to grab some sleep, Chance stayed so he could take her home. The shock of learning about the baby hadn't worn off, but his trepidation had.

His brothers would spend the bulk of tomorrow following up on what happened tonight—finding out what they could about Bert and Ernie and checking all the footage from the apartment building. He trusted them to handle it thoroughly, because he wouldn't be there.

Maci was pregnant with his baby, and he was going to be there for them both. Whatever it took. He'd already sent Weston by to get a bag of his clothes and necessities, because he wasn't going to leave Maci alone. Not today. Not tomorrow. If he had his way, not *ever*.

The sun was starting to come up as they got her discharged and wheeled out to the car.

"What's with the bag?" She nodded to the duffel in the back seat.

"Clothes for me. I'm taking you home and I'm going to stay with you for a few days."

She let out a small sigh. "Chance, this isn't

necessary. The stalker isn't after me, he's after Stella. I can take care of myself."

"That's all true, but I want to be there anyway." He sighed, running a hand over his face. "It's been a rough twenty-four hours, and I'd just feel better if I was close to you. You and the baby. Is that okay?"

She looked like she was going to fight him until she caught sight of his face. Something in his expression convinced her otherwise. "Okay."

"I thought you were going to fight more on this," he admitted with a laugh.

"I know Dr. Ashburn wants to make sure I'm monitored for a while. And you're right. We've all been through a lot the last few days."

It wasn't until Chance put the car in Drive that he realized he didn't know where she lived. They'd spent nights at his house and days together in the office, but he'd never gone to her place.

Not that he hadn't wanted to. It was just how things had always ended up. Was that part of the reason she hadn't wanted to immediately tell him she was pregnant? Part of the reason she stopped wanting to see him a couple months ago? She thought he wasn't interested in her life?

"Uh, I don't know where you live."

She nodded then gave him directions as he

drove. The farther they went, the more Chance's frown grew. It wasn't the worst area of town, but it wasn't anywhere he wanted Maci and their child to be. When she directed him to pull into an older apartment's parking lot, he tried to refrain from making any comments. The window frames drooped with water damage, and the squat buildings themselves had definitely seen better days.

Maybe he could convince her to move in with him before the baby came. It would be a tough sell, but he would try. Even as uncertain as everything was, he wanted the three of them to be a family.

In the meantime, he'd stay with her wherever she was.

He found a spot close to the doors and helped her out of the car—despite her grumblings that she wasn't an invalid—giving her space once she was steady on her feet.

They made their way to her apartment silently, with Chance taking everything in and Maci watching him. She seemed to shrink the closer they got, like she was embarrassed.

"It's not pretty, but it's home."

He shrugged. "I've lived in worse places."

Hell, he'd spent most of his childhood in worse places.

"Yeah?" She glanced at him as they rounded

the final bend in the stairs. Chance tried not to read into her expression too much.

"Yeah. I didn't always live with Clinton and Sheila. Some of my group homes left a lot to be desired. So yeah, I've lived in worse places than this."

"Me too," she said quietly, stepping into the hallway and leaving him to trail after her. For a moment, he couldn't.

Had Maci Ford grown up like he and his brothers had? Had she been forced to grow up too soon, to take care of herself when no one else would? Had her home situation been something no child should have to go through?

And why hadn't he ever asked?

She'd had him listed as her emergency contact, for God's sake. Didn't that state a lot about her relationship with her family?

He was so lost in his own thoughts he didn't realize Maci had stopped in the hallway not far from her door.

"What's wrong?" Out of instinct he wrapped an arm around her waist and pulled her behind him. But other than a middle-aged woman standing in front of one of the doors, he didn't see anything amiss.

"Going to introduce me to your friend, May May?" the woman asked, her eyes traveling over Chance's body. While he didn't like her ogling him, he could definitely see a resemblance between her and Maci.

"Mom." Maci stepped around and in front of Chance and moved to the door. Her knuckles were white as she gripped her keys. She definitely wasn't excited to see the woman standing at the door. "What are you doing here?"

"Can't a mama come to visit her only child every once in a while?" She looked at Chance again. "Aren't you going to introduce me to your friend?"

"No."

That was it. Just no. Maci's mom looked irritated but not surprised. It was easy to see in the way Maci kept her eyes angled toward her mother that she didn't trust the woman. Chance stepped closer to her on instinct.

Maci unlocked the door and shoved it open. She moved to step inside, but he grabbed her arm.

"Can I clear the apartment first?"

Maci nodded. Without another word, he stepped inside.

The one-bedroom apartment was just as small as he expected, but neatly furnished. Everything looked well used, but it was tidy and clean. Pops of vibrant colors bled through the white-on-white color scheme, reminding Chance of

Weston's gardens. It was beautiful and homey, just like Maci.

He took his time clearing each room, even going so far as to check the window locks. There were a few things he'd do to up the security of the place if he couldn't convince Maci to move in with him.

Once he was satisfied that the apartment was clear, he went back out to Maci and her mother. The two were talking to each other in low, tense voices. They stopped when he approached.

"We're clear."

"I need to talk to my mom for a minute alone."

He had to fight the urge to push himself into their conversation. Maci looked tense and almost scared. This definitely wasn't a good relationship.

But pushing now wouldn't do him any favors. They had to learn to trust each other, and there was no better first step than giving her the space she needed. "Okay. Are you hungry?"

He almost slipped and mentioned the baby. That would've been a huge error, given the nonverbal interaction between the two women.

"I could eat. Grab whatever you want to eat or drink too," Maci said, nodding toward the kitchen with her chin as she gripped her mother's arm. Maci practically dragged the woman into the bedroom without a single glance back.

Chance tried to think of logical reasons that Maci would be so detached from her mother, but nothing good came to mind. The desperate need to do a background check on Maci's mom pressed against him until his skin felt tight, but he wouldn't. Not without Maci's permission first.

If she wanted him to know about her past, she would tell him.

Though it was a solid reason, it still chafed—especially knowing the woman was his child's biological grandmother. The reminder that they'd eventually have to tell his own mother filtered through his brain, and he actually smiled. Sheila Patterson loved children, and she had been not so subtly hounding his brothers for more of them since Brax's son, Walker, entered the picture.

She was going to lose it when she found out Maci was pregnant. The two of them had met quite a few times since Maci started working for San Antonio Security.

Finally, the ladies came back. Maci looked even more tense, but her mother was smiling.

"See you soon, May May!"

Maci didn't respond and she definitely wasn't smiling. The second the door closed on her mother, Maci collapsed onto the threadbare couch in the living room. As suddenly as she dropped, she was on her feet pacing again.

He cleared his throat, gathering her attention. He pushed the sandwich he'd made toward her over the counter, but she shook her head, obviously too wound up to eat.

He wanted to push. This was part of the secrets she was keeping and he wanted to know. But when he looked at her, Chance could see the exhaustion setting in. It had already been a traumatic night, and the strained relationship Maci had with her mother was taking a further toll.

He pushed the sandwich toward her again. "I'm not going to pry, but I'm sorry having your mother here made things more stressful."

Maci rubbed at her eyes. "Mom has a gift of making everything more stressful."

"Does she show up a lot?"

"More than I'd like."

That didn't tell him much, but it gave him an idea. "Would you like to come home with me instead of us staying here? It'll be a lot calmer there, plus no unexpected visitors."

He held his breath, fully expecting her to say no. And if she did, he'd honor it. But at least at his house he felt like he could better protect her.

Even from foes he didn't even know she had.

"Yes, please."

No arguments. No complaints. Nothing. Chance couldn't help the grin that spread over his face, one that got bigger when she let him hold her hand. "Let's pack a bag and take you home then."

Chapter Eleven

Maci woke up the next morning in Chance's guest room feeling much better. Her head still hurt, but not as bad as it had. Plus, she didn't have to worry about going undercover as Stella anymore.

Most importantly, she didn't have to pretend like she wasn't pregnant. It was okay if she got sick, okay if she needed to sit down, okay to be completely overwhelmed. She didn't have to hide it.

Chance had taken the news much better than she'd thought he would. She definitely hadn't expected him to want to stay with her. If she could've thought of a reason to tell him why she shouldn't go back to her apartment, she would've done it.

She wasn't embarrassed by it, per se. But compared to his place, hers was pretty rundown. Everything was clean, but secondhand. The place fairly screamed that Maci was barely on her feet financially.

And then Evelyn being there... Maci rubbed her eyes. It could've gone much worse than it had. Once she'd gotten her mom back to the bedroom, she'd offered her all the cash she had on hand to leave.

Long-term, it wasn't the best way to deal with Evelyn. But Maci hadn't been thinking long-term. She'd just wanted Evelyn out before she revealed all Maci's sordid secrets—or the few she was sober enough to remember.

At least Evelyn wouldn't be showing up here. That was the most immediate reason why Maci had agreed to stay at Chance's house when he offered.

She'd slept most of the day, so there hadn't been much chance for them to talk. She knew he must have questions. She was less sure whether she had answers for any of them.

When they ate dinner across from each other, it was mostly silent. Chance's life had changed practically overnight, and she wanted to give him time to digest everything. He deserved a second to breathe. Truthfully, she wanted the time too.

She wouldn't avoid the big conversations forever. She just needed a second to get her bearings.

When Chance sat down on the same couch she'd curled up on after dinner, Maci knew her time was up.

"We should talk—" he started, only to be interrupted by a knock on the door. Frowning, he turned to her. "Were you expecting anyone?"

"Nope." Especially not here.

She stayed where she was as Chance headed toward the door, grabbing his weapon from the gun safe as he did. She heard him let out a sigh.

"Open the door, Chance! We want to see your baby mama." Claire's voice was muffled through the front door, but Maci could still hear her friend's cheerful pep.

"Incoming," Chance muttered, then opened the door.

It wasn't just Claire, Luke's wife. It was also Brax's wife, Tessa, and Weston's fiancée, Kayleigh.

"We wanted to come over and see how Maci was doing," Kayleigh said. "You know, have some girl time."

"Right." Chance met eyes with Maci from behind the women, eyebrow raised. He was making sure she was okay with company. She knew without a doubt that if she said she wasn't ready, he'd kick the girls out, even if it meant taking flak from his brothers for it.

His protectiveness did something to Maci. She'd never had someone care about her like that. She gave him a nod, letting him know it was okay. She knew her friends had questions, and she owed them a face-to-face talk.

He followed the women as they gathered around Maci. "Can I get you all something to drink?"

Maci hid her smile behind the blanket. Despite not having them their whole lives, Sheila Patterson had raised her boys right. The impeccable, gentlemanly manners proved it.

"No, no. We're fine." Tessa pointed at Maci. "We just want to talk to this one."

He nodded. "I'll go back to the other room and call the office. I'll get an update on what's been happening."

Maci knew he'd already done that today, but appreciated him giving them time alone. "Thank you."

As the others got comfortable, Chance disappeared into the kitchen again. When he came back, he dropped a sleeve of crackers, some ginger ale and a trashcan in arm's reach of Maci. When she arched an eyebrow, he grimaced. "In case you start feeling sick. Need anything else?"

Well, swoon.

Aware of everyone watching them, Maci shook her head and thanked him. Chance looked her over again and leaned down to press a kiss to her forehead. "Yell if these three get out of hand."

As soon as the home office door shut behind him, all three friends started talking at the same time.

Claire let out a sigh. "I hope Luke acts like that when I eventually get pregnant."

"That was the most romantic thing I've ever seen." Kayleigh fanned herself.

Tessa crossed her arms over her chest. "So, you and Chance? You're a sneaky one, I'll give you that."

Claire nodded. "We all knew you two needed to get together, but we had no idea you already *had.*"

Maci let out a sigh. "We were casually seeing each other a while ago."

It wasn't quite the truth, but it wasn't a lie either. They had been casual, but their time had mostly been spent wrapped up in one another.

"And you aren't anymore?" Kayleigh asked.

"I broke it off." Even that made her cringe. She hadn't broken it off, she'd ghosted him as much as she could with them working together. Suddenly, the half-truth didn't feel right in her mouth. "It was just sex."

"Not anymore," Claire quipped, grunting when Tessa nudged her in the shin. "So, why'd you break up?"

"I'm not the type of person someone like Chance should settle down with."

Kayleigh frowned. "Why not?"

Maci's past rushed through her mind, fragments of moments she barely remembered. Ratty mattresses and worn-down people. Broken bottles and dark, desolate places. Bad decisions that haunted her. Most days she used them as fuel to make a better life for herself, but sometimes they served as reminders of how far she could fall.

But her friends didn't know about her past either. "Let's just say that my history doesn't make me a good candidate for someone like Chance for a serious and long-term relationship."

"Who cares about your history?" Tessa frowned. "We've all got a past. All that matters is right now. You're a good person, Maci Ford. You're hardworking and kind and loyal to a fault. Anyone would be lucky to have you, especially Chance."

She knew Tessa was just being a good friend, but every part of Maci disagreed. Chance needed someone better at his side. Someone stronger and with far less baggage. Maci could fill an entire closet with hers.

"Did Chance demand long-term and serious?" Claire asked.

"No, but..." Maci couldn't finish. She'd cut Chance out of her personal life before he could even get close to that point.

"No, but you were afraid he'd go there," Kayleigh guessed.

Maci nodded. She'd intentionally tried not to dream of a future with him, but every time they gave in to their off-the-charts chemistry it became harder. She knew if he'd started talking about commitments, she'd never have the strength to deny them both.

Claire shook her head. "So, it's not that you're not with him because you don't have feelings for him. And I already know he has feelings for you."

Maci definitely had feelings for Chance Patterson. "It's complicated, you guys."

"It always is." All three women said it at the same time, then laughed.

"Can't be any more complicated than Brax and I," Tessa said. "He thought I was Walker's nanny, not his mother."

Claire shrugged. "Luke wasn't sure if I was a murderer at first."

Kayleigh grinned. "I thought Weston was the groundskeeper, not my bodyguard."

Maci couldn't help but smile herself. "I guess it is always complicated."

"So, what are you going to do?" Tessa asked.

"About what?"

Claire squeezed her hand. "About the baby, about Chance, about everything. You have the opportunity to point things in the direction you want them to go."

"Chance and I are going to be coparents and maybe friends. That's it." Even if she was the one who had to draw the line between them. Chance was always protecting her, and this was her chance to protect him for once.

"Uh-huh," Tessa said. "Do you still want to be with him?"

Yes. It wasn't even a question. Maci wanted everything with him, she just wasn't sure that she could have it. So, once again, she took the coward's way out. "I don't know."

Kayleigh called her on it, eyebrow raised. "Yes, you do. You just don't want to admit it."

"I already said—"

"We know." Kayleigh rolled her eyes. "You're not a good fit. You'll drag him down. Blah, blah, blah. Have you ever asked Chance what he wants?"

Tessa moved to sit on the coffee table directly in front of Maci, grabbing her hands tightly. "Instead of trying to protect him, why don't you let him make his own choices? It's what you would want if the roles were reversed."

She winced. "But he doesn't know—"

"Then tell him." Kayleigh squished onto the table with Tessa, setting a hand on Maci's knee.

Claire slipped an arm through Maci's and

suddenly they were all connected. "Chance is a big boy who knows how to weigh risk and rewards. He's capable of choosing whether he stays or goes and in what capacity he wants to be in your life, but it's unfair of you to take that choice from him."

"I'm scared. I don't want to hurt him."

"You already have," Claire said softly, grimacing when Maci flinched. "I don't say it to make you feel bad, but you have to know. Pushing him away when anyone can see that he wants to be closer is hurting him. Especially when he has no idea what he's done wrong."

"He hasn't done anything wrong."

"So, tell him that. Talk to him. It's okay to be scared, but you two are going to have to find a way to coexist for the rest of your lives. Wouldn't it be better to do it with a clean slate?"

Maci didn't even have to think about it. The girls were right. Chance deserved to make his own decisions, but how could she tell him everything he needed to know? How could she give him the reason he needed to walk away from her?

And how would she survive once he did?

"You don't have to do it right now, but just think about it. Okay?" Tessa pulled Maci off the couch and into a hug. "We're here for you."

"Anytime, anywhere," Claire added, snuggling into Maci's back.

"Whatever you need." Kayleigh slid an arm around her waist.

Wrapped in her friends' arms, she heaved a deep breath for the first time since she found out she was pregnant. Tessa, Claire and Kayleigh—because of their connection to the Patterson brothers—had become pillars of her life and the best friends she'd ever had.

They were just pulling away when Chance came out of his office. "I can come back if you need more time."

"Actually, we're heading out." Tessa pulled Maci back into a hug, whispering, "Let him make his own choices."

After the others said goodbye too, she ushered them out the door.

Chance closed the door behind them, but didn't move. He stood by the entryway and stared at Maci. Something in the way he watched her made Maci feel almost vulnerable, and she wrapped an arm around herself as if the added barrier would help.

"What are you doing?" she finally asked.

"Looking at you."

Uncomfortable under his gaze, she fell back to her default snark. "Obviously. Why are you doing it?"

"Because you're beautiful."

Maci opened her mouth, but nothing came out. What was she supposed to say to that? The air thickened around them as the silence grew, and suddenly it was too much.

"I'm sorry," she blurted.

Chance's brows lowered, shadowing his eyes. "For what?"

"I should have told you about the baby. I should have told you—" She cut herself off. It wasn't the time to invite her demons into the conversation. Not yet. They'd have to talk about them eventually, but that was a problem for future Maci.

"Why didn't you tell me?" His tone held no malice.

She walked back into the living room and plopped back onto the couch and looked down at her lap, twisting her fingers over and over. Finally, she decided that if they were going to have a chance at coparenting—*or more*—she had to be honest with him. They'd never be able to be anything if she kept hiding the truth. Baby steps.

"I was scared."

"Oh, honey." Just like that, he was kneeling at her feet, big hands cradling her face. "What were you scared of?"

Nothing. Everything.

She wanted to tell him, but she knew she couldn't. He didn't need to see how big of a mess she was. Eventually it would be clear, but for now, she wanted him to never stop looking at her the way he did. Like he cherished her. Like he understood her. Like he wanted to know every thought she ever had.

As if he could read her mind, he leaned in so close that their breath mingled. "You don't have to tell me right now. There's no rush." He pressed a soft kiss to her lips, the barely-there touch making them tingle. "Keep your secrets for now, Maci Ford. I'm not going anywhere."

Maci's chest ached at the tenderness in his voice and the way he held her. As she reached for him, pulling his face to hers, she knew that she was already gone. There was no avoiding the path back to each other that faith had put them on.

She wasn't optimistic enough to believe they'd have forever, but for now, she'd enjoy having Chance at her side again.

They kissed slowly, eventually moving to Chance's room where they relearned each other's bodies. Every kiss, every touch, stoked the need that months of distance had created. Maci's skin burned, aching for more with every sweep of his hands, and when they came together again, the look on Chance's face was like nothing else.

His eyes spoke his truth in waves of reverence and awe. The way he touched her, the way they moved together, felt a little like worship.

When they were spent, Chance curled his body around hers with his hand resting protectively on her stomach, his lips pressed softly to the nape of her neck. The steady counts of his breathing lulled her to sleep, and though she told herself not to fall for the dream, for the first time since she'd run from him, Maci felt at peace again.

Chapter Twelve

For the first time since he and his brothers had opened San Antonio Security nearly five years ago, Chance didn't really want to be here in the office.

He'd left Maci curled up in bed and hadn't wanted to leave this morning. She hadn't wanted to let him go either, but he was pretty sure it was more because she wanted to get back to work than because she would miss him.

Promising to bring home dinner from her favorite Italian restaurant if she took the day off to rest had finally worked. She'd agreed, though she'd glared when he suggested spending the day in bed napping.

He chuckled. Maci wasn't someone who enjoyed a lot of idle time. The food bribe had worked today, but he had no doubt it wouldn't work for long. Especially since she felt guilty that he was going out of his way to get it.

He didn't mind. He liked taking care of her. *Wanted* to take care of her. Wanted to make up for lost time when he hadn't taken care of her.

Chance had spent the morning holed up in his office, mostly because he needed to catch up on the intel his brothers had been gathering while he'd been gone. He read about Bert and Ernie—real names Daniel Neweth and Miles Dary—although official questioning of them hadn't led to much more info than what they'd said the first night. Someone had paid them; they didn't know who nor had they seen a face.

Dead end.

He also spent time writing up the report for Maci's attack and the car chase. He forced himself to tamp down the terror that still wanted to overwhelm him just at the thought of finding her lying so still on the floor. And that was before he'd known she was pregnant. He got the report done and sent it out.

But the real reason he was hiding in his office was because he knew his brothers were waiting to pounce. They wanted the details about Maci and the baby.

He couldn't avoid *the talk* forever, but he could avoid it for now. They were scheduled to meet Nicholas LeBlanc today for an update.

By the time Chance came out of his office, it was past lunch and time to leave for the meeting.

"He lives!" Luke joked, but slid him a travel mug of coffee and a deli sandwich. "Thought we were going to have to smoke you out to get you in the car."

"Just trying to get caught up on everything. Especially paperwork."

Luke's pronounced shudder at the word made Chance laugh into his cup. Coffee in hand, the pair found their way to the SUV out front where Brax and Weston were already sitting.

"So, Maci…" Brax said as he drove. "She feeling better?"

Chance hoped this wasn't the start of the inquisition. "No residual issues from the attack. She's feeling tired and sick, but said it's just normal pregnancy stuff."

He took a sip of his coffee and made a note on his phone to pick up a pregnancy book or two. "I promised to grab food on the way home if she'd just stay home and rest."

Home. He'd let himself drift off to the idea of walking through his door after a long day and finding her in his house more than once. It was almost too much for Chance, especially when he'd woken up that morning with her hair on his pillow and the utter certainty that she belonged there. With him and their baby. Always.

"Good. Let's get this meeting over with quickly," Weston said. "The sooner we finish this, the sooner you can get home. No one wants to make a pregnant woman wait."

His brothers let it go with that—no further questions. Chance shouldn't have been surprised. They wouldn't push if he wasn't ready to talk. Especially when they needed to be focused on the case at hand.

They parked at VanPoint Tower and headed up to Nicholas LeBlanc's office, finding him with both Dorian Cane and Rich Carlisle.

Chance tried to hide his distaste for Rich as best as he could, but all he could see was the other man's hands on his Maci. It left a sour taste in his mouth.

LeBlanc shook everyone's hands, despite the obvious tension surrounding him. "Dorian let me know about your teammate's injury. The woman who was impersonating Stella. Will she be alright?"

"She's recovering, but we won't be using that style mission anymore." There was no way in hell Chance was allowing that. "Her cover was blown anyway, so it's a moot point."

"That's a shame." Rich's charming smirk covered his face, as always. "I enjoyed spending time with her. She's feisty."

Chance's hands clenched into fists at his side. It was only Weston's hand squeezing his shoulder that helped him remain focused rather than leap across the room and knock the smirk off Rich's face.

Dorian stepped forward. "Did the teenagers

who were paid to get you to chase them provide any usable intel?"

The idea that teenagers had been paid to send grown men on a car chase throughout the city didn't sit well with any of them. What if they'd crashed? What if they'd hurt someone?

"Nothing." Luke shook his head. "No phone number or contact information for the person who paid them. They never saw his face."

"We have contacts with the San Antonio PD so we called it in with them," Weston continued. "Kids were brought to the station, but they ultimately were only held for driving under the influence."

While his brothers talked, Chance kept his eye on Rich. Chance's dislike was definitely personal, but it was also more than that. Something about the man was beeping all over Chance's threat radar.

Rich's background check had come back clear when they'd run it, but something still felt off.

"How much did the guy pay them?" Dorian asked.

Weston shrugged. "Enough to get high a few times. That's all they cared about."

"So, you have an injured employee, we have two teenagers who are useless for providing info, and we are still no closer to finding Stella's stalker," Nicholas said.

Chance grit his teeth. The other man was correct in his summary of the situation. "Yes. Using a decoy isn't going to work anymore. Before knocking Maci unconscious, he told her he knew she wasn't Stella. We don't know when or how he figured it out."

"We know he knew where all the security cameras were in your daughter's apartment," Brax said. "He took out the one in the elevator completely and was able to avoid the hall and lobby cameras."

"Even the ones we set up in secret?" Dorian asked.

Chance nodded. "Guy kept his head tucked down and face averted for everything. Avoided the cameras but didn't seem to know where they were specifically beyond the elevator. Doorman didn't see anyone, so he came in through the service door."

Dorian looked as frustrated as all of them felt. It was like the stalker was always one step ahead of them.

And even worse, he was starting to escalate. No more letters and two violent instances in a row. When stalkers changed their MOs so abruptly, it could spell disaster for the object of their obsession.

"Stella isn't happy about keeping out of the limelight this long," LeBlanc said.

Brax quickly shook his head. "Coming back now could be the worst thing she could do. The stalker obviously doesn't know where she really is because there's been no attempts on her in Europe."

The rest of them, including Dorian, were quick to agree.

"Mr. LeBlanc, we're still committed to solving this case," Chance said. "Doubly so, now that the stalker hurt one of our own."

LeBlanc rubbed the back of his neck. "What's the next step then?"

"We'd like to look through the footage for the last few months of events to see if there are any guests or patterns that we can discern. We'll need a full accounting of Stella's schedule to match up the times she got the stalker's letters we've already got at the office."

"Full staff list too," Weston said.

Rich shifted slightly in his seat. He looked uncomfortable. Was he nervous? Bored? Hungover from going out last night? All were possibilities.

"We've got all the security footage already. I'll get that for you," Dorian said. "I'll make sure to include who was guarding Stella and her apartment as well."

Chance nodded, glad the other man wasn't offended by them wanting to double-check his work. "If we continue to work together, we'll catch this guy. Everybody makes a mistake at some point. We'll figure out a way to hurry that along."

Not long after, with the meeting over and a plan in place, the Patterson brothers headed home. No one spoke until they were pulling away from the building.

"Rich didn't like that we're investigating the past," Weston said.

Chance tapped his fingers on the seat next to him. "No, he didn't. He especially didn't like that we're going to have full access to the staff list."

"Could he be the perp?" Luke asked.

Chance shrugged. "It wouldn't make much sense. He's had unfettered access to Stella for years. Why start being a pseudo stalker at this point?"

His brothers all murmured their agreement.

"Who wants to bet money we're going to find him doing something shady on the footage?" Luke asked.

No one was dumb enough to take that bet.

"For now, let's just focus on the plan," Chance said. "We look through the footage and dig through employees and people closest to Stella. We look again at the people who message her or follow her obsessively on social media. I think whoever it is has to be someone close."

"Why do you say that?" Weston asked.

"They know too much to just be watching. This feels like intimate knowledge."

"They could have a mole in the staff," Luke suggested, writing the idea down on his phone's notepad for later.

They all let out a groan.

"Don't say that," Brax muttered. "That'll make our lives indefinitely harder."

Chance scrubbed a hand down his face. "We have to consider the possibility."

A mole would have enough knowledge to evade them for a long time, and all he wanted to do was clear this case up and concentrate on Maci. He didn't have time for chaotic stalkers when he had a baby on the way.

They made it back to the office and everyone started to pack up for the day. Funny how Chance wasn't even tempted to try to talk his brothers into staying late and working.

Having someone at home waiting made all the difference.

"I'll see you guys tomorrow."

Brax stopped him with a hand at his chest, pushing him back toward the office kitchen. "We've cut you some slack with the questions of what exactly is going on between you and our beloved office manager."

Luke smiled. "But there's no way in hell we're leaving here without a toast to our new niece or nephew."

Weston wagged his dark eyebrows. "And to you becoming a father, ready or not."

Luke pulled out a bottle of whiskey—the expensive one they used very rarely. "This is usually for celebrating big wins. I think Chance becoming a daddy is the biggest win of all."

With a grin at Chance, he poured them each a drink, and all four of them lifted the glasses in a toast.

"Chance," Brax started, "fatherhood is the wildest ride with the most amazing reward." He was the only one of them able to speak of fatherhood with intimate knowledge. "I know you're going to ace it."

Weston clapped him on the back. "You've been fathering everyone around you since we all became Pattersons. Probably did it before that too. That's how we know you're going to be so good at it. You've got a lifetime of practice."

Luke held his glass up and they all joined. "Congratulations on becoming a dad and making us all uncles again. To fatherhood!"

"To fatherhood!" They clinked their glasses and sipped.

Once again it hit him. *He was going to be a dad.* Maci was having his baby.

"So, Maci, huh?" Luke waggled his eyebrows, making Chance laugh.

"Yeah. It was...unexpected."

That really made his brothers laugh.

"Only to you," Brax said, shaking his head. "It was plain as day to anyone else with working eyeballs, despite the hostility you both threw. Tessa and I had a bet on when you'd get together."

Though he was curious, Chance decided he didn't need to know who won in the end.

Brax nodded. "You and Maci aren't a surprise. It was inevitable."

"Maybe," Chance conceded.

"So, are you two together now?" Luke asked. "Should we add another place for family dinner this week?"

"We'll see about dinner. Depends on how she's feeling." He finished the last of his whiskey. "And no, to us being together. At least, I don't think so."

Luke's eyes sharpened on Chance's face. "You can still be part of the child's life without being romantically involved with Maci. Do you want to be together?"

"I do." The answer was immediate. Chance knew months ago he wanted her as more than whatever they were. She'd just run before he could admit it. "Maci is… Well, you know her. She's great. She's funny and smart as a whip. I love how she keeps me—keeps all of us—on our toes. I like how easy it is to rile her up and that she can throw back whatever I dish up. We just fit."

"Have you told her that?" Weston asked.

He let out a sigh. "No. She's skittish. It feels like she's two seconds away from bolting at any given moment." Like she'd done the first time.

"I'm no expert on relationships or women, but why don't you start by telling her that? Maybe it'll help, let her put down some roots. It's hard to be real with someone when they aren't sure where you stand."

Chance knew Luke was right, he just didn't know how to tell her.

There was something fragile about Maci, despite her prickly exterior. She could argue and fight with him all day, but something still made him want to protect her even from herself.

"You're probably right," Chance admitted. "But for now, I've got dinner to pick up."

He headed out of the office, already looking forward to getting home to his girl, whether she knew she was his or not.

Chapter Thirteen

Maci lasted three days cooped up in Chance's house.

And while she loved the closeness the two of them had shared, she was ready to get back to work.

"Be reasonable," Chance said, snatching the sweater out of her hand and throwing it back onto the bed. "You just got out of the hospital."

She picked up another sweater and pulled it on, only to realize it was Chance's. She debated taking it off, but it was too comfortable. Dressed, she faced him again. "Three days ago. I'm fine, Chance. I'm not an invalid."

"You need more rest. So does the baby." He crossed his arms over his way-too-sexy chest.

But if he thought bringing up the baby—or crossing his arms over his chest like some supermodel—would help his case, he was wrong.

"The baby needs a mother who isn't bored out of her skull, especially since I'm not planning on being homebound for the entirety of my pregnancy. Besides, I have things to do at the office."

"One more day. Relax here for just one more day."

Maci had done nothing but relax for days.

She was done. She looked him over with narrowed eyes. His casual work clothes weren't the suits he wore when bodyguarding, so she knew he was likely doing desk work. "Are you doing anything dangerous in the field today?"

He frowned. "No."

"You guys scoping out another hostage situation?"

"No." His jaw clenched and she smiled. He already knew he was on the losing side of this argument.

"So, why can't I go into the office?"

Petulant silence. It was almost enough to make Maci laugh.

"That's what I thought. I heard you talking to your brothers about going over the party footage today. That's desk work. I can help with that."

"Maci…"

"I'm not made to sit around and eat bonbons. I need something to occupy my time or I'm going to go nuts and start redecorating this house to look like a ninety-year-old cat lady threw up everywhere. I'm talking doilies and lace on every possible surface. Pink walls. The works."

He stared at her and Maci could tell he wanted to argue, so she went for broke.

"Please, Chance. I don't want to fight. I just need to get out of the house. Plus, I was there at those parties. My insight might be useful."

He sighed, running a hand through his hair. "Fine, but only for a few hours, and if I see even a single wince, you're leaving and you'll stay home tomorrow."

Maci didn't bother to hide her giddy smile. She hopped across the room and popped a kiss to his cheek. "Deal!"

Stepping into the office after so long away was like coming home for Maci. She'd missed the soft gray walls and warm wood. Even the sticky note reminders everywhere put her at ease.

Seeing the mess the brothers had left in the kitchen was far less enjoyable.

"Did we get rid of the dishwasher while I was gone?" She raised an eyebrow at Luke, who was in the process of leaving his dirty cup in the almost-full sink. He froze, eyes wide when he saw her hovering in the doorway.

"I forgot?"

"I'll just bet you did," Maci grumbled. Luke wisely loaded the dishwasher before turning back to her.

"Didn't know you were coming in today, Maci."

"That's because she should still be home resting," Chance said from directly behind her. He'd barely given her an inch to breathe since they walked in the door.

Maci waved his words away. "Ignore him. He's annoyed because he lost the argument."

"I didn't lose the argument. I chose to stop fighting because you asked me to."

That took the wind out of her sails. He was trying. Chance was overprotective of everyone on his best of days. Her pregnancy certainly hadn't quelled that behavior in any way.

He didn't like her being here, but he was *trying*.

She made herself some tea and found her way to her desk. It wasn't until she pulled out her chair to sit that he spoke again. "What are you doing?"

"I have hundreds of emails and dozens of invoices to get through. Thought I would get started doing the job you guys pay me for." Maci turned on her laptop and waited for it to boot up.

When she glanced up, Chance was back to scowling. It wasn't fair that he was so handsome when he brooded. "We're all working in the conference room."

"It's easier for me to work out here."

"I want you in there."

She wasn't about to delude herself that it was because he wanted to be near her. Nurse Chance just wanted to micromanage her choices.

"I've only got a few hours in the office, at

your request, so I'll work here where I can actually get things done."

She moved to log in and Chance pulled her chair back, spinning it so she faced him. "It's not a request, Maci. You wanted to come back to work and I'm respecting that—"

"I hardly consider badgering me at every opportunity respecting anything."

"—but I'm going to keep an eye on you while you're here. I know you won't tell me if you're hurting, so consider me your shadow until it's time to go."

Now it was Maci's turn to glare. "You going to follow me to the bathroom too?"

"If I have to." He didn't look a bit like he was bluffing.

Maci debated arguing more. That's what they did, argue. Chance didn't have any right to tell her what to do with her time or her body, she knew that. But she could see the furrow in his brow and the tenseness in his shoulders.

He was *worried* about her.

The attack had scared him, and now that he knew about their baby, he was doubly afraid. What was the harm in letting him coddle her a bit longer? Especially since she had every intention of moving back into her own place soon.

"Fine. I'll stay in eyesight, but so help me, if you really follow me into the bathroom, I'll be using those defense moves you taught me to take *you* down."

He kissed the top of her head, then moved her things into the conference room, greeting the others. She pretended not to notice as he brought in extra water and snacks for the table as well, knowing they were actually for her.

And definitely didn't let her heart get all gooey at it.

While the brothers talked about the case, Maci put in her headphones, falling into her spreadsheets and files with easy bliss. She'd missed her desk job. Missed answering emails and doing paperwork. It suited her much more than her single attempt at undercover work did, that was for sure.

She dug through the backlogged emails, sending invoices to clients and vendors, and getting caught up on everything the guys had let slide the last few days. By the time the scent of takeout filled her nose, she was feeling pretty tired and hungry, but the sense of accomplishment she'd been missing filled her with joy.

Chance rapped his knuckles softly on the table at her side. She pulled out her headphones, and he nodded to the white foam boxes everywhere. "Time to eat. You've been in the zone for hours."

"Perfect timing. I'm almost done." With a few

more keystrokes, she finished her last email and sent it off. Shutting her laptop, she moved everything to the side and grabbed the container Chance set in front of her. Chow mein with extra sauce and egg rolls. Perfect.

"This is so good." Chance smiled at her as he and the others pulled their usual orders out of the bag. It didn't escape Maci's notice that he'd gotten her food out first.

The guys were mostly quiet as they ate. "Anything with Stella's case?" she asked.

Chance stabbed a piece of meat with his fork. "We've been going through party footage from the last two months trying to find any repeats or patterns that we didn't notice before."

Luke ate a big bite of ramen. "So far, we've got nothing. No leads, no patterns, no suspicious faces. And the boys we chased were a dead end—they didn't know anything. Nothing on Stella's apartment security feed either."

She pushed her food away from her, not feeling as hungry. "I guess I was pretty useless too."

Chance pushed the food back toward her. "No. You survived and are healthy and whole. That is definitely not useless."

"Would you mind if we ask you a few questions about the voice you heard?" Weston asked.

Chance turned and glared at him. Obviously, Chance had told them not to ask her about it.

Enough was enough. "Yes, please do. I want to help if I can."

"You don't have to," Chance muttered.

She rolled her eyes. "What harm exactly do you think is going to come to me by trying to remember how the stalker sounded?"

"I don't want it to upset you."

She folder her arms over her chest. "You know what upsets me? Possibly being able to help stop a stalker but someone deciding for me that it's too much, rather than allowing me to make my own decisions."

There were snickers around the table but she kept her eyes on Chance.

He gave in with ill grace. "Fine."

Now she turned to Weston. "What do you want to know?"

"Did you recognize the voice at all? Or maybe there was some sort of accent or noticeable trait?"

"It was a weird, spooky whisper. Like he was trying to be menacing." As if him breaking into the apartment hadn't been menacing enough.

"Do you think it could've been anyone you talked to at one of the events?" Brax asked.

She shook her head. "Not that comes to mind."

"What about Rich?" Chance asked.

"Rich?" Maci turned to Chance. "Do you think it was him?"

"We aren't sure. We're trying to eliminate all possibilities."

Maci thought back to the attack, to the voice echoing in her ears. "I don't think so. Rich's voice is warm all the time. The man who spoke was cold. Empty."

Lifeless. The man who grabbed her had sounded lifeless.

"But then again, it was a sick whisper," she continued. "I've only ever heard Rich's regular voice. But still, I don't think it was him."

The brothers glanced at each other. Chance frowned again. "Alright, so not Rich. Could you pick the voice out if you heard it again?"

"Yes." Maci knew that for certain. "It's not something I'll ever forget."

"I know you didn't get a look at his face, but what about smells or strange sounds?" Brax asked. "Anything you can remember will be helpful."

She tried to think back, but other than the voice, everything else was a blur. "I'm sorry."

"Would you mind if we try something, since he was behind you?" Weston asked.

"Sure."

"Stand up for a second." Weston offered her his

hand to help get her to her feet. "Okay, so think of the voice, when the guy was behind you."

She nodded.

Weston looked over at Chance. "You go stand behind her."

Even knowing it was Chance, that she was completely safe, she was already tensing.

"Where did you hear the voice when he was behind you?" Chance asked. "Think about it. Was it high above your head, like where I am now? Or maybe a little lower."

She closed her eyes and forced herself to really think about it. "Lower. Closer to my ear."

She opened her eyes, not wanting to relive that any longer.

"So could be someone around five foot ten," Weston said. "Someone as tall as Chance would've been higher."

That made sense.

"But the guy also could've been leaning in toward her," Brax pointed out.

Maci sat back down in her chair but didn't reach for her food. She'd definitely lost her appetite.

"I'm sorry I'm not more help."

"It's fine. You're doing your best." Chance rubbed his thumb across her knuckles. "Why don't you help us look through some footage for a bit? Your half day is almost up anyway."

He was giving her an out and she was beyond grateful for it. "I'm going to come back tomorrow. Do you even know how many emails came in while I was gone?"

"We're supposed to check emails?" Luke joked, wincing.

They got out the footage and she pulled the screen closer. Maybe she'd be more useful this way. But as minute after minute scrolled by, she didn't hear or see anything that reminded her of the man in the apartment.

It was mind-numbing to sit there and watch it all. She had no idea how the guys did it.

She was only an hour or two in before her back was a tangle of knots and everything hurt. She leaned back in her chair and grimaced at the sharp ache in her muscles. Of course, her nursemaid saw and immediately swooped in.

"Alright, you're done," Chance said, ushering her out of the building and into his SUV, barely giving her time to grab her things and say goodbye.

She didn't even argue. She was exhausted.

And even worse, she hadn't been useful at all.

Chapter Fourteen

Chance arrived at the San Antonio Security office the next morning, coffee in hand, glad he'd been able to talk Maci into sleeping late and working a half day in the afternoon. She could talk tough all she wanted about how she wasn't an invalid. But the truth was her body had been through a trauma with the attack and was already exhausted from the pregnancy.

His phone pinged with a reminder as he stepped inside the building and he smiled. Maci had an ultrasound the next day and he was going.

The thought that they'd be able to actually see their baby—at least the heartbeat—had Chance shaking his head.

He was going to be a dad.

"You are a godsend." Brax snatched a cup of coffee from Chance's tray, gulping half the drink down in one go. "Walker is in the middle of sleep regressions. I was up most of the night."

Brax's two-year-old son was technically his biological nephew, but his son in every way that mattered—getting him to sleep included. Brax had officially adopted him once he married Tessa, Walker's mom.

"Maci and I are going to the ob-gyn tomorrow. Check on everything." Chance handed out the other two coffees to Luke and Weston.

Brax grinned. "Exciting, terrifying stuff, isn't it?"

"You better believe it."

Weston wasn't paying attention to any of the baby talk. He was zoned in on the footage in front of him. "The stalker has been inactive for too long. Something's not right. He's going to strike soon."

Chance met eyes with Brax, then Luke, behind Weston's back. Weston was definitely the quietest of the four of them, but his intuition was generally spot-on.

If Weston was saying the stalker was going to make another move soon, all of them were willing to believe him.

"I'll get on the phone with LeBlanc and Dorian. Make sure the security around Stella is tight." Luke was already walking out of the conference room, phone in hand.

"She's still in Europe, right?" Brax asked, all traces of tiredness gone.

Chance nodded. "Switzerland, unless they've moved her again." It was possible. Stella didn't like staying too long in one place.

Chance looked over at Weston, who was still

studying the footage. "Is there something in particular that has your spidey senses tingling?"

He shook his head without turning from the screen. "No. It's less this footage and more talking to Maci about the guy in the apartment. Do you remember what she told us he said at the apartment?"

"That he knew she wasn't Stella?"

"Actually, the part about battle and honor. That there was honor in staying when Stella had run and hid. It tells us something about his mindset."

Chance rubbed the back of his neck. "That he sees this as some sort of war or competition."

Now Weston turned to look at him. "Yes. All this time we've been searching for the stalker as someone who's obsessed with Stella. And honestly, he may be. But I also think he's obsessed with the *process* of stalking."

Luke came back in the room. "LeBlanc has Stella on lockdown. Guards have eyes on her and will be preparing for a possible attack."

"Did you talk to Dorian?" He had enough experience to understand that sometimes a gut feeling was actionable intel.

"Not directly. He's handling some other business for right now. But I did talk to his second-in-command, and we should be getting a call from Dorian soon to provide any info we can."

"We have reason to believe the stalker might

be former military or even law enforcement. Let's run guests at Stella's past events based on that filter and see if we can come up with anything useable."

For the first time they didn't feel like they were looking for a needle in a haystack.

They were maybe thirty minutes in when Chance's phone buzzed. He looked down, expecting a text from Maci or maybe Dorian. But it was from an unknown number.

Are you particularly attached to your office's front window?

"What the—"

"I just got some sort of weird text about the front window," Brax said. Luke and Weston had gotten it too.

"Sales promotion?" Luke asked.

"From an unknown number?" Brax responded. "Not going to get much business that way."

This wasn't right. All of them knew it. They moved into the office lobby, but the only things there were Maci's empty desk and a few other pieces of furniture.

The window shattered in front of them as a bullet struck it, a sea of glass flying everywhere.

All four of them dove to the ground—Chance

behind Maci's desk, Luke and Brax behind a couch, Weston at the corner of the room.

They paused, waiting for another shot to come, but there was nothing but the sound of tinkling glass.

"I have a feeling the stalker just brought the war to us," Luke said.

"Yeah, Weston, why do you have to be so damned right all the time?" Brax backed away from the couch. "How about next time your intuition tells you I'm going to win a million dollars rather than someone shooting at us."

Chance was staring at the chair Maci normally would've been sitting in. It was covered in glass. Rage was bubbling in his gut. "If Maci had been here…"

"There aren't too many places that someone could have made that shot from," Weston said. "It had to have been from the building across the street."

Chance nodded. "The roof. Let's go. If we move now, maybe we can catch him."

It was an office building with three stories. The shooter would've had a clear range.

Luke was already running toward the weapons room. He yanked out bulletproof vests, throwing them to each of his brothers. They all grabbed their weapons from their desks.

In under a minute they were running out the

back door. They all knew this could be a trap, but they weren't going to let that stop them. Not when they had a chance to get the upper hand.

As they rounded the corner from the back alley and had the building across from their office in sight, Chance barked out the plan. "Weston and Brax will clear the top two floors, while Luke and I do the roof. Good?"

His brothers called out their affirmations. They kept their weapons holstered as they ran for the building. It was already pandemonium on the street.

"You think they heard the shot and are panicking?" Luke asked.

As they got closer, the problem became evident. Someone had set off the fire alarm.

He and his brothers looked at each other. "He's giving himself an easy way to escape."

"Split up and look around. Let's see if we can catch anyone acting strange." Weston pulled out his phone and started recording as he walked inside. "I'll try to get as much footage as I can, see if we can match someone to one of Stella's events."

Brax grabbed Chance's arm as someone rushed by, sobbing and yelling about smoke. Maybe the stalker had started an actual fire to make sure there was real panic. "We need to get up on that roof."

Chance shook his head. "There's no way, not

with so many people pouring downstairs. Plus, he's already gone. You know he's around here somewhere. Let's record like Weston said."

They spread out, Chance checking every face he passed. He didn't bother looking for a gun bag. The shooter wasn't stupid. He'd either stored the weapon to come back for it later or got out of Dodge immediately after taking the shot.

Chance tried to ignore the most panicked people and the ones who didn't fit the profile. He looked for those who were more calm despite the chaos, and concentrated on recording those.

When the fire engine parked in front of the building and the firefighters began crowd control, Chance knew there was nothing else they could do. They'd talk to local police about the shooting and hopefully get the footage from any security cameras around, but they were limited in what they could do until then. He walked outside as the firefighters demanded it.

Annoyed at the situation, Chance yanked out his cell with a growl when it rang. Weston. "Please tell me you have good news."

"Unfortunately, nobody walking around with a shirt saying I Just Shot Out a Window. I didn't see anything or anyone who seemed too suspicious," Weston said. "You?"

"A few people who were too relaxed, but nothing concrete."

"Let's get back to the office. We can compare footage and start calling in favors to get the local security feeds. Maybe we caught something."

"I'll meet you there."

A flash of something in his peripheral had him turning, eyes locked with the back of a plain black hoodie. Besides standing slightly taller than the crowd, the man blended in with everyone around him.

Except he was walking away rather than watching what was going on around them.

Chance knew from experience it was human nature to stay at the scene of an emergency. Curiosity and the desire for drama had people sticking around.

Using one hand, he called his brother back.

"I may have something. Man in a black hoodie leaving the scene just to the west of the front door. I'm following."

"We're right behind you."

Chance sped through the crowd, having to jostle to the side as he tried to keep his eyes on the man in the hoodie. At the end of the block the crowd cleared out, and Chance could finally put on some speed. When he was close enough to touch, he reached out and clamped his hand down on the man's shoulder, whirling him around.

Not a man. Another damned teenager. The

kid ripped one of his headphones out of his ear with a frown. "Can I help you?"

"Were you in the building back there?" Chance asked.

"No. I stopped by because I heard the sirens, but it doesn't look like there's an actual fire. So I've got better things to do."

Chance still had him by the shoulder of his hoodie. "How do you know there's no fire? People were talking about smoke. Seemed pretty panicked."

The kid shrugged. "Whatever, man. There's no fire."

Chance wanted to push, but knew there was no way in hell this was the stalker. He let the kid go. "You see anything suspicious?"

The kid raised an eyebrow. "You mean besides a random dude grabbing teenagers? No."

Chance fished out a card from his pocket, telling the kid to call if he thought of anything strange. He snapped a picture of the kid's face while he was looking at the card.

They would run him and make sure he didn't have any ties to Stella they should know about. But besides that there wasn't much Chance could do.

He turned and walked back to the office, calling to tell his brothers the hoodie kid was another dead end.

When he got back to the office, he found his brothers hovering around Maci's desk.

"What's going on?"

Luke held up a piece of paper in a gloved hand. "The stalker left us a note."

You made me better, but I want to be the best. First one to the prize wins.

Chance didn't know what to make of that. "Is the prize Stella?"

Brax dropped his phone to the counter. "I just talked to Dorian, and Stella is safe. No attempts on her."

Chance rubbed his eyes. There were so many things he didn't like about this situation. The stalker actively communicating with them, and coming into their personal space. Him making it into some sort of game he wanted them to play.

But most of all he didn't like the fact that if Maci had been at work today she might have been at that desk when that bastard shot the window out. Might have been covered in glass.

"I need to make a call." He needed to hear Maci's voice.

Chance stepped into his office, dialing before the door was shut.

"Chance? Is everything okay? I was just about to leave so I can work the half day."

Just the sound of Maci's voice—relaxed and calm—soothed his frayed nerves. She was okay. That was all that mattered.

"You're not going to believe this, but we're going to need you to not come in today."

"Damn it, Chance. I am not going to let you—"

"I promise this is not me trying to get you to rest. The front window of the office...broke, and we're going to have to close everything early today and get it fixed."

"Oh, my gosh. Did you throw someone through it?"

He chuckled. "You're not here. So, no."

She laughed at that. "Ha-ha. I've thought about throwing you through that glass once or twice too. What happened?"

"I'll tell you everything when I get home. Do me a favor and make sure the doors are locked."

She didn't respond for a second. "Something happened, didn't it?"

He'd never lied to her and wasn't going to start now. "Yeah. But nobody was hurt."

"Okay," she finally said. He knew she wanted to demand details and appreciated that she didn't. "You all be careful. Come home safe."

Home. To her. "I will. See you in a while."

He walked back out to the main room. Although he hadn't touched it, Luke had found the bullet where it had wedged into the wall. Definitely a downward trajectory. The shooter had been in the building across the street.

"I called some friends on the force," Weston said. "They're going to come pick up the bullet and run it. Brax is on the phone with the window replacement company."

"Maybe we should put in bulletproof glass." Chance meant it as a joke, but Weston's bunched eyebrows said he was really considering it.

Luke stood from where he was studying the bullet. "Good news is that Weston did his voodoo, and because of the special circumstances of our ongoing case, the police have kindly offered to share the security footage from the high-rise to see if we spot anyone we recognize from our own research."

Chance looked over at Weston. He was the one who'd served on the San Antonio PD for a few years. He nodded. "Although, they're more interested in catching the guy who caused the fire panic in the office across the street than they are our window."

Chance shrugged one shoulder. "Since we're almost positive it's the same person, I'll take it."

Luke rubbed his eyes. "Means going through more footage."

It wasn't what any of them wanted to do.

But this bastard had brought the fight to their front door. Chance and his brothers were going to take him down.

Chapter Fifteen

If this was how Chance had felt when he'd found her unconscious in the apartment, then Maci probably needed to cut him some slack.

She was staring at the gaping hole at the front of the office where the wall of glass used to be. Chance had explained what happened last night, but until she saw it with her own eyes this morning, she hadn't truly been able to process it.

It was hard to believe that one bullet had done that much damage. The guys had explained that it had been a rifle bullet, so a big one, but still... *one bullet.*

What if one of the guys had been walking through the lobby, as they did a thousand times a day, when that bullet had hit? Only a little bit of glass had sprayed back far enough to hit her desk—well, hit where her desk *used* to be; the guys had moved it into the conference room where there were no windows—but if Chance had been standing there talking to her when the glass broke, it would have cut him to ribbons.

Now she understood his need to constantly keep her behind him so he was between her and any unknown threats. Because she felt like doing the same thing to him.

She knew if she stayed out watching the workers replacing the window for too long she'd get a lecture from one of the Patterson brothers. As it was, she was only allowed to peek her head around the corner—definitely was *not* allowed to stand in the open room.

But she wasn't going to argue. As long as Chance and his brothers didn't stand in the open room either. Protectiveness went both ways.

The guys were back poring over the new security footage from yesterday. Maci had work she could do at her now-conference-room desk, but could hardly focus. Between the shock of the window and her ob-gyn appointment later that afternoon, she was frazzled.

Her phone buzzed in her pocket and she took it out. Evelyn. Definitely not what she needed today. Maci hadn't answered any of the other five texts since they last saw each other, and planned to ignore this one too.

Maci knew better than to fall for the I miss yous or Let's catch up, babys.

Meet me at your apartment or I'm coming to you.

Maci grit her teeth as she typed back. Today really isn't a good day.

I can either come to that office or your boyfriend's house. Either one. Amazing how quick her mother could be when she wanted to.

Maci rubbed her eyes. She doubted Evelyn had Chance's address, but it wouldn't be impossible. Maci didn't want her showing up at either place.

Especially not today when she and Chance were going together to the doctor. Maci didn't want to produce proof in living color of the poor genes their child would be getting from Maci's side of the family.

Not to mention the questions it might lead to about Maci's mothering ability. *Legitimate* questions.

Ones she'd asked herself every single day since she found out she was pregnant.

Fine. I'll be at my place in twenty.

She headed into the conference room. The guys were so closely watching the footage, none of them even realized she was there. She walked over to Chance.

"I'm going to go and rest for a little while before the doctor's appointment."

Chance was on his feet immediately. "Are you okay? Do you feel sick? I can drive you home."

They'd ridden in together. She'd forgotten about that. "No, no. You have important and time-sensitive work to be done. I'm okay to drive myself."

He was torn, she could tell. She hated that she was deceiving him, but what choice did she have?

She reached out and touched his arm. "No smothering, remember? You can walk me out to the car, and I'll text you when I...get there."

That was vague enough not to be a complete lie.

He still didn't like it, but agreed. "Okay, I'll walk you out." He wrapped an arm around her shoulder and led her to the back alley, where they'd all parked today to avoid the front door.

He pulled her in for a hug at the car. She hugged him back. She needed his closeness.

"Be careful," he said into her hair. "And let me know you're okay. I'll see you at home."

Guilt ate at Maci. Chance wanted her to be safe and she was running off to meet with an unstable woman, but if she could spare him another run-in with her mother, she would. With a wave to Chance, she got in the car and headed back to the past.

MACI'S MOTHER WAS pacing in front of the door when she arrived.

"Took you long enough."

Maci ignored her, quickly texting Chance that

she was okay, before ushering them both inside. The sooner she took care of this, the sooner she could get back to the better parts of her life.

"What do you want, Mom?"

As if she didn't know. As if calling Evelyn *Mom* wasn't practically a joke.

"You could at least pretend to be happy to see me." Evelyn walked around looking at things in the apartment like she'd never seen them before and was fascinated by how Maci had decorated. "I don't even know what's going on with you. You rushed me out of here so fast last time."

Maci grit her teeth. She knew how this game was played. Evelyn was going to do whatever was the exact opposite of what Maci wanted.

If Maci wanted to spend time and try to connect, Evelyn would want to leave. If Maci was on a tight schedule, Evelyn would be clingy and refuse to leave.

It was a childish game, and they'd been playing it for as long as Maci could remember— even when she lived at home.

"I need cash."

Of course, she did. "What happened to what I just gave you the other day? You can't have run through it all already."

"You didn't give me that much."

"Because I don't have much to spare. Any, actually."

Evelyn spun around to stare at her, crossing her thin arms over her chest. "We both know that's not true. I saw the car your boyfriend was driving when he took you out of here. I know he owns his own company with those so-called brothers of his. I don't believe they all aren't loaded."

Maci hated hearing her even mentioning Chance or his brothers. The Pattersons were all good. Chance deserved better than to be dragged into Maci's toxic family drama.

"First of all, he's not my boyfriend. And yes, I may work for the Pattersons, who own their own business, but that doesn't mean they're loaded and it especially doesn't mean I have extra money."

Evelyn started walking around again. "But you could get it if you wanted to. Especially to help out family."

Maci sat down in the kitchen chair by the small table. This pattern with her mother was never going to end. Not if Maci continued to let it go on like this.

"Mom, I don't have money to give you. I need it for myself."

Her mother turned to scrutinize her. "I thought you were done with drugs."

"I am." She took in a deep breath, hoping she

wasn't about to make a huge mistake. "I need the money because I'm going to have a baby."

Maci's pregnancy was too new for her to have thought much about how she would break the news to Evelyn. But sitting here, she realized that she hoped the news would bring about some sort of positive change.

Evelyn had never been able to clean up for Maci, but maybe she would for her grandchild. Maybe they could have a relationship after all.

Her mother stopped and stared at her. "You idiot. You let him get you pregnant? You've ruined your life."

Knots formed in Maci's stomach. Definitely not the reaction she'd been hoping for.

"Thanks for the vote of confidence. Regardless of my *poor decisions* I don't have the money, so go find someone else to extort."

Evelyn was silent, turning back and walking around the room, peeking at all of Maci's things. Every time she picked something up, Maci ached to reach out and slap her hands away. This was her space, her sanctuary, and she wanted Evelyn out of it.

"You think I'm stupid?" Evelyn picked up a book and tossed it on the couch. "I know you have a rainy-day fund. I'll take that. You can ask your baby daddy for more money for raising some thankless brat."

"You should leave, Evelyn. I've made my decision."

Evelyn's eyes were flinty. She didn't like when Maci called her by her name instead of Mom. As if Evelyn hadn't just described her as a thankless brat.

"You've made your decision?" She picked up another book, flipping through the pages before tossing it to the side. "Do you think you're better than me?"

"This isn't about better or worse. This is about priorities."

"Oh, yeah?" She put her hands on her hips. "How do you think your little boyfriend would react if he knew what you used to do to get high? Don't you think someone should explain that to him so he knows what he's getting into?"

Dread pooled in Maci's stomach as she steeled herself against the memories. She refused to go back to that time, even in her mind. "I made mistakes. He would accept them, especially since I won't make them again."

Maybe if she said the words forcefully enough she could believe they were true.

Her mother laughed, a harsh bark of a sound. "I doubt that. He seems like an upstanding guy. A professional and respectable businessman."

"He is."

Evelyn's lip curled up in a snarl. "Men like

that have one thought when it comes to drugs—once addicted, always addicted."

No. Maci wasn't addicted anymore. She was in recovery. She'd done everything she could to get better. She *was* better.

"I'm not like you. I'm not going to keep doing drugs when I've finally made a life for myself. I'm not going to spend forever chasing a high I'll never be able to keep. I'm happy sober."

It was the wrong thing to say and it threw Evelyn into a rage. Maci stood there in horror as Evelyn swept out the rest of Maci's books off the bookshelf and onto the floor, then knocked the bookshelf over. The coffee table ended up on its side, with the empty glass that had been sitting on it shattering on the floor. Evelyn tore pillows and ripped the paintings and pictures from the walls.

It was impossible to believe someone as petite as Evelyn could do this much damage—the drugs in her system gave her the boost of strength. Maci knew not to get near. Evelyn didn't have these rages often, but her violence wasn't just targeted on inanimate objects. Maci kept far out of reach.

By the time Evelyn was done, the apartment that Maci had fought and scrounged for was nothing but scraps and trash.

"You ungrateful little bitch." Maci watched

her mother's chest heave with every angry breath. "You either get me my money or we'll see what your boyfriend says when he finds out his baby mama was a drug dealer and a whore."

There it was, Evelyn's trump card. There was nothing else to do. Maci knew it and so did Evelyn. Her smarmy grin was enough to prove it.

"Fine. Let's go find an ATM."

Twenty minutes later, Maci's bank account was empty—including the five hundred dollars she'd saved for emergencies.

And so was her heart. She felt hollowed out as she watched her mother slip away laughing, leaving her alone with her thoughts.

Now that Evelyn had a button to push, Maci would never be free. She'd lose everything she'd worked so hard for and Chance… Chance would eventually find out what Maci had done. The first time she tried to refuse Evelyn, she'd tell him everything and he'd hate Maci for it. It was only a matter of time.

Maci didn't know what to do with herself but she couldn't move yet, so she curled up on her couch and cried, as the future she'd been so desperate for slipped from her fingers for good.

Chapter Sixteen

Something wasn't right.

Chance told himself not to read into Maci's stiffness and slightly weird pauses as he walked her out to the car, but he couldn't help it.

Certainly, there were a lot of things for her to be stressed over...the window, the doctor's appointment, her head wound, the stalker in general. But something hadn't been right about how she'd left.

He'd still let her go and still forced himself to come back into the office once she was gone. He'd felt slightly better when he'd received her text—Made it okay—but something still didn't sit right in his gut.

He made it another hour before he decided to stop fighting it. "I'm going to go. Maci and I have that doctor's appointment this afternoon and... I don't know."

"You alright?" Weston looked up from his screen.

"Yeah. I just want to make sure she's okay."

None of them argued. Luke just tossed Chance his keys since Maci had taken Chance's car.

But when he got home neither his car nor

Maci was there. Normally stepping inside the house—especially since Maci had been staying there—made him relax, but not this time. Everything was silent.

Hoping there was some reason she was here despite the car not being in the garage, he called for her. "Maci?"

Pulling out his phone, he dialed her number and was immediately sent to voice mail. He sent texts, but got no response and no indication they'd been received.

He checked everywhere. The bedrooms were empty, the living room was clear and so was the backyard. There was no sign of trouble or forced entry. Every window was closed, every door locked.

Everything was exactly how it should have been, just without Maci.

Chance tried to focus. There hadn't been any other signs of attack. Nothing was out of place, no blood anywhere. Plus, no one except his family knew that Maci had been living with him.

So, she probably hadn't been kidnapped. Had there been a car accident?

No, because she'd texted him that she'd arrived safely.

He froze in the process of looking around again. Maybe she'd left? Like the night she'd snuck out of his bed and never returned. Maybe she'd decided she didn't want to be here with him anymore.

Maybe she'd decided to cut him out of her and the baby's life completely.

He rushed to the closet, heaving a sigh of relief when her clothes were still there.

He was about to dial his brothers to start a search party when he heard the garage door open. Relief warred with frustration so acute he had to take deep breaths to keep from losing his cool.

How he acted now was important. Because ultimately Maci was a grown woman and she didn't have to report any of her actions to him. He needed to show her that he was concerned but not smothering.

She walked in the door and his eyes combed over her—no injuries; that was good.

"Where the hell were you?" he barked.

Great, Patterson. Nice and calm.

She stilled on her way past, eyes narrowing. "I was driving around."

She looked tired, pale. Why?

"You were supposed to come straight home. Do you have any idea how—"

"I needed some time to think, Chance. Give me a break."

He could feel frustration bubbling up inside him. "You promised you'd come straight home and let me know you were okay. When I got your text, I assumed that's what it meant."

She flinched. "I had something to do first."

"Which was?"

Maci's hands clenched at her sides. "Nothing that concerns you."

"Everything about you concerns me."

"Well, it shouldn't! I'm a grown woman, Chance. I can take care of myself for a few hours."

Chance deflated. He was messing up…again. Letting fear drive him. If he wasn't careful, he knew he'd drive them apart.

He took a deep breath and tried again. "I know you can take care of yourself. I was worried. I came home and you weren't here and I couldn't get ahold of you. We have an active stalker who's targeting San Antonio Security, so now is a bad time to go AWOL without anyone knowing where. That's true for all of us."

Maci's eyes closed and she sighed. Chance watched the defensiveness in her posture slowly disappear. For a long moment they stood there in silence, then she came over and slid her arms around him.

The knot in his chest finally loosened as he clutched her tight. She was okay. She wasn't hurt and she hadn't left him.

When she spoke it was hushed. Apologetic.

"I'm sorry. I wasn't even thinking about all that. I thought I would make it home before you. I didn't mean to make you worry."

He stroked her hair, brushing it off her face so he could see it better where it rested on his chest. "I'm sorry that I snapped at you. Are you okay? You look pretty stressed. Is it office stuff? The window?"

He couldn't blame her if she didn't feel safe there anymore.

"No. I can't stand the thought of you guys getting hurt, but that isn't it. I was at my place with my mother."

He wanted to ask why being with her mom made her look so defeated and bone weary. But he wanted her to tell him because she wanted to tell him, not because he was prying. "Can I do anything for you?"

"This is good. I think I needed it."

He wrapped her up tighter, nuzzling his cheek against her hair. "So did I."

"It's almost time to get ready for the doctor's appointment," she murmured. "They're going to tell us the gender. Are you nervous?"

"No, not nervous. Are you hoping for a boy or a girl?"

"Maybe a handsome little boy like his father."

He grinned. "I think I'd like to have a little hellion of a daughter. She'd be the spitting image of her mama."

Maci stiffened against him for a moment, then relaxed. "Two Maci Fords in the world is probably one too many."

Chance wasn't sure what that meant, so he let it go. It sounded like a cliché, but boy or girl didn't matter to him. He just wanted both mother and child healthy.

MACI AND CHANCE sat in silence a few hours later in the ob-gyn's waiting room. She was feeling more nervous every minute.

When her name was finally called, Chance stuck by her side. He helped her into the gown and moved one of the chairs right next to the exam table. Although she didn't like to be fussed over, Maci couldn't help but admit it was nice to not be alone.

A nurse came in and did some medical basics, then the ultrasound tech entered, all smiles. For some reason that made Maci even more nervous.

"Have you seen the baby yet?" the tech asked. Both Maci and Chance shook their heads and she smiled. "You're in for a treat."

With a squirt of cool gel and a wiggle of the ultrasound wand, a whooshing sound filled Maci's ears.

"That hummingbird-like sound is the heartbeat," the tech explained.

Maci felt the pinprick of tears at the back of her lids. That was her baby's heartbeat. Chance's baby. As if she'd called to him, he reached for her hand, squeezing her fingers lightly. She looked up and saw the faintest sheen of moisture in his eyes too.

They watched the wiggling bean on the screen until it was over, and the tech handed them page after page of sonograms. The tech explained that the doctor would answer all their questions, including the gender if they wanted to know, and then left with as big a smile as she'd had when she came in.

"Alright, Ms. Ford. It seems like you're doing great!" Dr. Harris was also full of smiles when he entered. "You and baby both look healthy."

"So, the all-day puking she has sometimes is normal?" Chance asked.

Dr. Harris laughed and kept his eyes on Maci. "Yep. Morning sickness is a terrible name considering it has no internal clock, but it's completely normal. You haven't lost a lot of weight, so I'm not worried about it. Just keep doing what you can to take care of yourself. That part should be over soon."

"Thank goodness." Maci grinned. "I won't miss it at all."

Dr. Harris continued to go over test results from both today and ones that had been run at the hospital. He reassured Maci and Chance that the baby was fine. No damage had come from the attack, and there didn't seem to be any genetic issues either.

"You elected to get an early gender test. We have the results if you still want to know."

Maci looked at Chance. He shrugged. "Your choice. I'm good either way."

She looked back at the doctor. She wanted to know. "Tell us."

Dr. Harris smiled. "Congratulations. You're having a girl."

A girl. They were having a daughter. Maci couldn't pull her focus from that thought.

She was bringing a new Ford woman into the world.

The rest of the appointment felt like it moved at lightning speed, with Maci only partially aware of it. Dr. Harris provided suggestions concerning exercise and foods that might help settle her stomach. He answered all the questions Chance had while Maci sat there feeling numb. By the time she refocused on the world around her, Chance was bundling her into the car.

He slid into his seat and just sat there, keys in

hand while he stared out the windshield. "We're having a baby. A girl. *Our* girl."

There was awe and adoration in Chance's voice. When she glanced over, his eyes practically twinkled with joy. His smile was about to split his face.

So why did Maci feel the heavy weight of despair in her stomach?

A *girl*. She felt stuck on the knowledge that she and Chance were having a daughter. What did Maci know about raising a daughter when Evelyn was supposed to be her example?

Evelyn had been so deep in her own drug addiction, in and out of court-required rehab, that she didn't have the ability to protect Maci from anything. Then Maci had followed in her footsteps without a care. She'd found peace at the bottom of a pill bottle or heavier drugs.

It didn't matter that Maci had cleaned herself up, that she'd been sober for years. She was still always only one bad choice away from being back in that pit.

What kind of person brought a baby into the world to have a mother with addiction?

She put her hands on her stomach. Her baby was just one more cog in the chain of messed up Ford women. Maci didn't know how to break the cycle. She didn't know how to raise her daughter right. She didn't know anything about boundaries or parenting. She didn't know how she'd keep her child safe.

Her daughter was going to pay the price for Maci's stupidity. The thought made Maci sick.

She'd ruined her baby's life before she'd even got a chance to live it.

As they neared Chance's house, panic forced her breaths to come faster. The second he parked, she shot out of the car—she was going to be sick and it had nothing to do with morning sickness.

She couldn't be near him, couldn't speak to him. She'd ruined it all.

"Maci?" Chance grabbed her arm to reel her into his body, but she yanked it away.

"I'm going to go to bed."

"What about dinner? You need to eat."

The idea of sitting down and facing Chance made Maci's stomach clench even worse. "I'm not hungry."

She could feel Chance's eyes on her the whole way into the house, but she didn't turn back. She couldn't. Not when she'd ruined his life and he didn't even know it.

Chapter Seventeen

Chance barely slept a wink. All night long, his thoughts drifted to Maci. He couldn't stop picturing her after the appointment. The hunch of her shoulders as she bolted into the house, the stiff set of her lip as she tried not to cry.

Was it the baby? Did she not want a girl? Even if that was the case, he couldn't see Maci getting that upset over something like gender. It was something else, he knew it, but he had no idea how to find out. Maci had locked herself in the guest bedroom, refusing to come out for dinner, even when he'd asked as gently as possible. He'd almost decided to break down the door and demand to know what was going on.

Then he heard Maci crying.

Even through the door, Chance could tell that her tears were agonized. It wasn't just the typical fear of being a bad parent, she was terrified about something else, and that took the wind out of his sails. As frustrated as he was, Chance refused to badger her when she was obviously going through something difficult.

Worst of all, it was a reminder that, as much as he cared for her, he didn't know a lot about

Maci. So, as much as he wanted to demand answers, he stepped away and let her be.

It was the hardest thing he'd ever done.

By the time he'd gotten up this morning, the kitchen showed signs of Maci having made herself tea and breakfast. That was good. He wanted her to talk to him, but if she wouldn't, at least she was taking care of herself.

He'd barely made his own coffee and breakfast when his phone rang.

"We got another message from the stalker," Brax said.

A sliver of unease dug into Chance. He didn't like the way Brax's voice sounded—too careful and controlled for his free-spirited jokester of a brother.

"What did it say?"

"I think you should come in and see for yourself."

Chance didn't even have to think about it. "I can't. I need to stay here with Maci."

That got Brax's attention. He cursed under his breath. "I forgot about the appointment yesterday. Is everything okay with the baby?"

"The baby's good." Chance was careful not to let the gender slip. He wasn't sure if Maci wanted people to know yet. "Maci's just having a...tough time."

Brax was quiet for too long, and the foreboding got stronger.

"What's going on, Brax?"

"The message was a threat."

"Did you guys already let Dorian know? Is Stella secure?"

"It wasn't a threat against Stella."

Chance let out a curse. "Against us again?"

Brax didn't answer.

"What the hell is going on?" Brax was never this quiet.

A second later he heard a click. "Bro, it's Weston. Luke's on too. You and Maci both okay?"

This definitely wasn't good. "Yeah, we're fine. You guys need to tell me what's going on right damned now."

"The new threat is against Maci," Weston said quietly.

The world stopped. "What kind of threat?"

"I sent a picture to your email."

Chance reached for the computer, fingers slamming down on the keys as he found the picture of the letter Weston had sent. Curses flew out of his mouth as he read, fury burning through him with every word.

It's a pity when the innocent get caught in the cross fire of battle, don't you think?

But war is what this is and I'm determined to win.

With your queen as a prize, I'll do whatever it takes to defeat you. I'm looking forward to it.

You make me good, but she will make me better.

Included with the letter was a picture of Maci coming out of the office. It was impossible to tell how long ago it had been taken.

Every nerve in Chance's body demanded action. He wanted to move.

He wanted to *kill*.

Whoever this bastard was who wanted to drag Maci into his sick games... Chance wanted to erase him from the planet.

"Hang on," he said into the phone, before tossing it onto the kitchen table. He was tempted to throw his laptop across the room in rage, but knew in the long run that would only hinder his ability to protect Maci.

Right now he needed to see with his own eyes that she was alright. Especially after last night's disappearing act.

He knocked on the guest bedroom door. "Maci? I just need to know that you're in there and you're okay."

To his surprise, she opened the door. She looked pale and a little fragile, but otherwise fine.

Before he could stop himself, he yanked her into his arms.

"Chance?" she whispered.

"We've got trouble," he said, not letting her go. He wasn't going to keep this from her. He respected her too much not to tell her if she was in danger. "A threat from the stalker directed at you. I'm on the phone with the guys."

Her face got paler, but she nodded. He led her back out to the kitchen and grabbed his phone as she sat down in one of the chairs, pulling her knees up and wrapping her arms around them.

She looked so young and vulnerable. Her personality was so big, it was easy to forget that Maci was only in her early twenties.

He put his phone on speaker mode. "I'm back. Maci's here with me."

"Hi, sweetheart," Brax said. "We're so sorry about this."

"I'm okay," she said. "Let's treat this like it was any other case. Try to keep our emotions out of it."

The hell he could. But Chance just nodded. He spun the laptop in her direction so she could see the note.

"Where was the letter sent?"

"The office," Luke said. "It might have been

there a day or more, honestly. Mail hasn't been a priority."

"Guy is talking about war and battle," Weston said. "I think we were on the right track when we were narrowing the list to people who are former military or law enforcement."

"I don't understand what's made him change from Stella to me." Maci's voice was small.

Chance reached over and grabbed her hand, rubbing his thumb along her soft skin. "We think this has never necessarily been about Stella. Stalking is a game for this guy."

"Probably closer is that he considers it to be an exercise or a military mission," Weston interjected. "He's trying to improve his skills and feels like going up against us will help do that."

"So, targeting one of our own makes sure we're willing to engage with him," Luke said. "If he stuck with Stella, he has no guarantee we won't quit or get fired."

She shook her head. "Did I do something to make him come after me?"

Chance squeezed her hand. "No, honey. He thrives on a challenge. That's what all of us are to him."

But Chance damn well wished they'd never put Maci undercover to begin with. Then this bastard would've never known she existed.

"You and Maci need to get somewhere safe

until we can figure this out," Brax said. "Definitely can't bring her to the office or let her be at her apartment alone. Hell, I wouldn't even stay at your house."

"I'll take her to Mom and Dad's."

Luke snorted. "Finally, it's your turn."

Chance's mouth twitched into a small smile. It did seem like Sheila and Clinton's home had turned into an unofficial safe house over the past couple of years. All three of Chance's brothers had brought their women there at one point or another.

"I'll get Maci settled, then be back."

The brothers went over a few more details before Chance got off the phone. A quick call to his mother and everything was ready to go.

Maci was still sitting with her arms wrapped around her legs.

He brushed a strand of hair back from her face. "You okay? We should pack and get ready to go."

"I don't want your parents to get hurt. I know they watch Walker too."

"We'll leave if anything gets dicey for them, I promise." It was an easy promise for Chance to make. He didn't want his family getting hurt either.

"Does..." She trailed off and started again. "Do your parents know about the baby?"

"I doubt it. I know the guys know, but they wouldn't tell, and I didn't want to just drop it on them via text or something."

"Oh. Okay."

"We can keep it hushed for now if you want."

She nodded. "That would probably be best."

He wasn't sure exactly what that meant. He still wasn't sure why she'd been so upset last night.

Had she changed her mind about keeping the baby? The thought crushed something inside him, but now wasn't the time to get into it.

They packed up and twenty minutes later were on the road. Neither of them spoke much and the silence strained between them. He wanted to say something to make things easier for her but had no idea what to say.

The last thing he wanted to do was share Maci with anyone, even his parents. He wanted to sit her down and talk, to get everything out in the open—especially after yesterday's appointment and breakdown. But her safety had to come first. They'd have plenty of chances to talk about her past when the time was right.

Right now, Maci's past didn't matter. What mattered was keeping her safe from this stalker.

Chapter Eighteen

Maci felt like her life was falling apart on every possible level.

She was still reeling from yesterday's panic attack, then discovered she was the target of a stalker, and now had to stay with her not-boyfriend's parents who didn't know she was having his baby.

She wasn't sure which terrified her most.

Sheila and Clinton Patterson had always been kind to her. They'd often invited her over for holiday dinners and brought coffee for her on the rare occasion that they stopped into the office to visit their sons. They were good people.

But being nice to Maci as one of San Antonio Security's employees was much different than accepting her as the mother of Chance's child.

This was definitely something she'd need to keep hidden.

"You planning to stay in the car until you blend into the seats?"

Maci startled at Chance's voice. She'd been so stuck in her thoughts that she hadn't noticed him park. He stood next to her open door, waiting.

He held out his hand to help her out. "You ready?"

Not even remotely. But she nodded and got out of the car. At the door, Sheila Patterson stood with a smile on her face and her arms open wide. Even from feet away, Maci could see how much love she had for Chance.

She had that much love for all of her family.

"Chance, honey, good to have you home. Maci, welcome. You're looking well." Sheila wrapped them each in quick hugs before grinning. "There's someone here to see you both."

Chance smiled at his mom and took off for the living room, scooping the young boy from the carpet. Walker, Brax and Tessa's son, was babbling his uncle's ear off in unintelligible toddler language, but Chance didn't seem to mind. He gave the boy his full attention, nodding and adding to the conversation as much as he could.

Maci's heart turned to mush. What an amazing father Chance was going to be. She wished she could say the same about being a mother.

Walker continued to coo as Chance handed him over to Clinton. "Thank you for letting us stay for a while. We just need to get off-grid."

Sheila smiled. "At this point we're used to it. And you boys know this is your home too. You're always welcome. You can stay in your room, and I've made up the guest room for Maci."

"I have to get back to the office. There are

some things that need to be handled immediately, but I'll be back later." He kissed his mother's cheek and waved at his dad, who was getting an earful from Walker.

Then to Maci's surprise, he wrapped her in a hug, pressing a kiss to her temple. "Get some rest."

Well, it was obvious she wasn't just an employee anymore.

The tension felt thick, despite baby Walker's jabbering and giggling as Maci stood there with Sheila and Clinton.

"Why don't I show you up to the room where you'll be staying?"

Maci grabbed her small bag and followed Sheila. She showed Maci to a simple guest room, and Maci dropped off her stuff. The bed wasn't very big, but it looked inviting. She wished she could crawl into it and pull the covers over her head.

"Bathroom is just down the hall." Sheila turned and smiled as she opened a door to another bedroom. "And lest you think I'm completely old-fashioned or disapprove of you in any way, this is Chance's room."

Maci had to smile as she saw the twin bed and small desk. Sports posters all over the wall. There definitely wasn't room for a second person. "Oh."

"I know, I should redecorate. But I haven't touched any of the boys' rooms. They came in and made the space their own. For all of them it was the first bedroom that was truly only theirs."

"That's wonderful."

Sheila shrugged and led her back downstairs. "I guess these rooms are a reminder that sometimes families are formed in nontraditional ways, but that doesn't make them any less of a family."

Families definitely weren't Maci's area of expertise.

Sheila walked back downstairs, blowing kisses at Clinton and Walker still playing in the living room before leading Maci into the kitchen. "It's been a stressful day for you. How about some coffee? The boys got me one of the fancy espresso machines for Christmas last year. You like cappuccinos, right?"

"I, uh, I switched over to tea recently."

Shelia spun to look at her. "You're pregnant."

Maci wasn't sure what to say. "You got that from tea?"

"More that I knew the boys weren't telling us something. I thought maybe it had to do with a case. But Chance's protective hug clarified it all for me." She smiled gently. "Although it was the tea that clinched it. You love cappuccinos."

"I do miss cappuccinos." Maci chose a tea bag from the tin Sheila held out. "Are you mad?"

"Why would I be mad?"

Maci shrugged. "I don't think anyone in the family even knew Chance and I were...together. Maybe you think I'm trying to trap him or something."

It's what Evelyn had done to Maci's father... Gotten pregnant to force him to marry her.

Sheila gave a little laugh. "Honey, have you met Chance? Nobody forces him to do anything he doesn't want to do."

She relaxed and let out a little laugh herself. "Yeah. That's pretty true."

"We already considered you part of this family. You and that baby are Pattersons, and we'll have your back no matter what. Even if it doesn't work out between you and Chance."

"That means a lot to me."

They fell into a comfortable silence as Maci sipped her tea and they listened to Walker and Clinton play. She thought of Chance's interaction with his nephew.

"Chance will be such a good dad," Maci whispered.

"You'll both be great parents."

"I'm not so sure about me."

"I am." Sheila reached over and patted her hand. "Parenthood is more about instincts than anything else. I've seen you with Walker and you're great with him. I'm not worried one bit."

Sheila thought she knew Maci, but she really didn't. Maci frowned into her cup until a hand on her shoulder lifted her gaze again.

"I know my son. He's been enamored with you since the day you met. All the fighting? Everybody knew that was you and Chance's way of flirting with each other. Like kids on a playground."

Maci gave a half smile. "Yeah, we definitely have a tug-on-the-pigtails vibe."

"There for a bit a few months ago, Chance was happier. Smiling more and laughing. Then it was gone."

Because Maci had come to her senses and left him sleeping in his own bed. She didn't want to explain any of this to Sheila.

When Maci didn't say anything, Sheila eventually nodded and leaned back. "Regardless of what happened, I think you two can make it work."

"I don't," Maci blurted. She was not in line to be the next Mrs. Patterson. Chance needed someone better. "I wish we could, but regardless of everything that's happened, there's a lot he doesn't know about me. I'm not who he needs."

"I'm not so sure that's your choice, but if there are things he needs to know, tell him."

"You say it like it's easy."

"I don't mean to," Sheila admitted. "Baring your soul to someone you care about is the hardest thing you can do, but I will say that it's usually worth the pain. My son isn't a weak man. He's not going to run at the first sign of trouble with you. He hasn't yet, has he?"

No, he hadn't. Chance had been right there at Maci's side every day. He'd given her space when she needed it, yet still pushed her to talk to him whenever he could. He wanted answers, but he hadn't been cruel or malicious.

He'd been gentle. Not a word anyone would normally associate with Chance.

As if she heard Maci's thoughts running wild, Sheila grabbed her hand and smiled. "Chance is a born caretaker. It's how he shows his love. Trust him to take care of you and the baby. He's always going to do right by his family, and you can be the heart of that if you just tell him what you need and what scares you most."

Maci bit her lip, processing the words.

"Trust that what's in his heart for you is enough to keep him at your side," Sheila continued. "It may not be easy to fight your natural skepticism, but the battle will be worth it. I promise."

Maci had nothing to say to that, but Sheila didn't seem to need her words. This woman seemed to understand more about Maci than her own mother ever had.

Emotion urged Maci forward and she drew Sheila into a hug. "Thank you."

"There's nothing to thank me for." She ran a hand down Maci's hair, and for a moment, she knew exactly what a mother's love felt like. It was beautiful.

"Now, give me your cup and go take a nap," Sheila said with a playful smile and nudge toward the stairs. "Growing my grandbaby is hard—but very important—work."

Feeling lighter than she had in ages, Maci went upstairs to rest.

Chapter Nineteen

Chance could feel exhaustion weighing him down by the time he got back to his parents' house. It was well after midnight, so everyone was already in bed. Dad had kept him updated via text throughout the day just to reassure him everything was okay on the home front.

He was glad stuff was okay somewhere, because it surely hadn't been in the office.

Weston had called in every favor he had left with the San Antonio PD to get a rushed lab report on the stalker's letter, only for the report to come back with nothing. The letter was completely clean—not a single fingerprint or hair, nothing that could give them a clue. Even the stamp hadn't been licked.

It was a complete dead end.

They'd pored over more footage. Ran faces and names through every program they had available to them. Dorian and his team had shown up to help too. Just because the stalker seemed to have moved on to Maci didn't necessarily mean Stella was safe.

They all wanted to catch this bastard.

But he was still one step ahead of them, because once again, all their work had amounted to nothing.

Everyone had finally decided to call it a night. His brothers went home to the women who loved them. Chance went home to the woman who seemed only a half breath away from taking off in a dead sprint.

Chance scrubbed a hand over his face as he sat down in the kitchen. He didn't know how to help Maci with whatever was going on in her mind any more than he knew how to stop this stalker.

Uselessness wasn't a feeling he was accustomed to or liked.

Chance sat on a stool in the dark kitchen and thought about the past twenty-four hours. The doctor's appointment, Maci's silence, the note—he wasn't sure the best way to handle any of it. He wanted to wrap Maci in bubble wrap, to insulate her and their daughter from the world, but that wasn't his call.

Their *daughter*.

When they heard her heartbeat for the first time, he'd been overwhelmed by emotion. He could already see a little girl with Maci's nose and his eyes. He was ecstatic.

The baby and Maci were every dream he'd never let himself have. He had no recollection of his own biological parents. And while he would lay the world at the feet of Sheila and Clinton, this baby would be the only biological relation Chance had ever really known.

But where he was full of joy, Maci was shutting down and shutting him out. Running. *Again*.

Why did she always run?

Even after all the passion between them. Even when they could hardly be in the same room with each other without touching one another—magnets drawn together in a way they couldn't resist.

But still Maci refused to truly get close to him.

Chance wasn't surprised when he heard his mother's soft footsteps come down the stairs. Had he ever sat in this kitchen having a crisis without Mom somehow knowing and making her way here?

"Hey, Mom." He stood to put some water on for tea. Maybe something warm with no caffeine would help him settle down.

"Hey, baby. You just getting home? Long hours for you."

"I've been home for a little while, but yeah, long hours."

"You've got a lot on your mind. And not just what's going on with this case. I had a talk with Maci today."

"You know about the baby." He gave her a shrug and a smile. "I'm surprised she told you. But I shouldn't be, I guess."

"It was more that I put the pieces together than she actually told me, but yeah. Congratulations."

She wrapped her arms around him and he let himself sink into his mother's hug. Sheila Patterson had always been his safe space. From the moment he'd finally stopped fighting them, his parents had become his rocks, grounding and centering him when nothing else could. They'd earned his trust over and over again.

It was what he wanted to be for Maci, if she'd let him.

They finally broke apart when the kettle whistled. Sheila moved to put tea bags in the mugs.

"We found out we're having a girl yesterday."

"You excited about that?"

"I didn't care either way, but yeah. To think about a little Maci running around, that makes my heart happy."

He thought of Maci's reaction and his smile faded.

"But?" Sheila prompted.

"Maci seemed fine and then she just shut down. I'm talking practically catatonic. She hid in the bedroom as soon as we got home."

He stood, pacing the length of the kitchen as he tried to work out his thoughts. "I always seem to mess up with her, Mom. She runs away, and I don't know how to make her understand I would do anything for her and the baby."

His mom was silent as she watched him move, sipping her drink with that calmness that made it so easy to share his feelings. Finally, she set the cup down and folded her hands.

"You've been taking care of others since before you could take care of yourself. It's your first instinct with the people who are important to you."

Chance frowned. "Yeah."

"I know you've been taking care of Maci, that's what you do. But when's the last time you listened to her or even asked what she wanted? Do you even know if she wants to be a mother?"

Panic seared through Chance. He wanted his baby, but he wanted her with Maci. He wanted them to be a family. The idea that Maci might not want it too was almost too much to take.

His mom reached out and grabbed his hand. "Do you want to know what I see when I look at Maci? I see someone who's scared."

Chance shook his head. "Maci's the strongest person I know. She's not scared of anything."

But there was something in the back of his

mind that was screaming at him, that maybe his mother was right.

Sheila shrugged. "That could be exactly what she wants people to think. I think maybe her past is haunting her, and with a baby representing such an important future, it's scary for her."

He rubbed his eyes. "Why doesn't she just tell me this?"

"I think our Maci's been alone for a long time. She might not know how to."

She didn't know how to say what she needed to say, so she ran instead. Put walls up.

"There's nothing she could tell me about her past that's going to change how I feel about her."

His mother smiled gently. "In this house, we've always believed in second chances. We've always believed that the past didn't dictate the future. I think you're going to have to introduce her to those concepts."

"Yeah, I think you're right."

"I'm going back to bed. I hope you'll get some sleep too." She stood up. "And, Chance, when you talk to Maci, really listen to her. Take off your I'll-fix-everything hat, and just really listen. I think that's what she needs most of all."

JUST AFTER DAWN, Chance woke, rubbing grit out of his eyes as he stumbled into the kitchen. He'd gone to bed right after his talk with his mother and gotten a few hours of sleep, but what she'd said still kept playing in his mind.

He needed to listen to Maci. Not do. Not fix. *Listen*.

He found a note from his mother on the counter.

Dad and I are out for the day. Be home by dinner. Make your girl some breakfast and talk. Love, Mom

Chance hunted down the pots, pans and food he'd need to make a great pancake breakfast, something he knew how to do, since he and his brothers had been in charge of breakfast on the weekends. Maci shuffled into the kitchen just as he was finishing.

"Perfect timing," he said with a smile.

She stopped in the doorway. "I thought you would be Sheila."

"Mom and Dad went out for the day, but I was instructed to make you breakfast. I made pancakes, home fries, toast and even some eggs if your stomach is up for them. There's some cut fruit in the fridge too."

"Wow. That's quite the spread. What's the occasion?"

Chance shrugged. "You need to eat and we need to talk. Might as well kill two birds."

"Talk?"

"Talk," Chance said firmly. "Well, you need to talk and I need to listen."

She sat down at the kitchen island, and he pushed some food toward her to get her to eat. She took each bite slowly, as if each mouthful brought her closer to a firing squad.

He sat down next to her with his own plate. "Before we start, I wanted to say I'm sorry."

She looked over at him, still chewing. "What do you have to be sorry for?"

"This whole time, I've been more concerned about myself and my feelings than yours. I didn't even ask the most basic question."

"Which is?"

"Do you want to be a mom?"

"You did ask me. You asked me in the hospital if I was keeping the baby."

He nodded. "I know. But that's not the same thing. What I'm asking you now is if you *want* to be a mom."

She swallowed, setting her fork down. "I do, but…" She trailed off to silence.

"But what? Whatever it is, speak it."

"My mom is pretty unstable. She was addicted—*is* addicted—to drugs." Maci stared down at her plate, moving a piece of pancake around in circles. "When I was younger it was mostly booze like my dad, but by the time I was a teenager she'd moved on to harder stuff. The type of drugs you don't get away from without professional help. Not that she's ever wanted help."

His heart ached for Maci already. "That's really hard. I had no idea."

"Studies show that addiction can be genetic." She stared down at her plate. "That was true in my case."

Chance's stomach dropped, but he forced himself not to say anything. He needed to *listen*.

"I started dabbling in middle school. Pot first, then harder stuff as I got older. By the time I was seventeen, I dropped out of school to be my dealer's live-in girlfriend. If I wanted a fix, all I had to do was ask. And do whatever he wanted, of course."

The implications of what she was saying made Chance want to throw up.

She looked up at him. "Whatever you're thinking to put that expression on your face, you're right. I did it all. Prostituted myself for drugs. I'm not the type of person who should be raising a child. Especially not yours."

He frowned. "Especially not mine? What does that mean?"

"It means, look at your life!" She waved her hand around. "You have this great, tight-knit family who would do anything for you. You're the best person I've ever met, and you'll be an even better father. Why do you deserve to be saddled with my baggage forever?"

"Stop." He'd promised his mother he'd listen, but he wasn't going to let Maci tear herself apart like this. "The past only defines us as much as we let it."

She rolled her eyes. "Tell that to a greeting card company, Chance. This is real life. Our choices always come back to haunt us."

"Maybe they do, maybe they don't, but that doesn't matter. You're clean now, right? Been sober for at least as long as I've known you."

There was no way she could've run the office with such efficiency if she had a drug problem. She was never late, rarely called in sick and was way too sharp to be intoxicated. They would've noticed.

"Yes, I finally got sober a little after my twentieth birthday. My boyfriend got violent one night and I ended up in the hospital. A nurse helped get me into a program and I got clean."

"You got your life together."

She shrugged. "The program helped me. Helped me get clean, helped me get my GED, helped me get some work-training classes under my belt."

For the first time, she'd had a support network, and look at what she'd done once she had it—dragged herself completely out of the pit. "You accepted the help that was offered and changed your life. Everybody would call that admirable."

"Did you not hear the part where I spent years basically selling myself so I could get high? It's amazing I didn't end up dead or with some disease."

He reached over and grabbed her hand. "Yes, I hate to think of you living like that. It absolutely guts me."

"And yet that's what the mother of your child is. A person with addiction who did sex work for drugs."

"The mother of my child is *recovering* from addiction, who survived and got out of a situation that would've destroyed many others. The mother of my child is strong and courageous and capable."

She shook her head, so sadly it broke his heart. "My mother has promised to get sober and fallen off the wagon so many times. What if I'm the same? Addiction runs in my family and I'm passing it along to our daughter. How could you want to be involved with someone like that?"

He had to make her understand something he'd thought about for years. "What about my family and what's passed down?"

Her brows pulled together. "What do you mean?"

"I don't know who either of my biological parents are. There's no info on them. The only thing we know for sure is that they both abandoned me, so they're obviously not the most upstanding of people. Who knows what sort of genetic mess I might be passing down."

"I—"

He put a finger gently over her lips. "Neither of us can stop what we pass down genetically to our children. But both of us can be there to show that any deficiencies we start with don't have to be what defines us. To help them navigate the rough waters."

"I'm afraid I'll be a horrible mom," she whispered.

"There may be patterns from our childhood that both of us have to undo. But, sweetheart, you did so much already with just a little help from the program. Think of all you can do with the full support of all the Pattersons behind you."

She gave him the tiniest smile. "That's a pretty great support network."

For the first time, he had a ray of hope. "You think Tessa or Claire or Kayleigh are going to let you be anything less than the best mother possible? You would do anything for them. They'll do anything for you too."

"I know," she whispered. "I love them. I love your whole family."

"And they love you too. We don't have to tell them all the details, but if you open up to them, you know they'll support you in whatever way they can. I will too."

"Really?"

He pulled her into his arms and rested his forehead against hers. "Yes. And not just because of the baby. You mean the world to me, Maci Ford. We can't change the past and it doesn't matter anyway. I didn't know that Maci, and although I wish I could've helped her, she's gone."

He kissed her gently. "But I know this Maci and she's amazing. All that matters is the future. Our future. Do you understand?"

"No."

He chuckled, pressing his face into her neck so his next words were spoken into her skin. He wanted to imprint them there so she'd never forget. "It means, I'm all in with you, Maci. You and our daughter are my family and I choose the both of you."

He wanted to tell her he loved her, but that could wait. Baby steps.

She sighed and burrowed into his chest. Chance wished he could spend the whole day holding her like this.

"I'm glad you told me everything," he whispered into her hair. "No more running. If you start to feel overwhelmed, we work through it together. Deal?"

"Deal."

Now all he had to do was stop the stalker after her.

Chapter Twenty

Maci was still wrapping her head around the conversation with Chance as they finished eating and did the dishes.

He was still here. Hadn't told her to leave. Hadn't told her he wanted nothing to do with her or the baby. He wasn't acting weird or awkward.

It was more than she could've hoped for. Honestly, more than she could even understand. But he was touching her more, not less. Smiling at her gently in a way she could hardly resist.

And the thing was...she didn't have to resist anymore. He knew all the ugly parts of her past and was still here talking about baby names and something he'd read about pacifiers.

For the first time she had hope for a future that included Chance—which was more than she'd ever let herself dream of.

But a reminder that she had other very real problems came way too soon. Chance's phone chimed and he frowned as he looked down at the message.

"We've got incoming."

"Your parents?" she asked.

"My brothers. They're here."

Chance went and unlocked the door and let them in. All three men looked grim.

"We need to talk," Weston said. Chance nodded.

Luke took a seat at the dining room table. Brax grabbed a cup of coffee and did the same. Weston stood on his side of the table, his body tight with tension. Whatever he was going to tell them, Maci knew it wouldn't be good.

"Should I stay?" she asked.

Luke nodded. "This concerns you most of all."

Chance grabbed her hand and led her to the table, taking the seat next to her.

"First—" Weston rubbed his eyes "—when I got to the office, there was another note from the stalker. Hand delivered this time. It had been slid under the door."

He handed them a note inside a sealed plastic bag. There was also a picture of her and Chance leaving the ob-gyn yesterday.

It looks like congratulations are in order and the ante has been upped. I am up for the battle and will defeat you despite your attempts to stop me.

"He knows about the baby," she whispered. "He was there. He saw us."

"Actually, that image is from the medical complex's security camera," Luke explained. "He probably wasn't there, he just grabbed it later."

That didn't make Maci feel much better. She glanced over at Chance. Fury was burning in his eyes.

Weston held out a hand toward him. "I know you want to lose it right now, but you can't. Believe it or not, it gets worse, and you're going to need to focus."

She could see Chance fight to release the rage enough to focus. Finally, he nodded.

"Even before this delivery this morning, something has been bugging me about the wording of the stalker's notes," Weston continued. "I decided to cast a wide net to see if anything came back. It did. This is—*was*—Brianna Puglisi."

He slid over a printed newspaper article from three years prior in Dallas. Maci frowned as she read about a local hairstylist found dead in her apartment—strangled. She'd barely been twenty-five, but was a favorite of the wealthy ladies in town. More than one of them had lamented over her loss in the article.

"What's this got to do with us?" Chance asked.

"There was a note found with the body. It

wasn't published in the paper, of course. I found out about it through some police connections." Weston laid down a printed police report. "I highlighted the relevant part."

*Battles require sacrifices. War demands it.
I must be the best.*

Chance looked up at Weston. "Battle. Wars."

Brax nodded, hands around his coffee mug. "Exactly. Same language as our guy."

Chance muttered a curse. "And he killed her. Not just a stalker."

Weston nodded. "Report states that Brianna had mentioned some weird notes she'd gotten, but she didn't show them to anyone and police didn't find any at her home or work."

"This escalates things," Chance said.

"You have no idea." Luke slid a file across the table. "Once we started looking we found three more. All women in Texas or connecting states. Some stalkings that turned into murders. Some with no proof of stalking, but still a dead woman. But all with the *war, battle, cross fire, be the best* sort of language in notes that were found."

Chance flipped through the police files of the other murders. "So we know there's four dead women."

Brax nodded. "At least. That's what we found in just a few hours this morning by looking for cases with this sort of language involved. There may be more."

Chance didn't look up from the file. "We're dealing with a serial killer."

"A smart one," Weston said. "Killed in different ways so that law enforcement didn't put together what they were dealing with. Even the notes weren't always associated with the killings. Sometimes they were left in a way that made them look like they belonged to the victim."

Maci couldn't stop the whimper that fell from her throat.

Chance pushed the file away and grabbed her hand. He entwined their fingers, stroking his thumb alongside hers in soft, soothing motions, as if he could feel the absolute panic rushing through her.

There was a serial killer on the loose. One who'd announced he was after *her*.

Luke attempted a comforting smile. "As scary as it sounds, it makes sense. We were confused why the stalker was getting violent with little to no provocation when it's not typical for this type of fixation. But if he was a serial killer all along, violence was always the end goal."

She could understand the logic of what he

was saying, but it didn't change the fact that a serial killer had set his sights on her.

Chance leaned back in his chair but didn't let go of her hand. "Let's work our way backward. He targeted Maci and us because of our connection to Stella. But I don't recall notes to Stella containing the same war/battle language."

Weston nodded. "You're right. There's nothing in Stella's notes with those words."

"Are we sure we're dealing with the same guy?" Luke asked.

"Definitely the same as those dead women." Brax took the last sip of his coffee, then pushed the mug away. "That language is too specific and similar for it not to be him."

"It's Stella who's the anomaly," Weston said.

Chance's eyes narrowed. "Or…"

He faded off and Maci could almost see his mind spinning, working through various scenarios. Chance was a master at strategy and seeing patterns.

His brothers knew him well enough to give him silence while he worked it out. Maci squeezed his hand, then let it go as he stood up to pace.

"The other victims besides Brianna Puglisi, what did they do for a living?" he asked after a few seconds.

Luke grabbed the file. "Waitress in Houston.

Photographer in Albuquerque. Clothing store salesperson in Austin. No evidence that they knew each other at all."

Chance continued pacing. "They didn't have to know each other to be connected. See if they have any connection with Stella."

Weston caught on to his line of thinking first. "We have online access to Stella's calendar. We can look at back dates."

Chance nodded. "Start with the salon Brianna worked at. It catered to the upper echelon. Stella would've been willing to travel to Dallas to get her hair done by the stylist everyone was raving about."

Weston sat down and got out his computer. "Okay, this is going to take a few minutes. Most of Stella's appointments from over a year ago have been archived."

Maci grabbed her phone. There was another, easier way to get this information. It may not have as many details as what Weston would pull up on the calendar, but...

"I've got it," she said. "Stella was at the salon roughly eight months before Brianna was killed."

All four men turned to face her. "How do you know?" Chance asked.

She spun her phone around so they could see. "It was on her social media. She said she liked Brianna and the style, but didn't know that it would be worth coming to Dallas for every time, so she'd stick with her local stylist in San Antonio."

Maci grabbed the file and flipped to the clothing store salesperson who'd been killed. It was a high-end boutique in Austin. She turned to her phone again and within just a minute had social media proof Stella had been there too.

"Stella has shopped at that clothing boutique in Austin multiple times. No direct proof that she knew the woman who was killed..."

"But the fact that she was there at all ties those two women together." Chance looked around at his brothers. "Stella is the link."

"You think she's the killer?" Maci asked.

Chance shook his head. "No. But somebody close to her probably is."

Weston began typing frantically on his computer.

"But what about all the notes Stella got that aren't the same MO as the war/battle guy?" Brax asked. "Inconsistency doesn't seem to fit for him."

Chance shrugged. "Maybe after the first note he changed his plan or realized his normal language might get him caught. We don't know that he ever planned to harm Stella. Maybe he was just trying to up the ante."

Luke nodded. "This guy wants to be the best. But the best what? Killer? When he talks about winning, what is he referring to?"

With your queen as a prize, I'll do whatever it takes to defeat you.

Maci shuddered as the words he'd written in the note about her came to mind.

Chance rubbed his eyes. "I think we were on the right track when we said this is some sort of professional challenge to him. A matter of pride. He wants to be the best at…whatever it is. Killing, stalking, keeping ahead of law enforcement. Who knows? Stella and her level of security and exposure just upped the challenge for him."

Weston finally looked up from his computer. "I concur and want to take it a step further. I think we were right when we said this guy was former military."

Chance nodded. "We need to check the full security team. Get Dorian in on it. He'd be the best one to say if there's anyone on the team who fits the profile and maybe has been acting strange."

"Before we do that, there's someone else we need to look into. I think your instincts were right all along, Chance." Weston spun the laptop around so everyone could see it. It was a picture of Rich.

"Rich?" Maci asked. "He's not military."

Weston hit a button that brought up a picture of a young Rich in a military uniform. "Nope, but he was Junior ROTC in high school. And his father, who died five years ago, was a decorated marine. Definite military ties we didn't look closely enough into."

"You really think Rich could be a killer?" Maci whispered. She thought of how much time she'd spent with him so close to her and felt sick.

Chance's eyes were already filled with rage. "That smug bastard has been toying with us from the beginning. It damn well is going to end now."

Chapter Twenty-One

Maci went upstairs soon after their discovery, claiming to need a nap, but Chance knew better. She was terrified and he didn't blame her.

If Rich was the stalker—now killer—then she'd been in his grasp more than once. He could have taken her at any time, especially knowing all the security measures in place.

He hadn't done it because it would've made it too obvious they were up against an inside man. Instead he'd bided his time, set the game up for extended play.

Bringing Maci into it as his target had been a mistake. There was no way in hell Chance was going to let anything happen to her.

"We need to figure out a plan of action," he told his brothers.

"We have to be careful who we bring in on this. If Rich is definitely our guy, we don't know what sort of internal measures he has in place to get info."

Chance had no doubt Rich was their guy. "He could have phones tapped. Hell, he could have someone else working with him."

Brax got up to get himself another cup of coffee. "Nobody in the LeBlanc organization would think twice about giving Rich intel. He was handpicked by LeBlanc himself."

Chance rubbed the back of his neck. "The last thing we need is for him to go to ground because he figures out we're on to him." Maci would never be safe.

"I say we go see LeBlanc in person and let him know what we suspect," Luke said. "He needs to make sure Stella is in a safe place where Rich can't get to her."

"Agreed. Then we can check the dates of the murders with Rich's known whereabouts." Chance was ready to move. "Let's get Mom and Dad back here. Someone needs to stay here too, just in case."

Weston pointed at his computer. "I'll stay here and see if there are any more cases I can tie this to. And we're going to have to come up with more than a couple years in ROTC in order for the police to take this seriously. Rich isn't just going to roll over and confess."

Chance nodded. "You're right. Let's make sure everyone is safe, then we'll figure out a further plan. Start pressing your PD contacts. Let's see what we would need for them to make an arrest."

"Once I show all this to my colleagues on the force and they see it's a serial killer, believe me, they'll want to make an arrest. You guys be safe and keep me posted."

Chance ran up to say goodbye to Maci, but she was sleeping. Good, she needed the rest.

He reached over and kissed the top of her head. "I'm not going to let anyone hurt you." He was talking to both mother and baby.

And he meant every word.

LESS THAN FORTY-FIVE minutes later they were back in LeBlanc's office.

"Gentlemen, should I call in Dorian and his team?" LeBlanc asked. "I'm hoping you actually have something useful for us this time."

The man was frustrated. Chance couldn't blame him.

"We'd actually prefer to speak to you alone, if that's okay," Chance explained. "We've had a breakthrough in the case, and we have reason to believe the stalker may be working inside your organization."

LeBlanc's eyes got wide. "What?"

Chance didn't want the man to panic, so he chose his words carefully. "We've found some similar cases from the past few years that we believe were committed by the same person."

Brax gave the man his most comforting smile. "We have some questions we think will help us nail down who the perp is. But first—do you have confirmation Stella is still safe?"

Once they started making their case against Rich, it was going to tip him off. They needed to have everyone secure before that.

"Yes, I spoke to her not long before you arrived. She's safe, but we're not going to be able to keep her out of the limelight much longer. She's doing a photo shoot at castle ruins in Scotland. That will hold her off a few more days."

Chance glanced over at his brothers. "And Rich? He didn't go over there, did he?"

"No, he stayed here in case he was needed."

"That's good. We might need him. What can you tell us about Rich?"

"He's worked for me for five years. Stella responds well to him so I've kept him around. My one rule was that he wasn't allowed to sleep with her and he's not broken that. Why do you ask?"

Brax shot Chance a look. Chance understood what his brother was communicating: this needed to be handled delicately.

"Before we get into specifics, we need to run a few dates by you and see what you, Stella, Rich, Jason Rogers and your office manager were doing on those days."

LeBlanc was confused. "Marguerite?"

Chance nodded. He'd tossed Jason, one of the

main security guards, and Marguerite Frot into the mix for subterfuge. If Rich was listening or had means of accessing what they were talking about, maybe it would throw him off the scent.

LeBlanc sat down at his desk. "Okay, fine. What are the dates? My system will allow us to pull up schedules. It should list what security teams were working also."

Chance wasn't a huge computer person, but he was thankful for this program that was about to make their lives much easier.

Luke read off the dates. They waited as patiently as they could as LeBlanc started with himself and listed what he'd been doing on each day. Then moved to Stella.

Chance grit his teeth when he next listed what Marguerite then Jason had been doing the dates of the murders. Since both of them were red herrings, they didn't matter.

Finally, he got to Rich.

"On the first date, Rich wasn't working. He generally takes Mondays and Tuesdays off since Stella's calendar doesn't tend to be full for those days."

Chance glanced at Luke and Brax. Rich not working meant he'd been free to commit the murder.

"Date two, it looks like Rich had a doctor's appointment. I vaguely remember that. A few weeks later he had a spot taken off on his shoulder that he was concerned might be cancer. Stella was distraught and did a six-week segment on different sunscreens."

"Okay," Chance said. They would have to follow up on that. He may not have gone to the doctor's appointment at all or it could've been very short. It was inconclusive at this point.

"Third date, Rich was not working again."

Chance grabbed his phone, ready to contact Weston. They were three for three with Rich, and Chance was sure LeBlanc was about to say the same for the date of the fourth murder they'd found.

They needed to be ready to move. Brax and Luke had the same tense body language Chance did.

"Okay, date four." LeBlanc clacked on his keyboard. "Oh, I could've given this to you earlier. Rich was with me the whole day that day in Los Angeles."

Chance's brow furrowed. "Are you sure?"

LeBlanc nodded as he looked up from his screen. "Yes, I remember it now. Half the office and Stella had that stupid virus. Rich was one of the few who tested negative, so he came with me to the opening of a new LeBlanc office branch there. He was acting as part personal assistant, part pretty boy for the press and part security."

Chance spun to face Luke. "What was the time on the fourth case?"

"Midafternoon, Texas time."

Chance looked back at LeBlanc. "You're absolutely sure Rich was with you that whole day? He didn't take a later flight or something?"

"I'm positive. I remember because we were almost late. Flying at that time during the height of the pandemic was problematic, even on a private plane."

Brax handed Chance his phone. Pulled up on it was the press report of the office opening. It had been a bold move on LeBlanc's part, considering most people were working from home, with no indication of returning any time soon.

There was Rich, smiling beside LeBlanc. The footage was time-stamped in a way that meant it was impossible that Rich had killed the fourth woman. When they looked further into the first three, they'd likely find the same thing.

Chance's jaw ached at how hard he was clenching it. Rich was a smug bastard, but he wasn't the killer.

"So, does all this information help you with your theory?" LeBlanc asked.

Brax and Luke looked as frustrated as Chance felt.

"Yes," he finally managed to say. Eliminating suspects was an important step to solving anything. But that didn't make Chance feel any better.

"Then can I ask exactly what this is about? What these *other cases* you're referring to are?"

Luke recovered quickest. "We've come across some disturbing facts, and we need to gather more information before we give you details. For now, let's keep this conversation between us, please."

Chance was trying to wrap his head around the fact that they would have to start back at square one when Dorian entered LeBlanc's office.

"I saw you guys on the door roster. Has there been a breakthrough in the case?"

Nobody answered. Neither Chance nor his brothers wanted to mention the words *serial killer* in front of LeBlanc.

It was LeBlanc who finally took charge. "Evidently, there is some sort of breakthrough but nobody wants to tell me what it is."

Brax tried his charming smile. "Only because we want to make certain of a few things first."

They were about to get fired, Chance could feel it. That was the last thing they needed. Access to information surrounding Stella was going to be critical.

Dorian came to their rescue. "Nicholas, sometimes security teams have to work in ways that don't make sense to the client. You and I had to learn that about each other early on. Let them do the job you hired them for."

"Fine." LeBlanc threw up a hand. "Take them to the conference room and help them with whatever they need. I have a business to run."

Once they were in the conference room, they explained the situation. They were going to need Dorian's help to catch this bastard.

Dorian sat down hard in one of the plush leather chairs as he took it all in. "Holy hell. We're dealing with a serial killer, not just a stalker?"

They gave him a little time to process it. They'd all felt the same way.

Dorian ran a hand over his jaw. "I need to double Stella's security now. Even though the guy's focus seems to have moved on to someone else."

Maci. Chance would be taking her to ground until this was over. He wasn't taking a chance with her. If he had to move her to a different country too, he'd do it.

"So, what's the killer's motive? How'd you put together that we're dealing with more than a stalker?"

They explained the similarity of terms used

in the notes at the murder scenes and the ones the stalker had sent to their office.

"The guy wants a challenge," Dorian said after hearing them out. "Has the need to be the best."

Chance nodded. "That's what we concluded too. We've been looking at people who fit that profile—former military or even law enforcement."

"Agreed." Dorian was studying the reports Luke had brought with him. "I'd also widen the search to look at martial arts or MMA fighters. They use that kind of language also."

"Hell, gamers use it too," Brax muttered. "Maybe we tried to narrow it down too much."

"Honestly, we thought it was Rich," Chance explained. "He had some ROTC experience and his father was military, but it can't be because LeBlanc just provided an alibi for one of the murders."

Everybody grumbled about that.

"And this whole thing with Stella felt like the stalker always had the inside scoop on what we were doing," Chance continued.

"It definitely feels personal. Like he's taunting everyone. And that the choice of victim feels less important than the actual challenge. First Stella, now Maci."

Chance agreed with Dorian's deduction, but

the choice of victim was *very* important to him. "This still feels like an inside job to me. Or at least that the stalker/killer is getting inside info from someone."

"We'll run a complete security diagnostic. If there's info being leaked inadvertently from someone on my team, we'll find it."

"And if it's someone leaking it on purpose?" Luke asked.

"We'll find that too. It may take a little longer, but I promise you it will happen."

Chance walked over and shook Dorian's hand. "We're going to keep at it. See if there are any more murders we can link to this. We're bringing in some law enforcement contacts."

Dorian nodded. "That's one of the reasons Nicholas wanted to bring you guys in in the first place—your local contacts and influence here. I'll admit I was skeptical when he first mentioned it. But you've done nothing but prove me wrong."

"Let's just catch this guy," Chance said. "He made it way too personal when he targeted Maci."

Dorian gave him a tight smile. "I completely understand. He's messed with the mother of your unborn child. I'd stomp him into the ground."

"That's exactly what I plan to do."

Chapter Twenty-Two

When Maci woke up from her nap, she wandered downstairs. Weston was sitting at the kitchen table with his computer. His face was grim. Sheila and Clinton were back. Their faces were grim too.

"Chance, Brax and Luke went to meet with LeBlanc, see if we could get details about Rich. I have law enforcement waiting to move once we do," Weston said once he saw her.

"Okay." She was still having a hard time wrapping her head around the fact that she'd been so close to a possible killer. How many times he'd touched her.

"Do you want something to eat, honey?" Sheila asked.

"No." The word came out as a croak. "Chance made me a really big breakfast."

"Did you two talk?"

Maci nodded. It had only been a few hours ago, but seemed like forever. "Yes. It was good. You were right. Chance could handle my past."

Sheila pulled her in for a hug. "My boy can handle anything. He's going to handle this other thing too. Just you wait."

Maci hoped so. She felt like she couldn't

breathe. "I think I might go take a shower, then lay back down."

The older woman smiled gently. "Absolutely. Hopefully you'll be more hungry at dinnertime."

Maci looked back over at Weston. "Did you find anything else?"

His face was almost haggard. "At least one more. I'm still searching."

Five murders.

She couldn't think about it too much right now or she was going to panic. She showered, then got back into bed, pulling the blankets up to her head, trying to shut out the world.

When she awoke the second time, things were actually worse. Her phone was buzzing with a call from her mother.

"What do you want, Evelyn?" Maci kept her voice barely above a whisper so none of the Pattersons would hear her.

"Maci, baby, I'm in trouble."

Maci really didn't have the time or mental energy to deal with her right now. "You're always in trouble."

"Baby." Her mother's voice was small, shaky. "I'm really sorry for how I treated you a couple days ago. That was wrong."

Maci rolled her eyes. "You can't blackmail

me for more money. I've already told Chance everything."

"It was wrong for me to say what I did. So wrong. I thought about you being pregnant, and I knew you would need your money for the baby."

"Yes, that's true."

"My dealer has been trying to get me to sell for him for a while, so I told him I would. That way I wouldn't need money from you."

"Timothy?" He was low-level and not organized. Barely more than a thug.

"Yes."

Maci rubbed her eyes. This wasn't what she wanted. "Mom, that's dangerous."

"I know. I—I..." Evelyn let out a sob. "I was robbed last night. They took all the product."

Maci sat up straight in the bed. "Are you hurt?"

"No, but Timothy has given me twenty-four hours to come up with the money or he will hurt me. You know, he has to set an example." She listed the amount she needed.

"Mom, I don't have that much! Especially not since you just cleaned me out."

"I know. I know." Evelyn began to cry in earnest. "I don't know what to do. And it gets worse."

Oh, no. "What did you do?"

"Timothy was threatening to break my wrist when I told him I didn't think I could get the money. So I mentioned where you work." Her voice got smaller. "I think he's planning to jump your boyfriend or his brothers to get the money if I don't pay him back."

Maci thought through finances. If she pooled everything from every account and maxed out the cash withdrawal on her one credit card, then she might just have enough.

At least enough to keep Timothy and his buddies from attacking the Pattersons unawares while they were in the middle of a crisis. Maci could handle this for them. They would never even need to know.

And she could admit that, even though Chance already knew about her past, she'd prefer not to dump this on him in life-size Technicolor.

"Where are you, Mom?"

Her mom spit out an address on the south side of town near the warehouse district. Not the safest place, but not where Rich Carlisle would be hanging out, so at least she didn't have to worry about a serial killer.

Just run-of-the-mill family drug drama. No problem.

She disconnected the call and got dressed. There was no way Weston was going to let her go handle this, so she wasn't going to tell him. He had more important things to do. So did Chance.

She left a brief note on the pillow explaining she was going to see her mother in case someone wandered up to check on her. She didn't want them to think she'd been kidnapped.

She could hear Weston talking to his parents in the kitchen as she crept downstairs and out the back door. Luke had brought her car over a couple nights ago and left it parked on the street, so she slipped around the house and inside it.

She winced as the car started, hoping Weston wouldn't hear. Chance would kill her if he found out what she was doing. She pulled away from the curb.

So, she'd make sure he wouldn't find out.

"Weston has found one more murder tied to this guy and is checking further into another," Luke said as they walked back into the San Antonio Security office. "He's shown everything to his PD contacts, so it's more than just us looking into it now."

"Good. We need as many eyes on this as possible." Chance didn't care who figured out the identity of the killer. He just wanted Maci safe. "I'm going to take Maci out of town. Get us into a safe house nobody knows about. Mom and Dad's place is too easily connected to us."

Weston had been providing all clear updates since they'd left, but Chance didn't want to leave Maci there any longer than necessary.

"Agreed," Brax said. "Maybe we can get Stella to impersonate Maci to catch this guy."

Chance managed a grim smile at his brother's joke.

"You decide on a place to hide out with Maci. I'm going to start looking harder at the ob-gyn angle. How did he know you guys were going there?"

Brax froze. "We were talking about it here at the office before you went."

Luke and Chance froze too. If the killer had heard their plans, that meant he was either using a parabolic mic or had planted a bug in the office.

His brothers had realized the same thing. They all started searching for hidden recording devices in the office.

They found three.

Chance tilted his head toward the back door, and they went out into the alley so they could talk without being heard.

"Planted bugs means the person was in our office," Chance said. "He would know about

Mom and Dad's house. I've got to get Maci out of there right away."

"Okay, we'll look into moving the office to a secondary location until we can make sure it's clean," Luke said.

"Good news is, this narrows down our pool of suspects quite a bit," Brax said. "There's only been a half a dozen of Dorian's team members here over the past few weeks. It's got to be one of them. I'll call him."

Chance was about to nod when Dorian's parting words when they left LeBlanc's building came back to him.

He's messed with the mother of your unborn child.

The curse that fell from Chance's mouth was vile. Both brothers turned to stare at him.

"Did you guys tell anybody at LeBlanc's office that Maci is pregnant?" he asked.

"Hell no," Luke said. "We didn't even tell Mom and Dad."

"It's Dorian," Chance whispered. "He's the killer. He knew Maci was pregnant today when he shouldn't have."

All three men sprinted back inside to cut to the front door and get to their vehicles. Chance had his phone in his hand and was dialing Nicholas LeBlanc.

"Patterson," LeBlanc answered. "Unless you have some sort of—"

"Lock down your building," Chance cut him off. "Do it right now."

Locking down the building would keep Dorian trapped inside.

"What? Why would—"

"Do it!" Chance yelled.

He heard LeBlanc initiate the lockdown.

"Okay, it's done. In fifteen seconds no one will be able to get in or out."

"It's Dorian Cane. He's the stalker. He's not only a stalker, he's a killer—that's what we found out with the other cases."

"That's impossible." LeBlanc's tone was heavy with shock.

"I'll prove it later. Right now, keep your office door locked until the police get there. Don't let Dorian in there with you for any reason." The last thing they needed was a hostage situation.

He could hear LeBlanc clicking at his keyboard. "I don't have to worry about that. Dorian left just a couple of minutes after you did."

Chapter Twenty-Three

It was depressing how little time it took Maci to liquidate nearly every cent she had available to her name. Twenty minutes after leaving Clinton and Sheila's house, she had the cash in hand and was on her way to meet Evelyn.

She parked outside the warehouse address, surprised her mother wasn't there to snatch the money out of Maci's hand like she'd done in the past.

Maci got out of the car and began walking toward the warehouse. This was it. This was the last time she was helping Evelyn in this way. The only thing Maci would be willing to help pay for from now on would be some sort of rehab.

"Evelyn?" Maci didn't know where her mom was, but she needed to get back to the Pattersons' house before they discovered she was gone. "Come on, Mom. I don't have time for this."

She called Evelyn's phone but got no answer. She got all the way to the warehouse before deciding to turn back. There was no way she was going into an abandoned warehouse by herself, and for whatever reason Evelyn wasn't here.

She turned and shrieked when she found a man behind her. Fortunately, she recognized him quickly.

"Dorian Cane, right? Oh, my gosh, you scared me."

He smiled. "Sorry, wasn't my intent."

"Oh, no. Did Chance send you to get me?" Damn it, had he already figured out she was gone? She was in so much trouble.

"Um, yes. Chance sent me. Wanted me to escort you somewhere safe. Things have escalated."

She nodded. "Rich, right? Ends up he's a killer, not just a stalker."

"Yes, Rich. Fooled us all. Chance really didn't want you out here alone and... I was close by, so I offered to come get you."

"I was supposed to meet my mother. You haven't seen an older lady around, have you?"

"No, I haven't. We should go."

"Yeah, I'm sure Chance wants to yell at me as soon as possible too."

Dorian smiled. "Only because he cares. I understand that."

They began walking back toward the cars.

"Yeah, you two are probably cut from the same cloth. It's what makes you good at your jobs."

"Yes, this job is a battle. Getting to know

Chance and the other Patterson brothers has certainly made me a better me. I've always strived to be the best."

Maci tensed at his words. They were way too similar to the notes that had been left. She stopped.

"You know what? I should probably make one more sweep to be certain my mom's not here. Do you mind waiting just a second?"

There was no way she was getting into a vehicle with Dorian until she talked to Chance. Maybe she was being paranoid, but under the circumstances, that could be forgiven.

She forced a smile at Dorian. "Just hang out here for two minutes. I'll be right back." She turned back toward the warehouse. "Mom? You here?"

She walked, calling for Evelyn as she pulled her phone out. She was just hitting Chance's number when a soft voice spoke behind her.

"You're not a pale imitation at all, are you?"

Maci tried to breathe through the terror. This was the voice from that night at the apartment when she'd been knocked unconscious.

Dorian was definitely the killer.

She turned to face him again. "You. Why?"

"Someone has to be the best. Learning how to stalk, learning how to kill… It made me the best security expert available."

"But you're Stella's stalker. How can you be the best at protecting someone when you're the one putting her in danger?"

"I never planned to hurt Stella—she's not worth the time or effort. I wasn't even her real stalker at first. I eliminated him early on and took over. Especially once Nicholas brought in the Pattersons. I quickly realized how much I could learn by going up against them. And knew I could up the ante when I targeted someone they cared so much about... *You*."

Maci took a few steps backward, trying to figure out what to say. "I'm just their employee."

He tsked and shook his head. "You're the mother of Chance Patterson's child. He would burn the world to the ground to get you back. His brothers would hold the matches for him."

"I'm not going with you."

Dorian smiled and slowly pulled up his pants leg at the calf, showing some sort of knife holder. "I don't think you're going to have a choice."

Without another word, Maci spun and ran. She didn't make it far before Dorian's arms wrapped around her from behind, stopping her progress. At least he didn't have the knife out yet.

She remembered what Chance had taught her in their training. She used her legs to kick back, aiming for his knees, groin, whatever. Dorian let out a curse as her foot connected to a sensitive spot and let her go.

She dropped her phone in the skirmish but didn't stop to pick it up. She sprinted as hard as she could for the warehouse.

She knew if Dorian got her into his car, she and her baby would be his next victims.

"WHAT DO YOU mean she's not there?"

Chance was ready to put his fist through a wall. He'd called Maci's phone half a dozen times, and each time it had gone directly to voice mail.

"We all thought she was taking a nap," Weston said. "She left a note on the pillow saying she needed to meet her mom and would be right back."

He'd already explained that Dorian was a killer and law enforcement had an APB out for his arrest.

That wouldn't help if he already had Maci.

The door to the office opened and Chance turned to bark that they were closed. "I'll call you back," he said to Weston when he saw who it was.

Evelyn Ford. And she had seen better days.

He rushed to her and helped her sit down. She

had blood seeping from a head wound. "Mrs. Ford, where's Maci? What happened?"

His brothers rushed in to see what was going on, but remained silent.

"I needed money. She was supposed to meet me about a half hour ago."

"She didn't show up?"

"I don't know. Some man saw me, said he worked with you. Offered to give me the money I needed to pay back my dealer."

Chance grabbed a file and showed her a picture of Dorian. "This man?"

"Yes, that's him. I thought I was doing Maci a favor, not taking her money. You know, so she could save it for the baby. But then the guy knocked me on the head and dragged me into an alley."

"Evelyn, where's Maci? Her phone is offline, so we can't track it. I've got to find her."

"Guy left me with the money. I paid someone a hundred of it to get me here. I needed to tell you that my dealer may be coming after you."

He didn't understand what she was talking about and didn't have time to get her to explain.

"Evelyn, listen to me. My brothers and I can handle any drug dealer. We'll get you someplace safe so he can't hurt you either. But if you know where Maci is, you need to tell me right now."

Every second they wasted gave Dorian more time to hurt Maci.

"I was supposed to meet her at the warehouse district. I needed the money to pay back Timothy, my dealer. I promise I didn't mean any of those things I said to Maci." Evelyn started to cry.

He and Maci were going to have a talk—*again*—about the things she was keeping from him. But he needed to find her first.

"Where, Evelyn? Focus."

She got out the address.

"I'll stay with her and make sure no drug dealers do whatever she was talking about," Brax said. "I'll get PD there immediately too."

"Give us five minutes. Sirens may spook him into hurting her."

Brax nodded and Chance sprinted for his car, Luke on his heels.

MOST OF THE warehouses in this section of town had been abandoned years ago after a storm had caused massive flood damage. Maci could scream, but there probably wouldn't be anyone around to hear her.

And screaming at this point would tell Dorian exactly where she was.

She found an open door and rushed into a building. Hiding was her best option. It was dark in here, the only light from an emergency exit sign near another door at the side.

She ran for the far corner, zigzagging around various piles of crates and abandoned machinery. The door behind her opened and closed, and there was silence.

Maci struggled to hear anything over the pounding of her own heart.

The most important thing is to keep your head. Use your strengths.

She could hear Chance's voice in her mind. He was right. If she panicked, this was over.

"Now, now, Maci," Dorian taunted. "I love a good game of hide-and-seek, but this isn't your style, is it? You're more of a confronting things head-on type of gal, aren't you?"

She wasn't about to answer and give away her position. She needed to make her way around to the other door and try to get out.

He flipped on a phone flashlight, and she jerked her head back behind the crate she hid behind. The light would give Dorian more of an advantage.

"Do you understand the need to be the best at something, Maci? I was the best in my platoon until a stray bullet ended that part of my life. Do you know what it is to have the thing that is most important to you snatched away?"

Like a murderer trying to end you and your unborn child's lives? Yeah, I do, asswipe.

How she longed to say the words out loud.

"Then I had to find a new career pathway on which to be the best. Private security fit the bill."

He got quiet after that and the light switched off. She crept farther away from where she'd last heard his voice, keeping her body low and small.

"I've killed nine women."

Maci struggled to keep her surprised gasp silent. He was trying to get a reaction from her—any indication of her location.

"But listen, Maci, before you think bad of me... I did it for a purpose. Do you understand? With every woman I killed I became better at personal security. I learned more about how killers thought and what could be done to protect someone from a killer. Those women's deaths had *meaning*."

He was a complete psychopath. Could see no wrong in what he'd done.

The flashlight switched back on, aimed for where she'd been just a few moments ago. Damn it, he was expecting her to stay low to the ground. She needed to get higher, climb on some of the machinery all over this place. Dorian hadn't shone any light up there at all.

You're smart. A quick thinker. Use that to your advantage.

She found some debris on the ground—a piece of metal that had broken off something—and grabbed it. She threw it with all her might in the opposite direction of where she planned to go.

Then she scurried up onto what seemed to be some sort of bottling equipment piece, careful not to make any noise. That allowed her to move onto a conveyer belt a few feet higher that held her weight easily.

Dorian's light switched off once again when he heard the noise. When it came back on, it wasn't pointed in the direction she'd hoped. It was right where she'd been five seconds ago.

If he pointed his light up now, she would be caught.

She swallowed her whimper.

The light switched off again. "Your death will have meaning too, Maci. So will the Patterson brothers'. I can't leave them alive. Leaving your enemy alive means you always have to be looking over your shoulder."

She held still. He was waiting for her to make a mistake. The slightest one and she'd be dead.

"Your mother too, probably, if she doesn't take care of that herself. She's got a pretty severe drug habit, you know. Was more than happy to take the money I gave her, although was probably less happy when I knocked her unconscious. I traced her phone. That's how I found you."

Maci had to push thoughts of her mother aside. She had to push everything aside but this moment.

Survival is always the most important thing.

She was going to survive. She had too much to live for not to.

The light came back on, once again looking in hidden corners and in low places to hide. It wouldn't take much longer for him to figure out she wasn't down there.

But in the silence, she heard the most beautiful sound: sirens.

The light switched off again. "Looks like the game has changed, Maci, and we won't be able to finish today. What a shame. But don't worry, I'll be back for you. For all of you. I'm the best, so you can count on that."

In that moment Maci knew she couldn't let Dorian leave. He was telling the truth: he would be back. And one by one the people she loved would fall to his madness. Including her daughter. Maci had no doubt Dorian would hunt her too, even if it took years.

Maci could stop this right now. She *had* to stop it right now. Even if it cost her everything.

She stretched out her hand and found a small metal pipe. It wouldn't be much against that knife he'd taunted her with earlier, but she just needed to stop him long enough for the police to get here. The sirens were getting louder.

She shut everything out and listened for Dorian. As he passed under her she grit her teeth and let herself fall off the side of the conveyor belt on top of him.

Light flashed inside the warehouse from the far door as she fell, but she ignored it. She would only get one chance at this.

She landed hard on Dorian, swinging her pipe and yelling as loud as she could to let the police know where they were. She got two hits in before a blow to her face threw her backward.

She tried to get back to her feet but he was already over her, knife in hand. He grabbed the pipe out of her hand and threw it to the side, then pulled her up by her shirt.

"I am the best," he said simply.

He slashed the knife toward her chest, and she knew this was the end. She closed her eyes, waiting for the pain, distraught that she'd failed. Devastated she'd never told Chance she loved him.

But the pain never came.

She heard multiple cracks of thunder over the roaring around her but didn't open her eyes.

"Maci! Maci, open your eyes, baby. Come on."

Chance? She could barely hear him.

"Stop screaming, sweetheart. It's okay. I've got you. Dorian is dead."

All that noise was coming from *her*. She hadn't even realized it. She closed her mouth and silence surrounded them.

"Are you okay? Did he hurt you?" Chance was frantically pressing his hands all over her body, searching for wounds.

Luke was standing over Dorian, weapon raised. Dorian wasn't moving.

"I'm okay," she managed to get out. "I'm okay. I had to stop him. He was going to hurt you. Hurt everyone. I couldn't let him—"

Chance's lips pressed hard against hers and he pulled her against his chest.

"You did it. Dorian Cane will never hurt anybody ever again."

Chapter Twenty-Four

Three weeks later

"No, don't you dare touch me, Chance Patterson! If we are late to family dinner everyone will know what we've been doing."

Chance grinned from where he was stalking Maci in the kitchen of his house, loving the way she laughed as she threw her arms out in front of herself to keep him away.

As if she could keep him away.

As if anything was ever going to keep him away from her again.

He grabbed one wrist and used it to yank her closer. "We both took a full week off work and locked ourselves in this house without talking to anyone. I'm pretty sure everyone knows what we've been doing."

But they'd needed it. They'd needed a chance to decompress after what had happened with Dorian. Needed a chance to rest and be with each other.

Chance had definitely needed the opportunity to hold Maci close to him and reassure himself that she and the baby were really okay.

That could've so easily not have been the case.

Getting to Maci at that warehouse had been the longest twenty minutes of his life. Kicking open that door and watching her drop down onto a serial killer? Watching Dorian lift that knife to end her life?

Even knowing he and Luke had each plugged three bullets into Dorian, he would have nightmares about the image until the day he died.

Nicholas and Stella LeBlanc had been traumatized too by the thought that someone they'd trusted had been so evil. Stella had then figured out how to use it to become even more popular on social media.

Maci pressed her lips against his. "We can't be late. Mom is going to be there."

It was a first step for Evelyn, one they were delighted she was taking. She was a long way from kicking her drug habit, but joining them for dinner was at least a step in the right direction. Hopefully they would be able to show her some rehab options and she'd agree to treatment.

Maci had made it clear to Evelyn that if she wanted to be a part of the baby's life, she was going to need to be clean. They would help her as much as they could, but ultimately the choice had to be Evelyn's.

He kissed Maci tenderly. He'd kissed her so often over the past few weeks that they both should've been tired of it by now, but neither of them could get enough.

"I love you," she whispered. He would never get tired of hearing her say it.

"I love you too." And he would never get tired of saying it back.

He planned to do it every day for the rest of their lives.

Epilogue

One year later

Sheila Patterson's favorite place to be had always been the kitchen. As a child, it had been the heart of her parents' home, and she'd been determined to make it the heart of her own as well.

Though their usual Sunday dinner was still hours away, the house was already overrun with family.

Weston and Kayleigh had arrived first, their arms loaded down with drinks and snack packs for the kids. Instead of offering to cook, which wasn't always her strong suit, Kayleigh had kept Sheila company, talking all about her newest photography series and how Weston had transformed yet another elderly neighbor's garden into a little piece of paradise.

Sheila listened as Kayleigh spoke about her husband with pride, peeking up from food prep occasionally to see her son glancing at his wife, their eyes equally full of love and devotion. It soothed something in her to see her quietest child find the love of his life.

Halfway through an anecdote that involved a

rampaging Weston and a mole he couldn't catch, Brax, Tessa and Walker arrived. The moment Walker saw his favorite auntie, Kayleigh's attention had been stolen, but Sheila didn't mind. She'd sat Tessa on a stool in the kitchen and talked baby names while sneaking her treats before dinner.

Tessa and Brax were pregnant with another boy, and the way Brax looked at her...it was like no one else existed when she was in the room. Like she was the light his life had always needed. And Walker? He was overjoyed at the idea of a baby brother to play with.

Luke and Claire's arrival was followed by much shrieking from Walker once he saw they'd brought their Maine coon cat, Kahn. Claire, once shy and quiet around them all, immediately began telling a story of a second cat they were adopting. Luke kept a firm arm around her waist, his eyes brimming with love too.

Sheila was putting the final touches on everyone's favorite potpie when the sound of cheers told her the last of her family had arrived. First through the door, Maci was glowing, even though little Autumn was five months old and had barely slept since she'd arrived earth side.

Still, there was a calmness that motherhood—and Chance—had brought Sheila's final daughter-in-law. A peace that had allowed her to settle into the family and really open herself up to the rest of the Patterson clan.

Evelyn had joined too. It hadn't been an easy road, and there had been more than one setback, but the woman was trying. For her daughter, for her granddaughter.

But most importantly, for herself.

Sheila looked around the chaos and couldn't help but smile. Her family was here, made up of every skin tone and bound together by love.

Clinton wrapped his arm around her waist and pressed a kiss to her neck. "Remember how distraught we were when they told us we would never have children? Did you ever imagine we'd have this?"

Sheila took a look around at the sounds of yelling and laughter, the mess of toys already spilling out from the living room, the crush of bodies crowded into the kitchen.

Not only did she have four sons, but she'd gained four daughters.

She had a family that was happy, healthy and so full of love you could see it the second you walked into the room.

"No," she told Clinton, burrowing farther into the comfort of his embrace. "I would've never imagined this. But the reality is so much better."

* * * * *

High Mountain Terror
Janice Kay Johnson

MILLS & BOON

An author of more than ninety books for children and adults with more than seventy-five for Harlequin, **Janice Kay Johnson** writes about love and family and pens books of gripping romantic suspense. A *USA TODAY* bestselling author and an eight-time finalist for the Romance Writers of America RITA® Award, she won a RITA® Award in 2008. A former librarian, Janice raised two daughters in a small town north of Seattle, Washington.

Visit the Author Profile page at millsandboon.com.au.

CAST OF CHARACTERS

Ava Brevick—A nature photographer, she's dismayed to find she's not alone in the snowy mountain landscape. Another snowshoer seems to be pursuing her and armed men on a ridge above her must have crossed the Canadian border illegally. Operating on instinct, she photographs them...only minutes before a monstrous avalanche breaks free to roar right down the mountain at her *and* her pursuer.

Zach Reeves—A cop intent on finding solitude snowshoeing in the backcountry, he too is stunned to find he's far from alone. Is it possible the internationally sought terrorist Zach's border patrol friend warned him to watch for is among the heavily armed crowd on the ridge? Time for spec op soldier Zach to reemerge. The gutsy woman who saves his life needs him, given the pack of Russian terrorists intent on hunting them down.

Grigor Borisyuk—Proud of his reputation, a ruthless assassin and a fanatic for his causes, Borisyuk doesn't tolerate mistakes—and being seen and photographed by a woman who could give away his presence in the US means going to any length to eliminate her before she can share that picture.

Chapter One

In her rare glimpses of the sky, Ava Brevick marveled at the stunning blue, made richer by the contrast with snow, ramparts of rock and the deep green of the forest cloaking the North Cascades Mountains.

Picking her way among the infuriating tangle of willow and alder near the river and having to watch for the fallen trees and rocks hidden beneath the snow, Ava hadn't been able to maintain anything close to the pace that was possible on a stretch where snow lay smoothly on top of a trail maintained during the summer. Her snowshoes felt clumsy right now, almost more trouble than they were worth. This was nothing unexpected; even during the kinder time of year, most of the Cascade Mountain wilderness didn't welcome two-legged intruders.

After unsnagging her snowshoe from a whip thin stem that was part of a thicket she thought was alder, she paused for the second time in the past ten minutes to look cautiously behind her.

She'd been alone out here in this snowy expanse for two days now. Trails in the park were closed during winter—and May was still very much winter high in the mountains. A respected wildlife and wilderness photographer, Ava had been dropped by helicopter to work her magic, seeking the extraordinary moment when sun slid through a snow-laden branch or glanced off water dancing between the ice and rocks. She hoped to capture some good photos of the animals that weren't hibernating—or would be emerging from hibernation anytime. Not given to feeling lonely, she loved what most people would say was profound silence, but which to her ears was filled with the crack of a far-off branch, the whisper of wind, the occasionally ominous settling of ice and snow on steep slopes, the high cry of a bird or the scream of a small creature that had just become prey.

She'd already captured enough images she thought would delight the organization that had funded this expedition, but planned to set up another blind this evening in hope more nocturnal animals would wander her way. There were plenty of those deep in the Cascade Mountains, from mountain beavers and porcupines to the red fox, as well as the northern saw-whet owl she had yet to glimpse.

For herself, the only predators to fear in these mountains up by the Canadian border were grizzlies, reintroduced into the Cascades some years back, or an unusually aggressive black bear. She felt pretty confident neither would be emerging from hibernation just yet. Mountain lions could be a threat on rare occasions; she kept a sharp eye above when she passed below a tall rock upon which one might crouch. But a world without other humans was one where she relaxed her usual wariness.

What unnerved her now was the suspicion she *wasn't* alone out here anymore. It was like walking through a dark alley, certain you heard footsteps behind, except they stopped when you did…only, a fraction of a second too late. Someone was behind her, and fleeing would do no good. She couldn't exactly hide, given the conspicuous track she left in the snow, and if she parted from the almost-path following the bank, she wouldn't be able to bull her way through the rampant growth. Unfortunately, the dense vegetation kept her from seeing who might be back there.

She had heard a helicopter yesterday, although she didn't see it and had no reason to think it had landed. When the sound of the rotors had faded until silence reclaimed the wilderness, she'd dismissed any worry. Park rangers might keep an eye on the land they guarded with an occasional flyover.

But if it *had* dropped someone off, it had been a distance away, and how had he—or *they*—gotten close enough behind her that she heard the swish-swish of snowshoes and thought she'd gotten a glimpse of movement? And no, there weren't a lot of alternate choices of paths around here, not with the steep flank leading up to a sharp peak on her one side and the rock-and ice-strewn river to her other.

If she stopped, would he? If she decided to turn around to go back, would he nod and politely let her pass?

She was being ridiculous; why would anyone want to sneak up on her?

She didn't know whether to be glad or sorry that the trail was parting away from the river now and climbing above a jumble of huge boulders deposited by long-ago slides or avalanches, now surrounded by a clump of evergreens she identified as western red cedar, Sitka spruce and hemlock. Sunlight ahead dazzled her eyes as she emerged into the open.

The way was easier here, and she achieved a smooth stride in her snowshoes even as she continued to gain elevation and evaluated this open bowl of land. Now she had another cause for nerves: avalanche danger was high in this country, and it looked as if the trail led her across a curved, open slope she'd guess slanted at a forty-or forty-five-degree angle. She didn't have an awful lot of experience with winter dangers, but anyone with common sense could see that the long-broken tree trunks poking jaggedly out of the heavy snow weren't a good sign. An avalanche had plunged down this chute in the not so distant past. And yes, the warming conditions—although the day felt damn cold to her—contributed to the danger.

Still, she could see a clear line with the snow lying differently where the summer trail stretched across the way ahead. A single person stepping lightly wouldn't put any significant stress on the weight of snow, ice and rocks higher up.

Except now she felt exposed because of that uneasy feeling that she was being pursued.

A couple of minutes later, Ava couldn't resist stopping and turning. She'd been right. There he was, just emerging from the trees near the frozen river bank, moving fast and with surprising grace, climbing effortlessly to close the distance between them. She saw it was a big man wearing a dark green parka and carrying a huge pack. Only three or four hundred yards separated them.

Foolish instinct said to run, but her attention was abruptly jerked away from him when, out of the corner of her eye, she spotted movement high on the forested ridge across the river from her. To her shock, in an open stretch that had to be the result of a wildfire, a group of men were silhouetted against the blue sky. To her naked eye, they were nothing but small figures that didn't belong there, at least this far north. There was no trail heading down that ridge, summer or winter, Ava was quite sure of that. What's more, they were moving southbound, strung out, picking their way slowly. On snowshoes? She couldn't tell.

Habit had her lifting her camera with the enormous lens that she always had ready hanging around her neck. She snapped off the cap and zeroed in on them, until she saw them as if they were startlingly near, if still very small. They all wore white, including their packs. Or something like white capes draped over the packs? Most had carriers of some kind slung over their shoulders, too, although those were black. Could the group be skiers dropped off by helicopter? She couldn't imagine that kind of commercial venture was permitted within the national park. Besides, they were nowhere near an elevation high enough to be above the tree line. No slope *could* be skied in this vicinity, and she was pretty sure there wasn't one on the other side of the ridge, either.

Suddenly apprehensive, she stared at the sharp image of the man in the lead. Distant as he was, even through her lens, she was shocked to see that he held a rifle, one with a shape that had become all too familiar from constant news reports about mass shootings and war. That had to be something like an AK-47, not a typical hunting rifle—and, anyway, hunting was banned in the national park.

Not even sure why she was doing it, she took photos, moving from one man to the next. A couple of them wore what were probably fleece balaclavas. Several didn't, or had pulled them down. Maybe the sun felt warmer up there, she thought in some distant part of her mind. Those faces she saw clearly, and she photographed them without conscious thought.

Several of them had come to a stop while she studied them. At the same instant, she saw the glint of sun off glass and knew someone up there was looking back at her.

Men carrying automatic weapons, men who shouldn't be where they were, were looking at her.

She hastily let the camera drop and snatched

up her poles. Apprehension made her want to turn around and race back toward the trees, nearer if she went back instead of forward, except the stranger was closing in fast on her now.

Go, she thought.

She broke into a near run, wishing futilely that she was on cross country skis instead of the far clumsier and slower snowshoes, but that had never been possible in this difficult terrain.

Go, go, go!

ZACH REEVES HAD spent the past couple of hours speculating on who could be out here in the remote wilderness he'd expected to have to himself. He'd looked forward to cutting his own tracks in the snow.

Call him selfish—he'd *wanted* to be alone. The whole point of this expedition had been to escape the pressures he felt from coworkers, neighbors and crowds at the mall or competing with him for a corner table at the café. After ten years as a spec ops warrior, he wasn't adjusting well to normal life.

Life on the military base between operations had been fine, if not his favorite. He'd always managed during his rare visits home to Minnesota where his sister and brother lived. Now, he almost wished he'd gone to work as a Washington state patrolman or sheriff's deputy who patrolled miles of roads instead of the job he'd taken as a detective for the Whatcom County Sheriff's Department. The work was more interesting, but on patrol he'd have been covering a lot of empty country in the rural county, likely going hours at a time without having to interact with anyone.

This was Zach's vacation, damn it. He'd sought solitude and found a way to achieve it. It was bad enough that he had company, but what in *hell* was a woman doing out here alone?

Given the hefty pack she carried, it had taken him a while to realize the snowshoer ahead of him was female, but he no longer had any doubt. How had she gotten into this remote area, unreachable by road at any season or by trail in what was still winter in the North Cascades? Who did she think would bail her out if she got into trouble? He sure didn't have cell phone service in this deep vee between a high ridge and a higher mountain. He supposed she might carry a satellite radio, as he did.

He evaluated the white slope above before breaking from the trees to climb after her into a bowl carved in the ridge. He knew an avalanche path when he saw one; in July or August, wildflowers and shrubs would dominate in the sunlight, free of the tree cover he'd been traveling through. He'd have avoided this stretch if he could, but a couple of snowshoers were unlikely to tip the balance to bring the icy monster down on them.

Zach raised his head to see that the damn woman had stopped dead, lifted an enormous camera and was staring up at the ridge above the river. Now what? Zach flicked his gaze the way she was looking, and his muscles locked. His radar jumped into the red.

He hadn't heard a helicopter in the past day since his drop-off. Those men almost had to have crossed the Canadian border to get here, and this route wasn't ever an approved border crossing. Right now, with the border patrol stretched thin and on high alert to watch for a known terrorist sneaking into the country, that group had to have slipped in, taking advantage of the remote countryside that couldn't be adequately monitored. They must have expected to stay cloaked in dense, northwest forest, except that a wildfire had burned that cover in the past year or two.

He had razor-sharp vision. Even without lifting his binoculars, he recognized the weapon the guy at the front carried. A flash of light up there had him blinking; the sun must have reflected off the lenses of binoculars. Had they noticed him yet, or were they watching her?

Either way—

A very faint crack that might have been a gunshot came to him. From this distance, that wouldn't have been a concern, but a flash of fire arced across the sky.

A rocket-propelled grenade. He was racing toward the fool woman in front of him even as he evaluated what he'd seen and knew they hadn't fired directly at her.

No, they had a better way to kill a lone traveler who'd seen them.

An explosive burst came from the slope above the two of them on this side of the river. For one instant, nothing changed but for the white puff where the shell had landed. The sound of a second shot came to him. Before he had a chance to react, an enormous crack began to split open in the surface of a thick layer of snow and ice at the top of the slope, at first moving in slow motion in each direction.

Even before Zach saw the increasing speed the crack spread across the slab, he shouted, "Avalanche! Get out of the way!"

She gave a startled look at him, then up.

A loud *whuump* came from the sliding slope.

He wouldn't get to her, he realized in the compartment of his brain that kept him making logical decisions under fire. Couldn't help her, anyway. None of the old-growth trees with their massive boles had survived in this gully to provide shelter. He wouldn't make it out of the path, either. Farther ahead of him, she might reach the edge of the avalanche zone if she put on the burners.

A boulder ahead provided the only hope. It wasn't large enough to protect him, he knew, but he saw no other possibilities and raced to throw himself behind it.

Then he curled low, braced his pack against the cold rock and waited for one of the most brutal forces of nature to smash into him.

SHE RAN, cursing the need to lift each foot high to clear the snowshoe from the snow. It was as if she were moving in slo-mo even while the monstrous white slab fractured at what seemed a leisurely pace. She knew, *knew*, that appearances were deceptive. Snatching a quick look, she saw in horror that a mass almost as wide as this open bowl of land was gathering speed as it first slid, then thundered into motion down the slope. One last look at the guy behind her. There he was one instant, the next he vanished behind a boulder. Lucky guy. Her thighs burned, her breath whistled. A roar drowned out everything else.

It hit her like a semitruck on the freeway, slamming into her even as it tossed her, flipped her. A last instinct had her wrenching at the handle on the chest strap of her pack. Then her thoughts became nothing coherent. She had the terrifying sense she was upside down as she saw her snowshoes snatched from her feet to disappear in the white tsunami. Her poles were long gone. Winded, Ava flailed for a grip on anything at all, her hands finding nothing. She had to be screaming, but the sound was too puny to be heard even by her own ears. It was like leaping off an Olympic ski jump and not coming down. Weightless, she was flying, but also being buffeted from every side. It hurt, it hurt, it hurt.

THE NEXT THING she knew, she lay still. Astonishingly, when she shook her head, she saw a sliver of light. Had she lost consciousness? She had no idea. Something was choking her, and she gagged. Her legs felt as if they were encased in concrete that she prayed hadn't quite hardened yet, but her arms—yes, she could move them, although it was a struggle. Her groping hand found a flap of nylon, blue rather than the green of her pack. Avalanche airbag. *Oh, thank God, thank God.* She'd remembered to pull the rip cord. It must have inflated immediately, creating a brightly colored pillow that acted to make her more buoyant, lifting her toward the surface.

She broke through the snow and saw sky. The airbag had worked. Fumbling, she discovered her camera had been whipped around her head, and it was the strap throttling her. Awkwardly, she untwisted the camera strap from around her neck. It was a miracle she hadn't lost it. How damaged it was… Not important.

Now she just had to find a way to crawl free from the hardening snow.

She kicked and flung handfuls of snow away, widening the hole around her shoulders and head. One glove was gone, she saw, but she didn't even feel the cold. That wasn't a good sign, but if she couldn't dig herself out, what was a little frostbite?

It couldn't have taken more than a couple of minutes. It felt like forever before she found herself on her hands and knees, facing downhill. Her pack weighed her down, but the fact that it hadn't been torn from her body had saved her life. Would save her life again. She couldn't whip out a phone and call for help. She hadn't even brought an avalanche beacon, because she'd known that, isolated as she'd be in the back country, no one would come in response. With a sleeping bag, tent, food and more clothes, though, she could survive. She could.

She let out a cry. She was alive, but what about *him*? Ava had quit caring why he was following her; he was a fellow human being. He'd yelled a warning to her, hadn't he?

She staggered to her feet and looked at the devastation around her, frantically trying to orient herself. She'd ridden the avalanche almost to the end, but what about him? He'd started slightly lower than her, but right in the center of the chute. The boulder. Where was the boulder?

It took her a minute, and that was a minute he couldn't afford. In preparing for a trip in Alaska a couple of years ago, she'd read the horrifying statistics: someone who was really buried would start to lose consciousness in only four minutes from breathing their own carbon dioxide. The odds of surviving even after being dug out decreased dramatically as the minutes ticked by.

There! she thought. All she could see was a faint curve of rock surrounded by the tumble of snow and ice, but that had to be it. She didn't remember seeing any other boulders so high above the river.

She scrambled the distance to it on her hands and feet and even knees.

"Can you hear me?" she yelled.

Nothing. No, something stuck out of the snow. Ava tugged it out. A snowshoe. *Oh, my God.* He had to be near, didn't he?

She called out again, waited for an answer, tried over and over as she dropped her pack and unzipped it with fingers too numb to want to cooperate. She'd bought the airbag at the urging of mountain-climbing friends, but otherwise hadn't planned much for an avalanche.

"I'll be careful," she'd told everyone.

Famous last words.

For whatever reason, she'd added a folding probe to her gear. At last she pounced on it. By accident, she spotted her other gloves and hastily, gratefully changed. Then she unfolded the long probe, stood and began stabbing it into the snow. The chances of her finding him weren't good. If he'd been swept too far to the left or right of the boulder, she could poke the probe into the snow for days and not find him. If he was buried too deep…

Ava didn't even want to think about that.

She prayed as she'd never prayed before, and stabbed the probe repeatedly into the avalanche debris.

Chapter Two

Hell of a thing, to die here and now, on vacation, after surviving countless firefights and bombs, silent raids and HALO jumps from aircraft in every war-torn part of the globe.

Zach's struggles slowed. He might as well be in a casket six feet under for all the good kicking and battering with his shoulders and fists had done. It wouldn't take long to burn up all available oxygen.

His mind drifted. He tried to slow his breaths but knew how useless that was. The woman. Was there any chance at all she'd survived? He hoped so. For all his irritation that she was out in this wilderness where he'd wanted to be alone, she'd moved well, as if she knew what she was doing.

Damn, he was cold. He struggled a little more to prevent himself from freezing solid, even if keeping himself from stiffening up wouldn't do a thing to change his fate.

Something poked him. Had to be his imagination, unless...? It poked again. And then he'd swear he heard a voice calling to him, even if he couldn't make out words.

"I'm here!" he bellowed, the effort causing darkness to swim in front of his eyes.

Then all he could do was lie there and wait: for rescue, or for death.

AVA SCRAMBLED BACK to her pack and pulled out the folding shovel. Back at the probe she'd left standing in the snow, she started to dig. The probe might have struck a rock or a solid chunk of ice. It could have been anything. But she gambled. If this was him, she might get to him in time. Otherwise—

No, she had to believe this was her fellow snowshoer.

She flung snow to each side, her muscles burning. Digging as if her life depended on it, only it was *his* life instead.

Dizziness claimed her; she needed to rest, to take some deep breaths, but any pause could condemn him to death. *If it's him.*

The shovel scraped across dark green. Her heart expanded in relief. She threw herself onto her stomach and scooped snow out of the hole with her hands. He wasn't moving, he wasn't moving... Oh, God, which way was his head? If she resumed using the shovel, she might hurt him.

She realized she was talking to him, or maybe pleading with him. *Be alive. Don't leave me alone out here*—even though fifteen minutes ago she hadn't minded being alone at all.

With what had to take massive effort, he wrenched himself upward and gave his head a shake that scattered snow every which way. He gasped for breath.

"Are you all right?" Ava asked. Begged. "Are you all right?"

He turned his head enough so that he could see her. Snow-frosted brown hair, glassy eyes, a day or two's growth of beard on a strong face. Frozen blood in his hair and down his cheekbone and jaw.

"*God*. How did you find me?" Before she could answer, he shook his head again. "I'm stuck. I can't feel my legs."

"I'll keep digging." She calculated. "At an angle so I don't hit you."

He watched with what she guessed was unusual and maybe worrisome passivity.

Something made her look over her shoulder and up to the ridge that reared above the river. If those men had seen the avalanche, they might be scrambling down even now to help.

Or…maybe not. Either way, she didn't see anything, and it would surely take them hours to a full day to get this far.

She dug as hard and fast as she could, until he grunted and she realized the blade of the shovel had scraped over his knee. Now that she could see how his body lay imprisoned, she was able to dig with more confidence. She wasn't even aware of the soreness in her shoulders and upper arms anymore, or of the sharper pain shooting down her spine.

The man groaned, planted one hand on the ice to the side of the hole and heaved upward, twisting as he came. Agony flashed across his face. His leg broke free, but it appeared the other one was still trapped.

"You're injured," she said. *Duh*. How could he not be?

"Just get me out," he said from between clenched teeth.

Ava glared at him. "I'm doing my best."

His eyes closed. His voice became grittier. "I know you are."

Okay, foolish to take offense.

Moments later, he was free. He half pushed, half rolled out of the hole. That was the moment when she realized with dismay that *his* pack was nowhere to be seen.

Looking uphill toward the rock, she did see

something she'd missed: the other snowshoe, lying on the surface as if he'd casually tossed it aside.

He lay on the uneven surface, his head bare, and shook. As cold as she'd been, now she was sweating, but what she could see of his face was bone white, and he'd clamped his teeth together in a grimace that she felt sure was to keep them from chattering.

"We have to get you warm," she said. Decided. He was way worse off than she was.

She surveyed their surroundings and made herself think. Finding a way to warm him came first, ahead even of assessing his injuries.

Get him off the avalanche path. Pray he was able to walk, even if he had to lean on her to do it. Find a place to set up the tent. Laid out her sleeping bag. Maybe both of them would fit in it. She knew she needed to lie still, evaluate *herself* for injuries, gather herself for whatever needed doing next.

For the moment, she left the probe and shovel both in the snow and pushed herself to her feet. Her pack... There it was. She slung it onto her back again, the weight almost buckling her knees.

"You have to get up," she said. "I'm going to crouch down and help you."

He moved his head in agreement and, with what she guessed took superhuman will, pushed himself to his hands—no, one hand, she saw, his left arm dangled—and knees. She immediately became more aware of his sheer size. It wasn't only that he had to be several inches over six feet tall, but that he was broad. Shoulders, chest, powerful thighs. All of which meant he'd outweigh her by a sizeable amount. Nonetheless, she tucked herself under the crook of his uninjured arm and said, "Okay, let's do it."

They fought their way upright. His weight had her wanting to crumple, but she kept lifting. "That's it," she encouraged. "Upsy daisy."

The man lurched to his feet and his eyes met hers. He bit out, "Now…what?" before clamping his jaws together again. Shudders rattled his entire body.

"Down, toward those trees. It looks…kind of flat. I have a tent we can set up."

As they staggered, one step at a time, she kept talking without really knowing what she was saying. It hardly mattered; she couldn't imagine he was taking any of it in. The shaking came in waves, receding, then gripping his body again. She tried to time it so they could pause. If he went down, she had to wonder if she'd be able to get him up again.

Finally—*thank you, God, finally!*—they clambered awkwardly off the bottom of the avalanche flow onto snowy ground that was almost flat. Under the protection of evergreens blocking some of the sky, the snow wasn't as deep here as in most places, or they might have foundered.

Ava looked around, her uneasy remembrance of those men on the ridge making her want to find someplace that was out of sight. Yes, there. Low cedar branches hid a shadowy space behind. She steered the man there, pushed aside scratchy branches and finally had to help him lower to a sitting position so she could take off her pack and locate the tent.

When she bought it last winter to replace her old one, she'd almost chosen a bright red one, but now was glad she hadn't. She'd gone with dark green so it didn't stand out in a wild place, where she tried to pass as close to unseen as possible. Seeing that *her* hands were shaking now, too, she still unrolled a tarp and set out the tent. It was the kind that sprang up almost on its own. She also had a pad and sleeping bag that she unzipped.

"We need to take off your boots and some of your clothes," she told the stranger, who nodded jerkily but had to wait until she scooted close enough to untie his boots and yank them off, hoping she wasn't damaging an already injured knee or something like that. Gloves—they were really lucky his had stayed on, since he'd never have gotten those big hands into hers, even assuming she wasn't already wearing her backup ones. The glove had protected a watch, too. No hat to remove; that was gone. She unzipped his parka, the same color as her tent, and laid it atop the sleeping bag for some extra warmth.

Then she eyed the ice clinging to his snow pants and said, "I think these had better come off, too. I'll put them between the pad and sleeping bag and maybe they'll warm up and the ice will melt."

His expression showed no comprehension, but finally he looked down and nodded. With his one hand he unsnapped the waist but couldn't handle the zipper. Desperate to get them both warm—her sweat was making her feel colder by the second as it dried—Ava had lost all sense of personal boundaries. She unzipped his pants and, with another effort on his part, got him onto his one hand and knees again so she could peel the pants down and urge him to hop/crawl inside the tiny tent. She shoved the pants under the sleeping bag and helped him, wearing long underwear and a fleece top, scoot the rest of the way into the unzipped sleeping bag.

Aching to climb in after him, she listened to the uneasy voice in her head and made herself find a broken branch, which she used like a broom to brush away any clear signs of their trek from the edge of the ice-bound avalanche flow to their hidden refuge. Since they hadn't been able to go any distance, finding them wouldn't be hard, but...she'd done her best.

Only then did she take off her own gloves, boots, stretchy pants and quilted parka, and remove her fleece hat to pull it over his head before she lay down beside the big man who seemed worrisomely helpless.

Her parka she bunched to create an initially cold pillow. Zipping up the sleeping bag wasn't easy. She had to practically climb atop him to manage, then found herself pressed tightly against that long, hard, terrifyingly rigid body.

At last, at last, she burrowed her face into the crook between his neck and shoulder, let herself rest for a moment, then slipped her hands up under his fleece top and the waffle weave one that was beneath it. She began to rub his muscled torso with wide, sweeping movements.

"Warm," he mumbled, before he arched in another spasm of the shakes.

Since *she* didn't feel in the least warm, she was even more frightened by how cold he must be.

ZACH HAD BEEN seriously wounded twice in his army career, and he didn't think he'd ever felt as all-around terrible as he did right now. Still, hints of warmth began to penetrate; her heat must have lingered in the hat, and her breath on the bare skin of his neck felt like nirvana.

She was finding a lot of places that hurt as she moved her hands over his torso, but those hands felt deliciously hot, too, and he craved them. Higher, higher, he'd think, then lower. She didn't go quite as low as he really wanted, and he had a moment of wry humor. If he could convince her that was a top-notch way to warm him up... Yeah, probably not.

If he could even imagine getting horny or laughing again, he was probably going to survive, Zach decided.

"You hurt?" he managed to mumble.

Her hands paused. "I...don't really know," she said, sounding perplexed.

He understood. His head felt like a jackhammer had mistaken it for pavement that needed to be broken up. He knew something was very wrong with his shoulder, but otherwise...everything bloody hurt, so how could he identify any particular complaints? Once he was warm again, he decided.

"Your shoulder, or is it your arm...?" the woman said tentatively.

"Shoulder. Dislocated, I think." His damn teeth clattered every time he relaxed his jaw enough to speak. Given the spasms that shook the rest of him, the muscles surrounding his shoulder would be doing the same. Not good.

With a tremor in her voice, she asked, "Do you know how we can put it back into the socket?"

"Hope so, but... I need to get warm first." A vague memory suggested he had the order wrong—there was some reason the reduction should be done immediately—but he couldn't hold on to it.

"Okay." She snuggled closer, if that was possible.

He was able to press his cheek against her head, even though his stubble was probably going to tangle her disordered hair. It felt silky, though, and he'd seen some spilling out from beneath her hat when she was digging him out of the ice and snow. *Chestnut*, he thought was the right word. Her driver's license probably described her hair as brown, a lighter shade than his, but mixed in was a hint of something warmer. Red, he thought. It felt thick, warm. He wished he could bury his whole face in that tumble of hair, but suspected that wasn't logistically possible.

The movement of her hands slowed. Zach tried to zip his head so he could see her face, but their position made it almost impossible. Her rate of breathing dropped, too. She was falling asleep, he realized. Stress and exhaustion did often lead to a crash. He lifted his good arm enough to wrap it around her, securing her to his side. One of her hands slipped from beneath his shirt and she curled it next to her body, but the other remained splayed on his belly. Warm, comforting. He closed his eyes and wished he could zone out, too, but pain wouldn't allow him to surrender to unconsciousness.

He worried for a few minutes. What if he had internal bleeding? What if *she* did? More than most, he knew people could achieve heroics despite catastrophic injuries. Given how slender she was, the very fact that she'd dug him out quickly enough to save his life was astonishing.

Hell, finding him in the first place was downright miraculous.

Let her sleep, he told himself. *Pay attention*

in case she starts to struggle to breathe. He couldn't watch her, not as dim as the light was in the tent, nestled beneath heavy evergreen branches, not to mention how tightly the two of them were squeezed in here. As long as her breathing stayed even, she was okay.

Reality was, he might not be able to do anything to help if she did have a crisis.

Closing his eyes, shutting out the helplessness, he focused on her breathing alone. In, out. The tiny puff of air against his neck. The regularity reassured him, but also freed his mind to wander.

Automatic rifle. Worse, an RPG. Backcountry hikers in the US of A did not carry grenade launchers. He'd blanked both of those memories out since finding himself buried in what could have been an icy grave.

How *could* he have forgotten? Would those bastards be on their way to be sure they had successfully buried the witnesses? Or witness, singular, if they hadn't seen Zach?

Didn't matter; if they made it here, and he guessed anything like a straight line would be impossible, they'd see the huge hole the woman had dug to free him. Had she left any possessions there when she helped him down? Again, did that matter? The hole spoke for itself.

That she'd retained her pack was a miracle

itself. Not so much if she'd evaded the avalanche flow in the first place, but he guessed that wasn't the case or she wouldn't have sounded doubtful about whether she was hurt. Did she realize those men had deliberately triggered the avalanche?

Zach wondered, though. He hadn't been all there while she was setting up the tent, but she'd chosen an inconspicuous spot. By chance, because it was a level place she could find? Or because she was trying to tuck them out of sight?

Yeah, his mind wouldn't let up now that worries gathered, and he dealt with the unusual circumstance of not being able to do a damn thing to protect them. He'd curse the fact that he was unarmed because weapons were forbidden in the national park, except his Glock would have been in a pocket in his backpack. The one that could be anywhere beneath the snow and ice.

If at all possible, he needed to go back out onto the avalanche to try to find his pack and snowshoes. He could only hope she'd found her own. They were in trouble if their mobility was that severely limited.

And, hell, did she have enough food in her pack to feed both of them? For how many days? He presumed she at least had a phone that would give them hope of contacting the outside world when or if they emerged from this deep cut between a mountain and a high ridge, but that might be days away. The sat radio he'd carried, on loan from the border patrol, made finding his pack even more essential.

He realized his body had become rigid with tension. Not helping. Focus on her even breathing, the comfort of her supple, female body clasped to his, the lifesaving fact that she did have her pack with a tent, sleeping bag and at least minimal supplies. Without those, he'd be dead, and she wouldn't have had much hope.

Be damn grateful she was so gutsy.

AVA GRADUALLY SURFACED to realize that she must have fallen asleep. That was strange! She never napped, and now to drop off like a baby while she was squeezed into a sleeping bag with a strange man who'd scared her when she first realized he was chasing her down...

Fear tripped down her spine. No, she couldn't have left him to die. That had never been an option. But...now what?

Her body had obviously needed to take a time-out. She extended her senses to feel the entire length of his body, pressed against hers. He hadn't hurt her. He cradled her with one powerful arm. Her hand rested on his bare flesh, beneath his shirt. Right over his heartbeat, she realized, disconcerted. She felt the steady beat along with the tickle of chest hair.

Was *he* asleep? Instinct said no. There was too much tension in that body, and his breathing wasn't slow enough.

Ava cleared her throat. "Are you awake?"

He moved his head. "Yeah. How are you?"

That was a really good question. "Bruised all over," she decided, "and my back hurts, but more like I wrenched it than anything." She wriggled her toes. "Basically okay, I think."

"Good." There was a long pause. "'Upsy daisy'?"

"What?" Were her cheeks heating? "I don't know where I picked that up."

A vibration beneath her hand, breasts and cheek suggested a chuckle.

After a moment, she said, "I feel like I should get up. Except—"

When she broke off, his arm tightened. "We need to talk about what happened, and what we need to do to get out of this alive. We may as well be warm while we do that."

"I need to see your face."

After a pause, his arm relaxed. "Okay."

She squirmed until she could reach the zipper, then pulled it down enough to permit her to escape. Shivering, she took her parka from beneath his head and put it on.

He hadn't moved. Crossing her legs, she looked down at him. Then she swallowed and said, "Who are you? And...why were you following me?"

Chapter Three

"I've been asking myself who the hell *you* are and what you're doing out here on your own," he said with deceptive mildness, "but I don't mind starting. My name is Zach—Zachary—Reeves. I'm on vacation. I had a chance at a helicopter drop so I could enjoy some solitude in the wilderness." He wouldn't tell her yet that his ride had been courtesy of the US Border Patrol. "I was surprised to find out I wasn't alone, after all."

Yeah, that was suspicion in her eyes. Eyes that appeared dark in this light, but he suspected were blue. Bruises discolored one of her cheekbones and her forehead on the same side, but under other circumstances she'd be a beautiful woman, he realized for the first time.

"We must have chosen the same route," he continued. "I came across your tracks yesterday and…" He hesitated, then moved one shoulder. Even that sent a stab of agony through the other, although he was more disturbed by the numbness in his arm. "Was curious, I guess. I was faster than you, so I gained ground."

"Vacation," she said flatly. "Most people go to Honolulu in the winter."

"What are *you* doing here? This backcountry is closed for another couple of months."

"I'm a wildlife photographer. One of the magazines I sell to pulled some strings, and park officials dropped me off and arranged to pick me up again...um, three days from now?" She frowned. "I think. My name is Ava Brevick."

Wasn't familiar to him, but he couldn't remember ever glancing at the photographer's name when he did see photographs of wildlife, however spectacular.

"Well, we have some big problems now," he said bluntly.

Her eyebrows rose. "You think?"

"How did you find your pack?"

"It was still on my back." She reached over to lift at some loose nylon fabric. "I had an airbag, and just long enough before the avalanche hit me to pull on the cord to activate it. It's supposed to help keep you on top, and in this instance it worked."

"What about your snowshoes? Your poles?"

He hadn't noticed her camera and asked about that, too.

"My poles and snowshoes are long gone. My camera strap held. In fact, it tried to strangle me." She pulled down her turtleneck to reveal ugly bruises that made it look like she'd been garroted. Carefully covering her neck again, she said, "I did find your snowshoes. They didn't look damaged. I guess I left them out there, but they'll be easy to find."

"Poles?"

Shaken head.

"Maybe if we poke around, we can find my pack."

"We can try," she said doubtfully.

He gave a slight nod to acknowledge her pessimism. Or call it realism. He'd hold off explaining why recovering his pack was so critical.

"You know we didn't set off that avalanche."

She frowned. "You're saying it was just chance that it went while we were in the way?"

"No. Those men you were watching up on the ridge," he said bluntly. "Did you notice the weapons they were carrying?"

"Yes." It was almost a whisper, and she blanched. "I think they saw me. I noticed sun reflecting off glass. It almost had to be the lens of binoculars."

Or the scope on a high-powered rifle. But he didn't say that.

"Probably. They didn't expect to encounter anyone out here. I'm reasonably sure they sneaked across the Canadian border."

The woman—Ava—nodded. "That's what I thought, too. It was so weird seeing anyone up there. A wildfire must have opened up the top of the ridge. Even so, it has to be really difficult terrain."

"They used something like an RPG—a grenade launcher—to set off the avalanche. Whatever they fired was visible crossing the sky. Pretty sure they fired a second one, too, just to be sure. I don't know if they noticed me. Either way, they thought they'd take care of any witnesses."

Ava stared at him for a minute, making him think of an owl blinking in bemusement. "I... almost forgot about them."

"I did, too. We've had more pressing issues."

"Oh, God. You don't think—"

"I don't know," he admitted. "It was smart of you to set up the tent out of sight."

"I was glad it wasn't red."

He tipped his head, but decided not to ask about that.

"And...after you got in the sleeping bag, I went back out and used a broken branch to smooth away our tracks." She made a face. "More or less. So I guess I didn't completely forget them."

"You were smart," he said approvingly. He wished she hadn't left his snowshoes behind, but did that matter? Little as he liked the idea of either of them spending time in the open, he had to search for his pack.

She gave herself a shake. "You're hurt worse than I am. I should take a look…" In fact, she reached into her pack and pulled out some sterile wipes.

"Like I said, I think my shoulder is dislocated." He hoped that was what was wrong. A dislocation was fixable; shattered bones weren't under the circumstances. Shattered bones might have done nerve damage that would explain the numbness and the weird tingling he felt in his fingertips. If that were so, even if he made it to a hospital, he might have done too much damage for surgical repair to be possible. Even though it was on his weak side, the injury had the potential to end his newfound career.

He held still while she used one of the wipes on his face. Stinging told him there were cuts and scrapes, at the least, but she sat back, looking satisfied. "Anything besides the shoulder?" she asked.

He had one hell of a headache, but why tell her? He'd probably suffered a concussion. There'd been a few moments of double vision, and he was currently nauseated. None of that meant he could afford to lie around waiting to feel better.

"Bruises, like you," he said. "Maybe a cracked rib or two."

"You said you thought we could put your arm back in the socket." The idea clearly made her feel queasy, and he didn't blame her given that she wasn't a medical professional.

The hot coal of pain in his shoulder was making it hard to think, and would surely prevent him doing anything else, though. "I was...a soldier. I've done it for other people a couple of times." And no, he hadn't loved the experience, even though he'd had some medic training. "It works better if you have an assistant, but as it is..."

She took a deep, visible breath and gave a choppy nod. "I'll do whatever I have to do."

His admiration for Ava became something else he didn't let himself examine.

HE ADMITTED THAT they should have done this much sooner, that muscle spasms could prevent the bone from being manipulated back into the socket. He'd *known* that, but in his misery, had pushed the knowledge back.

"On the other hand, I guess you could say we iced it."

Ava gave a small, choked laugh that made his lips twitch.

Hey, he'd have been screwed if he'd been alone, as he'd expected to be.

"Might be easier if I weren't wearing anything, but I'm not about to try to wrestle my shirt off."

"And we can't cut it off, given that none of my clothes would fit you."

"Yeah." He described accomplishing a reduction of a shoulder dislocation as well as he could, keeping it simple. Ideally, he should sit up at about a thirty-degree angle. Maybe they could manage that if she propped her pack behind him. She would have to gently pull, applying traction while also rotating the arm outward until she felt the pop of the ball going back into the socket. It would help if he wasn't screaming. "If there's too much swelling or the muscles object too violently, it might not work."

"Then we'll pack your shoulder with snow and try again later," she said sturdily.

She was quite a woman, he thought again, even as he couldn't help also noticing the delicacy of her bone structure and the firmness of a chin that some would call stubborn. Stubborn was fine by him.

"I wish..." she began, before falling silent.

"You wish?"

"That there was someone else to hold you in place."

That would be ideal, but he'd do what he had to. He blinked against sweat dripping into his eyes. The pain was getting to him. He wanted to get this over with.

"I'm going to bite down on something to keep myself from yelling. Don't want to draw attention."

Her head bobbed. Her eyes were huge as she maneuvered in the small space, inevitably bumping into him a few times and making him wince, to wedge her pack behind him and punch it into a shape that let him half recline.

"Okay?"

"Yeah," he said hoarsely.

Now she half crawled until she was beside him on his bad side, forced to bend over by the curving roof of the small tent.

"One hand here." She gripped his upper arm. "The other on your wrist."

"Yeah. You might want to move down a little so you can pull harder."

She nodded and adjusted her position.

He'd begun to feel like someone waiting for the executioner to do his thing. If this didn't work—if something else altogether was wrong with his shoulder—would he be able to do his part getting them out of this remote country before they starved, froze...or were cornered by men he guessed were terrorists?

Too well armed for mere smugglers, anyway.

I CAN DO THIS.

Ava repeated the few words as if they were a mantra. Except, wasn't that the concept she already lived by? After years of having next to no control over where she went or how she lived, she'd dedicated herself to changing that. She'd made a success of a career defined by independence. If she could do that, she could do a little thing like this.

She gulped, took a deep breath and began applying pressure, pulling an arm that was easily twice as thick as hers, so muscular that, uninjured, he could probably pick her up with just that arm and toss her over his head.

His back arched. Tendons stood out in his neck, and he bared his teeth around the clean sock she'd offered for him to clench. She didn't dare look into his dark brown eyes, but she knew they'd dilated and never left her face.

Continuing pressure. Rotate outward. You can do this.

It seemed an eternity before she felt and even thought she heard the pop. Ava almost let out a whimper and slumped, but instead followed the remainder of his instructions and gently rotated the arm back toward his body, bent it at the elbow and laid his forearm across his torso.

He shuddered, spit out the sock and swore a few times, creatively.

"Thank God," he finally mumbled.

"It worked." She really hadn't expected it would, Ava was ashamed to realize. Something like that should have been done in a hospital ER, or at the very least by experienced paramedics.

"Yeah." His throat worked. "Pain let up."

"It...can't possibly be fixed that easily."

He grunted. "No. I should wear a sling, but maybe we can figure out how to brace the shoulder. We can't just sit here and wait for rescue."

No. They couldn't.

"You don't have poles, anyway," she pointed out.

"We can make some out of sticks." He frowned, reaching with his good hand to knead the injured shoulder. "If I had my pack, I could jury-rig snowshoes for you. Any chance you carry some cord I could use to tie branches together?"

"I do. It seemed like it might come in handy."

"Good girl." His grin changed a face that had so far seemed grim into one that was both warm and sexy.

"What do you do for a living?" she heard herself ask. Why hadn't it occurred to her to wonder before?

His expression returned to impassive. "I'm a cop."

"A cop." Did she believe him? She wondered again about the chance of him appearing at the same time as those men on the ridge.

"Whatcom County, the northwest corner of the state. Other side of Mount Baker. I'm a detective." He hesitated, watching her. "I got out of the service a year ago. Adjustment to a civilian life isn't as easy as you'd think."

"I've never thought about it." She pushed herself up to an awkward, bent-over position and clambered over his legs. "It's still light. I think I'll go grab everything I left out there. Maybe…maybe I should kind of fill in the hole."

"You're not going alone." He sat up.

"Yes, I am." She hoped he heard the steel in her voice. "If those men show up, they'd just grab you, too. You're not armed." As far as she knew. "If you won't rest *for even a few minutes*—" she leaned hard on that "—you could scout around for some branches that might work to make me snowshoes. I have a pocketknife you can use to cut the branches."

He didn't seem to like her being the one to put herself out there and argued against it, but he had to know she was right. Even if the men who'd triggered the avalanche had continued on their route along the ridge, putting from their mind the two people they'd gone out of their way to bury in snow and ice, Ava and Zach would have a difficult trek out of here with such limited supplies. They had to plan to leave first thing in the morning, and keep moving to the extent of their physical ability. Even fully equipped and in peak condition, they would be looking at a minimum of two to three more nights spent along the way. Now—

They would do the best they could.

"I'm not talking convenience, here," he said, voice clipped. "I have a satellite radio in that pack. We need to be able to call for help, and your phone isn't going to cut it."

He talked some more, although he'd already convinced her. The idea that he might be able to call for help *right this minute*—although she hadn't thought to ask if the thing had any limitations—was compelling.

She did win the argument about who would be going out to search, though. Dressed again, Ava felt like a mouse creeping out of hiding, excruciatingly aware that the cat might be watching her every timid move.

SHE MUST HAVE napped for a surprising length of time as they'd struggled to recover from the avalanche, because the light was already going, and fast. Days were still short in the Pacific Northwest at this time of year, and they were a lot shorter with mountains shadowing the valleys cut deep by rivers formed from glacial runoff.

It didn't take Ava long to return to the gaping hole that could well have been Zach Reeves's grave. Lovely thought. She stood still for a long moment, looking around, listening, but neither saw nor heard any evidence that other human beings were in the vicinity. Apprehension stuck with her, though—crawling up the back of her neck.

She seized the probe first, and began stabbing it into the much hardened avalanche flow, starting below where she'd found him, then working her way uphill from where he'd ended up. Nothing. She hit hard objects over and over again, but when she uncovered them, all she found were blocks of ice or rocks. Finally, she grabbed his snowshoes, then debated climbing up to see if there was any chance she'd missed seeing her own.

A shiver crawled over her, reminding her how exposed she was, how easily someone from quite a distance away could see her. Say, someone descending the ridge behind her.

Exhaustion already had her shaking. Rested, she could try again in the morning to find his pack. He'd convinced her that radio could be their salvation, and she was scared enough to believe him.

Finally she picked up the shovel and started scraping the snow and chunks of ice she'd dug out of the hole back into it. Her muscles burned and her back protested, but she kept at it until…well, she hadn't one hundred percent disguised the hole, but given how uneven the surface of a fresh avalanche flow was, it probably wasn't visible from very far away.

Zach, she suspected, would have searched longer and harder for his pack, the contents of which would come in really handy above and beyond the radio, but she'd reached her limit. She might have to sit on him to keep him from coming out here to poke and poke in a widening semicircle as darkness fell, but so be it.

She might have to sit on him to keep him from doing it, anyway.

Not that sitting on him would have much effect, she feared; he'd probably just pick her up and set her aside like a toddler who'd gotten in his way. Except that he'd damn well better not try anything like that, given the stomach-turning unpleasantness of…what had he called it? *Reduction of a dislocated shoulder.* That was it. And she did not want to repeat it, even assuming it would work a second time, because he was too foolish to recognize that, however temporarily, he had limitations.

Once again, she found a branch she used to brush away her footprints as well as she could, discarding it once she pushed between the feathery limbs of the cedar tree. Zach sat cross-legged in the doorway of her tent, head up as he watched her approach. His gaze swept over her from head to toe, taking in the few items she carried.

He'd found a way to halfway support his left arm using a cotton turtleneck from her pack. The gloved hand emerging from his minimal sling gripped a long branch he was stripping of smaller offshoots with the blade of her pocketknife. He had a fair pile of similar branches lying in front of him.

"You think that will work?" she asked doubtfully.

"In theory. I take it you didn't find the pack."

"No." She dropped the snowshoes at his side and thrust the shovel into the crusty snow, then folded the probe so she could stow it in her pack again.

He continued to study her with those penetrating dark eyes. "You have to hurt more than you're letting on. And be in shock."

"I'm not—"

Ignoring her protest, he said, "Come closer so I can measure the length of these against you."

After he'd learned whatever it was he needed to know, he muttered, "I hate to start cutting up the cord. If I screw up, we can't tie it back together."

She moved over so she could get into the tent and sat with a groan she hoped he didn't hear. His broad back blocked much of the light as she poked around in her pack.

"I have a stove. I could heat up a meal," she offered.

He turned. "How many meals do you have left?"

Counting was what she'd just been doing. "Um…five." And that only because she'd brought two or three extras, just in case.

"Then I'm going to say no. If you have any snacks, let's stick to those. I had an adequate meal last night, and I'm guessing you did, too."

Ava nodded.

"Worse comes to worst, I can try my hand at trapping rabbits or other small mammals, but that would mean starting a real fire, and until we're sure we're alone, I don't want to do that."

Her head bobbed again. She *wanted* to argue, but couldn't reasonably do so. Her stomach was growling, but she wouldn't starve in the next day. A handful of almonds would suffice.

Zach had already gone back to work, only saying over his shoulder, "See if you can find something that might work as a strap across the front of your boots."

Oh, lord. There had to be something.

"My camera strap," she started to say before changing her mind.

But he turned again, his suddenly intense gaze boring into hers. "You watched those men. Did you get any photos of them?"

She couldn't look away from him. "I...yes. But...what difference does that make? It's not as if either of us would *know* any of them."

"If you got their faces, there's one guy I might recognize. He's on a watch list I just saw."

He'd seen a watch list because he was a cop?

Her thoughts took a jump. "You're border patrol."

He shook his head. "No, I told you. I have a friend who is, though. We served together. He's the one who gave me the lift out here. There have been rumors about an assassin whose bomb making is notable, too, available for hire to select fanatic causes, who rumor also says is on his way to the US. You know, the northern border of the US is considered the longest undefended border in the world. It's something like fifty-five hundred miles. Patrols are spread so far apart on the wilderness stretches with no roads, my buddy asked me to keep an eye out, even though the chances of me seeing anything were next to nothing."

"What would he look like, this assassin?"

"He's Russian."

Caucasian, as all the men had appeared to be. Shaken, she fumbled for her camera. "I can show you what I did get."

What if…?

Chapter Four

Zach wouldn't have been surprised if Ava found her camera to be irreparably damaged. The lens showed definite damage. But he held his breath as she lifted the camera and did her thing. An image showed on the screen, although he was too far away to make out more detail than to know he was looking at a snowshoe hare. That didn't mean she'd captured a face clear enough to identify from such a distance, but he couldn't drag his gaze away from the images that continued to whisk by.

Then there was one, a figure clad in white that stood out against the intensely blue sky. A man.

"You mind?" he asked, and when she shook her head, he maneuvered himself closer to her. He ignored the jab of pain trying to persuade him to stay still. Tough. Blocking pain was nothing new to him; he could do it again. He was already ignoring the fact that his skull was splitting open.

Maybe literally fractured? He couldn't let himself think about that.

He studied the digital photo in amazement. There was no visible face; the guy was wearing a balaclava, at a guess, but small as the figure was, the image was still sharp enough he could see quilted pants, heavy boots—and the weapon slung across the man's shoulder.

Ava glanced at Zach, and he nodded. Two pictures later, one of the men had his face uncovered. It was almost in profile. Thin, tanned face. After close study, he shook his head, and she moved on. Two more wearing balaclavas, and then came a man looking directly toward the camera.

Zach hissed in a breath. Ava turned her head and, wide-eyed, stared at him.

"That's him. I'm almost positive. Those cheekbones are unusual. Jaw broader than usual, too. You can't see his widow's peak, but—" He broke off. "Grigor Borisyuk has only been caught by a camera once that the US government knows about. It was a news photographer who took the photo. He was strongly advised to transfer to a domestic beat after that."

"Did he?"

"My friend didn't say. He'd have been foolish not to." Although foreign news correspondents and photographers were known more for guts than common sense.

There was no saying Borisyuk would have bothered hunting down the photographer, of course; once the picture was out there, what was the point? He was known to be ruthless and utterly lacking a conscience, though, according to Reid. Zach didn't imagine Borisyuk as the sort of fellow who'd shrug and say, "Ah, well."

And now a second photographer had recorded his face, with him staring straight at her. He might not have known she held a camera, but someone in their party had seen her through binoculars, which increased the odds that it was Borisyuk who had snapped out an order to kill the observer.

Zach's instinct screamed: pack up *now* and get the hell out of here.

If only it was possible. They weren't going anywhere until he finished the crude snowshoes he was constructing and they found sturdy sticks suitable to serve as poles, by which time it would be dark.

The sky had deepened; the change subtle enough he hadn't noticed. He had to get back to work. They wouldn't want to show a light, that was for sure.

"Straps to hold your boots?" he asked, scooting back to where he'd set down the peculiar bunch of branches. He still had some cord, but less than he'd like.

"Oh, ah..." Looking shaken, Ava didn't move for a minute. Then, "We can cut pieces off the straps on the pack." She twisted and turned her backpack so he could see the tough compression straps used to lessen the bulk of the load, as well as straps dangling after she'd adjusted the fit for her relatively small body.

"Perfect," he declared.

She held out her booted foot for him to measure the lengths he'd need, then watched as he used the pocketknife to cut several lengths. Then, little as he liked it, she left to hunt for straight, solid sticks long enough to serve as poles for both of them.

Her absence split his attention, but he made himself keep working. Right now, she was fitter than he was, smart and capable. A protective instinct had kicked in the minute he saw the avalanche begin its roaring descent toward her, but he had to rein it in. The only way to get out of here was to trust each other.

Turned out she had a small folding saw in her pack, which she took with her. He couldn't believe the crowd from the ridge were near enough to hear even if he and she burst into song, but he was just as glad she didn't have to snap off any branches she found, even if that recognizable cracking sound was common in the backcountry when heavy snow weighted tree limbs down.

She came back sooner than he'd expected, and presented four only slightly curved or crooked sticks that looked sturdy and which she'd stripped of any growth.

"Those look good," he said with a nod.

He saw a flicker of something in her eyes at his approval—humor?—but then she sat down just inside the tent with a sigh. Pulling her pack to her, she rooted around and handed him a small packet of mixed nuts and a box of raisins, the kind his mom had put in his school lunch when he was a kid.

The mother whose face he had trouble recalling, given how long ago she'd died.

Ava produced a water bottle and they both took sips, Zach accepting another couple of ibuprofen. He thought about suggesting she use her stove to boil water, but the bottle was the only one they had, and it was still three-quarters full. Wait until midday or later tomorrow, he decided. They didn't dare let themselves get dehydrated.

Unsure if his unsettled stomach would accept anything he sent its way, he ate the nuts and raisins anyway, before taking another couple of sips of water, as did she. Then they moved out of the tent so she could try the crude snowshoes. He had to make several adjustments and still wasn't convinced the bootstraps would hold.

"Take a few steps," he said. "Better lift your feet higher than usual."

She did and looked down in surprise. "They're heavier than my snowshoes were, but...it works."

"Green wood," he told her. "I hope we don't have to break into a run. This isn't the most solid construction ever, but in theory it should work." He glanced around. "Damn, it's getting dark."

"It happens fast here."

"I know." He shoved himself to his feet. "I need to, ah, use the facilities, then let's try to sleep as soon as possible. I want to go back out there to try to find my pack—" even though the chances lessened as the avalanche flow hardened "—and that'll have to be at first light. We can't afford to take long."

Despite what had to be fear on her fine-boned face, this nod was as sturdy as all her previous agreements had been. He'd prefer to have an army teammate as backup, someone with serious muscle who also happened to have a weapon secreted in his backpack, but—otherwise?—Zach was astonished at how lucky he'd gotten that the woman who had catapulted them into this by taking a few photos was also gutsy, strong and determined.

Now, if only they could escape and contact the people who needed to see that photograph before Grigor Borisyuk succeeded at disappearing into the American population.

"WE'LL NEED TO sleep together," Ava said as matter-of-factly as she could manage. Why she'd felt compelled to say that, she didn't know. What else were they supposed to do? It just…felt like the elephant in the room. Well, the tent. "I hope we *can* sleep so squished together," she added. Although she'd already proved to herself that she could. Ava suspected he hadn't dropped off at all earlier, though.

With the increasingly murky light, she couldn't make out Zach's features any better than he presumably could hers. Lucky, since she suspected she was blushing.

And how ridiculous was that? She hadn't hesitated to wedge herself into that sleeping bag with him when the necessity had been so dire. Well, it still was. To survive, they had to sleep, and they had to share. *So get over it*, she told herself.

"We've had practice," he said drily, his deep voice having more impact after the darkness had shuttered her vision.

She pushed aside the sleeping bag and laid her outer layer of clothing onto the too-thin pad. From rustling sounds, movement and a grunt that was likely pain, Zach was stripping, as well. A moment later, he handed her his garments and she laid them out, too.

Then she shook out the sleeping bag atop the clothing and pad.

"Um…are we more likely to bump your arm if you get in first, or if I do?" she asked.

"I'd better go first. I can't prop myself up very well, and given our respective weights, I should be on the bottom, anyway."

Well, that was true enough, and he'd certainly been tactful. "Respective weights" indeed. He surely out-weighed her by eighty pounds, and perhaps as much as a hundred.

So she waited while he lay down, shifted a few times, then said, "Okay."

Ava zipped up the bag more than halfway before squirming until she was far enough in to rest her head on his chest. Then she groped for the zipper and pulled it up, excruciatingly aware of his contours.

Pretend he's a body pillow, she told herself. *Don't think of him as a man with big bones and powerful muscles.* Especially *don't think of him as the stranger he is.*

The stranger she had no choice but to trust.

She did her very best to lie still, even though one arm was bent awkwardly beneath her and she couldn't quite figure out what to do with the other one.

He shifted and wrapped *his* arm around her. "Try to get comfortable," he ordered.

She rolled her eyes, but wriggled until her position was the best she could manage. She hoped she hadn't hurt him. Then she sighed.

"I'm not very sleepy," she said after a moment. "It's early, and... I took a nap."

His chest vibrated in what she took as a laugh. "So you did. You needed it."

"Yes. It's just..." How to put into words how shaken she was by all the shocks, slamming one atop another? They tumbled through her head: the anxiety awakened by her awareness that she was no longer alone, was possibly even being pursued; the peculiar and then worrying sight of armed men where they shouldn't have been; the terror of being caught in an avalanche, followed by the possibly greater terror of thinking she wouldn't be able to find and dig out the other person caught in it. Never mind squeezing into the sleeping bag with the stranger who'd scared her, the icky task of manipulating his arm back into the socket—she still shivered, thinking about it—and finally the horrifying discovery that she may have photographed a terrorist sought throughout the free world. A terrorist who could only be sneaking into the US for a purpose that chilled her blood.

"I understand," he said quietly, his breath stirring her hair. His arm tightened slightly around her. "I'm...used to combat, but I don't love the night before I know there'll be action."

She tried to lift her head and failed. "You think there will be tomorrow?"

The pause felt longer than it probably was. "I hope not. I won't lie, though. If that is Borisyuk, he has damn good reason to want to ensure no witnesses are able to report his arrival in this country. That said—" the hand that had been tucked around her torso made a movement that might have been a waggle "—from their perspective, odds are good the avalanche took you out."

"Could they have seen that I pulled myself out?"

"I doubt it. From what you said, you were carried way down the slope. Both of us were. Tree cover is heavy along the creek."

She let herself relax a tiny bit, her mind wandering as she considered how intimate this felt, talking quietly in the night while wrapped in each other's arms. Not something she'd had in a very long time.

"The smartest thing they could do is go on their way," he continued. "Even if you survived, even if they had a glimpse of me, any experience at all would tell them how likely it was that if one or the other of us survived, we'd have been injured, and we'd be hindered by losing some of our equipment. If they got well ahead of us, they can tuck Borisyuk into whatever bolt-hole was planned, and assume we couldn't identify any of them. In fact, even seeing your camera, why would they think you'd have actually gotten a photo of him?"

She appreciated his reassurance, but couldn't take it at face value.

"You think that's what will happen, then? They'll go on?"

Another pause had her stiffening. "I don't know," he admitted. "The guy hasn't been so successful, moving like a ghost until he completes his job, then disappearing again, if he isn't ultracareful. Paranoid."

Her mouth suddenly dry, she swallowed against a swell of panic. "We should be—"

He gave her a little shake. "You know we

can't travel in the dark. Even fully equipped, it would be foolish. As it is, a good snag will tear one of your snowshoes apart. I'm confident that they will have as difficult a time dropping down to the river valley, assuming that's what they're thinking of doing."

"They'd have to, at some point."

"Yes, but doesn't a trail drop down off the ridge farther south? It'll be buried under snow, but will still be more navigable than heading out cross-country."

She bobbed her head.

"I'm...not sure I like that option, either, though." He spoke more slowly. "It's fine if they drop down the west side of the ridge, but I don't like the idea of them popping out in front of us."

Don't like the idea. What a splendid euphemism for a squad of terrorists spreading a net to catch Zach and her.

And yet, the two of them had no options at all. They couldn't hunker down where they were and hope their nonappearance convinced the bad guys they were dead and buried under the avalanche, because they didn't have enough food to survive for more than a handful of days, plus they'd need to trek out to where they might have cell service. Her ride had been prearranged...but they'd never make it there in time, not inadequately equipped and injured as they were.

Also...while she had never so much as considered joining the armed forces, she didn't like the idea of she and Zach protecting themselves at the cost of their nation. They *had* to get the word out.

If he'd told her the truth about himself and his background, it occurred to her, he must be utterly determined to do whatever was required to stop an evil man from carrying his war of twisted ideals into their home country. Wasn't that what he'd dedicated his life to?

His concern for her had been evident so far, but however calming his deep voice was in the darkness, however comforting the hot length of his body and the solid shoulder beneath her cheek, saving her had to be second on his list of priorities. And, while she couldn't blame him for that, the realization was...frightening.

What could she say? Nothing came to her, and he remained silent, too, even though she knew that, for the longest time, he was no more asleep than she was.

HE MUST HAVE awakened at least hourly all night. At one point, he'd have gotten up to use the john, but the impracticality of that persuaded him to shove the mere thought to the back of his mind. They had to sleep while they could.

A part of him, sleeping and awake, was listening for any sound that didn't belong. He hated knowing the enemy carried fully automatic weapons while he didn't have so much as a handgun. If only he could get his hands on one of those rifles...

Could he use it, given his present disability? He tightened his fingers into a fist a few times without any noticeable increase in pain. Yeah, he thought he could. Certainly if it was life or death.

He made himself slow his breathing, courting sleep. How long it lasted, he didn't know, but this time when he opened his eyes, he was able to make out the peak of the tent above him. The light, if you could call it that, held barely a hint of gray, but it was enough.

He tipped his head toward Ava's ear. "Up and at 'em."

"Is that sort of like upsy daisy?" she mumbled.

He grinned. "Yeah."

She didn't move right away. "I *ache*."

Now that he thought about it, so did he, and it wasn't just his shoulder and head. Of course they hurt. They'd both been beaten within an inch of their lives yesterday. When he said so, she groaned.

"I haven't forgotten. Ugh."

"You can stay cozy for a little longer while I go poke around for my pack," he suggested.

She rolled her eyes. "Don't be silly. Just… give me a minute."

Her minute was brief enough, so he didn't have to push. She sighed and wriggled her way against his body until she was free of the warm sleeping bag. Zach couldn't help thinking he'd be aching in a different way if they didn't both hurt, and their situation wasn't so urgent.

"Brr!" she exclaimed. "Roll over!"

He obliged, and she snatched up first his clothes, thrusting them at him, before grabbing her own and scrambling into them.

His shoulder and arm had stiffened up during the night, not surprisingly, and getting his quarter-zip fleece top on was a challenge. By the time he succeeded, Ava had shoved her feet into her boots and was separating the flaps of the tent.

"Wait!" he said sharply.

"We're still alone." She slipped out, and he heard a hint of a footfall and then nothing.

Damn it! She probably had to pee—now that he'd thought about it, he was near to desperation himself—but he didn't like her taking the lead.

As if he could have protected her if a terrorist materialized in front of them, Zach thought, disgruntled at his own weakness and frustrated anew at being unarmed. He used his left hand to help him get his boots on, then half crawled, half hopped out of the tent before rising to his feet. Ava pushed aside a feathery, low-hanging cedar branch and stepped into sight.

"I'll dig out something for us to eat."

"Thanks." He went the same direction she had, relieved himself, then detoured for a glimpse at the avalanche flow. The light was brighter up above the peak; down here in the vee of the valley, details were still elusive. He wondered how firmly the ice and snow had set, whether it would even be possible to dig a hole in it now. Damn, he hoped the hole Ava Brevick *had* dug wasn't visible to eyes looking for just that.

She'd already rolled the sleeping bag when he returned but left the pad open for them to sit on as they quickly ate more nuts and some dried apricots. His queasiness lingered, but if he had to expel this small amount of food, it wouldn't take more than a minute, and he could hope to do it without her noticing. He chased the bites with a few swallows of extremely cold water. Worse came to worst, he reminded himself, they could drink from the river where it appeared between sheets of ice and snow. Becoming infected with a possible bacteria wouldn't kill them in the near future, although odds were good she carried tablets to purify water.

He was left feeling useless as he watched her roll the pad and dismantle the tent, stow the tent in her pack and finally strap the roll and sleeping bag together where they'd rest on her lower back.

"I'll carry that," he said.

She yanked it toward herself, her expression indignant. "Don't be ridiculous! You're *injured*."

Ready to argue, Zach opened his mouth, but she added, "Besides, I'd rather have you able to keep watch and…and respond or at least make decisions if you see or hear anything."

He glared at her, then let his head fall forward. Fine, but he had no weapon. How was he supposed to "respond"?

The very question pulled him back from the frustration that served no purpose. She was right—and he needed to start thinking about what he *could* turn into a weapon, or how, if the opportunity arose, he could take out one man—and acquire ample food, weapons and equipment for him *and* Ava.

"We'll talk about it again once we really get started," he said roughly. "Okay. You all set?"

There was the nod that caused a squeezing sensation under his breastbone every time he saw it. He thrust his feet into the snowshoe bindings, saw her do the same with her makeshift ones, and they both gripped their sturdy sticks.

He stepped out from the shelter provided by the cedar tree, took a good look around and started out over really difficult ground. This would be a test of her snowshoes.

It didn't take them five minutes to reach the foot of the avalanche flow, which he really took in for the first time. A hundred and fifty yards wide or more, he estimated, stunned. The sheer amount of material flung down the slope was frightening. It was a miracle they'd survived—particularly that she'd found him. Good God, what made him think there was a chance in hell of stumbling on his pack in the vastness of this avalanche field?

He had to try.

They tried, at the stubborn woman's insistence, but he weakened fast. A couple of times dizziness brought him to his knees. He waved off her concern, pretending he thought he'd spotted something.

It was a relief when the hour he'd given them for the search was up. Premature relief, given the day facing them. A short rest was all he allowed them. Increasing awareness of the sun rising and the enemy that might be in pursuit drove him to ignore his physical limitations.

Once they were on their feet, on their way, he just hoped Ava's snowshoes held up until they reached the trail they'd both traversed yesterday, where the way would become somewhat easier. Trail or no, though, they wouldn't be able to move fast enough to stay ahead of any serious pursuit.

Chapter Five

Ava fell down twice in the first twenty yards or so. The first time, she failed to notice a rock lurking just beneath the snow and crashed down with an *uumph*.

Zach swung around in alarm, but fortunately she'd come out of the snowshoes, which didn't appear damaged. She made a face at him, ignored what was sure to be a new and painful bruise on her hip, and levered herself back up with the help of her pole. Booted toes back under the straps, she started out again behind him.

The second time, a springy whip of alder or something equally bedeviling snagged her. Now, a couple of the more fragile crosspieces in one of the snowshoes snapped, but after Zach crouched and examined it, he said, "I think it's still solid enough."

He was kind enough not to add, *If you don't put too much stress on it*. But she'd known, as well as he must, that this stretch where there never had been a trail cut, never mind maintained, would be the hardest going. Next to impossible, if not for the snow cover that buried some of the rocks and teeming growth the river valleys in this temperate rainforest were known for.

Their pace felt, and undoubtedly was, glacially slow. He'd have been able to go way faster if he wasn't stuck with her, she thought, but then it wasn't her fault that her snowshoes had been lost in the avalanche. She more than made up for that handicap with the supplies in her pack she *had* held on to.

Between each stride, she held her breath, however fleetingly, so that she could listen for the sounds of anyone else moving behind them. Zach must have been doing the same.

Despite her own struggles, she became aware that he wasn't moving with the smooth efficiency she'd seen when she spotted the man gaining ground on her yesterday. Of course he wasn't! What if his arm popped out of the socket again?

She took a couple of hurried steps and said, "Are you all right?"

He stopped and turned at the waist to look at her. "What?"

"Your shoulder. What if you reinjure it?"

For a long moment, his expression didn't change. Then he grimaced, deepening lines she'd already seen on his face. Yes, he hurt.

"I'm wondering if we can strap my upper arm to my torso so that only my lower arm is free."

He must've hated having to keep admitting to any vulnerabilities, but he was doing it, anyway.

"It'll be hard for you to use your pole effectively, but... I don't see why not. Why don't you look for someplace we can at least set the pack down and maybe sit?"

"How are you doing?" he asked, his gaze holding hers.

What her body needed right this minute was a spa with hot bubbling water loosening painful muscles, but he must feel worse.

"Fresh as a daisy."

His grin took her breath away. "Like daisies, do you?"

"As a matter of fact, I do."

She soaked in the power of that smile and the glint of warmth and humor in his eyes until he inevitably turned away and started out again.

Two steps later, her right stick plunged into a hole. Leaning on it as she was, she stumbled, barely saving herself from falling to her knees.

Although she regained her balance, despair grabbed her. Even aside from possible pursuit—or an ambush set in front of them—how could they hope to cover enough miles with her walking sloppily on a bunch of small branches, and falling every ten minutes?

Zach must not have noticed her latest mishap, because twenty feet opened between them before she braced herself and resumed the clumsy, knees-high marching steps. What was she going to do? Drum her heels and whine, *I can't do this*? They had no choice at all. This was life and death, and not only for them.

I'm stronger than this, she told herself, and fixed her gaze on the man leading the way despite his own pain.

FOR THE NEXT ten or fifteen minutes, it was all Zach could do not to turn his head constantly to check on Ava. He didn't like the fact that she was both the one to have to struggle with the jury-rigged snowshoes and to carry a heavy pack while he strode ahead unhindered.

He'd have suggested he try to convert his snowshoes to fit her smaller feet so they could switch, except his greater weight on the flimsy snowshoes she wore would ensure his progress was even more difficult than she found it.

And...he needed to be able to move fast should something catch his eye.

Move fast to do what?

And...how was he going to do it with a splitting headache and a tendency to get dizzy if he turned too fast?

Finally spotting a downed log covered by a six-inch coverlet of snow, he stopped. He'd have liked to feel relief, but the truth was, he felt as if his shoulder had been pinned together with a rusty spike.

Ava wasn't as far behind him as he'd feared. She lifted each foot in an exaggerated move and strode forward without hesitation, her concentration intense enough she was only a few feet away when she noticed he'd stopped and did the same.

She shuffled forward, planted her improvised poles and shrugged the pack off her back. Zach grabbed it with his good arm and lowered it to the log.

"We should see our tracks from yesterday anytime," he said.

She grimaced. "That'll have to be an improvement."

"Yeah." He sat down carefully, and she did the same. "I wish it would snow."

"Not likely this late in the season, but—" She tipped her head back and gazed at the sky. Seeing the same thing he had, she said, "I didn't pay any attention this morning, but that cloud cover does have a certain look to it."

Glad she'd confirmed his instincts, he said, "A few inches would hide our tracks."

"Not just behind us, but ahead, too."

"Right. If we can keep going even if it's coming down hard..."

"They might conceivably think we were buried in the avalanche. Except..."

She'd seen the fatal flaw.

"We're taking the logical route out of the mountains. They'll be behind us, and able to move faster."

"Unless they kept going along the ridge."

He hoped she couldn't hear the deep apprehension in his voice. "And are maybe waiting ahead for us. Yeah."

Zach hated being the walnut that would be crushed by the nutcracker. The situation was familiar to him, but this time he was as vulnerable as any civilian, and needing to protect Ava besides.

"You holding up okay?" he finally asked. They'd been on their way a ridiculously short length of time and shouldn't have stopped, but, damn, he hurt, and she was having to work at least twice as hard as usual to make any progress.

"Fine. And it so happens..." She raised her eyebrows. "I carry ace bandages."

Zach found a grin for her. "Mary Poppins."

Ava's laugh lit her face. Damn, she was beautiful, bruises and all. He couldn't look away. He wasn't sure what she saw on his face, but wariness stole her amusement. She proceeded to dig in her pack, finally producing a red canvas bag with the classic Red Cross symbol on it.

He pressed his upper arm to his side. "Do your worst."

That earned him a distracted smile as she unrolled the first stretchy bandage. "I think I'll need to use both. These are designed for a knee or some such. Your chest and arm together are wide, especially when you're wearing the parka."

Zach held still as she stretched the bandage over his arm just above the elbow, then across his back and chest. There wasn't much overlap, but she fastened it securely, then duplicated her effort with the second bandage.

"I'm not sure it'll hold if you yank against it," she said doubtfully.

"I'll try to be good."

"You inspire me with confidence."

Hearing her teasing, he smiled again. "I have my moments."

Her chuckle warmed him. "Wait—I think there's some cord left that's about the right length."

She was right. He just hoped they could untie the sturdier cord when they needed to.

With his movements even more hindered, Zach was irritated to discover how little help he could give her, even with something as simple as lifting her pack and slipping her arms through the straps.

She didn't say anything when he set out again, figuring he should pick out a path given his vastly lighter and stronger snowshoes. Plucky as she was, she stayed close behind, although she had at least a couple of mishaps in the next few minutes, judging from her under-her-breath grumbling. He probably swore a couple of times himself as he adjusted to the even more limited range of motion, as well as moments of double vision.

He'd been right, fortunately; maybe ten minutes later, he saw their tracks veer up gradually to cross the formerly open bowl of land. Those tracks ended abruptly at the edge of the now impassable mass of snow, rocks and ice.

Which would slow their pursuers down considerably if they came this way.

Zach would have said that he and Ava had

been unbelievably lucky, except their survival wasn't all due to chance. Contrary to his original incredulity at the sight of a lone woman traveling in these mountains, Ava had planned well. She'd escaped the avalanche because she'd made the smart choice to prepare, and had had the presence of mind to trigger her airbag. *He'd* survived because of her determination—and because she'd brought the probe and folding shovel she'd needed to find and dig him out.

He liked everything that told him about her.

Zach gave a last, frustrated look back, wishing there'd been some way he could have held on to that damned pack, and told himself to give it up.

With the going becoming easier, he waved her ahead of him. This way he didn't have to constantly look back to judge her pace and see whether she was struggling. She was unlikely to notice his brief stops to clear the dizziness.

Initially glad they both wore parkas and pants in shades of green and gray that blended with the foliage, he began to wish they wore white, like the men on the ridge had. Zach had seen a documentary about the Tenth Mountain Division fighting in World War II. They'd been mobile in conditions not so different from this on Nordic skis and wearing white from head to boot. They would have moved through a blizzard like ghosts. He wondered if the terrorists—or only one terrorist and a pack of mercenaries to escort him—had gotten the idea from those mountain troops, but doubted it. All you had to do was study photos of this daunting country, glaciated and snow swathed, to see you'd blend in the best clothed in white.

Unfortunately, Ava hadn't had the least warning of any danger, and even Zach hadn't taken very seriously his buddy's suggestion he watch for anyone looking like they'd gone cross country over the Canadian border. What were the odds?

He was still stunned. There had to be hundreds, thousands, of easier places to slip across the border. Short of taking the same risks in the Rocky Mountains around Glacier National Park, this had to be one of the more challenging routes.

Which also made it one of the least patrolled, of course, especially at this time of year with the backcountry closed.

Even as he watched Ava struggle ahead of him and tried to block out his own pain, Zach did his best to frame a plan that might allow them to survive. The options were few, and shaky, unless Borisyuk and company used their heads and ran for it.

Unfortunately, his gut said that was unlikely.

PICK UP MY FOOT. *Now the other one. Left. Right.*

Ava focused her entire concentration on each step. It reminded her of swimming laps, when she counted how many she'd done. It worked like meditation, she'd always thought: *ten, ten, ten*—flip turn—*eleven, eleven, eleven.* No room for stress.

Left. Right.

At least now she had tracks to follow.

She had no idea how much time had passed when Zach spoke to her back. "Let's take a quick break to talk."

Surprised, she came close to stumbling but managed to right herself. There wasn't any place to sit down here; the vegetation was thick. Ava laboriously turned herself to see him looking grimmer than she liked. She hoped the expression was a result of the pain getting to him versus him having heard or seen something—

"I've been thinking."

Her heartbeat quickened.

"I'm betting they split up. Possibly the main group moved on, but sent two or three men to make sure no one survived the avalanche."

She could only stare at him.

"Those men might have started descending the ridge, but it would have been extremely difficult going. Impossible in the dark, even if they have headlamps. Either they somehow set up camp partway down—and it couldn't have been very comfortable—or they used their heads and didn't begin the descent until first light. Which means they'll be well behind us even though we didn't set off until this morning. They'll take some time to try to find evidence of anyone surviving."

"Which they will immediately."

He nodded. "Our tracks. I thought about trying to wipe them out, but it would have been painfully slow. And once the men reached the trail on their way to rejoin their group, they'd have seen that two people are moving ahead of them. They'll be able to move one hell of a lot faster than we can, too."

"But...why wouldn't they have all gone on?" She was begging, but couldn't help herself.

Muscles bunched in his jaw. "As I said before, I really doubt Grigor Borisyuk would be willing to leave a witness alive. On top of that, as a group, they were counting on going unseen. They may not have known there are stretches burned in recent forest fires where they'd be exposed. Why would they, unless they'd looked at Google images? As it is, suddenly they realized that not only had they been noticed, but the person watching them wasn't just seeing small figures from a great distance. She had the kind of lens that meant she *really* saw them. Put yourself in their shoes. They'd be desperate to get under cover. What if she—and that's assuming they realized you're a woman—was in radio contact with someone? If a spotting plane or helicopter passed over, they'd be dead ducks or else have to take actions—say, shoot down a helicopter—that would bring even more attention to them. I believe they scuttled for tree cover, then decided to descend from the ridge to make sure the avalanche took care of you."

Ava didn't know what to say. She'd led a more adventurous life than most people, but none of that had involved human beings out to kill her. Or people who were capable of shooting down a helicopter. Thank God Zach had been close enough behind her yesterday! Otherwise, she'd be alone, unaware that the men up on the ridge had triggered the avalanche, never mind that one of them was a terrorist hunted throughout the free world. She might have figured out an even more primitive snowshoe design and set out to head back down the valley, but when those strange men caught up with her, she'd have no idea that they intended to kill her.

A shudder rattled her, one Zach saw. His eyes narrowed. "Ava?"

"You don't think they saw you."

"I doubt it." He hesitated. "Once they spot our tracks, though..."

They'd know there were two of them.

She nodded numbly. "It still looks like it might snow." But it hadn't. She let that go. "You're saying we need to really hurry."

He was watching her intently as he hesitated. "Yes, for now. If we keep moving, I doubt they can catch up with us today. The closer we can get to being able to call for help, the better."

She was torturously slow. It was like the turtle and the hare. No, a bicyclist on the freeway being chased by a sports car that didn't even have to exceed the speed limit to go sixty miles in an hour to the cyclist's...what? Five miles? Ten?

Zach had to know how far they really were from being able to call anyone at all. But that had to be their goal. If they could reach a point where the vee of the valley widened and a few alternate trails separated from the main one, she wouldn't feel quite so trapped.

"Then...then you think we can hide?" she asked.

"I hope I can find someplace off the trail to set up camp for the night."

And then what?

His expression hardened. "After that, at some point my goal will be to hide *you*. If I can take down even one of those men, I'll be armed. I may be able to arm you. That changes the odds."

Horrified, she opened her mouth, then closed it. Those odds sounded *abysmal* to her. She decided not to bother pointing out that she'd never in her life fired a gun, and she wouldn't remind him that he was already injured. So he'd been a soldier; how much combat experience did Zach actually have?

"I hate that idea," she said, straight out, "but I don't have any alternative to suggest."

A nerve twitched in his cheek and his eyes softened. "I'm not wild about it, either, but I think our only chance is to go on the offensive."

She lifted her chin. "Right now, we'd better get moving."

"Afraid so."

Ava shuffled back around so that she was pointing south, more or less, and picked up her right foot. Then left.

Trying to run would be a mistake, she felt

sure, but she was in good physical condition. She'd increase her pace.

Right foot. Left. Right.

He'd seen how she blanched at his plan, but clearly, crumbling in fear wasn't in Ava Brevick's nature. He should have asked whether she'd done any target shooting, but he could do that later. It was safe to say that a wildlife photographer didn't hunt wildlife as a hobby, which meant any experience she had handling guns was extremely limited.

That didn't mean she wouldn't pull a trigger if she had to.

Don't get ahead of yourself, he reminded himself. *Keep a sharp eye out, both ahead and behind. Think about how an unarmed man could set up an ambush.* Once he had her in hiding, he'd have her remove the ace bandages and cords strapping his arm to his body. It would be bad if the arm left the shoulder socket again because he hadn't given it time to heal, but sometimes you just had to gamble.

He couldn't help second-guessing himself. If they could have stayed completely hidden at the foot of the avalanche, maybe the group would have been satisfied and gone on their way. Sure, he and Ava would have been short on food, but humans could go on for a long time with nothing to eat.

Only—what if they'd made a single mistake? Say, missed a track one or the other of them had made below the foot of the avalanche? Dropped something from Ava's pack?

We'd be dead.

If the terrorists hadn't headed south on the ridge as fast as they could go, which was the smart thing to do, he reminded himself.

Ava fell in front of him. Zach helped her up and crouched to examine her snowshoe, pulling off his gloves to tighten the strap designed to hold her boot in place. Straightening, he said, "I wish..." but made himself break off.

His father would have growled, *Wishes are horses, boy, and you don't know how to ride. Life's hard. You need to be hard, too.*

He shook his head slightly. *Thanks, Dad.* No, his father had never, in Zach's memory, been anything Zach would call loving, kind, supportive. He hadn't ditched the kids he didn't seem to have any use for, though, and maybe the toughness he'd taught had been useful, in the end. Someday Zach would have to ask his brother and sister what they thought about it.

"You wish?" Ava prompted softly.

"Nothing helpful, I'm afraid."

She offered him a twisted smile. "I wish, too." Then she set out again, giving no indication she'd twisted a knee or ankle during any of these falls, or was suffering from the massive bruising she must have acquired courtesy of being flung down a long, steep slope by a behemoth of snow and ice.

Chapter Six

Every hour or two, he insisted they stop. She moved steadily, but he watched for tiny falters and would call a break. He chafed at their speed, but wasn't sure he'd have done that much better on his own without full use of his upper body. Twice he took more ibuprofen, too, for what good it did—especially since it exacerbated his nausea—and insisted she swallow some, too. He was grateful for all her preparations, especially the fact that she'd tossed a full bottle of pain reliever into her pack.

At what he deemed to be lunchtime, he spotted a decent place for them to sit down.

"We'd better have a bite to eat," he said.

"I'm...not really hungry."

If she was lying because she worried about them running out of food, that was one thing. If she really *wasn't* hungry, that was cause to worry given their extreme energy expenditure.

What if she, too, had suffered a head injury she hadn't mentioned?

He was the one to dig in her pack for the individual packets of nuts and dried fruits. He opened one of each for her and poured them into her gloved hand. She stared down incomprehensibly for a minute, then to his relief started to eat.

He followed suit, chasing down a couple of bites with a drink of water before handing her the bottle.

For a moment, he only listened to the silence. The sky felt heavier, almost oppressive, but not a single flake of snow had yet fallen.

"You travel a good part of the year?" he asked, going for conversational in part to hide his intense curiosity.

"Oh…more like three or four months out of the year. Choosing and editing the photos I want to use is time-consuming, and I have to market myself, too."

"Where do you live?"

"Right now, Colorado." Her shoulders moved. "I spend some time with…a friend in Maine." Her pause was almost infinitesimal. "Whales have become something of a specialty of mine. Oh, and my roommate from college is in Florida."

Was the friend in Maine a man? Ridiculous to dislike the idea so intensely.

All he let himself say was, "So when you need a little sunshine…?"

Her expression had become livelier. "Exactly. Plus…lots of wildlife in Florida."

He groaned and stretched. "I hate to say it—"

"No, you're right." She hastily zipped up her pack, eased herself into it and stood. "We shouldn't have stopped."

"I'm the one who insisted," he said mildly.

"I know, but… You'd be faster without me. Don't deny it. I'm fine, though. I can keep going as long as we need to."

"Yeah." He was already talking to her back as she took a first step, lifting her foot in that crude snowshoe high. He even believed her.

HER ENTIRE BODY HURT. Every bruise, every wrenched joint, every insulted muscle made themselves felt. Ava tried to remember the fluid stride that carried her along before. She capitalized the word: *Before*. It was as if she was a different woman now, in the After. Desperately fleeing for her life.

Right foot. Left. Right.

Trusting a man. A stranger.

No choice.

Her chest burned, her every breath seared until it froze as she released it. Her shoulders... She didn't even want to think about her shoulders. Half the time, the pole sank too deep, making her lurch; she stabbed each one forward, preparing for the next stride, with growing trepidation.

Her thighs and even her butt burned, too. Her feet and ankles hurt, which was new; having to lift the makeshift snowshoes higher than usual wasn't part of her practiced stride, the one that worked for snowshoeing as well as it did for running.

Right foot. Left. Right. Left.

She clung to the mantra, using it to—mostly—drown out the pain. The fear, too. Because this was all she *could* do: keep going, as fast as possible without breaking one of the snowshoes and slowing them down for as long as it would take Zach to make a new one.

She kept her teeth clenched, too, to hold back the faintest of whimpers. He was certainly stronger than her, but the shoulder injury trumped all her relatively minor aches and pains. And he had those, too, Ava didn't doubt. Maybe more than that. A couple of times, she'd thought his eyes looked as dazed as they had when she first dug him out of the snow. He did some odd blinking, too. Whatever was bothering him, she hadn't heard a single groan or bout of muffled swearing coming from back there.

"It's snowing."

Right. Left. Right.

She picked up her left foot, then had to think before she set it down. Her rhythm was broken. What had he just said?

She blinked a few times. A big, fat snowflake drifted down toward her nose. Going cross-eyed, she watched it continue on its way until it settled on her parka, remaining visible for a long moment.

Ava raised her face to the sky and saw not just a few stray flakes of snow descending, but enough to muffle the impact of the green of the trees surrounding them.

She twisted in place, so she didn't have to bother laboriously shifting her snowshoes. "It's snowing!"

His grin blazed at her. "Didn't believe me, huh?"

"Oh, my God! I *can't* believe it."

He shuffled forward until he was almost stepping on the back of her snowshoes, reached a big, gloved hand around her nape and planted an exuberant quick, kiss on her mouth. "Someone is on our side."

Shaking off the effect of his cold lips, warm

breath and the smile that made her heart jump, Ava said, "I hope it keeps on and buries our tracks."

"But doesn't drop two or three feet and bury *us*."

She wrinkled her nose.

Zach nodded ahead. "I hate to say it—"

She hated it every time he said that, but nodded. They had to keep moving, take advantage of being able to follow their own track as long as possible, because if the snow continued to fall, eventually they'd lose it. After that, finding the trail at all would be as hard as it had been when she traversed it days ago. Harder, if the snow kept falling, reducing visibility.

As she took the first step and then the second—*right, left, right again*—she wished vengefully that the men who might or might not be pursuing them weren't used to traveling on foot in a snowy, mountainous landscape.

Although... Russia had plenty of that, didn't it? Why couldn't this group have come from a sunbaked part of the world where the biggest challenge from nature was sandstorms?

THEY KEPT MOVING as long as Zach thought they dared. Longer. Not only couldn't he see any hint of a track ahead now, the quality of light was changing. He found it harder to make out the falling snow against the deepening sky.

The entire way, he searched their surroundings for a possible open spot well off the trail that wouldn't be painfully obvious to a passerby. A couple of times, he made some effort to give the impression they might have turned off, if only to briefly slow down any pursuers. He had no trouble catching up with Ava, and he wasn't even sure she'd noticed what he was doing.

They had crossed a stretch that was more open than he liked—a long-ago remnant of another avalanche or wildfire—then plunged back into the more typical, tangled vegetation he was really growing to detest. At the moment, he couldn't see or hear the river, although it lay off to their right.

He still hadn't picked up anything from behind them, but Ava was noticeably flagging when he finally saw what he'd been looking for.

"Hold up," he said.

She stopped so fast, he almost stepped on the tails of her snowshoes.

"Let me check this out." He stepped cautiously toward the river, able to slide between a thick growth of willows and alders and heaven knows what else. He bet this was, or had been, a game trail. Not obvious, but passable. If he could find a flat place large enough for them to set up the tent...

Ten minutes within what felt like a frozen jungle, he saw what he sought. He poked with his crude poles. No, this wasn't flat ground perfect for a campsite; there seemed to be a snarl of dormant growth below the snow, but he wasn't feeling real picky about where he laid his—their—sleeping bag right now, and he bet Ava would agree. Some nice, low branches of the cedar he'd just circled would veil them from anyone more than a few feet away, just as they'd been in last night's campsite.

He tipped his head, picking up the murmur of running water. A distant *crack* was easily identifiable, too: a branch breaking beneath a heavy load of wet snow. They'd hear that sound all night. Speaking of—

He took out the knife he'd pilfered from her pack and cut off a couple of stiff cedar branches.

Carrying them, remaining careful with each step, he made his way back to Ava.

"I found a place to set up camp for the night. I'd like to not break any of the vegetation—" he gripped some shrubby alder in his gloved hands "—if we can help it. I could carry you—"

She set her jaw. "Don't be silly."

"Okay. Follow my track."

She did, every movement exaggerated, gingerly. Satisfied, he turned to go backward, following her and using his branches to obliterate the tracks they were laying. Bending over, a couple of times he felt close to passing out. Had to be done. At the rate the snow still fell, he felt sure that within half an hour, their passage would no longer be visible.

By the time he caught up with her, satisfied, she'd slipped her feet from the snowshoes, set them against a nearby branch, removed her pack and taken out a tarp to lay across the snow. Tent next. She didn't argue when he helped her erect the thing, although it was easier than any tent he'd ever slept in. She half crawled in and unrolled the thin foam pad. Despite everything, he admired her taut butt in tight-fitting pants as it waggled before she turned for the sleeping bag. He set his snowshoes right next to hers and, one-handed, hauled the pack inside the tent.

Darkness had been falling with astonishing speed. Already he had trouble making out her features with any clarity. Last night, he'd had too much on his mind to be as aware of how cramped the quarters were. He couldn't shrink himself, but he suspected she wouldn't have cared if they'd had half the space.

He sat his butt down on the foot of the sleeping bag, letting her take the top. "Now if we just had a Jacuzzi."

"Room service."

He grimaced. "I'd settle for a hot shower." Yeah, he felt sure he didn't smell sweet right now. He'd worry more, except she'd been at least as long away from a last shower or bath as he was.

For what had to be a couple of minutes, neither of them moved or spoke. He felt as if they were inside a room designed and built to be soundproof. His eardrums felt odd.

"I'm starved," Ava said. "Do you think we can use the stove?"

"Yeah. We can set it up right at the opening here. We could both use an actual meal. We need—" He broke off. He didn't have to tell her that they needed to be strong tomorrow. For the moment, they could revel in the release in tension.

Assuming that was possible when stopping made him aware of every aching muscle, as well as the deep throbbing in his abused shoulder. At least his head was grateful for his stillness.

"Can you help me unwrap my arm?" he asked.

"Oh! Sure. It actually held all day."

He smiled crookedly at her. "It did. Solid construction."

Her laugh made him feel triumphant.

She scooted close to him, peeled off her gloves and picked apart the cord and then unfastened the two ace bandages. Then she very carefully rolled them up again before setting them aside.

He might let her put them back on in the morning—he thought he'd had some relief from the limited range of motion—but he couldn't hamper himself when he went on the offensive, so maybe it wasn't worth wearing them for what, if they were lucky, might be only a few hours.

Zach had no doubt that tomorrow was the day.

Unless, of course, he reminded himself for the umpteenth time, the whole party had stayed along the ridge and either continued on their merry way, or set up in wait for the survivor(s) of the avalanche. In that case, he guessed he and Ava would meet up with Borisyuk and company the day after tomorrow.

He needed to prepare for either possibility, but his gut said somebody was tracking them already.

Zach reluctantly gave her permission to do the cooking. Ava hid rolled eyes from him.

Sensing how intensely protective he felt for her, she wouldn't wish herself in this situation with a different kind of man. Or alone, God forbid. On the other hand, she wondered how controlling Zach would be on a day-to-day basis in normal life. Did he ever let up?

Well, she'd never find out. This intense closeness was temporary. It wasn't as if they had any kind of relationship that would go anywhere. They'd part ways; him back to western Washington, her to Colorado. Home, only it didn't quite feel that way.

All of this was assuming they both survived the next several days, of course.

She didn't even ask him for his meal preference, given how limited options were. She freeze-dried the meals for trips herself, and was rather proud of how good she'd gotten at it. Tonight, they were having teriyaki chicken with brown rice.

Zach thanked her when she handed him her one dish and a fork, leaving her to eat out of the pan using a spoon. He took a bite and looked up.

"Damn, this is good. Doesn't taste much like the MREs I'm used to."

"I'm assuming that's the military version of my meals?"

"Yeah." He took a couple more bites, obviously savoring each one. "In theory, they're better than they used to be. In practice... I'd usually prefer just about anything else."

"What kind of soldier were you?" she asked. "Or...no, I suppose you'd have said sailor if you'd been navy."

"Or airman if I'd served in the air force," he agreed. "I was an army ranger in the regiment that does special operations."

Her lips formed the words "spec ops."

"Yeah, constant action. We were...inserted in some pretty dangerous places. Rescued hostages, accomplished raids, gathered intel. I... lost a few too many friends, came back from a final injury—" he rotated his right arm—the good one—in remembrance "—and decided it was time to get out."

She just watched him.

"Which is easier said than done. They warn you, but you shrug it off."

Why was he being so open with her? Because he suspected they wouldn't live, and wanted to connect with her, the last person he could spend time with?

If that was so...she understood. Even felt the same impulse. Why hide anything from this man? Maybe...it would be freeing, to talk about some of the bad stuff. Part of her wished she could see his face, but that would mean he could see hers, and maybe talking was easier in the dark.

"Why the military?" she asked.

"My mother died when I was eight years old. Dad was career military. A colonel." Wryness sounded in his voice. "When I was being rebellious, I talked about college. He sneered at eggheads. Useless. The first to go down if violence erupted."

"Except that they invented most products he used, including weaponry," she pointed out.

"Try telling my father that."

"He's alive?"

"Yeah. We don't see much of each other. I do stay in touch with my brother and sister."

He fell quiet, leaving her to fill in the blanks, of which there were many.

After a minute, she said, "I think I'll just use snow to wipe these dishes out. We should try to refill the bottle in the morning." When he asked, she agreed that she had some purifier tablets.

Naturally, she rejected his offer to clean up, and he conceded, letting her crawl past him and do the task. Out of the corner of his eye, she saw him lift his newly injured arm and rotate it. He caught her eye, and said, "I have a better range of motion than I would have expected. Binding my arm today was the right thing to do. With a little luck, by morning the soreness will be reduced."

She and Zach took turns to find some privacy outside before each, in turn, scrambled back into the tent. The snow still fell, although she thought more slowly now. The temperature had definitely dropped with nightfall, though. What was spring down below sure as hell wasn't here.

When he started peeling off clothes, she pretended she didn't notice. They'd slept together last night. Why she felt nervous tonight, she had no idea.

Because he'd kissed her?

Maybe, although she didn't think he'd intended it in a sexual way. She *had* seen him watching her in a way that definitely was sexual and made her tingle, though, so she shouldn't discount the kiss.

They had absolutely no choice but to sleep together. Listening to the rustles as he slid into the bag, she undressed, too. He rolled over to let her lay her clothes atop his, then rolled back over, holding the bag invitingly open.

She slithered in, squirming until she was *almost* comfortable. He was able to zip up the sleeping bag tonight, after which he adjusted her position to suit him. She'd have complained, except she was definitely comfier.

Warmer, too. His big body radiated heat in a way hers didn't.

"Okay?" he murmured.

"Mmm-hmm."

As tired as she was, she couldn't imagine falling asleep immediately. She'd never been so aware of a man's body stretched out against hers, even on the few occasions she'd let anyone get that close. Of course, she wanted to move, to rub against him, to—

She told herself to knock it off. This was nothing but a reaction to the possibility that they might both die tomorrow. *Have some pride.*

Anyway, *he* wasn't doing a thing but lying there, his breathing completely even. He was no closer to sleep than she was.

"Tell me about you," he said after a moment. "Is this friend in Maine a guy?"

Talking. What could be a better distraction?

"No. Eileen is—" Oh, why not just tell him? "We went through two foster homes together. Aged out of the system and graduated from high school together, too. We've...stayed close."

"How long were you in the foster care system?" The low rumble of his voice, felt as well as heard, was more comforting than she would ever have expected.

"From the time I was a feral seven-year-old on. Nobody considered me adoptable, and I was difficult enough, so I got moved over and over."

She couldn't miss the sudden tension in the muscles supporting and enclosing her. "Feral?"

Ava had never, as an adult, told anyone this.

"My mother had drug problems. She just didn't come back one day. I…waited for a long time, then finally went looking for her. I was on my own for a while. Maybe as much as a year. No one, including me, knows. Turns out everyone assumed she and I had taken off, so nobody was looking for me. The house was vacant, after all. I was…too scared to look for help, I think. The stuff we left behind, well, no one would want it, anyway. Mom had never enrolled me in school. I didn't know any adults who weren't addicts. A cop pounced on me one day. I kept the picture they took of me when he hauled me in. I was skin and bones and filthy, and had this wild bush of hair. I hardly looked human."

After a long, fraught silence, Zach said in a constrained voice, "I've seen kids like that. In other parts of the world."

She bobbed her head, knowing he'd feel that. "Well, I got cleaned up, tutored so I caught up in school. Humanized. You know. Still, Eileen was the first person I really bonded with, and we were both fourteen by then. She'd been abused. I guess...we understood each other. That foster home wasn't so great, but a social worker rescued us, and we spent our last three years with a really great older couple. It gave me an idea what home might feel like."

"You still in touch with them?"

"Yes." John and Alice still treated the two of them like daughters, just way younger than their biological ones. They meant a lot to Ava, had maybe been her salvation.

"And the photography?"

"That was actually from an earlier foster home. The wife was a news photographer for a local paper. She saw how interested I was and gave me my first camera. I was hooked. At the time, it was way better than phone cameras. I never looked back."

It was true. She still thought about Jennifer long after most of her foster parents' faces and names had blurred. Someday, she should get in touch with her to say thanks, even if Jennifer and her husband had dumped Ava, too, at the first hint of problems.

"I want to hurt somebody for you," Zach said, in a voice that wasn't quite as expressionless as he probably intended, "but it's way too late, isn't it?"

"Yes. I'm…okay."

"Are you?" he asked softly, but not as if he expected an answer.

She didn't give him one.

Chapter Seven

Zach tipped his head back to look up at the sky. A few snowflakes still drifted down. Any and all tracks had been obscured the evening before, which was both good news and bad. His and Ava's pace was even slower this morning. He'd taken the lead instead of letting her risk her flimsy, primitive snowshoes.

Yes, anyone behind them would be moving slowly, too, but they were better equipped. He bet every single man they'd seen on that ridgetop was in excellent physical condition, prepared for winter travel in the backcountry. Unless somebody had taken a fall, none were injured, either.

He'd hoped the effects of what had to have been a concussion would have relented by this morning, but no such luck. There wasn't a damn thing he could do about it besides take the ibuprofen. That, and try to block out knowledge of his headache, a dull backdrop to the sharper shoulder pain. He consoled himself with the fact that the nausea hadn't recurred since yesterday afternoon.

He and Ava forged on for one hour, two, three. He kept an eye on his watch, glad he'd worn one. Sometime during the second hour he'd begun to feel an unpleasant but all-too-familiar itch crawling up his spine to his neck. He wanted to blame his imagination, but couldn't. He'd relied on this same feeling countless times over his years in dangerous parts of the world. It had saved his butt, and the lives of others in his unit, because he didn't let himself brush it off.

He felt like crap, but it was still time to set his plan into motion, he decided. Like yesterday, he kept a sharp eye out for anyplace he could stash Ava.

Fifteen minutes later, he thought he'd found it.

He said quietly, "Hold up," and made sure she'd stopped and sagged forward with her weight on the poles to rest. She must've guessed what he was going to do.

As he had last night, he left the trail, doing his best to stay on top of all the low-growing, tangled growth beneath the snow that wanted to snag his snowshoes, while pushing through the ubiquitous willows and alder and branches of smaller evergreens. Once again, he moved with extra care so as not to break a branch that would catch the eye of anyone looking for signs of human passage. An enormous log, the tree a real old-timer, had fallen about twenty feet from the trail. Given that it hadn't yet rotted enough to start service as a nurse log for countless seedling trees, he'd been lucky to notice it. What he was hoping…

Where the roots would once have been torn from the earth, he started probing with one of his poles. It immediately plunged deep. *Yes*. He couldn't feel any shrubbery filling in the hole yet, either. Probably it had come down as recently as this winter.

He turned and realized he could barely see Ava where she waited. The trick would be wiping out any trace of her passage—and his both going and coming. He hoped she wasn't given to flashbacks, since he'd have to leave her sunken in a well filled with snow, but he had faith in her resilience.

"This will do," he said aloud.

"Should I…?"

He'd carry her, he decided. He suspected her snowshoes wouldn't hold up to easing through such thick growth. They couldn't afford for her to fall and break branches off.

"Wait for me," he called, and began gingerly edging his way back to her.

It probably wasn't even noon yet, he realized. Maybe they could go on farther...but if he were Borisyuk, he wouldn't tolerate less than his own zeal in his underlings. Once again, Zach had deemed it futile to try to erase the tracks he and Ava had made.

The tracks between the trail where she waited and where he planned to stow her—those, he thought he could make less noticeable. Once he set out on his own, all he had to do was shuffle a little here and there to make it appear as if there were still two of them.

Or, he'd turn around and go back. He'd seen a couple of places that he thought would lend themselves to the ambush he had in mind.

Any way you looked at it, this was a long shot. His only real chance was if they'd sent a scout on ahead, knowing how much noise a group their size would make.

One man he could take out. Seven or eight at the same time, no.

The fact that there was only one path they could have taken made him and Ava incredibly vulnerable. On the other hand, short of continuing on the ridge, the bad guys had the same limitation.

He was gambling that he had guessed right,

and Borisyuk had sent only two or three men down to check out the avalanche while the rest of them proceeded on the planned route. It made sense. Delivering Borisyuk safely into the US was the primary goal, chasing what might turn out to be shadows secondary.

He still suspected that the main group would be waiting at the foot of the river valley. But Zach had enough confidence to believe that, if he could whittle the numbers down and, by so doing, arm and provision the two of them, he and Ava would have a good chance. How much actual combat experience would a group of mercenaries have? If they had any, it might have been gained invading Ukraine, and that wasn't the kind of warfare that would serve them here.

Right now...he had to go with his gut, and he had to give Ava the best chance to live if he couldn't return to her.

SO FOCUSED ON plodding forward—*left, right, left*—Ava had almost forgotten Zach's intentions until he'd ordered her to stop. When he emerged from the entangled growth to tell her he would be leaving her here, terror choked her.

"But—"

The expression in his dark eyes was both

kind and implacable. "We talked about this. There are not a lot of choices here."

"But...they could kill you."

"People have tried before. Now, come on."

He insisted on carrying first the pack then her through that vicious, scratchy growth. No man had ever slung her up in his arms like this. She wanted to struggle, knowing he couldn't feel much better than she did, but only held on tight to limit how much of her weight he had to support with his left arm. She kept her eyes fixed on his throat and stubbled jaw, which were generally not revealing. Once he set her back on her feet, she couldn't see what he had in mind.

"There's a big hole here." He stabbed his pole in a few times to demonstrate. "See that root bole there? It was torn out of the ground. This hole could be six or eight feet deep, maybe more. We're going to dig out enough for you to make a nest, then I'll build a wall of snow and try to make it look natural. If they're not familiar with old-growth forests, they won't know what they're looking at."

"And... I just *wait*? I don't understand how you think you can overcome even one heavily armed man, never mind several!" Did that sound hysterical? She didn't care. "You're hurt. I can tell."

"I know what I'm doing. Trust me."

Ava didn't argue for long. She grasped the shovel and began to dig out a mountain of soft snow, trying to envision the hole as an igloo.

"Let me look through your pack," he said absently, as if he might find—what?—a 9mm handgun she'd forgotten to mention? All she saw him pocket were the remaining pieces of line, a couple of stretchy bungee cords, the telescoped probe and, once he was satisfied at the depth of the hole, the shovel. Then, rising to his feet, he looked at her.

"Spread the tarp as a bottom layer. Wrap yourself in the sleeping bag. Use extra clothes if you have to. Staying warm will be your biggest challenge." His gaze was intense. "Nibble on food. Be quiet, whether you hear anything that worries you or not. Got it?"

"Yes, but—"

"I'll come back for you."

She had to ask, her voice on the verge of cracking. "What if you can't? How long do I wait?"

His mouth tightened. "At least today. Better through tomorrow. By that time, my guess is they'll have given up looking for you."

"Then why don't both of us—"

He shook his head. "They know by now that *someone* is ahead of them. If they get their hands on me, they may decide they weren't following two people after all. How could they ever find you?"

"But—"

"We need weapons if we're going to make it."

Hearing no give at all, Ava gritted her teeth to keep them from chattering. This was the worst thing he could have asked her to do, but he was right. She'd be a hindrance rather than a help when it came to trying to take down an armed combatant. He'd be so worried about her, he wouldn't be able to concentrate on what he needed to do.

"Yes. Okay."

He took her hand, presumably intending to help lower her into the pit, but went very still.

"Ava."

The intensity in his eyes was still there, but now he was utterly focused on her face. His gaze flicked to her lips. He bent slowly.

She suddenly wanted nothing so much in the world as for him to kiss her. Grabbing his parka with both hands, she pushed up on tiptoe. She met his mouth clumsily, but didn't care. Despite the cold, and the fact that he wore heavy gloves, he cupped her jaw and tipped her head to an angle that let him warm her lips, taste them, part them. She welcomed his tongue, tried to block out everything but this moment.

Which worked until he groaned, took his mouth from hers and leaned his forehead on hers instead.

"Ava." His chest rose and fell fast, hard. "We have to do this."

Her eyes burned, and she averted her face. "I know." As an excuse to avoid looking at him, she slid down into the hole, pulled the tarp from her pack and spread it, then sat down.

He already had the shovel in his hand, and in mere moments had shaped the pile of snow from the hole into a long, smooth rampart that even from her perspective could have been new-fallen snow atop a log.

He looked down at her, and it was all she could do not to let him see her fear.

"Be careful," she whispered.

He nodded, said, "I'll be back," and disappeared.

She heard him for a few minutes, brushing the snow so that no one could detect the path back out to the main trail.

And then she was alone in a hole that could have been dug out for a coffin.

ZACH DECIDED TO go back the way they'd come. When the first guy he intended to take on saw the returning track, he'd guess the person, or two people, he was pursuing had hit an impassable obstacle and were seeking another route. Since the actual trail was buried under snow, it would be easy to wander off it.

Except that those opportunities were few and far between, given the rampant growth in a river valley deep in a temperate rainforest. But one thing Zach felt sure of: these guys weren't from around here.

He hesitated briefly at the first spot he'd seen to believably turn off. Part of him wanted to go on, to set up this confrontation as far as possible from Ava, but he couldn't risk suddenly coming face-to-face with one of these guys. Plus, he needed to hoard his strength as much as he could.

The way was initially easy enough; he guessed it was a kind of spur off the main trail. Could be an animal trail, or ground worn by the feet of hikers deciding to take a break and have a bite to eat at a particularly pretty place beside the small, tumbling river.

He walked as far as the river bank, then circled around to set up by a particularly bushy group of small trees to serve as a blind. His chosen location was out of sight of the main trail—its other primary benefit.

Once he set out on the hunt, he became the soldier he'd once been, emotions buried, his mind occupied with imagining every possible outcome to every choice he made. In the end, he was left with his original plan.

He constructed his snare out of a couple of whips of willows, pulled across the way and knotted to the base of other wiry growth. Just in case his prey didn't fall for the first trap—he'd have to lift his snowshoes extra high at that particular spot—Zach crouched a couple of feet farther on to lay a second snare with one of the bungee cords he'd taken from Ava's pack. Then he stood to shake a couple of strategically placed evergreen boughs so that snow tumbled over the snares. Just enough to hide them. Natural seeming. If he or Ava had come this way, they could easily have brushed those branches. A deer could have done the same.

Then he chose where to wait, ready to spring. When the moment came, he couldn't hesitate. A single shot taken would alert all of those *other* heavily armed men, up and down the valley.

Zach was going to do his hunting as silently as was humanly possible.

IF YOU LEARNED one thing in special ops, it was patience. Hide or disguise yourself, and wait. The bursts of violence or hurry-up-and-go were scattered between long periods of waiting. He hadn't felt the humming tension in a long time, but it was familiar.

Eyes and ears sharp, he allowed his mind to drift, mainly to Ava but also to Borisyuk's agenda. Was he here for a single assassination, a death that would throw government and politics into disarray, or a high-ranking military officer whose insights and influence had become inconvenient for whomever had hired an assassin? Or had he been brought here for his bomb-making skills, the intended targets more plentiful?

Zach did wonder, and not for the first time, whether he could have imagined seeing the sought-after terrorist in that photo. If he hadn't just been shown the one-and-only previous photo of the guy and been asked to watch for him, would he have taken such a wild leap?

Since he had plenty of time, he ran through the same logic, the same arguments, that had convinced him in the first place. An especially distinctive face. The weaponry those men carried. That they'd fired an RPG to take out an innocent backcountry snowshoer who was no threat to them.

Because Ava's camera with the huge lens *was* a threat more significant than an automatic rifle.

Even if Zach had leaped to a conclusion about the one ugly face with singular features, why *did* those men sneak across the Canadian border into the US? What did they plan to do with more armaments than a typical army ranger unit carried? Why had they determined to set off an avalanche to take out one person who should have been too far away to disturb them? An innocent, at that?

It didn't add up to anything good.

If nobody showed up in pursuit, he might reshuffle his logic. He'd still believe somebody would be waiting for them where they emerged from the valley. And if that wasn't true—well, he'd call his buddy to show him Ava's photo.

His thoughts slipped, as they did every few minutes, to Ava. He had hated walking away from her. If he got back to find her dead because someone had stumbled on her… He wasn't sure he could live with that. This woman had gotten to him with stunning speed. She'd become a trusted teammate. But Ava was more because she was also a beautiful woman who had unhesitatingly shared the warmth of her body with him to save his life. She blushed when he betrayed his desire for her, which suggested she was having those same thoughts.

And last night, she'd decoded the mysteries of her personality for him, clawing him up inside. If she never showed him the photograph of the feral, hopeless child she'd been, it didn't matter. He could see it, blue eyes wild in the face of any of those skin-and-bone children clinging to life in war-torn parts of the globe.

He hadn't had to ask why she photographed nature and animals instead of humans. Or why photography, he thought now, defined her life.

He still didn't hear voices, however soft, or the shush-shush of snowshoes. He and Ava could have gone on for another hour or two—but if they had, he might not have found as perfect a place to hide her.

If I'm wrong... But the twang between his shoulder blades hadn't relented.

AVA HAD NEVER listened harder in her life. But then, what else could she do? Stare up at the sky, where she once saw the impossibly distant contrail of a jet, another time a bald eagle sweeping against the pale gray backdrop? Imagine the now scattered snowflakes coming more frequently? Envisioning herself, literally buried in snow, completed the horror she felt as she waited.

Would a gunshot be the first unnatural sound she heard? Careless voices as some of those men tramped past on the trail, oblivious to her presence? Or would it be her name, in Zach's velvet-deep voice?

Please let that be it.

Obedient because he was right, she made

herself nibble occasionally on peanuts and dried fruit. Sip the water that tasted of the tablet that had purified it. Keep her joints limber with small movements. Shiver and readjust so she could unroll the pad to lift her butt farther off the snow. Huddle, wrapped in the sleeping bag, and not let herself even *think* about climbing out of the hole and going looking for him.

After all, she knew how well *that* worked. She'd never uncovered so much as a trace of what had happened to her mother, not as a child, not as an adult.

But...*could* she make herself stay right here, alone, the rest of the day, and then the night, and then another day?

Ava didn't know.

Crack.

She tensed, even as she knew that wasn't a gunshot, only another tree limb giving way beneath the weight of snow. Head back, she glanced warily around, but didn't see any that would drop on her.

She heard a woodpecker at work, saw what she thought was a peregrine falcon soar overhead. A gray jay and a raven took turns sitting on a branch to study her, heads tipping first one way and then the other. Thank goodness a vulture didn't arrive to contemplate how much lifespan she had left. *Were* there any vultures in the North Cascades? She was pretty sure not, which made sense; in these perpetually damp woods, bodies decomposed quickly without help.

At that point, she descended into the kind of morose thoughts she abhorred. Still, it was probably inevitable to ask herself, who would even notice if she disappeared, never to be seen again?

Eventually Eileen, of course, but Eileen knew Ava was on assignment, off in some remote location without cell phone coverage. Post-trip she often plunged into editing her film, too, and forgot to even check voice mail. It would be a couple of months before Eileen would really worry.

Laura would wonder, of course; almost every winter Ava spent a couple of weeks with her in Florida, but they went long stretches without communicating the rest of the year. Plus, since Ava's last visit in January, Laura's boyfriend had moved in with her, which had made Ava wonder if staying with her for more than a night or two at a time wouldn't be awkward now.

John and Alice, but she'd spent Christmas with them so recently, and they, too, were used to long silences.

Some of the editors Ava worked with—except for Richard Vickers, who'd set up the funding for this trip and would be puzzled and irritated and possibly even litigious if she didn't submit the promised photos—would give her passing thought and start buying work from other photographers.

What a sad list that was. And really, did she care if a bunch of people out there wailed and beat their breasts at the word that she was presumed dead?

She gazed up at the sky, blinked away a snowflake and thought, *No*. She just wished there was one person who was more to her than an occasional phone call or visit, who would know *immediately* if something was wrong. Who truly loved her.

That wish feeling like a fist in her chest, she knew she had to try harder to open herself to relationships once she got out of here. No, there weren't a lot of men like Zach Reeves around, but maybe she could find one of them.

And then she growled, not quite silently. Oh, for gracious sake! She didn't do self-pity and wasn't going to start now. Of course she'd make it home! If she had to, she could wait as long as she needed to.

A greater truth crept into her consciousness: She had faith Zach *would* come back for her. Maybe that was foolish, when she'd known him such a short time, but this certainty felt bone deep.

Right now, the best thing she could do was hold on to it.

Chapter Eight

Zach moved often enough to keep from stiffening up. He rolled his shoulders, evaluating his pain level and dismissing it. He snacked a couple of times on dried fruit rather than the nuts he'd left with Ava; the fruit wouldn't crunch under his teeth. He hoped she was following his instructions.

One side of his mouth crooked up. "Advice" was a better word. In general, he doubted Ava was a woman who'd appreciate being given orders.

Despite himself, restlessness grew. Maybe he wasn't as patient as he used to be. Probably lucky he'd retired—

Swish, swish, swish.

He stiffened. The sound was subtle, not close. Rhythmic, though—and exactly what he'd been listening for.

Swish, swish, swish.

He turned his head, peering through branches

toward the main trail. There were no voices, not so much as a grunt. That sounded like a single snowshoer, although he might be mistaken. Would the man see the turnoff at all, or be too focused on what was directly ahead? If he did, Zach was still undecided about his course.

No, the guy couldn't be that foolish.

Swish, swish, swish. Getting closer.

Slower, too. Hesitating.

Zach rolled his shoulders, flexed his fingers a few more times and crouched.

Silence.

Then a few tentative sounds. The obvious track of one or maybe two snowshoers that Zach had laid was proving irresistible.

The swishing sound resumed, but quieter, as if the man was stepping carefully. He couldn't tiptoe, but he was doing his best. Ah, there he was, appearing around the bend. Clad in white, head to toe—yes, including the hood and cape that covered his backpack—but for the black automatic rifle slung to one side that clashed. Zach eyed the poles greedily. Those would be a big improvement.

No hint that the guy had company. If he did, they must be spread out.

Zach had already divested himself of his snowshoes. Now he peeled off his gloves and let them drop to the ground.

With a nice straight stretch ahead, the tracks leading out of sight ahead, nothing visible, the guy gained confidence and sped up.

That's it, Zach urged him on. Nice path, no reason to think about the snow that had obviously fallen from branches ahead. His prey passed him, head not turning. One snowshoe passed over the first snare, but he was sloppy lifting the back foot.

It caught, sending the man stumbling forward. He swore sharply, but not in English. Russian wasn't one of Zach's languages, but he knew the profanities from it.

He launched himself before the white-clad man could regain his balance, hitting him hard. A guttural cry escaped the man as they crashed down, Zach's weight forcing the other man to the ground. Zach had the advantage from the beginning, since the man's feet were tangled with the snowshoes and he had to release the poles to free his hands.

He twisted frantically. Zach was ready, slamming a fist into that face. Despite the fleece covering, blood spouted from the nose hole. Zach kept hammering him. The guy was groping for something beneath his parka—a gun? a knife?—but Zach drove his knee onto that arm, hearing a snap, followed by a strangled scream that gurgled from the blood that must be filling his throat.

Zach locked his arm around the Russian's neck, wrenching back to gain complete control. Instead of submitting, the man fought viciously to dislodge Zach, making him think of a hooked trout flopping on the bank. He tightened the vee of his arm just as the man bucked with his entire body. Zach heard another snap. No, felt it.

Oh, damn, he thought, sickened. Not immediately releasing the hold, he bent to let the suddenly limp body sag onto the snow to one side of the trail. He stayed cautious, pressing his fingers to where the carotid artery in the neck should be pulsing and finding nothing.

Zach rose to his knees and stared down at a man he hadn't intended to kill if he could help it. He yanked up the balaclava, seeing the face of a stranger.

He'd really have liked to question this guy. Whatever his native language, he surely wouldn't have been chosen for this trek unless he spoke English with reasonable fluency.

Also…aware of a level of discomfort, Zach realized he had acclimated more to civilian society than he'd realized. He had started thinking like a cop, not a soldier fighting terrorists in lawless parts of the world. No, he couldn't have arrested this guy. He had no cuffs, no jurisdiction, but he could have tied him up, left him with whatever he needed to stay warm and sent the border patrol back to pick him up.

That wasn't happening.

An urgent voice in Zach's head said, *Get him out of sight. He can't be alone.*

He heeded it, setting aside the rifle and removing the pack from the man's back, then putting on his own snowshoes before dragging the dead man around the back of the cedar tree, well out of sight of the trail.

Then, feeling angry and unsettled, he hefted the rifle and pack behind the tree and did the same for the snowshoes and poles. They were intact, he was glad to see. He'd expected the bindings on the snowshoe, at least, to be damaged. The man had much larger feet than Ava did, but Zach was confident he could adapt these.

He returned to the trail and found a couple of new long growths of willow or alder, flexible enough to be bent to lie level with the ground, and secured them in place. He used the shovel to do his best to erase any sign that a struggle had taken place. After brushing snow over the top of the new snare, he took a few strategic steps in his own snowshoes, making it less obvious that one set of tracks had ended rather abruptly. Finally, he backed around the tree, erasing his own tracks as he went.

No, he didn't believe for a minute that this guy had been entirely on his own. More likely one had lagged, maybe because he'd investigated an animal track. Zach hoped the companion or companions hadn't been close enough to hear that scream.

He searched the body for weapons, appropriating a wicked knife and sheath, but found nothing else of interest. Then, pausing every thirty seconds or so to listen, he employed the shovel to dig a shallow grave in the snow, roll the body into it and cover it. A predator could dig it out with no effort, but at least it wasn't immediately obvious.

Zach knelt beside the bulging pack but paused for a moment to scan himself for new and old pain. Yeah, he'd felt the hard blow to his thigh, but it wasn't anything to worry about. His shoulder…wasn't happy. He swung his arm in a full circle. It was functional; all he could ask. His head throbbed, but his vision hadn't been impacted.

Then he started his search of the pack with the outside pockets. That's where he would stow additional weapons. Worse came to worst, he *was* armed now, but what he needed to employ was guerrilla warfare, which tended to be silent. Pulling the trigger of an automatic rifle amounted to jumping up and down and waving his arms.

Here I am! Come and get me!

The first and most accessible pocket held goggles and dark glasses. Both potentially useful.

He recognized the shape of what was inside the matching pocket on the other side even before he touched it. A handgun was noisy, too, but...

He lifted it out, a grin splitting his face. Zach was glad Ava couldn't see him right now; he probably looked more like a winter-starved wolf about to bring down a caribou than the kind of man she'd ever known.

But hot damn! This was an American-made pistol with a suppressor screwed onto the barrel. It was all his Christmases wrapped into one—a nearly silent, effective way to fight their way out of the trap this deep-cut valley increasingly felt like.

He could just shoot the next SOB who came down the trail.

The breath he let out scraped in his throat. No. He couldn't do that. He'd keep it handy, though, in case his catch and—not release— hold wasn't going to work. Or if he faced *two* opponents.

He had time to take a look inside the pack, pushing aside changes of clothes to see packets of freeze-dried meals—descriptions in English, all presumably purchased at a Canadian store that equipped hikers, climbers and skiers—and lots of loose candy bars. Matches, a stove—

Swish, swish, swish.

Body aching now, Zach wished he could just arrest the next creep, haul him to lockup and go home to a hot shower, a bowl of something comforting like chicken noodle soup and the chance to lie down on a comfortable mattress in the dark until he felt better.

Instead, he crouched again in his blind, let his gloves fall to the snow at his feet and waited.

AT SOME POINT during the afternoon, Ava had lay down on her side and curled up, still clutching the sleeping bag around her, staring at the snow wall in front of her. Sitting up, keeping watch, wouldn't do her a speck of good, would it? What was she going to do, scrape her way out of this pit to attack one of those monsters with her bare hands?

Except they weren't bare, so she couldn't even use her fingernails. Which wouldn't be much use, anyway, because long, beautifully tended fingernails weren't compatible with her lifestyle.

She hadn't heard a single gunshot or voice. A snowshoe hare had hopped by, startling at the sight of her. More birds paused in branches high overhead. Once she did hear a piercing cry, as some small creature became prey. It sent a shock through her, because she felt as small, inconsequential and vulnerable as the mice and squirrels and chipmunks and hares that fed the larger predators.

The light was going, she began to realize, with a new chill of fear. Zach wouldn't wait until dark to return, would he? How would he find her?

Maybe he couldn't.

Would he dare call her name if he thought he was near?

God, she felt pathetic. She never, never wanted to be in this position again. It threw her back to that terrible time in her life when there'd been no safety anywhere for her, when *she* was the smallest, the most vulnerable.

She clenched her jaw. Zach said to wait, so that's what she'd do.

That was when she heard the swishing sound of someone approaching.

Ava strained, trying to decide which direction the person was approaching from, unable to be sure.

Whoever it was started coming directly *toward* her. Then Zach said softly, "Ava? Tell me you're here."

She let out an undignified whimper she prayed he didn't hear, and sat up. In an equally low voice that she thought came out remarkably calm, she said, "Where would I go? The mall?"

She heard his chuckle before she saw him, tall at the foot of the hole.

"We'll stay here tonight." He tossed a pair of snowshoes down and knelt to heave off a big pack. Two sets of poles followed the snowshoes, and then he lowered the pack, followed by—*gulp*—an automatic rifle.

That's when she really looked at him and saw his eyes. There was a wildness in them that made her shiver. He might sound completely self-possessed, but inside, he wasn't.

"You killed someone," she whispered.

The eyes flicked up and met hers. "Yes."

She swallowed and nodded, unable to chew him out, or not, or... What *could* she say?

Nothing.

"Let me wipe out my trail," he said, in that same, conversational tone. "Probably not necessary, but…" He vanished, and she transferred her gaze to his gleanings.

It finally registered that he had *two* sets of poles. Only one pack, but he couldn't carry more than one.

Unable to really even hear what he was doing, Ava just sat there until he reappeared, took off his snowshoes and jumped down into her hole.

"Are you okay? I was gone longer than I expected to be—"

She shook her head. "I'm—" Not bored. She hardly knew how to describe what she felt. "All right." Now she was.

He nodded and took a rolled sleeping bag from beneath stretchy bands at the top of the pack. A pad had been rolled up with it, she saw.

"You have two sets of poles." Ava hadn't even known she was going to say that.

"Yeah," he said gruffly. "I waited a long time to find out if anyone else would come along, but it appears only the two were sent on cleanup duty."

"Are they—"

"Both dead?" His eyes still didn't look right. "No. I…incapacitated the second man and left him tucked into his sleeping bag and tied up to a tree. We'll send someone back for him."

How did you "tuck" an unwilling man into a sleeping bag and then tie him up? Oh, duh—he must have been unconscious.

"I acquired quite a bit of food," he added. "Freeze-dried dinners and some desserts, too."

"Really?"

He smiled, and seemed to settle a little. "Our Russian terrorist had a sweet tooth."

Had. So he was the dead one.

"Are we really staying here for the night?"

"Where better?"

"I kept thinking—"

His eyebrows climbed.

"Well, that this looks an awful lot like a grave waiting for a coffin."

His head turned and he swore. "I'm sorry. That didn't occur to me."

At last, she could smile. "No, I shouldn't have said that. I had too long to think, that's all. Really, what could be cozier?"

Maybe he intended that sound to be a laugh.

"Shall I start dinner?"

"Yeah. I think we're safe here for the night. We probably don't want to break out in song, but I can't carry a tune, anyway, so that's just as well."

"Really?"

"Really. You?"

"I love to sing."

Now he openly grinned. "I love to listen."

Then they were a match made in heaven. Ava cringed, hoping he didn't read her thought.

She sat cross-legged and busied herself with her small cookstove. "These are my last dinners," she told him. "Pasta primavera. If you saw something better in there..." She nodded at the pack.

"I'm...not really hungry. Pick whatever you want."

She narrowed her eyes. "Why aren't you hungry?"

He opened his mouth, hesitated and then closed it. Thought better of lying to her? "I've...had a headache. Some nausea, too. Turns out extreme activity stirs it up."

"A concussion."

"Probably." He sounded amazingly unconcerned.

Mad, she said, "You didn't think to tell me this?"

Those eyes, not as expressionless as he probably imagined, met hers. "What could you have done?"

"We could have slowed down. Looked for a place to rest sooner! I could have—"

"No, Ava," he said, his voice both rough and gentle. "I'm not in that bad a shape. We have to follow the plan."

Frustrated, she wanted to keep arguing, but "should have" was pointless now, and she couldn't have set a snare, as he described it, bringing down the two armed men tracking them. He'd produced real snowshoes for her, food to sustain them and weapons she prayed she didn't have to use.

Her admiration for Zach swung higher, but she knew he didn't want to hear about it, and would shut down any attempt on her part to thank him.

Instead, she said, "Will you try to eat?"

One side of his mouth tipped up. "Okay. But make it pasta primavera. The ones I, er, acquired are store-bought. Which are better than MREs, but—"

She smiled, as he'd intended. Waiting for water to boil, she finally said, "Do you want to tell me about it?"

He seemed to be concentrating on the small flame. "Maybe after we eat."

HOW LITTLE COULD he get away with telling her?

Watching her as she prepared their meal, just as she had the previous night, he reconsidered his instinct to tell half-truths. No, she wasn't a soldier, but given her childhood, he suspected she wouldn't shock easily. They were in this together. He owed her the respect he'd have given any other teammate. What's more, the blunter he was, the more ready she'd be to pull that trigger if she had to.

He just hoped to God it didn't come down to that.

"You have a memory card in that camera?" he asked, nodding toward her pack.

"Yes, of course. Two different kinds. I've filled some."

"I want you to take out the most recent cards. We'll each carry one."

"Oh." She bent her head so he couldn't read her face well. "Yes, of course."

"Smells good," he offered. It did, and suddenly he was starved, too, but damn, what he craved most was stretching out in the sleeping bag and not moving for eight hours or more.

As they ate, they talked quietly. He told her a little about his current job as a detective for a rural county. "I like working independently," he said. "Using my head, figuring things out."

"Versus action?"

He grimaced. "Yeah. They wanted me on the SWAT team, but I said no. I used the excuse of my injury, but the truth is, I'm done with that."

"Except you're not."

"No." It was a minute before he added, "Lucky I haven't had time to get fat and lazy."

Ava laughed. "I just can't picture that."

He grinned. "You never know." The scrape of the spoon told him he'd eaten his entire serving. His stomach felt better enough, and he wondered if he'd mostly been hungry.

She talked about some of the outlets where she sold her work, telling him she had an agent, which was a good thing since she didn't have the right personality to do all the marketing herself. "Super outgoing and engaging isn't me. Of course," she said with a sigh, "I have to do a certain amount of it, anyway."

"You envision doing this forever?"

She set down the aluminum pan. "I know I can't. Once my knees go, you know..." When he smiled, she shrugged. "There are other types of jobs in the field. Sports, newspapers... I could sell prints of my work from an eBay shop."

If they stayed in touch—if they started something together—he was going to hate waving goodbye when she set off into the African bush or the jungles of Thailand or wherever the hell else she went to do her job. Except he guessed some of the time, maybe most of the time, she wouldn't be on her own. She'd have a guide, at least.

Okay, he could live with that. Except...what

he'd really like was to go with her. Carry, fetch, cook, watch her back.

And he was getting more than a little ahead of himself here.

He handed her his own dish and then dug in the pack he'd appropriated, producing a handful of candy bars. She pounced on a Twix; he went for Almond Joy and resisted having seconds when she did. Better be cautious.

Finally, watching her wiping out the dirty dishes with snow and stowing them away, he said, "I found passports."

Chapter Nine

Her head came up. "Real ones?" Her nose wrinkled. "You know what I mean."

"One was Russian, the other from Kazakhstan. The men flew into Montreal on different dates, close to two weeks ago. Both passports showed some previous travel, nothing likely to catch anyone's attention. Do I think those are their real names? No. When we get out of here, I'll give the passports to the border patrol."

"Do you think the man you left alive will survive until we make it out?"

He tried to keep his expression impassive. "Let's hope it doesn't take too long."

Her nod hid a lot, and he understood.

He talked more about the snares he'd set, and how well they'd worked on both occasions. "It helped that I had some height and weight on both of the men. That won't always be the case. I was also lucky because neither had a weapon in hand."

"Hard to use a pole if you're also clutching a gun."

He inclined his head. That would be a problem for him, too.

"There were eight men on that ridge?"

"No, I think seven. I can check for sure."

She twisted to take her camera out of her pack. What had to be a really expensive lens was obviously toast, but the camera itself came on for her. That had to be a super battery.

She brought up the photos again. She was right. Seven men. He took the camera from her and studied the three faces that she'd captured. None of those matched the two members of the group he'd taken down today.

"Five to go," he murmured. "And Borisyuk is one of them."

She didn't ask the obvious: Would the prime target expend his men before he got his own hands dirty, or would he enjoy killing two inconvenient Americans?

It was getting hard to see Ava's face, which Zach regretted. Even as tense as they both were right now, he liked seeing every flicker of her expressions.

"You brought your own sleeping bag," she said.

"You don't know how close I was to dumping it." He saw her startle. "I liked sleeping with you," he said wryly. "I'm afraid if I'm not, I'll wake up constantly, groping around to be sure you're there."

"We won't be far apart."

"I guess there's only so much space," he admitted, acknowledging the limited width of their hole.

She hadn't moved. He waited out her silence.

"We could...zip the sleeping bags together," she said softly.

WITH HER CHEEKS BURNING, Ava was grateful for the oncoming darkness. She also hoped he didn't take her invitation for more than she'd intended it to be. Sex wasn't casual for her. Truth be told, she'd never been able to relax enough, give enough of herself, for sex to be all that great—or, really, worth bothering with. She'd felt more intimacy sleeping in Zach's arms last night than she ever had when naked with any other man.

Maybe...

No. Don't even think it.

"I can go for that," he said calmly. "Shall we set up?"

"Yes." Woman of the world, that was her. "Then I suppose I'd better crawl out of here and, um, find some privacy."

"Ditto. Wait. You haven't stayed stuck in this

hole all day?" He was obviously frowning at her. "I didn't think…"

Could her face get any hotter? "No, I, um, used a plastic bag. Which I'll dump while I'm behind that tree."

He bent his head matter-of-factly. They took turns, Zach leaving the job of zipping the two sleeping bags together to what he described as her more nimble fingers.

He'd looked better over dinner than he had when he first appeared, but whatever good the meal had done him was already gone. His shoulders sagged. She caught him rubbing his temples when he didn't think she'd see. What bothered her most was seeing how…*still* he held himself. For a man who crackled with intensity, he seemed to have wound down.

She could not imagine that sex was on his mind.

Finally, in complete darkness he climbed into the sleeping bag, lay on his back with his head on a balled-up parka and waited while Ava slid in beside him.

She reached for his hand, which clasped hers firmly. "Are you okay?" she asked.

Long pause. "Been better," he admitted. "A night's sleep will do wonders."

She hoped so. If he looked this bad in the morning, she'd try to talk him into staying put where they were now that they wouldn't run out of food. She'd be even more strongly in favor of that if not for his injuries—the ones he'd told her about, and the ones he didn't want to admit to. He needed a hospital.

Also...would the terrorists, if that's what they were, really continue on their way minus their two compatriots? Or would they take the time to come looking for them—and for the problem they clearly hadn't solved?

Ava had a sick feeling that's exactly what they would do.

She'd have thought Zach had fallen asleep, except the hand holding hers hadn't relaxed. So she wasn't surprised when he spoke from the darkness.

"How are you?"

"Scared," she admitted. "Grateful."

He shifted. Turned his head to look at her? "For?"

"You," she said honestly. "I wouldn't have had a prayer alone. No, not just alone—even if I'd brought someone along on this trip. I've never met anyone like you."

"You must know some former soldiers."

"Yes, but..." They weren't warriors, but she wasn't sure he'd like that description. "You have different instincts, skills. How many people would know how to make snowshoes from some tree branches and a few cords? Would have the strength to go on when they were injured as badly as you were?"

"I'm okay—"

"You're not!" she said fiercely. "Don't lie to me!"

"Hey." His voice a gentle rumble, he rolled toward her enough to gather her up into his arms and settle her against his side. "I told you. I'm used to functioning with some pain. I'll bet you're a mass of bruises yourself, and you kept moving as long as you had to."

"It's not the same," she mumbled against his chest.

He seemed to be rubbing his cheek or jaw against her head. "Under the circumstances, my background has come in handy. You're right about that. I've faced worse odds and come out alive."

"But have you had to protect someone else?"

"Sure." He sounded surprised. "Locals in a bad spot, and my teammates, always. You…"

What felt like a hesitation drew out.

"Me what?"

"I…care about you. I'm not expecting anything from you, but if we'd met differently…" He huffed out a breath. "I need to keep you safe."

Her eyes stung. For an instant she listened

to his heartbeat. "I want *you* safe, too. I *hated* it when you left today, or thinking you'd sacrifice yourself."

His arms tightened. "I have faith you're capable of fighting if you have to."

Was he right? Ava tried to imagine how she could have brought down either of the men he'd surprised today, and knew she couldn't have done that. But could she pull the trigger of a gun to save his life, or hers? A hot coal of anger said, *Yes*.

"I just...want to say thank you. For being here."

"Which I wouldn't be if you hadn't dug me out of a snowy grave." That had to be a smile in his voice.

She sniffed, hoping he wouldn't hear, but something inside her relaxed, too. He was right. This partnership wasn't one-sided. She wasn't useless by any means.

"I got your arm back in the socket, too," she reminded him.

His chest vibrated with what had to be a laugh. "Yes, you did."

"Okay. Part of me wants to talk about tomorrow..."

"Let's wait until morning. I have some ideas, but I'll need to look at a map. Assuming you carried one?"

She bobbed her head. What she thought qualified as a hug followed. Really grateful she'd suggested they double up the sleeping bags, Ava concentrated on his warmth along her body, his heartbeat, his slow, deep breaths...and fell asleep.

ZACH'S EYES SNAPPED OPEN. Had he just shouted? His skin felt electrified, and he was desperate to jump to his feet, to be ready—

Taking in the silence but for the soft, rhythmic sound of Ava breathing, he made himself lie still. Damn, the nightmare had been a bad one; one of the worst. He'd been doing better, sleeping more peacefully.

Nothing like going to war again, killing, to stir up the muddy depths of a man's psyche.

He muttered a few foul words under his breath. Weirdly, except for the nightmare, he felt as if he were waking from a coma, no sense of time having passed. He'd been out until he was flung into an ugly moment of the past, and was now wide awake.

He became conscious that the night was exceptionally dark. Either cloud cover was heavy enough to hide the moon entirely, or the surrounding trees and high ridges did the same. After a long period of stillness, he didn't hear anything alarming. The wake-up call had been in his own head.

In fact, as he forced himself to relax, muscle by muscle, he realized that he was amazingly comfortable with Ava cuddled up to him. Her head still rested in the hollow of his shoulder beneath the collar bone, and their legs had come to be tangled.

He hadn't spent the night with a woman in so long, he could barely remember the last time. Since retiring, he hadn't even wanted sex enough to play the games required with a new partner. Apparently, he thought wryly, he was ready—except Ava wasn't the game-playing kind.

Because it was necessary, Zach ran the usual checklist: shoulder, not too bad, head still ached. How would he know if he was dizzy?

He slowly lifted his right arm and, without disturbing Ava, was able to punch the button on his watch to see that it was 3:00 a.m. Thank God his bladder didn't demand attention. He still had no desire to move. Lying here with an armful of woman suited him just fine. In the absence of another nightmare, he could get two or three more hours of sleep before dawn lightened the sky.

Not that they could get the same early start they had the past two mornings, he reminded himself. He'd have to tinker with the straps on the snowshoes to make them fit Ava's smaller feet. Then the two of them had to have a serious discussion about how they might evade Borisyuk and company.

His mind circled, not coming to any conclusions, until Ava mumbled something.

He bent his head. "Did you say something?"

"Quit worrying," she said drowsily. "I can hear you. Feel you. Something."

He smiled and pressed his lips to the top of her head. "Yes, ma'am."

She seemed to sink back to sleep immediately, and the exchange freed him to do the same.

Ava squirming to get out of the sleeping bag woke him come morning. In the gray light, he said, "What?"

"Have to pee."

"Oh." He lay back and enjoyed watching her wriggle into multiple layers of clothing, even though that meant she wouldn't be coming back to bed.

She grabbed something from her pack and scrambled up the bank, vanishing from his sight. With a groan, Zach pushed himself to sit up.

Damn. He felt even more battered than he had yesterday morning. His conditioning was sufficient for the traveling, but he hadn't needed two brutally physical fights, given his injuries. Curious, he lifted his fleece quarter-zip, along with the cotton tee beneath, and saw a motley collection of bruises that were a different color than the ones that lay beneath them. When he probed experimentally, he had to wonder if he didn't have a cracked rib or two, as well.

It wouldn't be the first time. He shrugged and winced. Good thing Ava hadn't seen that. He needed her to believe in him.

By the time she reappeared, he'd gotten dressed, too, not without wishing either of the men he'd tackled had been closer in size to him. He'd sure like a change of clothes. Standing, he groaned, wishing he'd had a chance to alleviate his stiffness.

"Oatmeal?" she asked.

"Sounds good." Boots on, he followed her path to the woods, and while he was there, he forced himself through some easy exercises to limber up his tight, aching muscles. The shoulder was improved today, he thought, despite what he'd put it through yesterday. The headache might have relented, too.

Neither talked much over breakfast. Ava kept sneaking looks at him he pretended not to notice. He suspected she was assessing his condition. He did the same in return, thinking that she'd visibly lost weight. They hadn't been eating enough, and both were probably getting dehydrated, too. The additional food and the second water bowl he'd acquired should help. He'd encourage her to drink more.

As she washed up the dishes and boiled water for what coffee she had left, he asked about her experience with firearms.

"I...did a little target shooting with a .22 rifle when I was a kid. It was fun, and I had a good eye, but that was a really long time ago. The target wasn't moving, and, well, it wasn't alive."

"No, you wouldn't have hunted," he acknowledged. She might be grateful right now for his capacity for violence, even the knowledge that he'd killed, but later, that might bother her. They weren't an obvious pairing.

He shook off more premature thoughts.

"I'm going to have you carry a handgun from here on out. I'll show you how to use it in principle, but even though the one I'm going to keep has a suppressor—a silencer—I'd just as soon not risk firing either gun."

"No! Oh, no."

He took out the Colt 9mm he'd lifted off his second victim, then showed her where the safety was and how to release it. He'd already verified that it was ready to fire, and that the magazine was full.

It was heavy for a woman's smaller hands, but she held it steadily, listening to his advice.

"Aim low. It'll kick up." He doubted the men hunting them wore any body armor. They were armed to the teeth, but hadn't really anticipated encountering anyone in the wilderness. If a helicopter had spotted them, they had come with the capability of shooting it down, which was different.

They must be cursing the chance that had led to them being spotted, and frustrated at not being positive the avalanche had taken the witnesses out. They couldn't realistically have expected the two scouts to rejoin them yet, not when they'd been ordered to take a lengthy detour. That said… Zach and Ava had lost most of a day after the avalanche hit, and then another full day when he went back to deal with the pair of hunters.

The question now was whether the main body of the group would simply wait there, or whether they'd proceed north again to pick up the two missing members, and potentially any survivors of the avalanche.

Before he started on the snowshoes, he asked for any maps she had, and they pored over the one she produced.

"Where were you dropped?" he asked.

She tapped a marked campsite.

His finger traced the length of the trail to roughly where the avalanche had caught them. "I was set down farther upriver, since I intended the trip to last no more than a week."

Ava looked rueful. "I was about to turn back. Just think, if I had before I set eyes on those men..."

"If you'd snowshoed downriver with no detours, you might have met up with them there."

She made a face. "I wonder what would have happened if I'd been able to call for a national park helicopter and they'd heard it coming."

Rather than reacting to that, he frowned at her. "Why *didn't* you turn back, if it was already on your mind?"

"I'm embarrassed to say it was because I suddenly realized someone was behind me."

"So you were running away from me." In other words, her involvement was his fault, one hundred percent. If she'd turned back that morning, he'd probably have exchanged a few polite words with her, then continued northward—and likely been alone when he saw the heavily armed group above. The binoculars he'd carried were fine, but he doubted he would have been able to pick out Borisyuk's face.

"I...suppose so. Except, it had long since

become obvious you were gaining ground on me." She looked perturbed. "I don't really know what I was thinking."

If not for the camera, would the terrorists have bothered to try to bury Zach under an avalanche? He didn't know, but if they had, at least Ava would have been safely going on her way, unaware of what she'd missed.

And he'd be dead, assuming he was in the same place at the same time.

Which was unlikely. Chances were better he'd have been deep in tree cover and unable to see the ridgetop on one side or the mountains on the other. He'd have enjoyed his trip, maybe wondered about the beautiful woman snowshoeing on her own out here—and Borisyuk would be passing unobserved through the wilderness, close to a planned pickup point.

He shouldn't regret anything, if there was the slightest chance they could stop that bastard. And yet, he did. He'd give damn near anything, including his life, to know that Ava was safe, even if that meant he had never had a chance to sleep with her pressed against him, her head on his shoulder.

Damn it.

Chapter Ten

"There are several trails turning off when we get closer to the end of this one," he said, tapping them with his finger.

"Yes, but one is where hikers on the ridge will emerge from—"

He conceded that with a nod.

"And this trail dead-ends at a lake." Her fingertip almost touched his. "I'm assuming they have this map, or a comparable one." Too bad the men weren't traveling aimlessly, but they were too well equipped not to have a compass and maps.

Zach told Ava what he was thinking. "There are a couple of possible alternatives. One is that, if we see tracks descending the ridge trail, we head up it." Assuming he and she made it that far.

She looked at him in surprise. "They'll just let us stroll by?"

He grimaced. "Not unless I can eliminate

whoever was left on guard there. If they plan well, the rest of them will be spread out across all the possibilities."

Emotion flared in her eyes. "I hate it when you say things like that."

"Eliminate?"

"Yes!"

"We're now either victims or victors," he said bluntly. "I don't know about you, but I want to be able to—" *Go home.* That's what he'd almost said. A picture crossed his mind of the small rambler on an acre he was currently renting while he decided whether to stay in the Bellingham area or not. Home? No, it was a place to lay down his head, no different than base housing. Funny time to realize what he *wanted* was a real home that included a family.

She was staring at him. Waiting for him to finish.

"I want to be able to get *you* home safely," he concluded.

"Home," Ava echoed, in an odd tone. Then she sighed. "Okay, what looks like the best bet to you?"

"We either head out cross-country—there are a couple of possible creeks—or think about the trail that climbs over this pass." He touched his fingertip to the map. "The zigzag line suggests it's steep, but it has to be doable. I wonder if the snow isn't year-round up there. Hikers and mountain climbers obviously navigate it. And once we get high enough, we'll have a better chance of cell phone coverage."

Her gaze met his again. "They'll surely be watching that route."

"Yeah. But all of them?"

Divided they fall. And he *was* armed now.

"There's not really a choice, is there?"

"No. Unless—keep checking your cell phone."

"Did either of them carry phones?"

"Both, but they're the cheap ones you pick up at the pharmacy. Who's your carrier?" When she told him, he nodded. "I'm betting you have better coverage."

"Okay."

Fortunately, one of the many smart decisions she'd made was to bring a couple of portable chargers. Her phone wouldn't run out of juice.

Except for a few necessary words, neither said anything else while she packed up and he worked on the bindings of her newly appropriated snowshoes.

Once he had her try them on, she offered him a crooked smile. "I deeply appreciate the expertise that allowed you to make my existing snowshoes. Really. But I'll still be thrilled to toss them into the woods."

Zach laughed. What he didn't say was that they wouldn't have dared take on what had to be a difficult climb to the pass if he hadn't been able to provide a replacement for the flimsy snowshoes that were already breaking apart.

Just before they set out, he changed into a white parka, even though it was a tighter fit than he liked, and utilized the white tarp to fling over the heavy pack. Ava looked alarmed, but only nodded when he said, "It'll give them pause at first sight."

As they beat their way back to the trail, Zach adjusting again to the weight of the pack, he couldn't prevent himself from running his own calculations, over and over. If the five remaining men continued on the ridge trail until its natural end, down at some other creek—if memory served—how long would it take them to head back up the valley, realize the two men sent on a separate errand should have appeared, and then figure out where he and Ava had gone?

What would he do if they came around a curve and found themselves face-to-face with any or all of the men?

Reaching the trail, completely untracked as it continued southward, Ava said unexpectedly, "We can worry ourselves in circles without helping."

How did this woman read his mind? "You're right," he said shortly, but planted a pole to free his hand long enough to pat the pistol he carried in the pocket of the parka, then reached back to estimate how long it would take him to get the automatic rifle in position to spray bullets.

ZACH INSISTED ON taking the lead, she presumed because of what he wore. The sight of that familiar parka and fur-lined hood might provide a critical couple of seconds before they realized he was a stranger.

Please.

It took her a few minutes to adjust to wearing the less cumbersome, modern snowshoes again, as well as having real poles, but after that she marveled at how fast they were now able to move. If Zach was being hindered by his shoulder injury or headache, she couldn't tell. A couple of times he opened enough of a lead on her that he paused after glancing over his shoulder so she could catch up. She didn't let herself feel chagrined. He was bigger, stronger and longer legged. After all, he'd gained fast on her even that first day. Still, Ava felt confident she wasn't holding him up much.

There weren't a lot of distinctive landmarks along this stretch. One small creek—mostly ice choked—crossed the trail. She poked with the tip of her pole at some ice and was surprised when it didn't so much break up as disintegrate. That was the moment when she became aware that she was too warm.

"Hold up," she called in a low voice.

Zach stopped and deftly turned his snowshoes so he could raise his eyebrows at her.

"It's warming up," she said.

He frowned, taking in the many snow-laden branches to each side of the trail. "Snow's not melting yet."

"No, but almost."

He pushed back the hood, as if testing the temperature. "That could be good or bad," he said thoughtfully.

Ava knew what he meant. A sudden melt would turn the trail into a slushy mess and expose whatever growth had happened since park personnel or volunteers had cut it back. Probably a brief warming wouldn't extend long; the park wouldn't really open to hikers until July. But she and Zach were at a relatively low elevation here, at the bottom of the valley.

"I'm going to take my parka off." She stripped off her gloves and unzipped, aware Zach was evaluating what she wore beneath. No, her next layer, a fleece quarter-zip, was not bright red, so she ignored his scrutiny but saw that he wasn't following suit. Of course not; that white parka with the hood was a disguise. Once she stashed her parka beneath an elastic strap, she pulled on her gloves again and said, "I'm ready."

His eyes lingered on her for a moment that felt...personal. Even warm. But abruptly he turned and set off again, Ava falling in behind him.

If we get out of this, I'll probably never see him again, she reminded herself, but discovered that she didn't actually believe that. Given what he'd said, would he let her go that easily? Would she go without making some effort to find out whether he might be interested in—

What? Spending a couple of nights together?

Ava was disconcerted to realize she'd take even that. She wanted to keep sleeping with him, and more.

The sound of something thrashing through the thick vegetation snapped her back to the present, and she came to a stop behind Zach, who'd raised one hand to signal her. A deer stepped out into the open in front of them, saw them, and took a giant leap into the tangled growth on the other side of the trail, going toward the river.

"She didn't expect us," he murmured, and resumed his long, easy stride.

An hour later, they had another unexpected encounter with wildlife. Zach stopped and said quietly, "Look."

A wolf stood so still beneath the branches of a cedar, his golden eyes on them, they might almost have passed without seeing him at all. Ava longed for her camera, packed away with the damaged lens. Reclusive creatures, gray wolves didn't show themselves any more often than did the lynx she'd hoped to see. She'd heard howling, but in the far distance. Now he evaluated them, then melted out of sight without making a sound.

"Suggests he hasn't met any other people recently," Zach said softly.

That was a heartening thought.

They made swift progress, finally stopping for a bite to eat beneath an old cedar tree much like the one the wolf had used for cover.

Ava was glad to shrug out of the pack for a few minutes. She felt stronger today, though, and it wasn't just the new-and-improved snowshoes. The avalanche had been…she had to think. Three days ago? Yes. Three nights had intervened. Her aches and pains were fading. She hadn't been able to see her face, but guessed the visible bruises were, too.

As Zach spilled some raisins into the palm of his bare hand, she studied him. His face was thinner, she felt sure, maybe even gaunt, although with the brown scruff that was swiftly becoming a short beard, it was hard to be sure. She'd noticed earlier without paying attention that he had dark bruises beneath both eyes. Not quite black eyes, but close. Now the almost purple color was muddied by some yellow. The lines carving his forehead seemed deeper, too, if she wasn't mistaken.

He'd moved today with the strength, grace and certainty that she'd seen when he first appeared behind her, but that had to be deceptive. He seemed determined to hide his pain, which might have offended her, except she guessed soldiers in the kind of unit he'd belonged to were always reluctant to show weakness. The fact that she was a woman might have nothing to do with his determination to disguise any vulnerability.

Or maybe he wasn't thinking about it at all; maybe he was utterly focused on what lay ahead of them. What he still had to do.

Yes, she thought. That's the kind of man he was.

He was looking right back at her, she suddenly realized, one of his unusually mobile eyebrows quirked. "Deep thoughts?"

"No, just thinking you look leaner. I suppose I've lost weight, too."

"Easily regained," he said lightly. "You ready to get going again?"

"Of course." Turning her face from his, she tucked the remnants of her snack—or was this lunch?—back into a pocket of her pack. While she was thinking about it, she took out her phone.

At his raised brows, she had to shake her head.

Shortly after they set out again, Ava realized the trail was climbing slightly to proceed higher above the level of the river. It now cut across a side hill. Although much of the undergrowth—the salal and gooseberry, the Oregon grape and lower clumps of devil's club—were mostly buried under snow, the trail here squeezed between a heavy growth of trees, the ubiquitous cedar, hemlock and spruce mixed with more deciduous ones than she'd noticed farther up the valley. She thought she recognized maples, even without any hint of budding leaves. She seemed to remember that dogwood was common, too, as well as aspen and the every-present alder and willow.

Zach had slowed down somewhat, although she didn't see any awkwardness in his stride or the way he planted his poles. He might be watching more carefully. He wouldn't like not being able to see far ahead, she knew, given the density of the forest, as well as the curve of the trail. She tried harder to listen, too, but was afraid she wouldn't hear an approaching snowshoer over the *swish-swish* of their own steps.

"I think I see a sign sticking out of the snow," he told her over his shoulder, voice barely audible.

She hadn't come from this far south, but of course national park employees would mark trails.

"Wait," Zach said sharply, but still quietly. "There are tracks on it."

Oh, God. Ava froze between one step and the next.

Then a voice called what sounded like an inquiry...in a harsh language she didn't recognize.

ZACH HAD REHEARSED for this moment since they started out this morning. With his hands encased in thick winter gloves, he couldn't get his index finger in to squeeze the trigger on the handgun he carried in the pocket at his hip. Given the warming temperatures, he considered leaving off his right glove, but the day still hovered around freezing, and he didn't dare let his fingers get numb or stiff. So he'd practiced, over and over.

Yank hand from the glove, leave it hanging

from his pole. Reach the short distance, take gun from the pocket.

He'd left the safety off to eliminate the one step.

He had run through it over and over in his mind, and practiced ditching the glove and reaching for the butt of the gun a dozen times. Either Ava was concentrating intensely on maintaining her pace, or giving what attention she had left over to watching and listening for company, but she showed no indication she'd noticed what he was doing or why.

Now, when the white-clad snowshoer appeared not fifteen yards ahead, Zach pulled the gun within three to four seconds.

The greeting, initially friendly sounding, gave him the time he needed. With five or six days' worth of scruff covering half his face and sunglasses over his eyes, Zach couldn't look that different at first glance from this guy's compatriots.

But when Zach didn't respond immediately, there was a gradual shift in body language and expression. The gaze slid past Zach, took in Ava.

This enemy's hand moved swiftly to the firing mechanism of the sniper-type rifle he carried slung over his shoulder, barrel pointing forward. Toward Zach and Ava.

Zach dropped his poles and braced his own gun in a two-handed firing position. With the suppressor screwed to the barrel, it was more awkward than what he was used to, but from this distance—

"I'm an American police officer," he said loudly, clearly. "Put down your weapons. *Now!*"

The man lifted the rifle, and Zach swore he was pointing it at Ava.

Zach fired, even as the man facing him did the same. Behind him, Ava cried out and either went down or flung herself to one side. He couldn't afford to turn.

He pulled the trigger three times, stopping only as he saw the white-clad figure folding in on itself, tumbling to the snowy ground. Zach had seen death take enough people to recognize it on this man's face. Still, he raced forward, yanked the rifle away from his adversary, and then spun clumsily and scrambled back to Ava.

Who, thank God, was picking herself back up. "He tried to shoot me," she whispered. "I think he *did* shoot me."

"What?"

"My arm stings, that's all, and—" She reached up to finger a tear in her parka on her upper arm.

"God." He fell to his knees beside her. "You scared me."

"*I* scared you?"

"*He* scared me." Zach had a bad feeling he was shaking, but he couldn't let himself yank her into his arms. The seasoned soldier he was had begun scanning for any indication of company before he'd even pulled the trigger. He wished he hadn't felt obligated to give a warning. He'd been desperate to prevent the other man from firing.

His brain was already turning that over when Ava said, "I didn't hear his gun go off. Or yours. Well, except for a few pops."

"You're really all right?" he demanded to know.

Her eyes were wide, shocked, but as always, determined. "Yes."

"Let me see," he insisted.

Wincing, she eased her arm out of the parka, and he was able to push aside the torn fabric of her fleece top and the turtleneck she wore beneath it to see a graze. Blood seeped, but treating it could wait. An inch or two to the left, and they'd be dealing with a real wound. Conceivably a shattered bone.

Heart racing from the close call, his thoughts jumped back to her comment about hearing only a few pops.

Galvanized by his realization, Zach pushed himself to his feet and returned to the rifle that lay where he'd tossed it, sunken in snow. He picked it up, astonished. Yes, it, too, had been fitted to fire silently. The AK-47s the other two had carried hadn't been; he wasn't even sure they *could* be. The shooter had to practice to achieve accuracy with the addition to any of the military's various sniper rifles, but they could be and sometimes were fitted with suppressors. There were moments when you had to go in quiet.

Zach couldn't believe his luck. He hadn't been primarily a sniper, but he'd gone through training at Fort Bennett and had utilized his skills plenty of times. He might still have qualms about picking off the remaining members of the terrorist group like ducks in a shooting gallery, but the fact that this man's first instinct on seeing Zach and Ava had been to gun them down sent a strong message.

"He's...dead?" she asked from behind him.

"Yeah. It was him or us."

"I saw." She'd stayed on the trail but advanced to within a few feet of the man. "What do we do with him? And which way do we go?"

God, he could love this woman, tough enough

to pass through terror into practicality and grit within a minute or two.

Maybe he already did.

This wasn't the time to become mired in the sinkhole created by emotions.

He still didn't hear any indication of other people nearby. They had to have spread out, the way he'd both feared and hoped.

That didn't mean he and Ava could afford to waste a minute.

He slung the rifle over his shoulder, straightened and looked around. "Get him out of sight, for starters." He evaluated the tracks. "Don't know how far he went up this trail before he decided we couldn't possibly be ahead of him and turned to come back. Maybe all he was doing was rejoining the main trail, but he might have been ordered to hang back out of sight, to lie in wait for us. Somehow, we surprised him."

"He certainly surprised *me*," she said dryly.

Zach spared a glance at her face, to see that for all her outward gutsiness, it was pinched. This was likely the only violent death she'd ever seen—unless at some point during that year while she'd tried as a seven-year-old to survive on the streets, she'd seen someone stabbed or shot. It was all too possible. He'd have to ask her what city she'd been in.

"Okay," he said. "You're going to stand guard while I carry his body back to the main trail and look for a good place to dump him. Then I'll get rid of his pack and snowshoes, too."

"Rifle?"

"That, we're keeping. In fact—"

To her obvious consternation, he gave her a one minute short course in firing a McMillan TAC-50, a sniper rifle used by Canadian military as well as by other countries. Zach had never personally fired one, but it made sense these guys had been able to get their hands on one on the black market.

Fortunately, for these purposes, she could ignore the scope. All she needed to do was point and fire. She wouldn't be shooting anyone from more than twenty, twenty-five yards, tops.

Ava did not look thrilled, but finally nodded, her teeth sinking into her lower lip. "Just… hurry, okay?"

Hanging around here at the junction of two trails was dangerous. "Yeah."

It took only a matter of minutes for him to drop his own pack, strip off the dead man's and heave the body over his right shoulder. Feeling the strain and the pain on the injured side of his body, he grunted. The guy was no lightweight, and Zach hoped he wouldn't have to go far to find the right spot.

He turned back the way he and Ava had come, and hadn't gone thirty feet before he noticed a particularly thick tangle of vegetation. He strode as close to it as he could, trying not to break branches, and did his best to fling a body that had to weigh 180 pounds or so. To his gratification, it disappeared.

He hustled back, seeing that Ava appeared frozen in place but still held the rifle in firing position, and crouched to conduct a cursory search of the pack. Another passport, this one from Uzbekistan. He pocketed that. Otherwise, the only thing worth holding on to was a handgun with a suppressor. He switched it out for the 9mm he'd given Ava earlier, then hauled the pack down the trail and threw it next to the body.

He took a few minutes to try to erase tracks, grimacing at his mixed success, and then smoothed over signs of the violent confrontation as best he could.

Finally, since no one else had appeared and he didn't hear any indication of someone close by, he gently took the rifle back from Ava and pulled her into his arms.

Chapter Eleven

Ava didn't know why she felt so traumatized now, after all the horrifying events of the last four days, but heaven help her, she might as well be a quaking aspen in a stiff breeze. She did a lot more than lean on Zach; she wrapped her arms around his torso, buried her face in his parka-clad shoulder and hung on for all she was worth. And shook.

He was talking, or only growling things under his breath. She couldn't make out a word he said. It had to be a couple of minutes before she realized she wasn't the only one shaking. The cold, bare hand that smoothed hair from her face definitely had a tremor. She rubbed her cheek against it, hard, and wished they were done, that this was the end and they could just stand here in each other's arms for the next half an hour or so.

But fear still squeezed her heart, and at last she lifted her head to look up at him. Eyes espresso dark met hers, and he said something else, still imperceptible. Then he wrapped her jaw with one hand, lifted her chin and kissed her.

This was like the other time, but more. He demonstrated with his mouth and teeth and tongue how desperate he felt, how hungry. Scared, too, she thought. *Like me.*

He all but devoured her, except she responded with equal ferocity. She *needed* this. Him. Her mind blurred, until she quit thinking, only wanted.

But then, with a gut-wrenching groan, he tore his mouth from hers. His eyes burned into hers. "Damn, Ava. You have no idea—" He bit off the rest, as if she couldn't guess what he hadn't said. His hand still shook, if for another reason now, when he stroked her face, as if that touch was precious.

Only, he straightened after that, and she had to loosen her grip on him and do the same.

"We have to get moving," he said gruffly.

She swallowed and squared her shoulders. "I know. I just—"

"This trail leads to the lake. I think we have to take it and then set out cross-country. I hope to God that's even possible."

She couldn't think, not without looking away from his intensity. "There's only the one track leading this way," she heard herself say.

"Yeah."

"But if he's already made it here, the others…"

"Must have divvied up the alternatives."

"Except, he thought you were one of his buddies."

"Momentarily, yeah. Maybe he assumed a teammate had cut back to report a sighting. Still, they wouldn't have split up and started investigating alternate routes the way it appears they've done if they'd hadn't started to worry. Even so, they're probably still pretty confident. For good reason. You and I haven't moved very fast, between the twenty hours or so before we were able to set off at all, and the slow pace because of your primitive snowshoes." He grimaced. "And my condition."

"So the rest of them have been expecting the two sent off to make sure no witnesses survived to zip along by now, or at least any minute, and say, 'No problem.'"

His mouth quirked. "Probably in another language, but yeah." His grimness returned. "Three down, four to go."

Her stomach rolled. "If they gang up on us—"

"We're still in deep trouble," he agreed. "I'd like to avoid that happening. And unfortunately—" he lifted his arm and checked his watch "—we've lost a lot of this day. If you're up to it, we should still keep going for a few hours, but that won't get us much past the lake, if at all."

"If only we'd searched harder for your pack. I'm sorry."

How many times had they had this discussion? The satellite radio he'd carried would have brought help within hours. If only *she'd* been smart enough to carry one, too—

"Knock it off," he said roughly. "We searched as long as we dared. It was miracle enough that you found *me*."

What more was there to say? Ava only nodded, taking in the sight of a man who looked as battered as she felt, yet also dangerous and still strong. His lips were a little swollen and had cracked. Averting her face, she licked her own and tasted blood.

Oh.

She felt his gaze on her face, and there was a discernible pause before he stepped away. He slung his pack on his back again, and the rifle over his shoulder. She saw him pat the right pocket of his parka where he carried the handgun, pull on his gloves and grip his poles.

"You lead," he said, moving aside.

Well, at least someone had broken the trail for her already. She set off briskly.

THE TRACKS THEY followed ended fifteen minutes later, where the latest dead man had turned around to go back. The unbroken snow slowed them down a little, since it wasn't always clear what was trail beneath the snow and what wasn't. They were left to flounder a few times before backing up and trying again.

Their next break, Zach and Ava studied the contour map again. That itch aggravated his spine constantly now, but however much he'd have preferred an alternative, it still looked like their best bet of cutting over to the ridge trail was from the lake, nestled in a high bowl. A fold of land lay between the two trails—not a high ridge, but steep on this side and forested. To his regret, with the sky high and blue, there was no possibility of another convenient, late-spring snowstorm to help them disappear.

That probably would have been asking for too much.

He turned so frequently to watch behind them, he'd have whiplash by the time they stopped for the night. He didn't dare miss anything, though. Any faint sign of a pursuer, he'd send Ava on ahead and set up himself with the rifle. He didn't need a snare this time; he could kill long-distance.

Not for the first time, he wondered how law enforcement would judge his choices, but he was damned if he'd second-guess them. Everything that mattered to him was on the line here: bringing Ava, an innocent civilian and a woman he could love, to safety; stopping a threat to the nation he'd spent ten years of his life fighting to protect; and, probably in last place but still meaningful, his own survival. He'd hoped never to kill again, but he intended to do whatever proved necessary to protect what mattered to him.

He paused where he had a decent sight line to the trail behind him between tall trees and scanned with binoculars. Still nothing. Where were the others? In the next hour or two, they'd know for sure that they had a major problem on their hands. Zach had to circle back to wondering what Borisyuk was thinking. Shouldn't his mission be at the forefront? He'd lost some men; Zach doubted this cold-blooded terrorist gave a damn. He was still in a position to get the hell out of this wilderness and on his way to the job awaiting him. Why *wouldn't* that be his choice?

He could have gone on with only, say, one of the men, leaving the others to clean up behind him. If that was the case, he might still be able to wreak havoc that could be devastating for this country. But he also risked having one or more of those men captured and, potentially, talking.

Zach hummed in his throat. If these were all dedicated terrorists, Borisyuk might believe he was safe from betrayal no matter what. If they were mercenaries hired to get him across the border, though...that was different. Did those men even know who he was?

When he wasn't snatching looks over his shoulder, Zach rarely took his eyes off Ava, which was distracting in its own way. Hard not to let his gaze linger on her long, strong legs and taut butt outlined in stretchy fabric. To picture her face, and aching at the memory of her passionate response to his kiss.

That wasn't what he should be thinking about now, though. Protecting *her* was too much of what mattered. In a way, she represented all the other Americans who would suffer if a terrorist accomplished his goal.

The psychology of his opponents, and particularly their leader, played in Zach's mind as he climbed the trail rising above the deepest cut of the river, following a creek that murmured in the background of his consciousness, but only made a sparkling appearance from snow cover and ice to tumble in mini waterfalls on occasion.

What Zach thought was that Borisyuk had an ego problem. Maybe he'd set out on his deadly path years ago with complete dedication to a twisted ideal, but he'd been too successful. He'd become a legend, and he *couldn't* let himself run like a frightened rabbit. He would not, could not, let himself believe he could be outmaneuvered, refused to believe anyone was smarter or more capable than him. Maybe it wasn't even the possibility of a photograph that still drove him. Once he realized three of his men had failed to stop whoever had survived the avalanche, his determination would harden. One or two people, mere backcountry travelers? Inconceivable!

At this moment, he probably still felt smug. One of his men would show up with evidence of the death of any Americans foolish enough to get in his way. But that smugness would wane as time passed. Eventually, he'd send someone to venture back up the trail, where the snowshoe tracks would initially be confusing, but eventually make clear that three people had met up—and only two of them had gone on.

No, Borisyuk wouldn't be prepared to quit, to say, "A photograph of me? What does that matter?"

Of course Zach couldn't be certain, but he thought he was right. And *that* was both good and bad. Good because it meant he and Ava still had a chance to kill or capture an infamous terrorist. Bad because they were still in great danger.

The trail broke into the open, and Zach paused to lift binoculars to his eyes and scrutinize the land below him. Still nothing, but that might only be because the dense Northwest rainforest hid so much.

Another hour passed, and the two of them paused for a drink and a handful of nuts. At Ava's worried look, he shook his head. They didn't talk at all, only went on. Two hours, three. The sun was dropping in the sky. In another couple of hours, it would go behind the mountains, and they'd lose light fast. They needed to take refuge soon. Not generally an optimist, he thought maybe he'd been expecting pursuit sooner than it could reasonably occur. The lake couldn't be far—not that it offered any safety.

His eye was caught by multiple deer tracks diverting from the trail. He'd seen them off and on all day, sometimes going off into the forest. This was different. It looked like a favorite route for the four-footed residents of these mountains. And, damn—that almost had to be a track left by a bear. Or Bigfoot.

"You seeing deer tracks up there?" he called.

Ava stopped and looked back. "Yes. I can see the lake, too. The ice is breaking up."

"Come here and tell me what you think."

She lifted her snowshoes in a quick turn and returned to his side.

He pointed with his pole. "Animal trail."

"Going the way we want to go."

"That's what I'm thinking."

"I say we take a chance." Her eyes widened. "Is that a bear track?"

"Has to be." His mouth quirked. "Probably just woke up. Can't be in a good mood."

Ava made a face at him. "Thank you for that. Do you want me to go ahead again?"

"Yeah, I'm going to try to muddy the tracks a little."

She nodded and set off. Looked like they'd face a steeper climb now.

Zach tramped all the way to the lake, made a mess in the snow then turned back. He went a little past the animal trail, snapped off a branch, swung around again and started swiping behind him as he moved backward. He did the same for ten yards or so onto the alternate trail, but going backward uphill was a strain, so he abandoned the effort. His best hope was that a few more animals would travel this way as the day waned—and maybe some nocturnal creatures, too. Someone hunting humans might not pay attention to the deer, rabbit and raccoon tracks that they'd been seeing everywhere.

Zach didn't relax his watchfulness any as he turned and sped after Ava.

AVA'S THIGHS BURNED. The trail meandered in a way one cleared and leveled by humans didn't. It turned out deer didn't think a thing of bounding straight upward, too. She had to pause every ten minutes or so, breathe deeply and wait for her muscles to relax. It was like doing sprints in training, she consoled herself; short, fast sprints divided by brief rests.

She hated that, when she caught a glimpse of Zach behind her, she couldn't read his expression at all, beyond obvious grimness. It was as if he'd pulled inside somewhere. His gaze didn't meet hers; his eyes were dark and curiously flat. He moved steadily but for his regular stops to search the landscape behind them. His head would tilt, and she had a suspicion he had better hearing than she did.

She hoped he did; she was depending entirely on him right now.

She didn't descend into the kind of exhaustion she had in previous days, when she couldn't think about anything but which foot to move next. *Gee, I've gained some conditioning*, she thought. But really, it was more the shock and fear of the earlier encounter sending her adrenaline into overdrive, and she still felt it circulating in her blood.

The speed with which the incident had erupted stunned her. Very few words exchanged, a gun barrel swinging toward her, the weird, compressed sound of silenced guns and the sting as a bullet creased her arm. The body collapsing, the *look* in his eyes—

Ignoring the momentary queasiness, she reminded herself to wash and bandage the still stinging place on her upper arm. She felt sure Zach wouldn't have forgotten.

The track curved to level out briefly, although they hadn't reached the top of the ridge. Just as it curved back and began to climb again, bear tracks continued straight. She had bigger things to worry about, but still exhaled with relief. She'd be just as glad not to stumble on an irritable, hungry bear.

Maybe he had a cave up here, it occurred to her. He might be like the famous groundhog; he or she had emerged to decide whether winter was past, and thought, *Nah. I'm going back to bed*.

A strange sound came to her ears. She froze between one stride and the next, trying to identify it. Zach exploded into action, catching up to her with shocking speed.

"That's somebody behind us. Don't know if there are two of them, or whether he stumbled, cracked his shin and swore, but that was a voice."

She clenched her teeth to be sure they couldn't chatter. When she was confident she wouldn't give away her panic, she asked, "What do we do?"

"Go on until we find a place I can set up," he said tersely. For the first time in the past couple of hours, she felt as if he was seeing *her*, and his expression was raw. "If I can hide you and my pack, I may climb a tree."

She bobbed her head. "You go ahead, then. You know what you're looking for."

Without another word, he passed her and set off fast, despite the crosshatch technique needed to climb in snowshoes. She did her best to keep up. The worst part was that she didn't hear so much as a whisper of sound behind her. It made her picture a little red dot centered on the back of her head. One pull of the trigger—

Go, go, go.

"Here," Zach said suddenly.

They weren't at a high enough elevation for the trees to be stunted yet. He seemed to have his eye on a cluster of big hemlock or Douglas fir, she wasn't sure, probably spruce and certainly cedar. The snow cover thinned to almost nothing beneath the spreading branches.

He pointed. "Get under cover, well back. Hunker down. Have your handgun ready to fire. Do you understand?"

"Yes. Yes."

He didn't move until she took a couple of

steps, then removed her snowshoes and kept going on the side hill, a foot slipping here and there, but she caught herself with a hand on the branches and rough trunks.

When she glanced back, she couldn't see Zach anymore. That scared her, but she had to trust that he knew what he was doing. Of course he did.

Finally, she crawled beneath a cedar tree. The feathery branches brushed the ground. Ava had to push them aside. With shuddering relief, she dropped the poles and snowshoes, eased off her pack and dug the gun she didn't even like to handle out of the outside pocket.

Then she crawled to a position where she could just see traces of her own tracks between the thankfully lush branches that she hoped would still hide her. She decided to sit up; a lot of positions would be hard to sustain for long. Then she took off her right glove, as Zach had taught her, pushed the tiny button to turn off the safety and listened to herself breathe. She just couldn't let herself get so scared that she accidentally shot Zach.

No. I have to wait to make sure.

MUCH LIKE HE'D done setting up the previous ambushes, Zach continued on ten yards until the trail curved enough that a pursuer was unlikely to notice that one of the two people ahead had peeled off. He'd see only tracks heading on.

Then Zach stepped carefully off the trail and circled back to his chosen trees. He stashed his pack and equipment out of sight and, with the rifle slung over his shoulder, started to climb.

This was an old enough cedar to have branches he hoped would hold his weight. If he could get high enough, he'd be able to step over to a spruce that would give him a better sight line down the trail. He'd kept his gloves on to give himself a good grip. If a branch broke and he fell, they were screwed.

Each scramble upward was made gingerly. He tested some of his weight on a branch, then all of it, but kept an arm around the trunk or a hand gripping the limb above to keep himself from plummeting.

He still didn't hear anybody approaching, but knew he couldn't be mistaken.

At last, maybe twenty-five feet off the ground, he found a perch that felt secure and gave him a hell of a view.

He was planning to kill in cold blood. He couldn't issue a warning, not when this SOB was likely carrying a fully automatic weapon that could spray bullets to cut him down along with half of this stretch of forest, too.

The shot wouldn't be long, which was just as well since he hadn't practiced at the range at more than two hundred yards since he got out of the service. The old skills were probably there, but he was just as glad not to have to test them. If all went well, this shot wouldn't even be a hundred yards.

Nothing to it.

He rolled his shoulders. Stuck both his gloves in parka pockets and worked at slowing his breathing. How many times had he done this?

More than he wanted to remember.

He rested the barrel of the rifle on another branch, needing to compensate for the extra and unfamiliar weight of the suppressor. Then he zeroed the scope. Details sprang out in what had been a faraway scene. The length of a football field. Now, he could almost reach out and touch.

Slow and easy. Breathe in, breathe out. Wait for the natural rest.

Ten or fifteen minutes passed. Longer. Then suddenly a white-clad man appeared without Zach having heard him. Despite the warming day, he wore the hood up so that the fur almost obscured his face. He blended in remarkably well, only his boots gray or brown instead of white. The AK-47 stood out, of course.

Zach could have fired, but waited. *Closer, closer.*

Some instinct had his opponent sliding the rifle off his shoulder to ease it into firing position.

Can't let that happen.

Zach set the gun sights over the chest, safer than a head shot now that he knew the others hadn't worn Kevlar vests.

He let out a breath and gently pulled the trigger.

Dead on.

He'd have new nightmares, but refused to feel guilty. These bastards were hunting him and Ava relentlessly, as if planning to mount their heads on a wall.

He'd done what he had to do.

Chapter Twelve

With no way to tell the time, Ava could only guess. Each minute probably felt like fifteen. She strained her ears and eyes. It already felt like forever when she thought she heard… something. A *pop* that made her feel queasy. Then she decided she must have imagined it, because nothing else happened. Zach didn't appear, or call out to her to emerge from hiding.

She rested the gun on her thigh, holding it with her left hand every so often so she could flex the fingers on her right hand. How *could* it be so quiet? Why couldn't she even hear a bird call? It was as if nature held its breath. Maybe these old mountains and this forest resented the violence that invaded an ancient landscape meant to be a refuge. Except, these mountains also were home to several of nature's top-of-the-line predators.

What if she had heard a gunshot, only it was *Zach* who'd been shot? The thought sickened her, but after some deep breathing, Ava convinced herself she didn't believe that was possible, not for a minute. Zach had brought down *two* men when he was hurting and unarmed but for a folding knife. The next one, heavily armed, had come face-to-face with them, and Zach had outgunned him.

Who knew she'd ever be able to think so matter-of-factly about stuff that was so horrific.

No matter what, she kept her guard up. She flexed her fingers again, peered in every direction and strained for any sound at all.

It had to be an hour or more before the low call came to her. "Ava? Where are you?"

"Here." Her voice croaked. Her next effort was better. "Here!" She tried to stand but found her knees had pretty much locked. Still, she sent the closest cedar branches waving, and within a minute she saw him turning his head as he came into sight.

She staggered to her feet just in time. "Oh, thank God!"

He gave a weak grin. "Now, now. You need to have faith."

"I do," she said quietly, almost hoping he didn't hear her. From the way his gaze sharpened, she thought he had. "What happened?"

Carrying the rifle, he ducked into her shelter. "There was only one man on our trail. I went down almost as far as the river to be sure there wasn't a second one." He rested the rifle, butt down, against the tree trunk.

"He's dead?"

In the act of lowering his pack to the ground, he gave a clipped nod as he glanced quickly at her before looking away.

"Did you, well, learn anything?"

"No." With a groan, he sat down a couple of feet from her, leaning against the tree trunk. If she'd thought she had seen him tired before, it was nothing in comparison. He pulled off a glove and scrubbed his hand over his face and dug his fingers into his hair beneath the fleece hat. "Damn."

On instinct, she reached to lay a hand on the forearm he had braced on his knees. "I'm sorry. I wish I could do more."

The turbulence was back in his brown eyes. "Like kill people?"

The sharp edge in his voice shocked her. She snatched back her hand. "I should have said, I wish you didn't have to kill people."

"I'm the one who's sorry," Zach said heavily. "I hated doing it, but there wasn't any option except raising our hands and saying, 'Here we are, execute us.'" His mouth twisted. "*I'm* the executioner instead."

Feeling tentative, she said, "You said yourself that this is war. We *can't* let that monster loose on our country! Isn't this every bit as critical as whatever you had to do in, I don't know, Afghanistan or the other places you were sent?"

His eyes met hers. He didn't so much as blink for a minute before he finally dipped his head. "You're right. I know you are. I guess I've been getting mushy in my retirement."

She snorted, and one side of his mouth curled up.

"Okay. I'll quit with the self-doubt."

"Thank you. You saved both of our lives today. *Twice*."

"Yeah, I guess so. Damn, I'm beat." His head turned again, as if he was evaluating her hidey-hole. "I'm thinking this is as good a place as any to spend the night. Maybe we can set up a little deeper in this stand of woods."

"Okay. Do you want to rest for a few minutes first?"

"Maybe." He tipped his head back and closed his eyes, thick dark lashes fanned on tanned, still discolored skin.

Ava let him brood, if that's what he was

doing. If he fell asleep...well, she'd find them a campsite and set up, then come back for him.

"This was another Russian," he said unexpectedly. "I'm betting ex-military. Probably all of them are. Were."

"That makes sense," she said softly.

"The odds are almost even now, except..." He broke off. "I wish I could keep you out of this."

"So far, you mostly have."

"If we could just get our hands on Borisyuk himself."

"Wouldn't it make sense for him to run for it?" She was practically begging for the answer she both wanted to hear and didn't, but also... There was no *logic* in a man whose goal was to disrupt this nation in some significant way wasting time to hunt down two snowshoers who, for all he knew, hadn't even had a good look at him.

Zach told her some of what he'd apparently been thinking about today, and she had to agree it was logical. And no, she didn't want Grigor Borisyuk to go on his way. Despite the struggles in her life, she'd never felt vengeful until now. She wanted that man to die next— or, better yet, for Zach to capture him and be able to hand him over to authorities.

THE END OF an operation was when you evaluated every decision, every pause, every command. Every hiccup. It wasn't Zach's habit to second-guess himself constantly mid-op, but he couldn't seem to help himself this time.

He did get himself moving so that he and Ava could find a secluded campsite even farther from the trail, but when she insisted on setting up the tent and rolling out the sleeping bags—and zipping them together again, his ears told him—he let her. He felt as if he'd been pounded.

He always had hated his rare sniper missions. He didn't know how the guys who did it day after day, month after month, came home even semisane. The combination of looking into someone's face so clearly, it was as if you could touch them, while they had no idea they were going to die, always sickened him. In modern warfare, it was necessary. He got that. But he'd rather any day be involved in a shoot-out across the street in some red-brown, dusty town, a straight-out battle where everyone involved knew what was at stake. Or having a hand-to-hand fight, as with the first two guys he'd brought down, even if he'd given himself the advantage from the beginning with the element of surprise.

Get it out of your mind, he told himself.

Which was fine, but then he devolved into thinking that, tired or not, he and Ava should have gone on, opened more distance between themselves and any pursuers.

Yeah, except it was likely one or two of these guys had also advanced up the ridge trail and would therefore be lying in wait for them. Better to face them after a good night's sleep. As good as he'd have, when he'd be keeping an ear out all night for any faint noise that didn't belong.

Ava broke into his brooding. "Any preferences for dinner?"

"Food."

She chuckled. "On our way out, maybe the helicopter would drop us in the parking lot at a pizza parlor."

"That sounds good to me." Now he was *really* hungry. He also liked that she pictured them together sharing a pizza. "I should have taken a turn cooking tonight. No reason for you to wait on me."

"An enlightened man," she teased. Then her voice and expression turned serious. "You're the soldier. I'm the one who has to wait. Of course I should contribute any way I can."

He frowned. "I'd be dead if it weren't for you, remember?"

"Yes, except if not for me, there probably wouldn't have *been* an avalanche."

"You're in a mood, aren't you?"

She closed her eyes for a moment, and her shoulders seemed to relax. When she opened her eyes, she fixed her gaze on his face. "I guess so. I *hate* waiting, not knowing what's happening to you. The last thing I should do is whine after you come back safe."

"Ava."

Her lashes fluttered a couple of times.

"You may be the bravest woman I've ever met. This has been a monumentally bad few days, and you've endured it all without any whining. You had to have passed the point of complete exhaustion and continued on for hours without a word at least a couple of those days." He smiled ruefully. "You cuddled with a complete stranger to warm him up. You popped his arm back into the socket. You let him leave you for *hours* in a hole that looked like an open grave. So let up on yourself."

Her mouth curved. "I will if you will."

He stiffened. "What are you talking about?"

"I know brooding when I see it."

Zach grimaced. "Set me up, did you?"

Wrinkled nose. "Kind of. I do feel useless, but I am smart enough to stay out of your way and help where I can. So let's eat, and go to bed the second it's dark enough to sleep."

He glanced around. "It's getting there fast."

"I know."

Dinner was a stew that he wolfed down, even though it wasn't very good. Ava had given him a much bigger portion than she ate. He saw that she'd opened three packets tonight instead of just two. Thanks to his scrounging, they had more than enough food.

See? There's a positive.

The candy bar was another positive, as was the cup of coffee. And knowing he'd be sleeping with Ava in his arms.

Tonight she boiled some water, and they took turns using a thin bar of soap, a washcloth and a towel. Each found privacy to scrub what they could. He imagined she was fantasizing about a hot shower as much as he was. He smelled his underarm dubiously before and after washing it, and couldn't decide whether there was any real improvement. Probably irrelevant, since he had no clean clothes. He hadn't felt he could afford the time, but he still regretted not ransacking the packs of the two men he'd shot in hopes one had been close enough to his size. But really, in the grand scheme of things, what difference did it make? On operations, he'd gone a lot longer than this without a shower.

None of this would have crossed his mind if it weren't for Ava.

He had reluctantly helped himself to a toothbrush from the first pack he searched, did his best to wash it clean of any germs and then used it. He wasn't going to subject Ava to his bad breath because he was squeamish about sharing spit with a Russian terrorist.

His outer layer of clothes went between the pad and the double sleeping bag. Lying down made him aware of every sore place in his body, yet was also such a relief that he groaned aloud. Ava, soon to join him, laughed, and he grinned at her. Her pencil flashlight lit up the interior of the tent enough to allow him to watch as she stripped off clothes, as well. Just not enough of them. As was their routine, he rolled, she spread them out with his, he rolled back onto the now double pad, and she turned off the flashlight before slithering in beside him.

Also as usual, she lay stiff for the first minute or two, until he reached out his right arm and pulled her into him. In no time, her head rested on his shoulder, her body pressed against his side and her hand lay splayed on his chest. He felt her fingers flex a little, and his body stirred. Making a move on her wasn't on the table, though, even if he thought she was attracted to him, too. He didn't like the idea she'd have sex with him because she was grateful, or how awkward it might be if she said hell no. A first for him, he might hate almost as much them making love only because she was thinking they could both die tomorrow and was grabbing for life with both hands.

Yeah, damn it, but what if they did die tomorrow, and had never—

He cut that train of thought right off. He wanted…something entirely new to him, and hadn't a clue whether she felt anything similar.

The remaining tension in her slowly eased. Eventually, she'd throw a leg over his. He also knew she wasn't asleep yet. Her breathing would change.

An owl hooted softly, not far away. He heard a squeak. Nothing to worry about, though. Letting himself relax toward sleep, he spoke without thinking.

"I feel as if I've held you like this every night for a lot longer than we've really known each other." He'd almost said, *For all my life*. Good catch, even if he shouldn't have said as much as he did. And, damn, suddenly he regretted every night he *hadn't* spent with her.

The ones to come, he couldn't let himself think about yet.

There was a minute tightening in her muscles before she whispered, "I…know what you mean. I've never been so comfortable before, or slept as well as I do with you, despite everything."

"I guess we fit together," he murmured.

"We do."

That sounded sad, which worried him, but he didn't know what he could do or say to make any of this better.

One more day, he told himself.

ZACH FELL ASLEEP before she did. Not that he snored, but...she could just tell. He was right. What would it be like in the imaginary future when she was able to go back to her life, crawling into a bed alone, shifting around, trying to find a place to rest her head that felt *right*? She'd never known before that she really needed, well, a body pillow to wrap herself around, too. Except, that body pillow wouldn't have a heartbeat; it wouldn't rise and fall in a gentle rhythm. It wouldn't be warm. And there'd be no strong arm around her, either.

She was grieving already.

I don't really know him, Ava tried to convince herself, but knew that was wrong. It was true they hadn't shared the trivial stuff people might on first dates: tastes in movies, music, books, favorite color, first celebrity or real crush. But none of that mattered. He'd told her things about himself that cut much deeper, giving her a glimpse of a complex man who probably suffered a degree of PTSD from his service. A man who, in an often-selfish world, was capable of enormous self-sacrifice. A man skilled at killing, who still showed kindness and an ability to understand what drove her, after knowing her less than a week.

She'd told him more about herself, and so quickly, than she had anyone else, too.

She was falling in love with him, Ava realized with less shock than she should feel. What to do about it...? Well, that wasn't obvious. Nor whether he felt anything similar for her. For heaven's sake, she hadn't even thought to ask whether he had someone waiting at home, a girlfriend or even a wife, although she believed he wouldn't have kissed her the way he did if that was so.

Worry about tomorrow, she lectured herself, and at last felt sleep claiming her.

Darkness was complete the next time she surfaced. Aware she'd half climbed on top of Zach, she puzzled over the big hand clasped over her butt cheek, while the other had found its way under her knit shirt to have a firm grip on her waist. First time that had happened. In her current state, she didn't mind. In fact, a hold so proprietary gave her a warm feeling of security. It let her slip back to sleep.

Some tension in the big body beneath her awoke her the next time. Was he holding his breath? Maybe he'd lifted his head slightly. She'd know, since she had tucked her face against his neck.

He was listening, she decided.

"Do you hear something?" she whispered.

After a long moment, he said, his voice low, "No. Probably came out of a dream."

He'd have plenty of nightmares to draw on, it occurred to her. As she herself did; frighteningly often, she reverted to being the hungry, desperate little girl who didn't dare trust anyone, who tried to be a ghost while stealing what food she could get her hands on and carrying it back to whatever nook she'd found that provided even minimal shelter.

She patted Zach's chest. A faint rumble rose beneath her hand.

"Comfortable?" he asked. And yes, that had to be a trace of amusement in the quiet question.

"Um..." She was suddenly unsure of herself. Okay, she'd been asleep, but she had taken an awful lot of liberties with his body. "Yes," she admitted.

"I like it." He squeezed her butt and rubbed his cheek against her head, catching hair on his short beard.

The position of her thigh, sprawled across him, had become a little less comfortable due to what felt like a bar on a sleeper sofa, but which she knew quite well was his erection. Arousal washed over her, tightening in her belly, melting down lower. Her nipples had to have hardened.

He'd notice.

Except...he was the one who'd started this.

"Ava?" he asked huskily.

She made a sound that might have been a whimper. When he wrapped both hands around her waist and lifted her, she went eagerly. Their mouths met clumsily in the dark. He had to pull back to swipe a long hank of her hair out of the way, but then they kissed with urgency like nothing she'd ever felt before. This contact was more important than anything in the world. His tongue thrust into her mouth, and she sucked on it, tangled her tongue around his, followed it back into the depths of his mouth. She tasted blood but didn't care.

She'd come to be straddling him, and even as they kissed, he gripped her hips and worked her up and down on his hard length.

"Swore I wouldn't—" he mumbled once, but she didn't let him finish. She didn't want to hear his qualms, or consider her own.

If she had any.

He found his way under her shirt to her

breast. Ava had never been more grateful that she had stripped off her bra every night for comfort. He cupped her completely, squeezed and rubbed gently, and oh, she wanted his mouth where his hand was, but even more she wanted—

"Let me," she said in a strangled whisper, and climbed off him enough to push her stretch pants and panties down. If only this was as simple as taking off a pair of jeans. Beside her, he had to be pushing his pants off, too, or did they zip or button open? Ava had no idea. At last, she contorted herself to grip the hem at her ankle and yank the wretched pants off that leg.

His fingers slipped between her thighs and her hips rocked.

"You feel so damn good," he said, in the voice like gravel. "I need you. Are you sure, Ava?"

"Yes." She'd given up getting the pants all the way off and flung her leg back over him.

"I don't have any—"

"I'm on birth control." A moment of sanity had her asking, "If you're—?"

"Yeah," he said hoarsely, even as he used his greater strength to position her, opening her.

As desperately ready as she was, he stretched her, filling her beyond capacity...except, after the first shock, she knew his size was just right.

We fit, he'd said, and they still did.

On her knees, she rode him even as he guided her, sometimes hurried her, slammed her up and down as she'd swear his entire body bowed up to meet her.

What hit her felt like the avalanche, a natural cataclysm, except being spun around and around was like flying, and she never wanted to come back to earth.

The pulsing inside her set her off again, something that had never happened before. She loved the raw sound he made that vibrated against her breasts as she collapsed against him.

In the sweaty, breathless, shaky aftermath, it would have been so easy to say, *I love you*. Instead, she made herself wait to hear what *he* would say.

It came after a minute, a ragged, "I never knew."

She'd never known, either. Scared as she was of making herself too vulnerable, Ava couldn't be a coward.

"Me, either," she whispered, closing her eyes to savor the way he stroked her, kneading occasionally, never stopping. *She* didn't move, because she didn't want him to slip out of her.

Turned out, she didn't have to worry, because faster than she would have thought possible, he was swelling inside her again, moving slowly, nudging her, until these impossible feelings rose in an inexorable tide, and they made love again.

Chapter Thirteen

Ava awakened to strong hands kneading her—butt, back, shoulders. It felt amazing.

"Morning," a gritty voice murmured in her ear.

She pried open her eyelids. "Not morning."

"Close enough. We want an early start."

She'd had such sensational dreams, and now came the hard clunk back to reality.

Not dreams. Oh, God. They'd made love *three* times, and each had been as good as the last. A quiver deep in her belly let her know that a fourth time would be absolutely fine with her, except… She let out a whimper. Or was it a whine?

"Sorry."

A last squeeze had her sighing before she squirmed her way out of the cozy, warm sleeping bag into frigid air.

He rolled the sleeping bags and pads with quick efficiency while she fired up the stove. Not fifteen minutes later, they were eating oatmeal with raisins in it and sipping coffee. Neither of them said a word about last night. She didn't know what to say, while he... Oh, he was a man. She'd been there, and why would they bother talking about it?

Ava suppressed a sigh.

Craggy and scruffy, his face came into focus as the sun rose. Ava was sure the lines beside his eyes hadn't been that deep the first time she'd climbed into a sleeping bag with him. His lips were even more cracked, as she could tell hers were. She grimaced, knowing she must look like something the cat had dragged in, as her last foster father had said. They'd both lost weight, despite the supplement to their diet. Think of the calories they were burning!

It didn't take her a minute to clean and repack the stove, pan and dishes, and not that much later she slid her booted feet into the bindings on her snowshoes.

"This is going to be rough," Zach warned.

She leveled a look at him that made him grin. Which lightened her heart, at least briefly.

He'd been right, she thought. Why bother getting into sticky emotions, assuming she wasn't the only one feeling them, when today might be the day they'd die?

The climb was a struggle. Occasionally, they had to remove their snowshoes to scramble up bare rock that tilted steeply upward. The rest of the time, they wound between stands of trees that became more stunted the higher they went. Obstacles lurked everywhere beneath the snow, some forming lumps, others dips: rocks, fallen trees, stumps, clumps of what might be huckleberry bushes or the like. Both kept having to untangle their snowshoes from whatever had seized them. Twice in the first hour, she went down and began to resent Zach's greater muscle mass that allowed him to stay upright even when he was tripped up.

He paused every twenty feet or so to scrutinize their surroundings. Ava appreciated the breather, but always felt her heart rate accelerate when his gaze paused on something or another and his eyes narrowed. She quit asking what he'd seen.

She was concentrating on where she put her feet when he said quietly, "There's the trail."

Lifting her head, she stepped on the back of one of his snowshoes and grabbed his parka for balance.

Crossing their current path, there were undeniable tracks on a level path covered in formerly smooth snow, but following those tracks with her eyes, she saw how the trail zigzagged to continue to climb steeply.

"Are they ahead of us?"

He leaned forward on his poles, studying what wasn't a clear-cut print. "Up and back, I think," he said at last. "This wasn't one man."

She absorbed that. "Do we dare—"

"Check your phone."

Ava lowered her pack to the ground, fumbled to open a pocket and removed her glove to touch the phone. She didn't have much hope, given that the trail had just started the steepest part of its climb, and if she turned in place she could see the surrounding Cascade peaks with dominating elevation. Still she stared at the phone in frustration. "Nothing."

"You've charged it?"

"You saw me!"

Ava stayed quiet and let him take out binoculars and scan, lowering them and frowning without saying anything. He was thinking.

Out of the corner of her left eye, she caught movement, or maybe the sun reflecting off something. Her adrenaline spiked.

"Zach?" she whispered. "Off to the left."

He whipped the binoculars in that direction just as she saw a flash of blue.

"Blue jay," she said in relief.

Zach studied the stunted trees growing amidst rock protruding from the snow for another minute. "Might have been scared into taking off."

She held her breath until, satisfied or temporarily dismissing any possible threat from that quarter, he turned the binoculars down the ridge again.

"Birds don't just hang out on branches all day, you know."

He didn't smile. She wished he would have.

"We have company coming," he said tightly. "Quite a ways down, but heading our way."

"They're afraid we went cross-country."

"That's my take."

"One, or the whole party?"

"I see only one man."

His eyes met hers. They were almost expressionless; this was the spec ops warrior looking at her. He'd quashed his emotions in favor of clinical decision-making and action. She would ache for the loss, but this part of him was the reason they were both alive.

"I need to stash you again," he said.

Somehow, she wasn't at all surprised by his pronouncement.

KEEP IN MIND *how fast two people heading toward each other will meet up,* Zach reminded himself as he strode as fast as the damn snowshoes allowed. *Set up an ambush, or gun him down.*

Zach didn't feel so much as a stir from his conscience this time. He no longer had the slightest doubt that this was life or death for him and Ava. Seeing the grenade launcher slung over this slug's back was the clincher. He had knowingly fired the shots to try to kill an innocent woman.

Never mind everything that had happened since.

Zach's mind seemed to have a split screen: his current surroundings and what he had to do, and Ava.

He didn't love the most recent hiding spot where he'd left her. The scattered clumps of stunted trees provided scant coverage because of the higher elevation. The best he could do was tuck her at the foot of a small drop-off along with both their packs. She couldn't be seen from the trail, but that didn't mean he felt comfortable with the choice.

She was armed, he reminded himself, but he lacked confidence she'd be able to pull a trigger to kill a man—at least, without hesitating too long.

Hell.

He'd done all he could. When he left, she'd had the handgun in a pocket of her parka where, worse came to worst, she could access it easily. At his last sight of her, Ava's bare hand had been buried in that pocket.

Concentrate on the war of attrition he was

conducting, he ordered himself. Four down, three to go. He couldn't afford a moment of carelessness.

His pace slowed. He'd rather set up, wait for the enemy to come to him. The idea of being too far from Ava ate at him. He hadn't liked the other times he'd left her, but this...

He traversed another switchback, finally spotting a small cluster of trees on top of a rock ledge that should allow him to see anyone coming up the trail before they saw him. Clothed in white, he should be hidden by the twisty group of mountain hemlock and subalpine fir.

He'd decided against setting any kind of snare. Lying in the snow, rifle set on a bipod, he might as well be in a shooting gallery. *Pop, pop*, done.

Zach used the binoculars sparingly under the theory that his target would be pausing regularly to use *his*. Best not to give him any warning.

He wasn't feeling real patient, though, and with every passing minute, his nerves stretched tighter. Could he have imagined seeing someone?

No.

Could the guy have halted before the pair of new tracks appeared on the trail and turned around to rejoin whatever compatriots he still had? Zach didn't believe that; any scout would have gone considerably farther before giving up. He wouldn't dare return too soon; Borisyuk would expect his minions to go to the last extreme.

Still, Zach detected no movement at all below him.

Disquiet had him feeling edgy and thinking hard. That peculiar, not-quite-itch crawled between his shoulder blades and up his neck.

What if the jay *had* been startled by humans? What if danger had been up the ridge, and the man Zach had seen was a decoy? What if that man had showed himself deliberately with no intention of advancing up the trail?

Without even knowing he'd made a decision, Zach was moving. Backing away from the edge, locking the bipod in place, hitching the rifle over his shoulder as he shoved his feet into the snowshoe bindings.

He was perilously close to panic. What if he was too late?

AVA WASN'T SURE she'd ever have the capability to wait patiently again, whether in line at the grocery store or to check in at the airport. This was torture, plain and simple. It had been all she could do not to beg Zach not to leave her. Only pride let her follow his instructions and do no more than whisper, "Stay safe," before he left.

Weird, when she thought about it, because her career was all about patience. She could lie for hours, impervious to stiff muscles or hunger, watching the entrance to a fox's den for a pup to emerge, or crawl into some absurd position in a tree where she could see the nest of a peregrine falcon. She'd been lucky enough that time to catch extraordinary photos of tiny beaks cracking open the shells, of the emergence of the babies and their first meal.

She'd like to think she could summon that kind of patience again, but right this second she wanted to scream.

He had a watch, but she didn't. Although, being able to see the seconds pass, wait for a minute to go by, then another, might make this worse. *A watched pot never boils*, right?

He'd asked her several times to have faith in him, and she did. Really. But he was one man against a terrorist sought by a good percentage of the governments in the world, and that terrorist had a squad backing him. Zach was still outnumbered three to one, and that was assuming their count from the photos she'd taken of the group on the ridge was accurate. There was no saying a couple more men hadn't been trailing well behind for some reason, or had gone ahead and already disappeared behind tree cover. What if there'd been a dozen more men?

For heaven's sake, she was talking herself into hysteria. Ava made herself take a few slow, deep breaths. So far, unless Zach had lied to her, he had hardly been challenged as he eliminated one opponent after another. There was no reason to think this would be any different.

Except she felt very, very alone.

A soft sound came to her. Her head turned sharply. Was Zach already back? Or—

A white-clad man reared above her on that rocky ledge. Her brain said, *Shoot him!* Her body tried to collect itself to move, but she was too slow. He sprang down, slamming her into the snow. Something cracked and pain shot through her. His gloved hand closed over her face, covering her mouth and nose. She couldn't breathe, couldn't scream. He'd broken her arm, Ava knew, which didn't prevent her fighting as viciously as she could to get out from under him.

She managed to get her mouth open and bit hard on what was probably mostly glove, but the man holding her down with sheer weight snarled something harsh.

He must have risen to his knees, because he wrenched her up, still stifling her ability to scream. She twisted and fought with everything in her. The next time she managed a bite, that big hand mashed so hard on her face she couldn't part her lips. Blood filled her mouth.

A calm voice behind her said something in that other language she assumed was Russian, and her captor turned her to face a second man who pointed a black handgun at her in a negligent way. If she hadn't already been terrified, the sight of him would have done it.

He was strange looking—not ugly, exactly, but as Zach had said, so distinctive no one would ever mistake that face. Cheekbones that, along with an exceptionally wide jaw, made the lower two-thirds of his face a square. As she stared at him, he pushed back his hood, and she saw the sharp widow's peak. The eyes that stared back at her were... No, cold didn't even describe them. Reptilian was closer to it.

Grigor Borisyuk himself. Ava knew this man would torture her to get what he wanted, and kill her with no more thought than most people gave to an ant on a sidewalk they'd accidentally stepped on.

It might almost be better if she was nothing to him but a problem he could solve with a snap of his finger. As it was, she and Zach had frustrated and inconvenienced him, and Ava suspected that wasn't a common experience for this monster in human form.

"You took pictures," he said, his English heavily accented. "I want your camera." He nodded at the other man, who loosened his grip on her mouth.

Could she talk without her teeth chattering? Her whole body wanted to tremble, but she made herself stiffen.

"My camera was damaged in the avalanche."

"You should have died." His eyes bored into hers.

"I was lucky." So lucky, she almost wished she *had* died, instead of being tormented by discovering hope and meeting a man she could—probably did—love.

"Give me the camera."

Scream? Ava knew she no longer dared. There was nothing to stop them from shooting her now and rooting through the packs on their own. She nodded as well as she could.

Another jerk of the head and the man holding her from behind spun her to face the packs. His rough handling must have grated the bones in her upper arm, because the pain that had been buried beneath shock and fear had her crying out.

She tried to reach out for the pack with both hands, but couldn't lift her left arm. She'd have to do everything with her right hand.

She'd still be able to shoot, she realized in a part of her brain that must be walled off from the emotional distress and pain. The man she'd fought, the one whose face she *hadn't* seen, must not have noticed the shape of what she had in her pocket.

She could dip her hand in that pocket right now.

No. She'd be dead before she could pull the gun out.

Wait.

With her right hand, she began fumbling with the zipper that opened her pack.

Was there any chance at all Zach would come in time?

SWEAT RAN DOWN Zach's face. It might be freezing, but he neither knew nor cared. Despite the steep climb, he was all-out running. His gut told him Ava was in trouble, that he'd been lured away from her. He'd felt a twinge of unease when that blue jay shot into the air. He'd have sworn if he could have spared the breath. He knew better than to ignore his own instincts.

At least one of the two remaining men had waited up above. Maybe both were there. If they'd seen where he rejoined the trail when he started down—they could go straight to Ava.

God. He needed to be more aware, not get himself shot because he was too single-minded, too afraid for her to care if he was the target instead.

He stopped, scanned. Continued, did the same. He didn't see any sign of life higher on the ridge.

That's because they weren't there anymore; he was terribly afraid they already had Ava.

Going up was slower than down, however hard he pushed himself. Sweat stung his eyes. He gasped for breath.

Soon, he had to get off the trail. Approach her position from an unexpected direction. Remember that he might still have one man coming up behind him.

Now, he decided, stepping gingerly onto a rock slab because he couldn't risk damaging his snowshoes. He took them off. Had to be quiet, too. Let Borisyuk and company think he was still down the ridge, fooled into thinking they had the upper hand.

AVA FUMBLED AS slowly as she could, which wasn't really pretense. The camera had settled down toward the bottom. First she pulled out the damaged lens, showing it, then dropping it on the snow when the Russian only sneered. She had to pull out packets of freeze-dried meals, rolled-up socks and wadded-up clothing, and let them fall, too. Finally she came to the camera and worked it out.

Borisyuk snatched it from her. The guy behind her tore off her hat and grabbed her braid, tugging her head back as if he enjoyed making her uncomfortable.

Of course he did.

Borisyuk brought the camera to life and began scrolling through photos. It took him time, but she knew the exact moment when he found his own face because he went completely still, not even blinking as he stared down at the screen.

His eyes scared her even more when he lifted them to her this time. "You have a… card. Or did you send this photo…?" He waved upward.

"I have a card."

"Do not play games with me. Show me."

Would he notice that there was a second slot for a different sized memory card?

Who was she kidding? Of course he would.

She indicated an empty slot.

"Where is it?"

"I—" Where had she put it? Her brain didn't seem to be working at top speed.

He backhanded her. Now her cheek hurt along with her neck. The man behind her laughed.

Borisyuk's cold gaze lifted, and he snapped out what sounded like a series of orders. The other man replied—argued?—and Borisyuk's face took on a cruel cast. He said a few more words that might have been ice pellets, but also raised the handgun to level it at her chest.

Her braid was suddenly released, and she bent her head forward in temporary relief as she sensed the second man rising to his feet. Finally, sidelong, she saw his back as he clambered back up the drop-off to where they'd presumably left their packs and snowshoes.

New fear squeezed Ava's chest painfully. He had been sent to watch for Zach—or even to join the hunt for him.

"Where is it?" Borisyuk asked again, and before she could open her mouth, the back of his hand connected with her cheekbone again.

Stunned, she had to blink a few times. If he knocked her out, he wouldn't get an answer...but maybe he didn't care. He could search her body and her belongings without any help from her. In fact, she wondered why he hadn't killed her yet.

"Where—"

"I have it," she interrupted, only her words didn't come out quite right. Her mouth must be swollen. She swallowed blood. She reached out again for her pack. She remembered slipping the card into a small, flat pocket near the top, probably designed for passports or driver's licenses or the like. It would have been easy to overlook, but refusing to produce the card would get her killed. Now, instead of later.

If he wasn't satisfied—no, she didn't *want* him to be, because then he'd be done with her.

She held it out, and he switched the gun to his other hand as he took the memory card from her. She dropped her own hand to her side and began inching it toward her pocket.

"There should be another one," he declared. "Give it to me."

Wham.

Her vision blurred. She wasn't sure she was seeing out of her right eye at all anymore. That meant *he* was right-handed, the way he was hitting her. Ava didn't know why that made any difference, but knew it did.

"My friend," she mumbled. "The man I'm traveling with. He has the other one."

She had never seen anything approaching the rage that built on Grigor Borisyuk's ugly face. His next blow knocked her over. She lay helpless on the snow as he glared down at her, the one memory card fisted in his hand, the gun pointing at her.

So much for her gamble. Why wouldn't he pull the trigger right now?

Chapter Fourteen

He heard voices and then a cry of pain, but also movement to his right. Zach threw himself flat onto the snowy ground, only slowly lifting his head. It was one of the men, but he passed out of sight before Zach could ready for a rifle or even pistol shot.

And did he dare do either? He gritted his teeth. Suppressors did just that, limiting the cracking sound everyone knew as gunfire. But they weren't true silencers by any means. Anyone with Ava was close enough to hear and recognize the peculiar *pop* if he fired now.

He wished he could be sure whether the guy had gone uphill or down. Or cut across the side hill to report back to Borisyuk, if that's who was with Ava.

Keep moving, he decided and rose. After taking a couple of steps that resulted in him sinking deep into the snow and leaving what looked like postholes, he awkwardly put the snowshoes back on. Soft as the snow was, he still sank, but at this point, tracks had ceased to matter.

Fear came close to clouding his ability to envision a scene and make a judgment. Ava cried out at nearly exact intervals, and each cry felt like a lightning bolt burning through his entire body.

Picturing the place where he'd left her, he realized he couldn't approach from below. Under the wide ledge, he'd be too low to effectively launch an attack, and too visible. Get back to the path he and she had used in the first place? That made him uneasy. There'd been a small bluff above her, which would have been the ideal way for someone to sneak up on her.

The cluster of trees didn't provide the kind of cover he'd like—they were too scrawny, too thin—but that still might be the best option.

Suddenly, two men were speaking what he thought was Russian. Ava was silent.

THE SECOND MAN came back twice to report to Borisyuk. Ava would have given almost anything to be able to understand what they were saying. Had he killed Zach and was now receiving congratulations? A growl in Borisyuk's voice suggested displeasure.

Where was Zach?

Through her daze of pain and with her blurred vision, she realized Borisyuk's attention was back on her. She was still on her knees, curled forward despite her best attempt at dignity.

"Why did you take my picture?" he asked.

"I—" She swallowed a mouthful of blood. "Whenever I'm looking at something, I click the shutter. I'm a wildlife photographer. That's why I'm here."

"You took—" he kicked her camera "—eight, nine pictures. Why?"

"Because..." She hesitated.

His hand blurred, coming at her so fast. Pain exploded.

She could only mumble.

"What? I cannot hear you."

"I was curious." She tried to form the words to his satisfaction. "Nobody should have been up on that ridge. I thought you must have crossed the border from Canada. There are no border checkpoints anywhere near."

The nearest she could come to describing his expression was displeasure.

"I saw the assault rifles some of the men carried. That...scared me. I thought I should report what I'd seen."

"Did you?"

Knuckles slammed into her face again, and she rocked in place.

Would he believe her if she lied? Would her answer, either way, make any difference?

No.

She swallowed more blood. Her tongue instinctively tried to find out whether he'd knocked out any teeth.

"No," she whispered. "Not yet."

"Your...*friend*?"

"I...don't know," she lied.

Wham.

This time she toppled sideways to the snow, landing on her broken arm. She'd thought it was almost numb, but now learned better. Had to keep her right arm free, though. Sooner or later, Borisyuk would get careless and she'd have her chance. Maybe the next time his teammate—no, his mercenary—returned.

"Do you know why I didn't kill you yet?" he asked in a tone of mild curiosity.

"No."

"You might be some use." He studied her. "You have a name?"

Nope, not me.

"Ava," she mumbled.

"Eva?"

"Ava. A-V-A."

He grunted, frowned and looked in the direction his man had disappeared.

She tensed, but before she could so much as stick her hand in her pocket to retrieve the gun, the Russian again turned that emotionless gaze on her.

She had to ask. "What use?"

"To, how do Americans say it? Ah. *Take care* of your friend."

Trap Zach. Persuade him to lay down his weapon with only the faintest hope they'd release her.

Don't do it, Zach, she pleaded. *They'll lie, then kill me, anyway.*

She was in enough pain right now, death didn't seem as frightening as it had.

Borisyuk bent and yanked her to her feet, his hand gripping her right upper arm with punishing force. "Stand." He pushed her a foot away from him. "You can stand," he said brusquely.

She could and did, but found it hard to keep her eyes open. Well, her left eye—she thought the right one was swollen shut. But she couldn't let herself sink into the dark abyss that beckoned, not while there was the slightest chance that Zach would save her—or that she could save herself. Or even him.

Borisyuk began to appear bored, if she

wasn't imagining things. *Yes, do think about your plans, your deadline, these irritating delays. Anything but me.*

He looked the same direction again. She squinted. No sign of that creep. Had Zach gotten to him?

But...was that movement, off to her left? The Russian hadn't noticed. She might be imagining that his boredom and indifference was shifting very slowly into tension.

She mustn't react at all. All she could do was wait.

Out of the corner of her only good eye, she could see a sliver of a man not quite hidden behind a wind-twisted tree. White arm, white hood framing his face, just as all those men wore. But it had to be Zach. What was he doing? Slowly, so slowly lifting a rifle into firing position.

Borisyuk was mostly behind her, so that she inadvertently blocked any shot. Would Zach risk it, anyway? That might be their only chance. Except, her captor thought she was helpless, and she wasn't.

If only Zach could draw his attention. The terrorist didn't seem to notice her hand creeping toward her right pocket. She couldn't pull the gun out unless he was distracted, but she could—her thumb found the tiny button that allowed her to turn off the safety.

With what felt like her last reserves, she ignored the useless left arm, all the pain, and poised on the balls of her feet to move faster than she'd ever moved in her life. She'd either shoot, or dive for the ground so Zach had no reason to hesitate. If Borisyuk heard anything and grabbed her, he could use her more effectively as a shield, and she couldn't let that happen.

She envisioned every action she had to take. Pull the gun out so smoothly it didn't get tangled with fabric. Or kick and dive.

"Grigor?" Zach called.

Borisyuk spun on instinct toward Zach. She yanked the gun out, leveled it, and just as the Russian thought to turn enough to grab her, she pulled the trigger, then pulled it again and again.

His gaze held hers as his own weapon fell from his hand, and then in eerie slow motion, he collapsed. It was like watching a puppet, animated one minute, losing all semblance of life when the strings were cut. He was dead before he hit the snowy ground. She could tell.

She backed up a step, then another, and finally dropped to her own knees to purge her stomach.

"Sweetheart." Zach was there, crouched beside her, hand on her back. "You're amazing. You'll be okay."

He kept his voice low, she thought in puzzlement. Didn't he know the monster really was dead?

And then she remembered there were still two more men, armed, alive and a threat.

SITTING ON HIS HAUNCHES, Zach wanted to haul her into his arms but knew he couldn't. Depending on her injuries, he'd hurt her, not give her comfort.

Deeper inside, he knew in horror how close he'd come to firing, despite the risk of hitting Ava. Thank God he hadn't. Thank God.

From the minute Ava looked up at him, rage joined the adrenaline-fueled emotions already so tangled he couldn't separate them. She looked bad, and would look worse once the bruises gained more color. Her right eye was too swollen to allow her to open it. She could have a broken cheekbone or jaw, or have had teeth knocked loose or out altogether. He'd seen pictures of women brutally damaged in horrific domestic violence episodes who looked better than she did.

Around the lump in his throat, he asked, "Where are you hurt?"

"My arm is broken." As swollen as her mouth was, the words were barely understandable. She touched her left upper arm in a tentative way that spoke for itself.

"I need to move you." He'd never hated saying anything more. "I assume that guy will come back—"

"Yah." Ava turned her head slowly, as if searching for her pack.

"No, for the moment, just you." He grabbed both handguns from where they'd fallen in the snow, switched on safeties and shoved them in pockets. He'd take Ava back the way he'd come, he decided. He had to pick up the rifle he'd dropped once Borisyuk went down, anyway, and he just needed to get her out of sight. "Can you stand?"

With his help, she rose shakily and showed no sign of collapsing. At his instruction, she put her right arm around his neck, and he scooped her up. Zach winced at the small cry that escaped her, but strode toward the tree cover, scanty as it was.

His thoughts scattered like a flock of pigeons at a clap of sound. He hoped there were still painkillers in that bottle she'd brought, or in one of the other packs. Borisyuk's and the other man's had to be nearby. What could he use for a splint? He could pack some snow on her face and the break—at least there was plenty of that. How quickly would the second man return—and what if the third one had joined him by now?

Zach wanted to get his and her packs out of there before reinforcements arrived. They wouldn't know how badly she'd been hurt, or how far away she could be. But he also needed—

"Is your camera working?" he asked.

She peered dazedly up at him. "Um...yah, if I can get...'nother lens on it."

"Photos with your phone would do," he realized.

A mumble answered him.

"Okay, I'm going to set you down here," he said, having seen a long crest in the snow that had to be a fallen log. Moving slowly to limit how much he jarred her arm or any other injuries, he bent and lowered her to a sitting position. "I need to grab our packs," he said. "I'll only be gone for a couple of minutes, but I want you to have protection."

That wasn't enthusiasm he saw on her face—truthfully, expressions on a face as battered as hers were next to impossible to read—but Ava accepted the handgun, flicked off the safety again and nodded at him. Her bare hand was probably freezing, but she didn't complain.

This was a woman who would never quit. The knowledge had his knees buckling with gladness that he'd met her, even as he wished she hadn't had to endure any of this.

Then he moved as fast as he could. He hurried to stuff her scattered possessions back into her pack before slinging it over one shoulder, his own over the other while carrying her poles and snowshoes. Now nothing remained in the vicinity except the body.

No—he frowned and scanned the trampled snow again. She'd have taken off the one glove to be able to shoot. But there was no sign of it.

He hustled back to where he'd left her, grateful to see her still upright and gripping the gun. He dropped everything in front of her and unzipped the pocket where he knew she stowed her phone.

She traded the gun for the phone and opened it for him, then they traded again.

As hard as he was listening, he wished he could swivel his ears like a rabbit, but no such luck.

Back to the clearing. As if he were a forensic photographer approaching a crime scene, he snapped pictures from a distance and then closer and closer before he rolled the body to get some clear ones of Grigor Borisyuk's dead face. Finally, he took a few more as he stepped back before dropping the phone in his pocket.

He broke off a couple of low limbs from an evergreen and used them to try to mitigate his tracks from going and coming repeatedly. At best he blurred them, but had to hope that was good enough.

Once he was beside her again, he gently removed the gun from her hand and laid it atop his pack where he could easily reach it. The magazine had been full, and she'd only shot three or four times, he thought.

He dug in the jumble he'd made of her pack until he found some plastic bags, dumping out the contents—dirty clothes, he thought—and filling them with snow before wrapping each in some of those same dirty clothes. "Where's your glove?" he asked.

"Pocket." Or that was his best guess for what she'd said.

He found it, held it for her to insert her hand in. "I'm going to put this on the right side of your face. Can you hold it while I get a look at your arm?"

Ava nodded. Once he'd positioned the first ice pack against her face to cover her cheekbone, brow, eye and jaw, she raised her right arm and replaced his hand with hers.

Under almost any other circumstances, he'd

have cut off her parka to avoid hurting her, but he was painfully aware of how swamped she'd be in one borrowed from any of the men. None of them were small. Continuing to wear her own would be best. They still had to get to where they could make a cell phone call. If he had to leave her, the inactivity would make her especially vulnerable to cold.

So he carefully removed the glove on her left hand, said, "This is going to hurt," and started easing the arm of the parka off. She couldn't entirely stifle a few whimpers and cries, and he apologized nonstop, grimacing the entire while.

He couldn't put either of them through this again. The fleece quarter-zip and turtleneck she wore beneath were replaceable, so he used the wicked knife he'd taken from one of the packs he'd rifled and cut the fabric at her shoulder. If only he had scissors—

Since he didn't, he sliced the sleeves from the top down to her wrist until they fell off.

It wasn't hard to see the break.

Still holding the ice pack to her face, Ava craned her neck to peer down at her upper arm. "I hab..." She licked some blood from her lips. "First aid kit."

The reminder was good. He hoped she hadn't used up most of what the kit held treating him. Once he dug it out, he marveled again at how prepared she'd been when setting out on her trek, knowing she'd be beyond help if she injured herself. He found a foam splint, and, though it wouldn't match a cast, it would help until they reached a hospital.

First, though, he pressed the other bag full of snow against the grotesque swelling.

Her slit of an eye fixed on him. "Otter mun?"

O... Other. Other man.

Zach shook his head. "I set up not far down the trail and waited for him, but when he didn't appear I got worried that he was a decoy."

"Was."

"Yeah. I hauled ass back to you, but I heard voices before I reached you."

She bobbed her head. "Knew you'd come."

He had to be getting better at understanding her thickened mumbles. He wished he could put an ice pack in her mouth, which was bloody. Had she bitten her tongue? Lost teeth? God. "I almost didn't." He was tortured with the knowledge of how close he'd come to being too late. The vicious ache felt as if a blow had cracked his sternum.

"Did."

Zach closed his eyes and bent to press his lips very softly to the cheek on the—mostly—uninjured side of her face.

Her worries now almost had to echo his.

"I could go out to the trail and shoot anyone who shows up, but that would mean leaving you alone." Vulnerable. "Not doing that again."

A tear had leaked from one corner of her eye.

"I wish I knew what they'll do when they find Borisyuk dead." Go for revenge? Or run for their lives? The answer depended, again, on whether they were hired muscle or dedicated zealots.

And where was the guy who'd left just as Zach arrived? Lying in wait along the trail, thinking he could pick Zach off? Meeting up with his buddy?

Zach wished he could be a hundred percent sure there *were* only two men remaining. He hadn't said anything to Ava, but he knew the group they'd seen up on the ridge could have been strung out far enough that they hadn't all been visible silhouetted against the sky. If so, they might be spread out watching other trails, per orders.

A faint, alien whisper of sound reached him, and he stiffened. Obviously watching him, Ava did the same. She set down the snow pack and picked up the handgun.

Zach cocked his head, waiting.

It came again, not quite a *swish-swish*,

but walking in deeper snow was a lot harder work than striding along a trail. One man, he thought. He rose to his feet, careful not to make a sound, and lifted the rifle from where he'd propped it against his pack.

That someone moved past them, higher up the ridge than where they'd holed up. Angling in to rejoin Borisyuk? Damn, Zach wished he and Ava had been able to move farther away. If this guy chose to use his fully automatic rifle to spray bullets in a circle, he could mow them down.

Zach held out a flattened hand to indicate that she should lie down. Without a word or so much as a cry of pain, she slid to her knees, then half rolled over the log where she'd been sitting so she would be behind it.

He eased behind the largest tree in this small clump, even knowing it was inadequate cover. Better than nothing.

Then he fitted the butt of the rifle to his shoulder, rested the barrel on a branch and focused through the scope. Through it, he clearly saw the one guy, who had seemingly left his snowshoes up above but jumped down and rushed to Borisyuk. The very clarity offered temptation. Had this man been guilty of injuring Ava? Zach's finger tightened slightly on the trigger, but he waited. Despite everything, he found himself thinking again like a cop instead of the soldier he'd been. That didn't mean, if this bastard made one wrong move—

But he didn't. Shock appearing, he made a hoarse exclamation, looked around in panic and then turned to scramble back up the steep rise. He made a lot more noise retreating than he had arriving.

Zach swung around and moved quietly in turn toward the trail, feeling Ava watching as he passed her.

A pack slung over his back now, the visitor was hustling down the ridge. Running. For help, or with the intention of fleeing?

Lowering the rifle, Zach wished on one level he'd killed the SOB, diminishing the count by one. Fine time to be hit again by how much he disliked killing, seeing death on those men's faces.

After a minute, he returned to Ava, who in turn lowered the handgun down. "I think we have time," he said. "Let me help you up."

Time, at least, to splint her arm to the best of his basic medic ability, get some painkillers and something to eat in her, and figure out whether she was capable of striking out for the ridgetop.

Chapter Fifteen

Zach had kept wincing as Ava tried to eat the snacks he poured into her hand. The raisins weren't too bad, but her jaw hurt too much when she tried crunching on almonds or even peanuts. Eventually, he'd conceded that she had done the best she could, and the super dose of ibuprofen he'd convinced her to swallow didn't seem to be upsetting her stomach. Not that she was sure she'd notice, given how much she hurt. No, not true—she distinctly remembered puking after she'd shot and killed a man, so close up she'd never be able to block what she'd seen from her memory.

Her arm felt marginally better after Zach set it—he claimed it was a clean break—splinted it and then constructed a sling from a turtleneck shirt he ripped and reshaped.

"It's getting later than I'd like," he said finally. "I'd hoped we could make it up high enough for cell service today, but I don't see how that can happen. We can't stay here, either, though, not without knowing whether the two remaining men will come gunning for us."

"Why would they?" she tried to say.

Seemingly understanding her, he shrugged. "Because they're enraged? I don't know what they'll do, and I don't like that. We can't forget they're out there."

She was in no danger of forgetting.

"I think we should combine whatever we think we really need into one pack now. My suggestion is that we go up the trail and watch for someplace we can camp for the night that isn't quite so close to, er…"

The body. The man she'd shot dead.

The farther the better, in her opinion. She felt weird, but also steadier than she had. Yes, she hurt, but Zach must have hurt as much after the dislocated joint and head injury, and he'd been able to cover miles. *His* head had been slammed by a wall of snow and blocks of ice. Borisyuk had wanted to hurt and scare her, but she doubted the force he'd applied had been remotely comparable. If Zach could go on after that, so could she.

"Head?" she asked, tapping his temple with a gloved finger.

His alarm was obvious. "Your head worse?"

"No. *Your* head."

He gave a bark of laughter. "You're worrying about *me* after you've been beaten to a pulp? Today's been eventful enough, I've kind of forgotten about my headache. I think it's mostly gone, though. No more dizziness or double vision."

She scowled at him, then wished she hadn't. "Didn't tell me—"

"I didn't want to worry you."

Ava would have rolled her eyes if she could have. Any woman would have had the sense to tell her partner that she was having worrisome symptoms so she'd have someone to watch out for her. Superman here hadn't wanted to worry her.

He'd also saved her life several times over, she reminded herself.

"Can go on," she managed to say.

After a sharp look at her, he turned his attention to inspecting the contents of both packs, discarding a good-sized pile, then repacking with an occasional addition or subtraction made by her. She was secretly glad he hadn't fetched Borisyuk's pack. She didn't want anything out of it.

As if their minds were in tandem, though, Zach sighed. "I need to find Borisyuk's pack. See if there's anything I should take from it."

"Don't want—" she protested, but he shook his head.

"He might have carried something that will tell us who his target was, the contact info for whomever he was meeting up with, that kind of thing. In case the pack isn't here anymore when the border patrol comes for the body."

"Oh." That made sense.

He left her with his usual precautions, and she listened hard until he returned fifteen or twenty minutes later, moving so quietly she didn't hear him until he was close enough to startle her. His grim expression didn't surprise her, but she didn't ask what if anything he'd found. There'd be time for that; she had to believe that, after all this, they'd make it.

He attached one of her poles to the pack before helping her into her snowshoes and to her feet. Eyes keen on her face, he was obviously watching for any hint she was about to collapse. Even though she didn't want to take a step, Ava was careful to hide how awful she really felt.

So, okay, she did understand why he'd done the same thing when they'd absolutely had to keep moving those first couple of days.

Progress was painfully slow as they slogged toward the trail, sinking into deep snow, tripping over the usual hidden obstructions. Seeing how desperately he wished he didn't have to put her through this kept Ava strong. The one time he had to pick her up and she tried to give him a reassuring smile, though, she saw immediately that the attempted smile had had the opposite effect. Not one of her best, apparently.

Once they neared the ridge trail, he left her again to reconnoiter. Returning, he said tersely, "Don't see anyone."

She nodded and followed him.

I can do this, she told herself fiercely, and kept repeating it.

The way was easier on the actual trail, especially because of the other tracks going both up and back on it. At least it had been maintained well enough through the autumn; it was mostly free of fallen limbs and rocks. What's more, at this elevation, they were leaving behind the tree line. She could tell Zach didn't like being so exposed, but he'd have been on edge no matter what their surroundings. The enemy was still out there, and he had to protect her.

She quit keeping tabs on him and bent all her concentration on the next step. Every movement hurt her arm and head. Even reverting to thinking, *Left foot, right, left*, was beyond her.

She plodded and focused on the tracks right in front of her, blocking out everything else.

She could and was doing this.

ZACH HAD SEEN teammates injured and going on with that same intense focus, but watching Ava moved him beyond anything he'd felt before. A couple of hours ago, she'd had her arm snapped and then been beaten; she could only use one pole, and he knew damn well the dose of ibuprofen he'd given her hadn't done more than slightly mute the pain. Yet there she was, marching on up the switchbacks of a precipitous climb.

If he asked her, he knew she'd say she could keep going as long as necessary, but unlike her, he'd been keeping an eye on the sinking sun. He was desperate to reach the top, prayed the phone could make contact from there to a cell tower, but no matter what, they didn't dare continue once the light started to fail.

What worried him was that she'd feel worse in the morning than she did now.

He bared his teeth in a grimace that she, thank God, couldn't see. No, that was one of a long list of worries. At the top was staying aware that Borisyuk's two or more remaining men could be hunting them. He stopped frequently to use binoculars to scan behind them.

Unfortunately, not even high-quality binoculars could penetrate the dense woods low in the valley. All he could do was be sure no one could sneak up behind them.

Remembering the grenade launcher kept that irritating prickle crawling along his spine. They were out of range now, he was confident—unless someone else awaited them at the top of the ridge.

At last he spotted what he'd been looking for—a small cluster of subalpine hemlocks, able to survive where other trees couldn't because of their slender profile and down-sweeping branches that shed heavy snow. Below them was a sharp drop-off, so no one could approach from that direction. He hoped there was a level spot that would allow two people to stretch out, but even if they had to sit huddled against each other, this was the best they were going to find.

"Ava. Wait."

She stopped but didn't even look back. Just stood there, confirming his belief she was at the end of her rope.

He came up next to her and pointed with his pole. "We'll spend the night there."

Still without looking, she nodded.

"Wait until I make sure it's accessible." Without pausing for a response, he left the trail, every movement cautious. He quickly discovered he was clambering along a rocky ledge. A fall wouldn't be great, and likely would ensure broken bones or heads. With each step, he stamped his foot a couple of times to bare the rock as much as he could. There'd be no hiding the trail he and Ava would make—but he already knew he didn't dare sleep tonight.

As he'd hoped, the trees had been able to take root because of a deposit of soil, however thin and rocky, left in a small dip on the mountainside. Zach poked around and found a clear place large enough to set up the tent, although he didn't plan to do that. He wanted a 360 degree view around them.

He set the pack down and went back for Ava. A dull gaze lifted to him when he appeared in front of her.

He'd rather carry her, but when he offered, she said, "I can keep going." Of course she did.

"Okay. Follow my tracks. The rock isn't far beneath the snow. I'll be right behind you."

With that same absolute concentration, she trod in the path he'd laid, one cautious step after another. Behind her, he stayed poised to lunge forward and catch her if he had to—but she reached his pack and stopped.

He laid out pads before he gently helped her step out of her snowshoes and sit down. Even with his arm around her, lowering herself to the ground clearly hurt like hell. Zach discovered how much he hated seeing her suffering, but all he could do was try to make her as comfortable as possible.

He wrapped the sleeping bag around her shoulders, then encouraged her to sip water. Without complaint, she held another snow pack to her face while he got out their stove, fired it up and peered into a couple of packets of freeze-dried meals before finding what he wanted—one that would probably taste more or less like the stew it purported to be, but didn't appear to have much texture.

In fact, heated, it looked a lot like canned dog food, but didn't smell bad.

To his dismay, Ava looked vaguely surprised when he held the pan in front of her. Had she not noticed that he was cooking? How bad was her concussion?

But then she mumbled what he thought was "Thank you" and took the spoon from him. He stayed close to wipe her face when she didn't quite get every spoonful in her swollen mouth, and to take over after her hand started to shake.

Most of it went down, though, and when he took the pan away she met his eyes.

"D'ank you."

She was all there. Thank God. He smiled.

"You're welcome. This isn't as good as the meals you brought, but..."

She lifted fingertips to her lips.

"Easier to eat," he finished, and she nodded.

Zach wolfed down his own portion, wishing it was a greasy burger with cheese and an extra-large serving of French fries, although pizza would have been fine, too, or real stew with tender chunks of meat and potatoes.

He'd have liked to think, *Soon*, and believe it, but couldn't quite. There was no guarantee they'd find cell phone service even at the top of the ridge. As for their next step... He hit a wall. Yeah, he was tired, but he would figure it out when he had to.

After cleaning up, he readjusted the sleeping bag so he was under it with Ava, and settled for cuddling her. She lay her head on his shoulder and just...rested. The unfamiliar warmth in his chest felt like happiness, despite their perilous circumstances.

It had to be fifteen minutes before she mumbled, "Missed pickup."

"Yeah." He'd had other preoccupations, but now that she'd reminded him... "I never heard a helicopter."

She shook her head, he assumed to say that she hadn't, either.

"When you didn't show, they should have mounted a search."

"Maybe just think I'm late?"

"Alone out here? They're irresponsible if they don't ask the park service to start looking for you." That would have cheered him more if he'd heard any helicopter however far away, but still, at the top of the ridge, he and Ava would be highly visible. Too bad there'd be no wood, dry or otherwise, to build a fire that would draw attention.

Against his upper arm, she tried to say something. He had to pull back and raise his brows.

"Wish we had…"

She was back to dwelling on that damn satellite radio. He shook his head. "None of that. We've made it this far. We'll make it the rest of the way."

Given her swollen face, he couldn't be positive, but he thought Ava was peering deep into him, seeing… Who knew? His confidence?

Or was it pretense she saw?

He said, "Why don't you lie down? You can use me as a pillow."

Not easy to arrange, but it worked.

BECAUSE OF THEIR increased elevation, darkness came a tiny bit later. Between mountains, Ava even saw a lingering, gradual deepening of the sky rather than the sudden plunge into night to which she'd become accustomed.

She held on until twilight made it hard to see at all, and despite the pain that tried to consume her, she fell asleep. Or lost consciousness. Rousing several times to darkness, shifting in futile attempts to find a more comfortable position, she knew Zach never slept. Each time, his hands were there, reassuring, helping her settle, his touch tender, his voice husky and words comforting. She couldn't have said whether she'd been in a coma or truly asleep. If there were dreams, they didn't linger.

This time when she opened her eyes, the sky had lightened enough she could see Zach's face above her. She lay on her side, she realized, arm propped on the pack, head on his thigh. He seemed to be staring contemplatively down at the intersecting valleys now far below them, until he must have become aware she was awake—she'd tensed, or her breathing had changed. Who knew?

"Hey, sunshine." He smiled, peeled off a glove and cupped the less painful side of her face with a big, warm hand.

She nestled into it.

"Don't suppose you're feeling your best," he murmured.

Ava thought about it. "Yesterday, I didn't think I'd live to see this morning," she pointed out. And, wow, her speech sounded clearer, didn't it? Had her swelling gone down?

His dark eyes never wavered. "Think you can sit up?"

Think about, maybe. Actually doing it…not so much. But…she had to, didn't she?

"Yes?"

He laughed at her. "Heartfelt positivity."

She'd have wrinkled her nose, but had a bad feeling it was broken. Maybe her cheekbone, too. Teeth… She ran her tongue over them. Thank goodness, they were all there, although a couple felt like they might be loose.

Just as well she hadn't brought a mirror.

He helped her as she raised herself an inch at a time, groaning. Zach supported her lower arm with one hand until she was upright, then tied her makeshift sling back into place. The water in the bottle was almost too cold to drink, but she washed several ibuprofen down with it, anyway, then waited eagerly for the pills to take effect.

If they did, the effect wasn't all that noticeable, but she was able to eat the oatmeal he prepared, and savored every drop of her cup of tea, even if he'd overloaded it with sugar.

Drinking his own, he scratched his jaw irritably.

"Itch?"

"Like crazy."

She'd almost forgotten what he looked like without the scruff that had now become a shaggy beard. At least it helped keep his face warm.

At last, reluctantly, she asked, "What's the plan?"

Regret in his eyes, he said, "I think we need to find out whether you *can* go on. I hate the idea of leaving you, armed or not. These guys can shoot from such a distance, you might not even know they're coming."

She shivered.

"Damn." He leaned forward. "I'm sorry. I shouldn't have said that."

"No. Should. Need a motivational talk."

He glowered at her. "Are you making fun of me?"

"Maybe?"

Zach grunted, but one corner of his mouth lifted.

"Not that far."

"No. Maybe a couple of hours should see us at the top. We'll have wide visibility there, which'll give us an advantage if anyone is behind us. Otherwise…"

She patted the pocket of her pack holding her phone.

"Yeah." He cleared his throat. "Might be worth a prayer or two."

THE WORST PART was getting started. Every joint creaked, every muscle hurt as if she'd wrenched it. Her head felt as if it had blown up to twice its size and her neck wasn't adequate to keep it upright. It throbbed. Her dark glasses didn't seem to block the glare; she kept wanting to close her eyes—okay, eye—but fought not to succumb. For Zach's sake.

But gradually, as she warmed up, she found she was moving more easily, the lift and stride in the snowshoes natural. She'd have given a lot to be able to use both poles, but considering the alternative—say, getting shot, her body abandoned like trash in the snow—this wasn't so bad.

To Zach, her pace undoubtedly felt like slow motion, but he never forgot about her long enough to let any significant space open between them. She knew he was pausing frequently to watch her, but she didn't let herself meet his eyes. Better to empty her mind as much as possible and just keep going.

He did insist they stop once, making her eat a handful of raisins and drink some water, but kept it brief. He must've been afraid her body would stiffen.

More than it already had.

For a while, she counted legs in the switchback, but really that didn't help, since she had no idea how many remained ahead of them. Her concentration waned. She kept moving, but wasn't thinking at all. Just step, swing pole, step. Once warmed up, her legs didn't feel bad, but her head and arm coalesced into blazing agony. The last coherent thought she had was, *How had Zach done this?* And for days?

"Sweetheart."

She liked him calling her that, but didn't let herself break stride. If she stopped now, Ava wasn't sure she could start again.

She collided with him, teetered, and let him catch her in his arms.

"We're here. You made it, Ava."

Here? After blinking a couple of times, she turned her head and saw that the trail had leveled off, and a dazzling panorama surrounded them. Even so, with her mind working sluggishly, it took her several minutes to understand. They'd reached their goal. He was right: she *had* made it. Only…

He said it for her. "Now's the moment of truth."

Chapter Sixteen

Ava's phone produced a single, flickering bar, and that was after Zach tromped knee-deep in snow in circles for a good ten minutes, pointing the damn thing every which direction. When he saw that small flicker, he froze.

"Got it." And if he so much as twitched, he'd lose it.

"Oh, thank God." Ava didn't try to get up from where she sat with the pack.

Trying to hold the phone completely steady, he tapped in his friend's phone number. Then he held his breath…to no avail. The call could not be completed.

Unsurprised, he thought some foul words.

"Text," Ava said from behind him.

Yeah, they sometimes went through when a call wouldn't. Naturally, he lost the bar while he wrote a short message saying, basically, Borisyuk dead, need pickup for two, the ridge identified. It took Zach two or three minutes to find the perfect spot again to recover that fragile, single bar. He pressed the arrow to send the text on its way, and held his breath again. He didn't so much as blink while he stared at the phone.

Was there any way to know if a message reached its goal? He had no idea. What if it had gone through fine but Reid was busy, didn't check his phone for five minutes or five hours? Zach wouldn't get any response unless he stayed as still as a statue—or found this exact spot again. Damn, he should start thinking about plan B—

A message popped up with startling speed.

What the???? Your ride on the way as fast as I can find a pilot and get the chopper in the air.

Blown away, Zach tried to take it in. He could only imagine the confusion, consternation, hope that his few words would have aroused on the other end.

He sent back a thumbs-up, pocketed the phone and turned to Ava.

"They're coming," he said simply.

Her mouth trembled and a couple of tears leaked from her open eye. She hadn't believed this would work.

He felt like whooping, picking her up and

swinging her around, kissing her until they both forgot where they were...but of course he couldn't do any of that. Who knew how far an exuberant yell would carry in the vast quiet?

So all he did was sit next to her, gently kiss her cold cheek and dig in the pack for something to eat and for the water bottle.

He couldn't find any raisins. The dried apricots and other fruits would take some serious chewing. He offered her peanuts again, and she stared at them with an expression of loathing before taking the small packet from him.

"French fries. *Salty* French fries."

He laughed, joy welling up from deep within him. "Hate to tell you this, but you'd be sorry if you ate anything salty with your mouth in that condition."

Her sound of frustration made him laugh again. For a few minutes, he let himself savor being able to sit beside her, his arm around her back, her head tipped against his upper arm. Along with a tangle of other emotions, he felt an unfamiliar sense of peace.

Of course, it couldn't last, since he wasn't foolish enough to forget their potential pursuers. He and Ava would have quite a wait...and they were more exposed up here than he liked.

He downed a good-sized handful of raw almonds, swallowed some water and made himself get back to his feet. The binoculars still hung around his neck, and the rifle leaned against the pack, ready for him to grab.

"DAMN." ZACH'S FRIEND Reid had to shout to be heard in the noisy helicopter. "That's really him." He hadn't torn his gaze from the screen of her phone. He sounded incredulous, for which Ava didn't blame him. Really, what were the odds that a noted terrorist had crossed the border here, in Washington State, and that in this vast wilderness, his retired army friend out for some winter camping had happened to stumble upon him?

Ava watched from her seat, *not* designed for comfort, and tried to keep her teeth from chattering from the vibration. She didn't mind flying—although she definitely preferred a big jet to a small plane—but really didn't enjoy helicopters. She'd had no choice but to take one to drop her in the midst of the park. This time, though... Well, it had appeared like an angel from on high. She hadn't fully believed she and Zach had survived until she saw that helicopter swooping toward them. She was afraid she'd actually cried at that moment, although she'd wiped away any tears before the copter gently settled onto the snowy top of the ridge.

Zach had wanted her to be conveyed straight

to a hospital, while Reid argued for them to first retrieve the terrorist's body and pack. Ava had shaken her head to silence Zach's protests. The border patrol agents and maybe somebody like the National Guard would undoubtedly swarm through this segment of the park once they heard the whole story, but that would take time to organize, and she understood their priority. She wasn't dying. What difference would another hour or two make?

Only to herself did she admit that the detour also gave her a little longer to watch Zach and to revel in his frequent, searching glances. He hadn't put her out of his mind the second that rescue had arrived. Once this helicopter did land on a hospital helipad, she knew she'd be whisked away while he involved himself in the hunt for the remaining terrorists and the maybe rescue of the one he'd left trussed up, to use his words.

Ava had no doubt she'd see him again. They'd become close enough that she believed he would come to see her, verify that she had arrangements in place to go home, and to say goodbye.

It was the goodbye part that she dreaded.

She'd lost track of how many days and nights they'd spent together since she had started across the avalanche slope with the uneasy awareness that a man was behind her, maybe even chasing her, and gaining ground by the minute. It had to be less than a week...but one of heightened emotions, physical exertion like she'd never imagined and a reliance that went both ways with an extraordinary man. The before felt...pallid, in comparison. Or maybe not even real. Her future was a blank.

It was silly to mourn the loss of a man she knew in one way, and not at all in others. There'd never been any chance that— what?—he'd throw over his life to follow her to Colorado? That he'd want to have her waiting patiently for him at home every day, once he could get away from his real life investigating crimes? That didn't sound like him, or her.

But for the first time in her life, she knew she'd make sacrifices to be able to stay with him.

Ava pushed at even that acknowledgment. The intensity of what they'd shared would fade. What felt most real now no longer would as the days passed, as she downloaded her photos and became absorbed in editing, settled into her usual routine.

She turned her head to see him watching her again, lines furrowing his forehead, concern in his dark eyes. She tried for a weak smile that failed to smooth those deep lines at all or lessen the intensity in his expression.

Habit, she tried to tell herself. The bond they'd formed would take time to thin and eventually disappear. Given his many deployments and the losses in combat, this experience was probably familiar to him. One minute, the people around you meant everything, the next, you said your goodbyes and flew back to a base where you had to reconnect with friends and family you'd left there.

Ugh. Knock it off.

Things became tense—snapped orders, cold washing in the open door of the helicopter as it hovered above the snow-covered ledge where she and Zach had left the body of the man she'd shot and killed.

Something else not to think about.

Apparently the body was still there. The pack, too, she saw, when Zach was winched up carrying it on his back. The body... Ava looked away at that point. The two men deposited it somewhere behind her.

Then, as the helicopter rose into the air again, Zach came to sit beside her.

"Hadn't been touched," he shouted. "The two survivors must be on the run."

"What about...?"

His eyebrows climbed. "The guy I left alive?"

She nodded.

"He's our next stop, if I can pinpoint the place from the air. Although—" now he sounded bleak "—I doubt he could hold out this long."

Of course he hadn't forgotten the one man he'd been able to leave alive. She reached over and squeezed his hand, rewarded by the way their eyes met and held.

She did know him. She did.

To Zach's astonishment, Jarek Krasnitskiy— or so his passport claimed him to be—was alive. In bad shape, but bundled for warmth, given oxygen and fluids, he would soon be in the hospital along with Ava.

Zach had known he wouldn't be able to stay with Ava until everything he knew, had done and had thought since he first saw those men silhouetted atop the ridge had been sucked out of him. He had no doubt agents would pounce on her, too, once doctors gave them the go-ahead.

After watching her get placed on a gurney and rushed into the hospital, he went to the local border patrol headquarters and submitted to the interrogation. He did his best to put

Xs on the detailed topographic map, showing where he and Ava had first spotted the men—and where the other bodies could be found. Somebody, somewhere, would have to decide whether he was justified in shooting and killing, but his conscience felt clear. He and Ava wouldn't be alive if he hadn't had the skills he'd brought home from his service in dangerous parts of the world.

When they were done with him, at least temporarily, he called a taxi to take him to the hospital. A receptionist directed him to Ava's room. The door marked with the right number stood half-open. As he pushed it fully open and started into the room, a nurse hurried toward him.

"I'm sorry. Visitors aren't—"

"We're friends," he said. "I was with her when she was hurt."

Her lips compressed, but she nodded. "Please keep your visit short. Authorities are eager to talk to her, but Dr. Chavez has refused them access."

Zach smiled at her. "Good."

His first sight of Ava in the hospital bed took him aback. Her face looked even more discolored and swollen against the white pillowcase. Her eyes were closed and her body appeared slight beneath the sheet and thin blanket. He couldn't see the vibrant woman who had dug him out of the grave made from snow, ice and rock, who had warmed him with her own body...until her eyes suddenly opened.

One was still a slit, but the deep blue color was apparent. "Zach. Is everything all right?"

Despite appearances, the swelling was definitely decreasing, giving her speech improved clarity.

"Yeah." He cleared his throat. "Let me find a chair."

He pulled one from under the window to her bedside, then sat down and reached out without thought for her hand that lay on top of the covers. Their fingers twined together, the action so fluid they might have held hands through years instead of days.

"I see you got a cast."

"Yes, and it helps." Her nose crinkled. "Whatever they're pumping into me through the IV helps even more, I suspect."

He grinned. "I have no doubt. You had to be dehydrated besides. I'll bet you've lost a lot of weight."

Her gaze seemed to drink in his face. "You, too. You've had something to eat?"

He cleared his throat. "Ah..."

"A cheeseburger. And fries?"

Had she caught a whiff of his breath? "Afraid so."

Ava made a sound that expressed indignation.

"Maybe I can sneak something in. I assume they're keeping you tonight?"

"Yes. They think I had a concussion."

No kidding.

She frowned. "You should get looked at, too."

"I'm feeling fine." Exhausted, relieved, grateful and scared about how she'd respond when he talked to her about the future, but the headaches were gone, and his shoulder... He rotated his arm experimentally. "Shoulder is good as new."

This time she snorted.

He laughed. "Really. And no, I haven't forgotten that it will be more susceptible to a dislocation if I get hammered by an avalanche again, but I'm hoping to avoid that."

"Me, too," she said quietly. It was a minute before she asked about Krasnitskiy, although she didn't remember the name.

No, Zach realized, he'd never told her any of the names, only the nationality claimed by the passports they carried.

"He's not up to talking yet, but it looks like

he'll make it. He'll even keep his fingers and toes."

"You bundled him up well."

"Yeah." Uncomfortable with the implication that he was a good man, Zach cleared his throat again.

Behind him, someone else did the same even as the curtain rings rattled. It was the nurse, he saw, who looked sternly at him.

"Ms. Brevik needs to sleep. I'm afraid you'll have to leave now."

He didn't move. "I'm not going anywhere. I'll spend the night right here."

She frowned. "That's against—"

Ava said, "Please. I…feel safe with him here."

To her credit, the nurse backed down, but insisted on turning out the light after taking Ava's temperature and pulse, and then reminded her that she could push the button at any time if she required assistance.

The darkness wasn't all that complete, light from the hall seeping around the curtains, but Zach felt himself relax.

"She's right," he murmured. "You need to sleep."

"You, too," she whispered.

"I will. I can sleep anywhere."

If anything, her fingers tightened around his hand. "Do you think...?" She hesitated.

Zach leaned forward. "Do I think?"

"You could lie down with me?" She sounded tentative, and vulnerable. "I'd...sleep better."

Heart squeezing like a fist, he answered in a low voice, "I haven't showered yet."

"I don't care," she whispered.

"Your guard dog will probably kick me out when she sees us, but...yeah. I'd sleep better, too."

While he kicked off his boots and pulled his quarter-zip over his head, Ava shifted herself sideways on the narrow bed. He carefully climbed on, stretched out beside her and helped her find the position they knew worked best—her cast lying across his chest and belly, her head nestled in the hollow beneath his shoulder.

He wanted to sleep like this every night for the rest of his life—minus the cast.

She sighed, squirmed a little and murmured, "Sleep tight."

Smiling, he closed his eyes, refused to let himself think about tomorrow and stayed awake only until he knew from the slowness of her breaths that she was asleep.

AVA AWAKENED WITH vague snippets of memory telling her the nurse had checked on her a number of times, making her answer questions and expressing her disapproval of Zach sharing the hospital bed, but she must have given up and left them each time. He was gone now, although Ava was sure he'd stayed through the night. Her heart sank when she saw the empty chair.

"Breakfast will be here in just a minute," a new nurse told her cheerily. "Do you need to get up first?"

Oh, heavens—she did. That chore completed, she climbed back into bed laboriously, feeling as if she were old and arthritic.

He'll be back, she told herself. That he'd wanted to stay the night meant everything. Today, though, she'd be released from the hospital.

"Do you know where my friend went?" she asked.

"I'm afraid I didn't see him. Nobody was here when I came on."

Ava could only nod. She actually was hungry, and the breakfast looked surprisingly good to her. Scrambled eggs and oatmeal, easy to eat, a slice of whole wheat bread, and tea and orange juice. Her jaw felt better, she decided as she ate. She started to think about practicalities.

Where was her pack? Obviously not here.

None of the clothing in it was clean, but what she'd been wearing—and she had no idea what had become of that—had to be indescribably filthy. Besides, she'd need her wallet, keys, phone. What day was today? Had she missed her return flight home? Probably. Ugh—replacing the ticket would be costly.

Just as she pushed away the tray, Zach appeared around the curtain. A new Zach—clean and freshly shaven, wearing cargos she didn't remember seeing and a long-sleeve, navy blue T-shirt. And he carried her pack slung over his shoulder.

"Oh, thank goodness!" she exclaimed. "I had no idea what happened to my stuff."

She'd almost forgotten how handsome he was beneath the shaggy growth of beard. Hadn't cared. What had mattered was *who* he was.

"Reid's wife offered to wash your clothes." He glanced down at himself. "He and I are close enough in size. He loaned me something to wear."

"I have clean clothes?" What a thing to get stuck on!

His broad grin sent her pulse into double time. "Best thing that's ever happened to you."

She laughed. "Well, not quite."

On a sharp pant, she knew: the best thing

that had ever happened to her was meeting him. The time they'd had together, however fraught with fear and danger it had been.

"So." He set down the pack and sat in the chair. "Do you have a plan?"

"I haven't gotten that far. I just finished breakfast."

He eyed her empty plate, expression dubious, but didn't comment. The silence felt uncomfortable.

Zach rolled his shoulders, which she'd learned was something of a giveaway for him. He had something to say he didn't want to. Was this the *Goodbye, I have to be back at work, you take care of yourself?*

"Will you come home with me?" he asked. "Heal up for another few days? My place isn't fancy, but—"

"I'd love that," she said in a rush. A reprieve. She was ready to seize that with both hands.

"Good." His relaxation was noticeable. "Maybe I should say this first, though. It could be awkward if you're not thinking anything the same."

The leap of hope plummeted like a stone thrown high in the air. She could only nod.

"We haven't known each other very long, but… I don't want to say goodbye to you." His voice was gruff. "You're the most extraordinary woman I've ever met. My life isn't all that exciting anymore compared to yours, but..." He appeared momentarily lost for words. "I've been falling for you. Hoping you might have room in your life for me. So we can figure out—"

His face blurred. To her horror, Ava realized she was crying. No, sobbing. She snatched up a corner of the sheet and tried to quell the flood, but failed. Salty tears stung as they found raw places.

On an exclamation, Zach moved to sit on the bed and gently lift her until he could wrap her in his arms and it was his shirt front she was soaking. His *clean* shirt.

"I'm sorry," he murmured. "Damn, I didn't mean to upset you. God, Ava. Please quit crying. Please."

"They're happy tears!" she wailed, but he probably couldn't make out a single word she said.

Only...he started to laugh. Rocking her, rubbing his cheek against her head. "It's okay, sweetheart. Damn. You scared me. I thought—"

She straightened, pulling back enough to gaze at him through even puffier eyes, knowing perfectly well how pathetic *she* must look. "I kept telling myself what I felt wasn't real, but it was. It is! I was terrified of having to saying goodbye."

He grabbed a handful of tissues from her bedside table and mopped up her face as tenderly as if she were a baby.

Tossing the tissues, he agreed roughly, "Yeah. Same. I'm…in love with you, Ava. I'll move to Colorado if that's what you want. I can get a job anywhere. I'll hate waving goodbye when you head out on expeditions, but I hope most of them aren't as dangerous as this one. And…maybe sometimes I can go with you."

"We can live here, you know. There's a lot of spectacular country around here. The Puget Sound, the Gulf Islands, mountains everywhere, the rainforest. I didn't leave anything important behind in Colorado. It's just…a place. I don't mind moving."

He absorbed that. "Then, once they let you go, I'll take you home with me. It's, uh, just a rental, but we can buy something we like together. I can afford it. I didn't want to commit when I first took the job."

"Yes." Oh, it hurt to smile, but she felt as if she must be glowing from some inner light. A niggling thought surfaced, though. "You're not in trouble, are you?"

Zach shook his head. "I have an official offer from the border patrol to join."

"Will you?"

He shook his head. "Too close to what I did the last ten years. I never want to go to war again. Regular policing, that's different."

"I wish you could kiss me."

He bent forward and rested his forehead against hers. "You have no idea how much I wish the same. Soon. And…we have time."

"We have time," Ava echoed, her emotions indescribable. She'd never expected to believe in something like forever with a man, but she had already given Zach her trust, and would keep giving it. He wasn't a man who'd ever let her down. "I can hardly wait."

* * * * *

INTRIGUE

Seek thrills. Solve crimes. Justice served.

Available Next Month

Marked For Revenge Delores Fossen
Texas Scandal Barb Han

Wyoming Mountain Cold Case Juno Rushdan
Pursuit At Panther Point Cindi Myers

Special Agent Witness R. Barri Flowers
Resolute Investigation Leslie Marshman

Larger Print

Available from Big W, Kmart, Target,
selected supermarkets, bookstores & newsagencies.
OR call 1300 659 500 (AU), 0800 265 546 (NZ) to order.

Visit **millsandboon.com.au**

Keep reading for an excerpt of a new title
from the Western Romance series,
HER OUTBACK RANCHER by Joanna Sims

PROLOGUE

"AND THEN HE took a shuttle to the airport and I haven't talked to him since," Jessie Brand told her best friend.

"Que idiota!" Valentina Flores-Cruz exclaimed.

"Si!" Video-chatting with her friend after her train arrived in Brisbane, Australia, it was the first time Jessie had felt like laughing since her boyfriend, Hudson, had left her. "He *is* an idiot. A total idiot. But, then again, so am I. I actually thought he was acting *off* because he was going to propose in the same place we had met several years ago. I couldn't have been further off base if I tried."

"You're not an idiot, Jess. You couldn't have known he was still talking to his ex-girlfriend."

"No." Jess had to agree. "And, I couldn't have known that he would dump me in Sydney and head back to the States to be with her. It all still feels like a bad dream."

"I'm sure. How could it not?" Valentina said. "But, *do not* stalk them on social media, Jess. Resist the urge!"

"Too late," Jessie confessed.

"Glutton for punishment."

"I know," Jessie said. "Salt in the wound. He actually uploaded a video telling all of his 1,500 followers that he was flying back to his soulmate, his one true love."

"Idiota!" Valentina reiterated.

After the breakup brunch and after they had retrieved their bags from the concierge, Hudson took a taxi to the airport, and she took a shuttle to the Sydney train station.

It wasn't until she was several hours into her trip that she realized that Hudson had accidentally taken her backpack. He had her passport and wallet and she had his backpack full of dirty socks and underwear. She was going to need to figure out how to get it back before she could leave the country. Now she was sitting in the Brisbane Roma Street Station waiting for a friend of her oldest brother, Bruce, to pick her up and take her to the hotel.

"You're better off," Valentina said bluntly. "I never liked him."

No one had really liked Hudson—not her family, not her friends. But despite that, she had loved him. Maybe it hadn't been the grand romance with all of the bells and whistles she had dreamed of as a little girl—but he had a genius IQ, shared her love of traveling and always knew how to make her laugh.

"Where *is* this guy?" Jessie suddenly felt exhausted. "I thought he would be here when I arrived. I just want to go to my hotel and sleep. I don't even know why I decided to come to Brisbane in the first place."

"Because you are obsessed with Steve Irwin, and you want to go see his zoo, that's why. You wouldn't be *you* if you let that *idiota* stop you."

Jessie was about to respond when a man wearing an Australian version of a cowboy hat, dark jeans and a neatly tucked button-down shirt strode into the main terminal of the train station. He was tall, lean and rugged; his skin was tanned a deep golden brown, giving him the look of a man who spent his time outside working with his hands. She was not the only woman in the building who noticed him; women were craning their necks every which way to get a better look at him. And she couldn't seem to take her eyes off him either. It was the way that he carried himself—self-assured and confident.

"Okay. Who are you looking at?" Valentina asked.

"An Aussie cowboy." Jessie flipped the camera around so her friend could see the man.

"Yes, please, Mr. Australian cowboy! Can you say, Hudson *who*?"

The man stopped near the spot in the terminal where Jessie had parked herself, waiting for Bruce's friend. The stockman looked at his phone and then looked around the station. He scanned the waiting areas until his eyes landed on her. The moment their eyes met, Jessie's heart began to beat faster, and she forgot to breathe for a split second.

"He's walking toward you," her friend said.

"He sure is." Jessie nodded, her heart fluttering in the most wonderful way.

"Is *that* Bruce's friend?"

"Lord, I certainly hope so."

Jessie's eyes were now locked with the man's striking light green eyes. She didn't look away and neither did he.

"When one door closes, another one opens to let a hot guy in," Valentina teased.

"I think I need to go."

"Call me later." Her friend ended the video call.

Jessie sat frozen while she waited for the man to reach her. His strides were long and determined; it felt like a split second, and he was standing in front of her.

"Are you Jessie?" he asked with an Australian accent that sounded so sexy to her American ears.

"I am." She stood up and offered him her hand. "Are you Hawk?"

"At your service." He lifted his hat politely, then shook her offered hand.

She slipped her hand into his large, callused, strong one. It reminded her of home and of the cattlemen in her family. "Thank you for coming to my rescue."

He picked up her two large bags, leaving only the backpack full of Hudson's laundry for her to carry.

"I hope it wasn't too much trouble."

"No worries," Hawk said. "Bruce is a mate."

They reached his sleek black Land Rover Defender; he opened the door for her, got her situated in the passenger seat and then loaded her bags into the SUV.

"Emporium Hotel?" he asked her when he joined her in the cab.

Jessie nodded, taking in the clean smell of Hawk's skin. The soap he used smelled like rum and cinnamon—a bit spicy and a bit sweet. Lovely. Every cell in her body seemed to be reacting to this Australian stockman; *all* of those elusive bells and whistles were suddenly going off! And why not? She was a free woman now, wasn't she?

"I got dumped," she blurted out.

"The bloke's obviously an idiot."

"That's what my friend just said!" Jessie exclaimed, partially with excitement for his compliment.

"So, what's next then?" he asked her as he pulled onto the road.

"Well—" she settled back in her seat "—my flight home isn't for two weeks. After I go to the zoo, I suppose I'll move my flight up and head back early. As long as my ex returns my passport, that is."

"Naw. You don't want to do that." Hawk glanced over at her with a broad, adorable smile.

She laughed at the way he said it—so direct, as if they had known each other all their lives. "I don't?"

"Of course you don't. Brissie's an awesome place," Hawk said, using the city's nickname. "I spend a lot of time here. You don't want to miss it. They have museums, botanical gardens. Kayaking. Pub crawl. Whatever you want. I'll be your tour guide." He smiled at her again. "We'll start with the zoo tomorrow."

"You want to be my tour guide?" She turned her body slightly in his direction, her arms crossed in front of her body.

"Of course I do," Hawk said without a moment's hesitation. "You're bloody gorgeous. Too gorgeous to be alone on your first night here. I'll take you to one of my favorite restaurants for dinner. Do you like Chinese food?"

She nodded, her mind whirling. It hadn't even been a full twenty-four hours since the breakup, and now she was having dinner with a handsome Australian cattleman? She certainly couldn't have predicted *that*!

"I'll take you to Donna Chang's. You'll love it."

"Did Bruce tell you to babysit me?" she asked, suddenly feeling a funny sensation in her stomach.

"No. He asked me to pick you up at the train station and make sure you got to the hotel safe. That's it."

"So, taking me out to dinner is your idea?"

"All my idea."

"You don't waste any time, do you?"

He gave her a quick wink with a confident smile. "A girl like you doesn't come around every day."

It was undeniable that this gorgeous man's unexpected interest in her took some of the sting out of being dumped in a foreign country by Hudson. Maybe a dinner date with a hot Aussie was *exactly* what she needed. And if dinner went well, maybe she would take him up on his offer to be her tour guide.

"So?" He prodded her out of her silence. "How about it? Do you want to come to dinner with me and see how we go?"

"Yes, Hawk," she said with her own smile. "I think I'd like that very much."

Brisbane was looking up.

OUT NEXT MONTH!

PERFECT FOR FANS OF YELLOWSTONE!

Grudges run deep between two ranching families — as do the secrets — in this first book in the exciting new Powder River series from *New York Times* bestselling author B.J. Daniels.

Available in-store and online September 2023.

MILLS & BOON
millsandboon.com.au